BROTHERHOOD OF APEP

The Gods of Chaos
Book Two

GLENNIS GOODWIN

First published in 2023 by Blossom Spring Publishing
Brotherhood of Apep: The Gods of Chaos Book Two
© 2023 Glennis Goodwin
ISBN 978-1-7393514-1-0
E: admin@blossomspringpublishing.com
W: www.blossomspringpublishing.com

CHAPTER ONE

Across the swathes of the southern grasslands, two figures could be seen slowly disappearing into the distance as they moved away off the Median Bridge. Around them, the lands opened up, and a cool morning light lit the tall grasslands which stretched ahead while behind, the trees surrounding the southern end of the arch gradually diminished.

Steadily progressing into the vastness spread before them, their shadows fell to the side as the sun appeared in the east. The wind remained cold, and Olor Ebon, the Black Swan and her companion Theroc, the elder, sat well-wrapped with their hoods covering their heads as the horses made their progress through the high vegetation. The view from atop their mounts remained constant as they rode with the Icon *Amaunet* wrapped safely beneath the cloak of the Black Swan, but behind them, they knew they had left their friends, and for Olor, the leaving of her daughter Shuma had given extra grief.

After the two had disappeared, Malian the altar tender, who the gods charged to reclaim the stolen Icon of his people, persisted in staring out across the bridge for many moments. He knew that it should have been him returning with her back to the snowbound valley in the south. But the responsibility of the gods had fallen upon him again, and his word to aid Tragen the warrior in reclaiming his own Icon, and Captain Gallius in the return of his daughter was bound by their pledges.

All he could do was keep hope alive and give best wishes for the safe arrival of Olor and Theroc back at the Sleeping Caverns, and his mind filled with great belief as he put his trust in the two to share the burden of restoring *Amaunet* back to the valley if he should fail to return.

Finally, he turned away, and focusing his attention on the north, he let the Icon go.

***

The weeks leading to this moment had passed long and eventful, with a rush northwards to reclaim *Amaunet,* the Eighth Deity, after her theft by the riders from the north. Alliances on both sides had fallen over time in the pursuit of the Icon, but success had finally come as the two groups converged at the Median Bridge, where the betrayed and wounded rider Gallius had been able to question Roth, his double-crossing second-in-command. Events had gone further as the traitor scribe Mentu had knowingly shown his true allegiance, and these two had endeavoured to steal away in the night, taking with them the Icon to place in the hands of Dedrick, king of the high city. Now their bodies lay beneath the greenery, and in the coldness of the morning breeze, their stiffened limbs were covered by a light mist that played beneath the trees.

Above the bridge where the light fell on the remaining group, the camp had been hastily broken, and in the clearing, the blackened ashes of the fire had cooled and been scattered around in the dust. A returning quietness descended upon the land and over the bridge as the horses were readied to ride off, leaving behind only memories of the past night as an indication of the turmoil.

***

Gallius took the lead as the group found themselves departing the meeting place of the great waters, his trusted kinsman Brann and the warrior Tragen following behind, each sitting their own horse as they rode off into the lower northern forest. The rest followed, Shuma, the wise woman from the valley, sitting at the back of Malian, her bow thrown across her back, while the young man Darric, his white hair shining in the growing light, sat in front of Anitta, the scarred swan woman. These last two rode together on Mentu's horse, which had seen fit to return in the night and guiding the remaining pony, which carried the packs; they brought up the rear as the group headed north.

The trail was easy to follow out of the clearing, past where the scribe had fallen after Shuma had released her bow and the arrow had found its target, and their mounts were given their head as the path widened under the tall pines. Eventually, the branches of the trees and the undergrowth encroached and became thicker, and the horses slowed as the track disappeared beneath the mixed woodland of the north and the grey of its canopy closed in.

Finally, the riders dismounted, and moving forward, they carefully made their way. The shadowy terrain was damp underfoot, and the fallen leaves and discarded pine needles of past years had left behind thick debris from which arose a musty smell that the chill wind failed to disperse. Here the odour of rotting foliage hung around as they walked through the dappled light, the overground roots of the trees allowing only for slow progress.

As they walked, Gallius again went over the last words Roth had said, for in telling of his instructions from the high priest over those of the king, it appeared he had given little thought to Gallius' daughter held by Dedrick and the leader remained bitter towards the man he had once thought a trusted friend.

At last, they came to a stop where a shallow stream appeared between the trees. Here, where the roots of the thick oak trees tangled together, the group came to rest, and the horses dropped their heads to drink.

Gallius could now take time to study the two talismans, the one taken from around the neck of Roth while the second had been found on the dead body of Mentu. Retrieving them from his pocket, he laid them side by side on the leaf-covered earth. They were both made of silver, but the one taken from his second-in-command appeared slightly smaller and was lighter and less intricate, its middle taken up with what looked like interlocking lettering, while around the edge, a thin band made up the circumference of the ring. Looking closer, the edging could be seen to be a snake coiled around with its tail in its mouth to make one complete circle.

The one taken from Mentu was thicker, the scales of the snake appearing more defined in the deeper band, while an inner circle, absent on Roth's disc, could be seen sitting on top of the lettering and towards the bottom. Gallius had seen such items before, and struggling to remember the one he had seen around the neck of King Dedrick, he was sure it was more in keeping with Roth's than Mentu's. Either way, he remained baffled and was unable to gain anything further from the metal discs.

"What do you make of them?" Malian asked as if reading his mind. "Some sort of ceremonial or ritualistic image, do you think?" Seating himself alongside the man on the cold ground, he hoped he could provide some advice. His years as altar tender had provided some little insight into the ceremony and order which had been placed upon his world, and in his capacity in the temple, he had often been witness to the hierarchy that positioned one man above the other. He had also known and could hold testimony to the lust which could so easily drive the search for such positioning and betterment. On seeing these talismans, he immediately recognised their significance of order and command, for the slightly larger one could only imply a higher status.

"Yes, I think that would fit," Gallius replied, picking them up and handing them across, "and possibly in their difference, they denote some sort of ranking or grouping. But for who or which group, I don't know."

Malian turned each one over and contemplated their worth, and continuing to turn them back and forth, he considered the markings on the objects. He had never seen these exact forms before. Still, on noting the outer edging, he knew the snake was to be recognised in its interpretation of fear and dread, and an unease brought about a sickness to his stomach as his fingers moved across the silvered surface.

"I've also seen one like this before," Gallius said, breaking the silence as he reached out briefly to touch the one that had hung around Roth's neck. "I think it's similar to the one worn by King Dedrick. But I can't be absolute in my remembering."

"Well, if it was this one, over this," Malian said, holding the lighter disc above the other, "then I think the king's powers maybe do not rise as high as we imagine."

Mentioning the king brought a worrying thought to Malian's mind, and he promptly asked, "But why did Roth steal the Icon, Gallius, when you were already taking it north to Dedrick? Why did he take *Amaunet* off you?" He stopped briefly before asking the most critical question, and looking hard at the man, continued, "And why are the Icons being collected in the first place?"

This last thought had been increasing in the mind of the altar tender, and after the recent violence on the bridge, had begun to bother him greatly and give cause for a deeper concern. Even in knowing that *Amaunet* was being taken back into the safety of the south, he still held a disquiet for the reasoning behind her acquisition and for those already collected.

"Roth told me in his dying breath that he was taking it to the high priest. To Serdos," Gallius angrily said, taking back both of the talismans from the outstretched hands of Malian. Again looking at them intently he sternly finished, "He said that the high priest had ordered him to take the Icon to him and not to the king. But that reasoning I don't understand. For to my knowledge, it was the king collecting the Icons, not Serdos!"

Standing quickly, he returned the discs to his pocket before walking off as he saw the others eager to be on their way. Pausing as he reached his horse, and as Malian caught him up, he added, "But to what final aim of their assemblage I never knew, for my daughter was my only regard and remains so."

Gathering the reins and lifting the horse's head, he continued his lead alongside the flowing stream, and the group followed behind, the horses walking with their heads lowered as they passed beneath the trees.

***

The day had also dawned for King Dedrick, and seated in his cold vaulted hall before his vast table, he dismissed his attendants as the high priest entered the chamber and strode up the middle of the meeting room.

Ensuring the area was free from witness, the king, with his cloak of thick fur gathered around his thin frame, slowly poured a hot drink into the two silver cups which sat before him. Placing his own to one side, he offered the second up to Serdos. Accepting the drink which was held out, the king motioned for him to sit, and the high priest dropped to the wooden bench, which ran the length of the table. Here the measure of the bare timber top stretched away from each of the men. After taking a drink, the silver cup of the priest was placed upon the polished surface, and Dedrick raised his own while looking down on the upturned restless face of the older man.

"One more Icon, Serdos," he said, his harsh voice disappearing into the beamed canopy. "Just one more and the Eight will be ours, and the forces of order will be reviled, and our world returned to its unified whole of *Apep*." He brought the cup to his lips and drank heavily, the strong mulled wine tasting bitter as its warmth filled his mouth and ran down his throat. Draining the cup to the last, he raised it in salute. "And darkness and chaos will again bring back its original shape to mankind." Wiping his mouth with the back of his hand, he ended, "We must now make ready and gather the brothers." Setting the drink down, he looked upon his high priest as they each felt a sudden gathering of power rising around them as they sat before the table.

The dark, piercing eyes of Serdos looked excitedly back upon the king, and his hands tapped nervously at the unique talisman he alone wore. The silver snake-edged disc, which enclosed the figure of eight shaped serpent within its bounds, hung long around his neck and fell heavy in his lap. The words *Hem-netjer-tepi*, meaning "high priest, the first servant of the god", were woven intricately around the snake symbol, illustrating the unending cycle of creation and the wish for an end to diversity and the return to a unified whole.

"Yes, we must make ready," he agreed, his voice making known its urgency. "The last Icon should only be days away, and each must prepare themselves as brothers for the coming ceremony." He dropped his eyes from the watch of the king before saying in ending, "The word has already gone out, and in total we shall all come together."

Having finished their warming drinks, the two left the table, and crossing towards where the fire blazed, they stood before its heat, the cold stone floor stretching behind as they faced the flames. Above the hearth, the Coat of Arms of the Northern Kings, the four crossed swords indicating domain over the north, south, east and west of these highland countries, sat high up on the chimney breast supporting the black and gold oval shield, its top of beaten armour disappearing into the gloom. Along the mantelpiece, the smoky dust of past fires had settled and sat thick over the trinkets and jumble of oddments that lay there.

Both men had little to say, the taller king standing above the shorter priest, for they knew they now had only to wait. But for both, their expectations had soared as they realised the approach of the coming collapse and the rise of upheaval, and they were both elated in their own beliefs.

The door at the end of the hall slowly opened, and Prince Edgar, the king's younger brother, appeared. Walking swiftly towards the hearth, he was blatant and obvious in his manner towards the two who stood there. Being some ten years younger than Dedrick, Edgar had been kept in ignorance of the brotherhood, and Serdos was quick to take his leave, glaring at the man as he passed. The intense dislike between himself and the brother had never been well hidden on either side, and no room appeared large enough to give each his own space.

"What's he doing here?" Edgar questioned, rubbing his cold hands at the warmth.

The likeness between the two was stark, for the king had a tallness in his favour but with a gaunt frame, while Edgar was short and stout, his shoulders broad with thick, muscular arms ending in generous hands. The dark, sharp features of the past king, however, remained noticeable in both, but the black hair, which had thinned considerably on Dedrick's head, remained lush on his brother's, and his beard remained equally as dense.

"We had things to discuss," Dedrick eventually replied, feeling no real need to explain himself or the actions of his high priest, "and we shall be in closed meetings for the foreseeable future."

The king left the fireside glow, and returning to his seat, he turned towards the man who remained at the hearth, the shadow of the flickering flames outlining the stockier figure.

"You will be well considered to keep your own company these coming weeks, Edgar, and not be bothering us," he gravely advised, his voice taking on a menacing tone as he continued, "For there is an unstoppable change coming, and the winds of unrest will gather and be welcomed not only within this city but also beyond among the farms and villages, and through the streets of the towns in the west, and all shall feel its breath."

"Change!" Edgar snorted, staring into the deep redness of the fire's heat. "Good, change is what this place needs!"

The younger man looked along the dusty mantel and around at the drabness which had grown throughout the room, and spinning back around, he strode forward to the table. Placing both hands down in front of his brother, he brought his face towards the king.

"And these winds of unrest you speak of, will they be for the betterment of all or the few?" he asked in challenge, his question appearing somewhat sarcastic but holding a note of concern. His nature was unlike that of his brother, being more akin to the chosen queen, and they had both grown up in the knowing of who had been favourite of their father. But age and birthright had always given precedence, and the families of power would forever be torn apart in their loyalties, for both

Dedrick and Edgar each knew who was best liked. However, on the old king's deathbed in the long past, it was Edgar who had been the one taken out of the room.

"Watch your tongue," the king slowly and firmly warned, "for you are ignorant of more than you will ever know or realise." Rising, he came around towards the shorter man and firmly lifted the large hands off the table. Forcing his brother across the hall, he guided the man unceremoniously towards the open door.

"Look to yourself, Edgar!" he said ominously as he pushed the man through, and dismissing the guards who stood outside, he closed the door with a bang.

***

On maintaining their travel north, the horses were brought to a night's stop at a junction where another smaller stream joined that of the one they had been following. At this intersection, Gallius held up his hand, and bringing his tired mount to a halt under the boughs of another giant oak, he calmly dismounted as the dusk crept slowly around. The forest was just beginning to waken for the night, and the creatures of the dark began to take over from the growing silence of the roosting birds, while the light of the sky was quickly disappearing as the leader's voice broke into the moment's stillness.

"We'll spend the night here," he announced, his weariness causing his arm and injured shoulder to ache, and he was quick to pass his reins to Brann and surrender up his command as the other riders, also tired and weary, came to a stop.

A camp was made with a small fire burning in a shallow stone-lined pit, and the group was content to come together in warming their hands at the flames. Gallius and Brann no longer felt a need to move apart from the others, for since the events at the Median Bridge, there had been some meeting and merging among the group. They had seemingly been accepted for the recent deeds they had done, although some usual order remained evident, and the two naturally sat down next to each other. Likewise, the two women Shuma and Anitta sat together, and Tragen and Darric each typically settled alongside Malian.

The warrior, however, with Malian on one side, found Gallius sitting at his right. Still, with recent incidents and with allowing the Icon of *Amaunet* to return south, his confidence and trust in the rider had risen to some extent, and doubt and suspicion had slightly fallen away.

Yet Tragen's anger and rage still burned deep and were never far from the surface, and he knew that he would never truly be free from his bitterness. The remembered faces of his long-dead wife and children would not yet allow that to take place, but he would use and employ these men to his benefit and work with them. In the doing, hopefully, he would reclaim *Naunet* and return her to his people. He had made that promise to himself and on his wife's memory, or he would fight to the death and kill all he could in the trying. Turning towards the leader, he asked the question that had been playing through their minds as they walked north.

"What's your plan, Gallius?" he charged, giving acceptance and acknowledgement to the rider of his command.

As the darkness fed its chill mistiness through the woodland, the leader addressed the group as a whole.

"We shall remain in a northern heading tomorrow," he began, the light from the flames reflecting into his face, "though still following the stream. Once we have passed through the woods, we shall see the lower ranges, and our travel will take us eastwards along the river and towards

11

the slopes." He paused and looked long into the flames. He knew eastwards lay the City of the Fosse, which sat on the edge of the Eastern Great Waters, its seeming isolation brought about by the mountains that sat at its back and the high cliffs that fronted onto the water.

Gallius and his men had come down this way from the north but had avoided the town, swiftly passing it by in the dark of night while the folk slept, for he knew they would not have been welcomed. This city's Icon was *Kauket*, the goddess of darkness, and she had been taken by men untold months before. Unaware and wishing to remain unknowing of the devastation caused by her absence, the riders had consciously urged their mounts past and onward.

"That will be for tomorrow," Gallius eventually continued, "but the day after, we should hopefully be into the ranges and will pass along the lower slopes before reaching the City of the Fosse on the waterside. We won't be stopping there or entering this city," he quickly advised. "We will follow the cliffs around at the city's back before entering the flatter lands, and there we'll again turn north."

Malian had heard of the City of the Fosse, for it was renowned in writing for its beautiful river, which surged through its streets. The water, it was said, rushed freely along the main avenue, dividing into deeper canals before plunging over the cliffs in huge fern-clad falls where it overflowed and dropped down in sparkling rivulets into the depths of the Eastern Great Waters. The writers had called the city "The Village of the Cascade", and in their description, had talked of the many waterside establishments which prospered along the tree-lined embankments. The whole city sounded like paradise in Malian's remembrance, but suddenly recalling his own devastated home, a nagging doubt made him wonder what they might find should they have cause to enter.

Their plan for the coming day and route forward had been finalised, and all agreed, with no more questioning, that the group would rest and hopefully find some sleep in the fire-lit darkness. Knowing that the next day they would be heading along the riverside before making their journey through the mountain paths between the two slopes gave some direction to their travel. But beyond that, the way north remained in Gallius' hands, and the trust given and placed upon him now came from all around the fireside, for any doubt in their hearts had long since passed.

***

On waking, the cold dampness of the forest wrapped itself around, and the need for action and warmth saw the group hurriedly packing up and moving on. Further into the wood, as the cold air began to disperse, the stream widened, and the boughs of the trees opened out overhead to show the pale blue of the morning sky. The path too, expanded and the horses were led on through its growing width and eventually out of the trees to where the flat open land leading to the Eastern Ranges was seen away on their right.

Before them, the central elevations came almost down to the tree line, and the snow-topped mountains made off into the west and the north, their peaked and crowned summits covered in high mists collected around their shoulders. A colder wind could be felt coming across the grassland through which the stream led, and the group pulled their cloaks further around and raised their hoods as they viewed the late morning sky, its darker blue span streaked with thin shredding clouds which chased off into the west.

Coming out of the forest, the land appeared firmer on the northern side of the stream, and wading through the cold depthless water, the horses were led across. Here they reached the solid grass of the northern bank and could once again be mounted, Gallius taking lead as they trotted and cantered alongside the water, and following the stream, they headed into the east. Twice they had to cross the shallow flowing stream, once onto the southern side as it cut across their path and then back along the northern bank as the water again changed its direction.

The panorama of the scenery surrounding them was unchanging in its vastness as they moved eastwards, but the ranges slowly crept closer, and the end of the day saw them having travelled a greater distance with the edge of the crags almost within reach. Gallius, however, would not go any further that day. For he dared not risk the start of the paths between the elevations as the sky darkened, and the night would be spent out in the open of the windy plain.

***

The next morning was again cold and breezy, and the sky was covered by scudding clouds as the group finally crossed the water. Following the eastern path between the mountains and trailing along the shallower side of the slopes, they quickly moved forward, leaving behind the openness that surrounded them, and entered the gorge between the ridges. Here the winds immediately settled as the northern side began to tower over, while the gentler southern side they travelled along made for a quicker, easier pace. Following the water flow, the stream cut directly through the bottom of the gorge and slowly widening became faster as it neared the city.

As the morning advanced, the ravine through which they rode with its cream and grey-coloured barren sides began to slope gently to the right, and the group followed its course as the city walls gradually came into view around the slight bend. The canyon widened into a spacious open area that spread off into the distance where the vast plain lay. Here the stunted growths of old dead palms poked up out of the shale and lay desiccated over the impoverished land, and the riders took care in guiding their horses across the uneven ground.

On approaching the City of the Fosse through this rock-strewn area, the gates appeared to be thrown wide with a number of tall, graceful palms surrounding and defining the doorway. But no movement, neither man nor beast, could be seen around them as the group continued alongside the southern edge of the river. The water eventually turned sharply to the right, flowing directly towards the ornate entrance, and before they reached it in the early afternoon, the horses were brought to a stop as Gallius raised his hand. In sight of the doors, he swung around on the path, and the riders gathered about him.

"Brann and I will not be entering," he said, "for men from the north will not be made welcome." He paused, before coming to a quick decision. "But if the women want to go in, then be swift, and if you can get fresh supplies, it will be to the good."

Quickly taking hold of Shuma's arm as she turned to leave, he advised sharply, "Don't say anything about your reason for travel into the north or say anything about us if asked." His hand let go of her arm as he gestured towards the group standing alongside the rushing water, and Shuma nodded in understanding. As the horses were led out of sight of the gates and back across the flowing water onto the northern bank, the two women having taken down their packs moved off in the opposite direction from the men.

"I think I'll go with them," Darric suddenly volunteered, feeling a swift sense of duty fall on his shoulders on seeing the two women step away. Quietly handing his reins over to Tragen, he quickly followed. As Anitta and Shuma walked slowly over the uneven ground towards the shade beneath the palm trees, Darric caught them up, and following the flowing water, the three passed through the massive gates on the southern side of the river. Here they entered the expanse of tree-lined boulevard, which led downwards into the distance.

The river, once through the gateway, could be seen continuing on its palm-fringed course directly down through the centre of the street, and with its many blockwork bridges crossing the two halves of the town, the two sides of the north and south banks were brought together. These two sides of the city had grown over many centuries, and the galleried walkways which stood back from the water wandered along its sides, giving it a feeling of shaded grandeur and prosperity.

This architecture remained, but inside the city, few people moved around, and the three wandered silently for many moments down the waterway, their heads turning left and right as the palm-lined avenues led off at intersecting junctions.

Eventually, as they came upon a central square, the river channel having sloped down and disappeared beneath its surface, a small number of people could be seen moving around in the afternoon light. Each appeared to fumble their way forward, holding their hands out before them or else moving along close to the walls under the shade of the raised walkways, their hands touching the smoothness of the stone as they stumbled ahead.

Some were in small groups, each holding another's hand as the main figure led them slowly along, and all had their heads at an awkward angle as if they struggled to see what was before them.

The sight of the city's people had been deteriorating since their Icon *Kauket* had been stolen, and its creeping and progressing onset had left them all in an increasing darkness that had not accounted for wealth, poverty or age, for even the children's sight had been eventually affected. The first symptom had started as a slow fading of colours, leaving a perception of the world in a two-tone grey, followed again slowly by a blurring of vision and an aversion to the brightness of the morning and then by extreme blindness itself.

The older men and women, and those already affected by poor eyesight, had gone blind the quickest and some without friends or family had simply disappeared behind their doors and had not come out. Their growing darkness then became a prison, and as time passed, their deathbeds. The bodies of the dead had initially been removed to the burial gardens, but as the sight of all became affected, and the city struggled in its day-to-day business, then doors were just boarded up and rooms left to the twilight of the gathering dust.

Looking across the plaza to where the river re-emerged on its far side, Shuma stopped, and noting the reservation and impairment of those who faltered in their steps, she exclaimed, "What on earth has happened here!"

Promptly walking towards the nearest group being led across the ornately paved sidewalk of the park, she came before them and addressed the stooped man who was their guide.

"Can you spare a moment, friend?" she softly asked, a concern noted in her tone. "We are newcomers to your city and are keen to gather your news."

On hearing the voice, the man hurriedly stopped in surprise and turned towards its source. He raised his head as he peered at the wise woman with the eyes of the old, and the squinting gesture reminded Shuma of her long-departed grandmother. The unshaven face into which she looked, however, was not in itself old. Still, the eyes had a grey hazy cloudiness about them more accustomed to those of older age which she straightaway recognised, and she knew the man was partially blind.

"Who are you? What do you want?" he uneasily made his demand as he continued to hold the lead hand of his line of followers. Swiftly stepping forward, he placed his body protectively in front of the children.

"I would like to know what has happened here?" the wise woman asked, her voice remaining in its anxiety. Introducing herself, she said, "My name is Shuma, and I am a visitor to your city, myself and my two friends." Naming Darric and Anitta, the man's eyes again scrunched up as his head turned to either side. "We have stopped to rest our horses outside your gates and have entered in hope of gaining supplies. But we are troubled by what we find."

"Troubled, yes, our city has certainly been troubled," the man bitterly said, his voice rising as he wiped his free hand across his tired eyes. "Let me tell you, Shuma, that this city has been blighted and long abandoned by the gods. For the loss of our guardian, *Kauket*, untold time ago, has thrown my people into such turmoil and ruin in her absence." The man let his voice drop as a sudden sadness took the place of anger. "I give note that a gradual darkness has fallen over this great City of the Fosse and upon its citizens, and none have been spared its touch."

He brought his hand up, and with his hazy eyes staring out, he reached forward.

"My name is Ansan," he presented himself, "and I am one of the city's physicians. With that, I know full well the extent of our dilemma and the torment it has caused." He peered towards the wise woman as she grasped his hand, and feeling the warmth that passed between them, he eventually stepped back and said, "These are my children, and we have been gathering food in the south for ourselves and our unfortunate neighbours, and are on our way back to the north bank with our finds."

The line of four young children, three boys and a girl, could be seen carrying laden packs slung across their backs, and each held tightly to the next hand in line, their gaze falling at their feet as they stood at a halt amongst the richness and opulence which spread across the palm-fringed plaza. Their eyes, when they lifted them, were completely white and their outright blindness came as a shock as their young faces looked out.

"Then let us help with the carrying," Anitta said, coming forward. Taking the nearest hand, she took down the heavy pack, and Shuma and Darric followed her example, relieving the thin shoulders of their weight.

The three escorted the line across the plaza and along under the colonnade, which shaded the north bank. Here Ansan, aware of his whereabouts, turned right, and taking the lead, piloted his children and the visitors away from the river.

"Where is everyone?" Darric eventually whispered as they moved away from the plaza. Around their feet, the gathered debris of fallen leaves and old desiccated animal droppings on the unswept streets showed the neglect and slow decay of the city.

"Most, I fear, remain indoors nowadays and stay safe," Ansan replied, stooping forward and staring intently ahead as they passed the grimy windows looking out over the walkway, "for what can we do when we cannot see?"

Ansan's home was on the north bank, past the opulent façades where the money men used to sit, and down past the back of the prosperous frontages where the city's elite lived, their view taking in the palm-lined canal walkways and parks.

Here, in the narrowed streets of the workers, the ordinary man and his family resided, and the closer to the outskirts, the less fortunate could be seen the occupant, the rear of the city's high surrounding wall providing its backdrop and support to the homes of the less affluent.

The streets leading off these colonnades appeared all the same with rows of unnumbered identical doorways, their cream colouring matching the small window surrounds, and here and there, in no particular order, some had been battened across with flat strips of timber and a certain despair was immediately apparent along the dirty empty terraces.

Ansan eventually turned left, and walking along the right-hand side of the street, his hands counted down the doorways until he reached the sixth. Here, on either side, the doors and windows had been boarded over. Pushing open the door, he ushered the line of children inside, and the three visitors followed him in.

The smell which met them when they entered hit with its heavy sour sweet odour and the obviousness of its pervading source came from the very walls of the house. The next-door residents on both sides had only recently gone quiet, but the smell had slowly begun and now invaded the very atmosphere, which the doctor and his children appeared unaware of.

"Is that you, Ansan?" a voice called anxiously from the rear of the house. Appearing at the end of the passage, a tall, sandy-haired woman emerged from the bedroom area, and with her hands spread out on either side of the wall, she made her slow way forward.

"Mari, we have visitors," the doctor shouted back to her.

On hearing his news, the figure immediately stopped. "Who is it?" came the demand, an alarm and anxiety sounding great in the voice. "Tell them to go! Tell them to go!" Turning, the woman instantly disappeared back the way she had come, a door banging shut to keep out the intruders, and the three neither saw nor heard from her again.

Ansan apologised for his wife's behaviour, saying that she had a great fear of strangers since her blindness. As he slowly and gently saw to the comfort of his children, he turned his head this way and that to see what he was doing, and the three became aware of his caring nature along with the distress at his loss of sight.

Turning his attention to the packs placed on the table, he explained, "I've enough sight to see where I'm going at the moment, but once that's gone, then..." The sentence remained unsaid as he turned away.

Picking up one of the bags, he left the room, and shuffling across the street, knocked sharply upon the opposite doorway. Shuma watched as the residents eventually opened up and accepted the offered pack with seemingly great gratitude, before they disappeared back into their darkness, and Ansan slowly returned, his hands feeling around the frame of the door as he entered.

"Sit down and rest," he said, holding his head forward as he peered towards the group in the greyness of the room. Opening the remaining packs, he spread out the food which they had collected that day, his hands sweeping across the assorted fruit and greenery which lay before them. "And please...help yourselves."

The three sat, unable and unwilling to take any food off the table, and looking around the single large room, took in the simple furniture and decoration which made up the home.

The cooking fire in the far corner was unlit and

appeared to have been like that for some time, for no wood sat at its side. It was clear that this entire family now relied on the sight of its husband and father as their lifeline. Once that was gone then it would, like many others, linger in its despair. Eventually, they would simply perish as most of the residents around had already done.

"Thank you for the hospitality and the welcome you have given us, Ansan," Shuma eventually said, as the silence surrounded them, "but please, can you tell us what happened to the city after your guardian was taken?"

"The city councillors sent armed men out the very next day," the man calmly began, seating himself between his children on the long bench after handing each a round fruit taken from the table, "for the thieves came in the night, and their tracks led north towards the edge of the cliff. And again, more than three times, men were sent out. But none ever returned, and eventually, they gave up and thought that all would be well." He stopped and caught hold of his daughter's hand.

"The blindness came slowly, you see," he explained, "starting first with the elderly, ailing already with their eyesight, and no one thought the worse of it or blamed it on the absence of *Kauket*." He stopped and passed a hand over his eyes as the remembrance came painfully back. "But eventually, as the colours began to fade for more and more, then a greater panic filled the city, and all became scared and angry. The doctors and priests were unable to provide answers, you see, apart from the absence of our guardian, and this, in the course of time, became our focus. However, in her loss, we could do little, and many wanted to leave while they had their sight."

"Did any leave?" Anitta questioned, watching as the

young boys became increasingly irritated at sitting. Eventually, they dropped to the floor, and crawling over to the far side of the room, they sat silently, their backs against the wall and their heads bowed, as they ate the fruit. "Did any get away?"

"I don't know," the doctor replied. "The councillors ordered the gates to be closed and locked in worry of spreading any disease. For as well as the absence of *Kauket*, that was one of the rumours passed around as to what was causing the affliction. So no one was allowed out, you see, and that's wise enough under the circumstance. But then the consequences of that decision had to be dealt with, and that has not been easy."

"We found the gates open on our arrival," Shuma said directly. "We just walked straight in. There is no barrier to either entry or exit."

"Well, possibly the gates were opened later to allow those to leave who felt it was the best or for those who wished to get help, for some of us had our doubts that any disease or illness was involved." He paused in his telling before letting go of his daughter's hand. Rising, he crossed the room where he stumbled forward, and using the edge of the table as a guide, he came to a halt before the cold fireplace. "Still, I fear that many are already beyond that, and each has had to look to their own."

"Is there no one in charge now?" Shuma enquired, her rising outrage becoming noticeable. "No one ensuring supplies and water to those unable to fend for themselves?"

"Not as far as I know," Ansan stated, his voice trembling in anger and despair. "We have seen no one and can only assume that all have succumbed. It appears we have been left to our own ends!"

The room became quiet as the hopelessness became even more palpable, and the feeling of utter misery collected around those sitting within. The only sound came from the children finishing their fruit on the dusty floor, and finally, even that came to a stop.

"What can we do to help?" Anitta eventually urged, her unhappy voice breaking into the silence of the cold room. "Can we collect more food for you? What about water, can we fetch some?"

"We are fine for water, thank you," Ansan came back, a smile fleetingly crossing his weary face. "And the fruit is best left on the trees to be shared. We take only what we need and leave the rest for our neighbours and their animals."

"Animals?" Darric quickly asked for he had seen evidence of wandering stock in the debris left behind in the streets of the plaza. "Are there many left?"

"I think maybe some goats and possibly a donkey or two, but they have also been affected in their sight and been taken to the south bank. The meadows there are spacious, and there is scope for them to wander and graze without harm. That is where we go to gather food. In the gardens, where the fruit trees remain laden, some greens can still be found growing." He paused before generously saying, "Please, you must help yourselves if you need supplies for your journey."

Darric left the two women in their continuing discussion with the doctor, and arranging to meet them later at the gates, he followed Ansan's directions and made his way back to the plaza. Crossing the bridge onto the south bank, he quickly found the orchards and gardens of which the man had spoken. He met no one on the way, the whole area being deserted in the gloom of the late afternoon.

The meagre vegetables and greens he found would not see many more weeks, and he was quick to pass these by, not wishing to deny the city people their only source of sustenance. The windfalls under the trees he also left for the pickers, instead reaching up high to take the less ripened fruit, and even then, he was frugal in his taking. He saw no donkeys, but the goats he could see had been shut out of the garden area, and they foraged further out in the long grass. Raising their heads as they heard Darric pass by, they turned their blank eyes towards him and were quick to move off, disappearing back into the pasture. Half-filling his pack, he returned to the watercourse and, following it upwards, made his way to the rendezvous and sat in wait beneath the palm trees as the darkness collected.

***

The campfire in the canyon, made from dried palm stumps, had been burning long as the dusk gathered, and the flames cast their flickering shadows against the dark empty backdrop of the canyon walls. The men had settled themselves and their horses in wait just above the waterline. As Shuma, Anitta and Darric left behind the persecuted city, they were drawn to the glow over the dark water, and the group met around the warmth of the blaze. Carrying the minimum supplies picked from the orchard, Darric placed them near where Malian sat, and crouching down before the fire, he rubbed his cold hands together.

"How was it in there?" Malian was first to speak as the others looked on, their faces warmed and lit by the fire.

"Dire!" came Shuma's quick reply. Seating alongside, she accepted a hot cup from the altar tender's outstretched hands, and after taking a deep drink of the sweet liquid, she lowered it to her lap. "They've all gone blind in there," she said, "or are going blind. And many have died. The place is in total disorder since their Icon, *Kauket*, was stolen."

"Did you say anything?" Gallius quickly asked, his voice harsh as he turned his dark eyes on the wise woman.

"No," Shuma said, looking back directly, her stare questioning his doubt, "it would not be right to instil any hope when it cannot be guaranteed. I just told them we were visitors. But I wish we could do something more for these remaining folk."

"They are, unfortunately, the same as the people of the valley," Malian declared, thinking of his friends in their anguish, "and only the swift return of their Icon, the restoration of *Kauket*, can help them." Bowing his head, he instantly became more aware of the burden placed upon them and the increasing enormity of the responsibility that appeared to be growing in their undertaking.

Staring into the red depths of the charred embers, he felt great despair wrap itself around him, and he sensed the approaching turmoil.

The group finally settled for the coming night beneath the shelter of the canyon walls, and the darkness of the city opposite gradually crept across the water and crawled its way along the rough sides of the slopes. Each eventually found rest, falling asleep in their own time, and Malian dreamt.

CHAPTER TWO

Olor Ebon and Theroc had seen enough of the grasslands, for the landscape remained unchanging in its vastness as they travelled south. But as Gallius and the men made their campfire on the northern slopes above the City of the Fosse, the two had almost reached the borders. As the light faded in the west, the sloping harshness of the covered domes of the Sleeping Caverns slowly reared up into view and the raised grassy areas fronting the tunnels could be seen in the distance.

They would be pushed to make the safety of the lawns that night, for the gloom descended rapidly. However, they were cheered that the journey was coming to a close, for the bitter wind had been a constant companion since they left the group. On this last night, as they came to a stop, the chill breeze dropped, and their final night amongst the grass became more tolerable.

The pack holding *Amaunet* had been shared between the two as they rode forward, the Black Swan carrying her the first day and Theroc the next. Here, on the third day, the small statue was once again safely tucked away around the shoulder of Olor, her cloak wrapped tight around to protect both herself and the Icon, and each felt some comfort in knowing that the task had been apportioned.

They had made no fires as they travelled, sleeping cold under the cover of their blankets with the clear moonlit sky providing its own illumination. Thankfully, this last night appeared to be slightly warmer, the cloud having gathered tight above their heads while its darkness gathered close, and the two could sleep with some ease of mind.

* * *

As they slept amongst the canyon rocks, the group around the fire in the north had slowly settled, and Malian's dreams again took him away on a journey.

Floating amidst the dark, uniform waters of chaos, he felt a great overwhelming power surge around and down his body, like the fall of cold rain rushing through his veins.

Gradually he began to rise and was lifted as the ground slowly came into being below his feet, forming the first landmass of order with its division between the waters of confusion. Around him in the darkness, the Eight Deities of Chaos moved, their properties of infinity, invisibility, water and darkness giving them their unique existence.

Now the god Atum *stood upon the risen earth, and with the lesser gods surrounding, the work of creation was begun. While he worked his magic, and disorder was supplanted by order, the Eight Deities seethed amidst the waters, uniting and joining to combine and create the god* Apep, *the Great Golden Serpent of Chaos.*

Emerging from the blackness and slithering around the base of the mound, he made his presence known and in encompassing the land, his head touching his tail, he brought into being the symbol for infinity of disorder. This image of a unified state of oneness becoming his purpose for existence.

Malian had been unable to move as the snake slithered around, and as the first sunrise of Ra *appeared and lit up the uplifted land,* Atum *raised his spear, and striking downwards, had overthrown the serpent, and the gold of his being had run hot. The Eight Deities had immediately been divided, and after each was re-fashioned out of the molten liquid, the Eight Icons were*

28

handed over to be distributed throughout the land, the intent for them to be kept forever separated as the light of day emerged triumphant.

Looking beyond the great god, Malian could see the black-clad figure of Mentu standing between the assembly of gods and goddesses, his arms tightly bound with the talisman of the snake about his neck. Remembering the shape of the fallen serpent at the feet of Atum *he could now see that the two symbols reflected that of each other, and very quietly, the words "Brotherhood of the Snake" were breathed into his mind.*

***

Waking with a start and with his thinking totally disorientated, Malian stood, and walking past the glowing embers of the dying fire, he strode down to the water's edge. Kneeling, he doused his face in the coldness which washed through his hands and let the water drip down his arms. His mind raced as he fought to hold the dream, and as his memory wandered, he constantly repeated the name *"Apep"* and the words "Brotherhood of the Snake" to stop the recollection from slipping away.

Looking into the darkness before him, the city below remained hidden in its slumber, but its presence could be felt, and he raised his head to peer across into the dark and desperation that he knew lay there. With his dreaming, he thought he had been given some small insight and understanding of their plight and that of his own people, and more importantly, of the enormous task that awaited the group as they travelled into the north.

***

For Shuma, the night had been long, and she had lain awake for many hours, unable to find sleep. Her mind constantly replayed the conversation with Ansan as she witnessed the awful dismay and hopelessness surrounding him and his family. Going over the situation, she could see no respite, and only further despair would be found, she feared.

On noticing Malian get to his feet and pass by the sleeping bodies, she too had quietly left her bed, and following him down towards the water, came up behind as he softly talked to himself.

"Malian," she whispered, "are you alright?" Sitting down close to the hunched figure, she dipped her long fingers into the coldness and brought them back up to soothe her tired eyes.

"Yes, I'm fine," his voice came softly. Turning his head away from the flowing water, he said, "I've just been dreaming again, Shuma."

Going on to tell of his dream as he remembered it, he struggled to explain to the wise woman all that he had been shown by the gods. He told how they had enlightened him to the reason behind the making of the Icons, with their link to *Apep* and the only possible motive and intent behind their theft. And he told of the showing of the talisman and the words that had entered his thoughts.

"This is why the Icons are being collected," he finally said, his voice becoming quiet as he pointed out the enormity of the situation that had fallen upon them. "They are being gathered by this Brotherhood of the Snake, the servants of the talisman, with their one aim to remake *Apep*. To unite the Eight and create once more the snake of chaos, and return the world to its original darkness!"

"But *Amaunet* is now protected and has been returned

to the safety of the south, so the Eight will never be complete," the wise woman rationally said, her face coming close as she strained to hear Malian's voice. Placing her hand on his arm, she continued, "So we have nothing to worry about except the return of Gallius's daughter and Tragen's Icon." Her voice slowly faded as her thoughts suddenly turned to those of the City of the Fosse and its people, with their gradual blindness causing their downfall as unseeing they struggled in *Kauket's* absence. Knowing she would be amongst the Icons so far gathered, her return to this city also had to be considered in their pursuit. However, in thinking about this, it brought up a further unexplained question.

"Malian, why have the cities been thrown into disorder and confusion now?" the wise woman asked, her mind wondering why the suffering had already begun. "For really, until the Eight are gathered together, then chaos shouldn't hold any sway in the world! So why are the people down there going blind?" She nodded her head towards the city's walls, "And why was our valley plunged into the depths of winter immediately after *Amaunet* was stolen?"

Mentioning again the Icon that Malian had once so lovingly tended in the temple, he again had cause to worry about her safety. If she was known to be travelling back south, then other riders would undoubtedly be sent out to reclaim her, and the Sleeping Caverns would no longer be a safe place and Malian had to push aside his fears and concentrate on the here and now.

"I don't know, Shuma, the gods did not show me the reasoning for that," he answered truthfully. "All I was shown in my dream was the making of the Eight and the reason for their dispersal, along with the token that both Mentu and Roth wore." He went on to explain, "The talisman was shown about the neck of the scribe as he stood between the gods, and that must surely be of great importance to us and give warning of the people we are dealing with. This so-called Brotherhood of the Snake."

The altar tender went quiet as he contemplated the reasoning and reality encompassing his dream. And as the water continued its flow towards the city gates, he and Shuma sat together on the bank. Watching as the depths of the darkness gradually began to lighten around, the new day slowly began in its greyness.

***

Gallius was quick to rouse the group that following morning, and wishing to swiftly move on and leave the persecuted city behind, he gave little chance for conversation, and Malian and Shuma were forced to hold their tongues and keep their night's insight to themselves. As the shadows began to lighten across the city walls, the horses and their riders were soon leaving the rushing water behind. Continuing through the gorge along the northern bank, they headed towards the cliffs which bordered the Eastern Great Waters.

The track initially swung round the back of the city before moving eastwards, and as they progressed, Shuma tiredly turned her head and watched the passing walls knowing they held behind them so much misery.

Speaking softly to Malian, who sat in front of her, she touched on their conversation of the night.

"Malian, are you sure about your dream?" she whispered, her voice hissing close to his right ear. "Sure about what it represents, I mean. For here in the light of the morning, dreams may sometimes hold a different message." She paused to let her words register before going on unfaltering, "But if you are sure in your understanding and there are no doubts in your mind, then

32

Gallius must be told before we reach the City of the High Places. He must be warned of this brotherhood and their association with the talisman!"

"I think he may already be wary of those in the city," the reply came back, "especially the king. And yes, I am sure and yes, once we stop, I shall immediately talk with him and accept no delay in doing so."

That said, Malian concentrated on the path ahead as they rounded the sloping foothills. Following the backs of Tragen and Brann advancing before him, they followed Gallius around the hillside to where the dark cliffs came into view as they led off into the sweep of the enormous bay.

***

The escarpment which enclosed the Eastern Great Waters went on for mile after mile, its craggy rock face dropping deep and sheer into the rough waters that played beneath. Leaving behind the slopes of these eastern ranges, the group, having been steered around the headland, came upon the expanse of the pathway that took them along its plummeting edge. Directly below, the waters of the eastern sea spread out before them, and the darkness of the mass increased, stretching out into the distance.

No islands or coastline could be seen out in the ocean, but close to the cliffs, the wind skipped across its surface, the foaming swells surging and expanding before crashing together and disappearing into the blackness. Further out on the horizon, the heaving waves appeared small and insignificant as they rose and fell away, and where the skyline met the water, it merged into a greyness.

The track they followed had slowly opened out on their left as the ranges eventually ended, and the beginning of the deep valleys could be seen extending onto the flatlands, their wide mouths yawning between the heights. Here the waters flowed freely from the heart of the ranges and the upland tarns. Before them lay the plateau, its stretch mirroring that of the vast water with its flatness broken apart by the many water-filled crevasses that intermingled and infused through the wilderness.

Meandering their way through the scrubland of the steppe, many of the larger streams mixed and merged before they met the path. Rising up the side of the walkway, they reached the stony ridge of the cliffs before cascading and trickling over its brink and disappearing into the depths. The plateau appeared to be treeless, but the small scrub bushes, which pushed up out of the moist soil and lined the waterways, gave a disjointed and rambling feel while their short, stunted leaves provided a richness of variation to the greenery.

Coming to the first cascade along the path, the group dismounted to lead the horses over. But the water was not overly deep as it crossed the raised pathway, and soon the riders had little concern for the spills, remaining seated as the horses splashed their way through. Again, the day spread out before them and cascade followed cascade before the light began to drop and Gallius, noting an area between two major streams, eventually brought his horse round to a halt and dismounted.

Immediately Malian dropped down, and leaving the tending of their mount to Shuma, he hastily walked towards where the rider had stopped in the half-light of the late afternoon.

"Gallius, I have urgent need to talk with you," he said, approaching the man face on as he slowly unsaddled his mount, and giving him no chance to turn his back, he continued, "for last night I dreamt, and the gods once again came to me."

The leader paused in his activity, his shoulder still not giving him its full cooperation as he looked towards the altar tender, then carefully lifting the weight away, he patted the horse on its back and allowed it to join the others in their grazing.

Their camp for the night sat just off the pathway with the precarious drop in the foreground, and here, the rest of the group had already begun to gather. At the same time, Gallius led the older man further along the path and into the growing shadows. Allowing some distance to fall between them, the leader stopped and turning towards Malian, he stood on the edge of the cliffs and stared directly back.

"The gods would seem to have been absent from you for a while, Malian," he said, his voice somewhat scathing as the constant pain of his shoulder tormented him. "Why do you think that is?"

"I don't know," Malian grimly replied, sensing the scorn and doubt of the rider, which was unhidden in his asking. "But I feel they come in their own time, not when invoked." His eyes looked directly and piercingly back, and Gallius's gaze dropped as he looked away over the darkening waters that boiled below.

"Well, I'm sure they came with wisdom and guidance," he eventually remarked, and realising his disdain was uncalled for, he smiled back grimly. "Please," he quietly said, "tell me your dream."

Malian explained his vision given by the gods and the making of the Eight Icons. Finishing with the sighting of Mentu and the talisman with the whispered words "Brotherhood of the Snake", he asked the rider if he could again take a look at the tokens, and Gallius was quick to retrieve the silver discs from his jacket and handed them carefully over.

"Well, at least we may know why the Icons are being

gathered," Gallius could say as he deliberated the dream. Watching Malian turn over each of the discs, his mind turned to his own knowledge and remembrance of his friendship with Roth, and he suddenly realised his lack of insight into someone he thought he knew. "And we also now know more about this 'brotherhood' which gives us a clearer understanding of these talismans."

"Yes, I feel they were specifically shown in my dream," Malian pointed out as he peered closely and intently at each token in the gathering gloom. "So I feel they must have some significance. Both Mentu and Roth wore one of these, and we know that they each wanted to steal the Icon even though you were already taking it north."

"I told you that the king also wears one," Gallius reminded him, recalling the shape of the token as it hung around the throat of Dedrick, "and it's definitely the same as the one from around Roth's neck." Replaying again Roth's words spoken as he lay dying, his message that he was taking the Icon to the high priest and not to the king instantly appeared more as a warning, and he added, "I think, Malian, we would be best advised to watch out more for High Priest Serdos and less for the king."

"I fear you may be right. But what if this brotherhood gets to know that both Mentu and Roth are dead? What then will be our chances of getting into the city?" He passed the talismans back to Gallius, and his agitation became apparent.

The questions poured into his mind as he paced further along the path. "And how will we reclaim the other Icons if we cannot get to them? And if they know *Amaunet* is not being brought north, how do we save your daughter?" He suddenly stopped and went very quiet before saying slowly, "If they find out that she has been taken back into the safety of the south, then I fear that further action would be their only choice," he turned quickly towards the rider, "and more men would be called upon and sent out to find her and she would never again be safe!"

"I need to give it more thought, Malian," Gallius quietly said, as the many doubts and questions turned over in his head and the distraught face of his daughter floated before his eyes, "for you've posed a few problems which I need to think on, and I have a few of my own to consider. But the next days should hopefully give some time and let me ponder each of these." He turned to look along the pathway towards where the group sat before cautiously asking, "Who else have you told about this?"

"Only Shuma, why do you ask?"

"I ask because I think it best to keep it between the three of us. What do you think?" His mistrust suddenly became apparent and caused Malian to once more recognise and think on his own fears.

"Well, if that is how you feel, then I agree," came the slow response. Knowing his doubts had been equally shaken at the shock of Mentu's dark and hidden side, he nodded his head before saying, "I'll let her know."

"No, I'll tell her," the leader replied, and easing his shoulder, he felt the sharp pain stab down his tired arm. "I'd like her to take another look at this shoulder, and I'll speak to her then."

As the two stood talking, the fire next to the camp became more intense as the darkness descended, and soon the nightfall overtook the day. With the conversation done for the moment, the two returned carefully along the path to the safety and warmth of the flames and settled for the cold night to come.

***

Far to the south, Theroc and the Black Swan had finally left behind the wild grasslands, and reaching the lush lawns late in the day, they bound their horses about the eyes and entered the tunnels of the Sleeping Caverns as the day came to its close. And as Malian and Gallius stood talking along the cliffs of the Eastern Great Waters, they retraced back a short way along the footsteps of Roth and his men before making their camp for the night in the darkness, where Theroc carried the Icon of *Amaunet* into the safety of the tunnels.

The relief felt by both was immediate and immense as the gloom settled around them, and for the Black Swan, her return to the safety of her home felt overwhelming, and she knew that the dark would be their saving.

***

Away in his own dark, Prince Edgar, Warden of the City of the High Places, also settled before a fire, his gloomy chamber in the lower halls of the stronghold lit only by one solitary lamp, while on the couch, his bedclothes remained straight and undisturbed. Sleep had not been sought that night nor the previous, for he had been constantly pacing within his rooms with the one thought continually returning to his mind being that of his brother and the high priest. He knew they were plotting something, but what it was had been the main question going through his head these last couple of days. The long nights had, however, failed to enlighten and remained fruitless in their answer.

His dismissal from the hall had given him great cause for concern, and he felt a need to cautiously ask questions of the guards stationed within the stronghold. But gaining nothing from them apart from a growing realisation of their loyalty to the king, he found it wise to be turning his attention to the downtown areas in the hope of discovering what was going on for himself. He had noted the rise of unease within the streets, and that, he knew well, is always where trouble breeds.

Joined by some of his men, known to be trustworthy and loyal to him alone, they had on a couple of occasions visited the taverns and gaming dens where the men gathered. As warden, it gave him free and easy access to all these establishments within the city walls, and his presence and questioning did not appear untoward to the citizens who frequented these areas.

The whole of the City of the High Places seemed on edge, and there had been constant comings and goings through the main gate in the last few weeks, which had increased as the days passed. Edgar had been informed of this while his main direction of questioning had finally been guided to a group of men known to have recently returned from the City of the Fortis in the western mountains.

Finding one of the group in a tavern frequented by the king's soldiers nearest the stronghold, he had been further pointed towards the eastern outskirts of the town where the less respected areas had developed and multiplied. Here was where the lanes narrowed into much poorer and simple walkways, the overhanging shadows of the tall houses blocking out the colour of the sky.

In the long past, this city had seen an enormous arrival of residents from surrounding towns and villages, and the walls gradually expanded to accommodate the influx of people. The outer walls became inner façades, and slowly the surrounding forest had been developed and enclosed. It had eventually grown in its vastness and spread, and some had made their fortunes. But there had always been an area where the less privileged and desperate had gathered or been pushed, and here amongst the poor and unsuccessful, Edgar brought his men.

Again he stood before a fire, while around him, the business of drinking and gambling was pursued even in the early hours of the day. As his men questioned the bartender, Edgar glanced around at the regulars who frequented these drab and dingy places. Most were of a similar character, hard men who would easily resort to a fight and whose presence on a battlefield could decide the day. Still, he knew he could rely on their greed, and with that, he would surely be accepted by the depth of his pockets.

Seating himself at a table close to the fire, he warmed his hands and stared hard into the flames. As a young server deposited a mug of ale before him, he turned to see his men bringing forward one of the gamblers from the gaming booths. He appeared somewhat reluctant to accompany the warden's men, and having to be dragged forward, was brought before Edgar.

"I know you," the warden said, immediately recognising the man who was roughly seated opposite. "You're Maddox, one of the king's scouts."

"Yea, that's right," the man answered back, his eyes anxiously looking around and showing evidence of the many ales already downed. "And I know who you are, so what d'you want?"

"We want to know about your visit to the Fortis," Edgar said, coming straight to the point. Looking at the dishevelled man seated before him, he raised his mug and took a long drink. Then nodding to one of his own, another mug was placed before Maddox, and the ale was filled to the brim.

"What's it worth?" the scout demanded, his inane face staring at the mug as the froth played around the edges.

"That depends on your answer." Edgar again raised his mug and took another long drink. "I just want to know why you went there."

Reaching into his jacket, he pulled out his purse and placed it carefully in the middle of the scratched and grubby table, the richness of the black money bag attracting more than just the drunken man's attention.

"We did a job for the king," Maddox slowly said, his eyes focusing on the purse before he looked up into the hard face of the warden. "And were well paid for our troubles," he eagerly added, remembering suddenly who he was talking to. "We brought back something wrapped up, gold, some say. But we never saw it ourselves."

He went on to tell of the expedition to the City of the Fortis, which had taken them over the lesser steppes and down through the lower ranges. Cutting along the edge of the plateau they had travelled along the Canyon of the Palms and up into the city itself. There had been one captain and six other men, he explained, but only the captain had entered the city, returning with a small wrapped-up package in the dead of night. They had then swiftly made their journey back, the weather around the base of the Mounts of Aquila causing an unwanted delay to their return.

"Who was your captain?" Edgar asked as the telling came to an end, and pushing the purse forward, he indicated that this would be his last question.

"Gregory, Captain Gregory!" the man finally declared before his hand reached towards the purse. Quickly taking it up in his greed, Maddox eagerly returned to the gambling booths, and before the end of the night, the money earned had been lost to the tables, and even the empty black purse itself had been stolen.

**

The cry of the gulls as they soared noisily overhead woke Malian to the cold winds of the morning. Carefully turning over beneath his blanket, he saw the Eastern Great Waters leading off into the far distance. Away on the horizon, the dark, sullen columns of storm cloud met the skyline, and the rain poured out its temper over the shifting expanse.

The massive thunderstorm out in the ocean had driven the sea birds inland. And away far in the north in the shelter of the northern bays, the enormous flocks had gathered, seeking refuge from its anger. On the plateau, they had descended along its cliffs, and upon the land bordering the coast had settled in their extent, the drifts of birds swooping and diving as they caught the harsh flurries of the morning breeze. Above in the lightening sky, their raucous cries mingled with the howl of the wind as it gusted overhead and the strident echoes poured out over the waters.

Sitting up, Malian could see Darric and Tragen tending the horses amongst the bright green scrub of the plateau, the dark ranges of the north giving a distant backdrop to the scenery. Brann was soon to join them as they brought the mounts away from their grazing and bringing them closer to the camp they made ready to saddle up. Rising, he joined Anitta where she sat alone alongside the warm embers of the night's fire, while around the camp, the water ran its ever-flowing course towards the cliffs.

"Shuma said you had not been sleeping well, Malian," the swan said, her hair pushed back to reveal the scarred face as she looked across to the man, "so we thought we would let you rest a while longer." Smiling at the altar tender as he sat down, her features took on an easier appearance, and the disfigurement of her past life appeared to fade as she passed over a warming drink.

"Sleep has long been a challenge in finding," he replied, accepting the cup, "and once it comes, it's good to be able to make the most of it." Thanking her, he stared off across the path to where two figures were positioned before him on the edge of the cliffs.

Gallius stood on the brink of the rock face, his back to the camp, and by his side, the wise woman had paused, her arms folded around as she fought to hold on to her wrap as the wind gusted upwards off the sea. Neither seemed fearful of the dizzying drop opening at their feet, and as they stared out to the darkened horizon, the two appeared in talk as they looked out over the view.

As their voices were thrown back over their shoulders, the updrafts carrying them across the pathway, the occasional disjointed word could be discerned by those seated around the fire, and Malian briefly caught the words "talisman" and "high priest" along with "shoulder" before they were whisked further away across the plateau. Glancing quickly across to Anitta to check on her observance, he was thankful that the swan appeared more interested in her packing over anything else, and the altar tender felt able to relax.

***

The brightness of the day saw them moving further along the pathway, the horses falling into place behind Gallius' mount as they followed the basin's gently curved contour around the waters. And throughout the course, the runoff from the plateau cascaded around their hooves and over the path before dropping away over the escarpment.

The dark clouds out over the water could now be seen to be slowly seething and roiling, their dense, heavy blanket spreading with a threat to make land later in the day, and Gallius did not hold his horse back as it trotted carefully along the sodden path.

Their next stop would be the last before heading inland, and he knew it should only take another three to four days, given good weather, before reaching the Highland Tarn of the lower ranges and then another two or so before the abandoned City of Muntani on the lesser steppes lay before them. The riders had come down this way from the City of the High Places on their quest to steal the Icon of the valley, and now on returning back, he knew this land from old. However, as Gallius and Brann slowly retraced their steps and neared home, many doubts began as to their next course of action.

Sitting again behind Malian, Shuma remained silent as they bounced along, splashing through the waters while the ocean breezes that coursed up the rock face brought with them a salty tang to their lips. But after several quiet hours passed in riding, Malian felt a need to break the silence.

"How's Gallius' shoulder?" he softly enquired, his voice hoping to hide any note of implication other than concern.

"It's slowly improving," came the brief reply, the wise woman's tone adding nothing further. And in her fleeting response, it allowed the quietness to wrap itself back around as they jogged along, each in their own thought.

Eventually, the sameness of the vast panorama to both right and left became monotonous, and the constant sight of Gallius, Brann and Tragen riding before them added to the unchanging view as they moved onward. Malian could feel a growing unease and restlessness as Shuma bounced around behind him before, finally, the stillness was broken.

"Malian, I've been thinking about that question that I asked you the other night," she began, "about why the disorder has already started." She stared out over the altar tender's shoulder as Tragen's horse splashed on through yet another cascade before continuing, "And I can only think it must be because of the Icons that have already been brought together, for then their governing powers would increase, and the forces of chaos grow."

"That would sound about right," Malian slowly answered back, his mind having been focused elsewhere at that particular moment, "and, yes, it would explain the quickness of the coming winter to the valley. For I feel right in assuming that *Amaunet* was one of the last Icons to be collected by this brotherhood."

"Yes, but I fear you don't understand," she said, her voice suddenly anxious. "That means we need to split up all of the Icons, just like they were in your dream," she whispered. "All of them, Malian, and they must be returned to the cities where the gods originally placed them. For even if just two are left together, then their powers are increased!"

Malian was not unexpectedly shocked, for he had already considered this aspect and had slowly come to the same conclusion. But he was suddenly aware of the concern in what the wise woman was really saying to him and how this would affect the entire group.

"So you see," she said softly, her voice filled with dread, "it's no longer just about Tragen's Icon and Gallius' daughter anymore, is it?"

"No, Shuma, I'm afraid it isn't," he declared, dismay heard in his voice as he acknowledged the task placed upon them. "We now have to ensure the rescue of all of the stolen Icons and restore them once more back to their god-assigned cities!"

***

As they progressed along the pathway, the clouds gathered, and the seabirds which had remained present as they rode disappeared further inland on the storm's advance. At the end of the day, the journey became wetter as the outlying rains descended, and the night's stop was forecast to be cold and damp. Gallius, aware they would be turning north in the morning, hoped their journey would be swift and the weather more on their side, for tomorrow, he would be leading them inland along the stream across the plateau. Then heading up past where the eagles soared and the Mounts of Aquila rose high, they would eventually reach the Highland Tarn in the lower ranges.

CHAPTER THREE

The night's stop was cold as they made camp once more just off the pathway but they had finally reached the stream which would lead them through into the greenery of the plateau and on north towards the lower ranges. Gallius, knowing well the tiredness passing amongst them, noted, at last, the moss-covered boulders that stood at this position and appeared thankful to have arrived at this point.

The wet weather, which had earlier threatened, fizzled out as darkness fell slowly over the upland, and the slight drizzle eventually stopped. And the thicker, heavier clouds remaining at sea disappeared as the increasing breeze pushed them away eastwards, and the dark blue of the night sky steadily became clearer.

Malian was again quick to take Gallius to one side as soon as they stopped, and this time, Shuma joined him as they walked back along the darkening path, leaving Anitta and the men to their now well-practised routines. Once they came to a halt away from the main group, their talk immediately went to the question that Malian and Shuma had been talking of.

Telling Gallius of their thinking behind why the chaos and disorder was spreading, Malian declared, "All of the Icons will have to be found and taken back, Gallius." Looking from the weary man back to the wise woman as she stood with her back to the vista of the great waters, he finished, "All of them!"

His voice then firmly stated the magnitude of their mission, "For until they are all restored to their rightful places, this turmoil within the cities will never be controlled, and this Brotherhood of the Snake will maintain the upper hand."

Gallius turned, and stepping away from the two, walked further off along the path, the dark of the plateau gathering itself around before he stopped for many moments, his mind taking in the words just spoken. Slowly, he returned out of the shadows. His face held a hard and decisive look about it, although the tiredness remained, and a weariness could be seen about his frame.

"Well, it seems quite a challenge has fallen upon us," he eventually said as he stood before the altar tender, his mind having come to a settlement. "But first we have to deal with getting into the city. Once that is achieved, I must find my daughter over and above anything else and check that she is safe." He paused before going on, "Only then will I help in finding these Icons."

"Agreed!" Malian affirmed, and looking to Shuma, he saw her gentle nod in accord. "We understand that your first action must be to find your daughter and check her safety, and in that, we will help all we can. And in return, you have offered your support to us."

"Good, if that is agreed, let us hope the weather will keep well for us and not cause a delay in the ranges."

Walking along the pathway, the three returned back to the night's camp and their last evening on the edge of the escarpment.

***

The next morning they tracked the course of the stream northwards, where it cut deep into the softness of this moist green land, and Gallius focused his attention on following it back to its origin high in the ranges.

The Highland Tarn from which it flowed was on the very borders of the eastern lower range, while the Mounts of Aquila led off one behind the other into the west. Here the pathway to the high city would take them between the two, with the blue water of the tarn guiding them upward from the first hill to the second.

Then they would turn northeast, and following the small valley between the hills, would take the path through into the lower ridges and upwards into the very heart of the high north. Here the vast vertical slopes of the lesser steppes rose before them, and here also lay the long deserted City of Muntani, which sat directly along their course. Behind these forgotten ruins, the steppes would lead further to the higher ground and their goal in the north, where the governing power alone held its position.

***

Captain Gregory was found at the arena in the City of the High Places. This stood in front of the stronghold where the high walls of its stone-clad enclosure formed the backs of the market areas. These sat around its outer perimeter and teemed with the activities and enterprises of the sellers and hawkers.

Between the walls and among the sand and dust of the square, a large number of thickset men were being schooled with various weaponry, and the captain was preoccupied with the unfavourable job of picking out the most skilled for security duties.

The high city had, over many decades, seen an expansion in its population, and for the majority, they had remained in law and order, and in general, the people had thrived. Only recently, however, the community had witnessed a sharp rise in public disorder, and a growing number of men and militia had been called upon to ensure some semblance of control within the back streets where the unrest appeared to foment.

"Gregory!" the warden's voice resounded across the

yard. "A moment of your time!" His harsh tone echoed above the constant clatter and clang of metal and gave little chance of refusal to its request. The captain seeing the arm raised in his direction was quick to turn the men over to his officer. Striding across the sand of the square, he joined the prince at the boundary gates, where after briefly lifting his hand, he turned to regard the men.

"I think the bottom of the barrel is in sight," he gruffly said, and watching the disheartening efforts of the assembled men, he turned his back on the scene and addressed Edgar. "You wanted me, warden?"

"I hear you have recently been to the Fortis?" Edgar said, coming straight to the point of his questioning. Dragging his gaze away from the combatants, he led the burly captain out into the crowded street where the bustle of daily life revolved. Heading right, they moved through the press of people and past the main doors to the stronghold. Here, just to the side of the fortified building, the hoteliers and bordello keepers had found it profitable to establish their trades, and with the many gaming halls and eating establishments proliferating in the area, it gave the city soldiers easy and convenient access for the spending of their income.

"The Fortis, yes, that's right," the captain eventually replied, his voice low and guarded as he walked alongside, his height slightly towering above that of the warden and the encroaching mass of citizens. "There were unpaid taxes to be collected."

"Taxes!" the warden said in surprise. "I've heard otherwise, Captain!" Guiding the man along the nearby smaller alley off the main pavement, he strode through the doors of the nearest beer hall and gestured for him to sit. He was quick to seat himself opposite, and the server, noting the uniforms of his fresh customers, was brisk to attend upon the king's brother and the officer.

While Edgar glanced casually around at the other clientele, Gregory maintained his account. "I was told to collect taxes," he repeated, his only defence to keep to his original story.

"Enough, Gregory!" the warden instantly said, his eyes returning to stare fixedly at the man. "Please don't think me a fool. I know you went in of a night-time, hardly the hour to be collecting taxes, I feel!"

"Well, yes," he had to agree. Lowering his voice, he continued firmly, "But we have been well paid to keep our tongues, and I have taken those words to have been said in their full meaning!"

Edgar, staring out over the brim of his beer mug, could see that the captain was afraid as his hands on either side of his untouched mug nervously tapped a rhythm out on the tabletop, and a certain fear could be seen deep in his eyes which glared back as he sat straight within his seat.

"I've already spoken with one of your scouts," the warden declared, already in the know, "and he told me you took something away, something gold and valued by that city alone."

"Who did you speak to?" the man instantly demanded, his voice whispering as the harsh tapping became slightly more erratic.

"Never mind that!" The warden reached forward, and grasping the heavy hands as they drummed away, forced the fingers down upon the hardwood and brought about a stillness. "I want to know what you carried back for the king! And as king's brother, you are entrusted with answering my questioning, or I will have you taken away."

He slowly let the hands go, and the captain knew he was being given no alternative and had a crucial decision to make. Edgar was his superior in being both Warden of the City and brother of the king, and the options were beginning to look slim whichever course he examined. He could either incur the king's wrath, or the warden would have him dealt with in the stronghold's dungeon.

Grasping the mug, he took a deep mouthful of the bitter ale and made his choice. Looking around the crowded beer hall, he pulled his chair around the table closer to that of the warden and hastily explained to Edgar that he and his men had been chosen to enter the Fortis to steal a treasure. A treasure that the city folk there held very dear. It was also made known to him that the job would be well paid upon his successful return. He then made clear that he had been advised by the high priest that this task would be best undertaken by himself alone and that it should only be he who entered the city and took the treasure. This would leave his men none the wiser to the artefact taken.

"What was it you stole?" Edgar quickly asked, unable to hold back his questioning.

"It was a small statue with a frog's head," the captain whispered, "a solid golden statue with eyes like rubies." He took another deep draught, and wiping his mouth across his wide sleeve, continued, "The job was easy enough done in the dark while the city slept, and we were well paid by the king on our return." He glared towards the warden before declaring, "It was that High Priest Serdos who told us to keep our silence or else he'd cut out our tongues." Emptying his mug before placing it down, he finished, "That's all I can tell you, Warden."

Another thought then occurred to him, and grasping Edgar's arm, he went on to say that there had recently been talk of another group that had also gone out to one of the cities, away in the deep valley of the south. But the talk had gone quiet of late, and the disturbances within the high city had become a priority, with the gossip naturally turning elsewhere. But it might be useful for the warden to pursue this avenue if needed.

Edgar now felt able to dismiss the captain, for he could see little sense in questioning further when no other information would be forthcoming. He had, however, gained something additional to contemplate even if he felt only somewhat the wiser, and he turned the thought over in his mind.

"Just a statue," he pondered as he remained seated. And while the empty mugs were gathered off the table top and a further overflowing one set down along with a plate of bread and cheese, he let the hum and liveliness of the tavern surround him.

***

High Priest Serdos wrapped his cloak tight around his thin body, and stepping north out of the palace gardens, turned and shut the wooden door behind him. Following around the enclosed walkway, the thick walls forming a colonnade, he walked swiftly towards the stronghold. The covered cloister through which he passed ensured some safety and privacy between the two buildings from the encroaching city and left the everyday world of its people unwise and little knowing of its existence.

The guard on the doorway was, therefore, the only person to see the approach of the priest as he strode around the far corner. Holding open the thick wooden door at this other end, he stood to attention as Serdos passed through. Once inside the stronghold, he headed directly along his well-walked route towards the halls in the north of the building, where he found Dedrick at meal, the king once again seated at his long polished table. This time, however, he was not alone, for he had a guest and one who sat upright and tense further along the bench on the king's right-hand side.

"Serdos, welcome," Dedrick said on seeing the high priest, "please come and join us, for we are ready to begin our meal." He held his hand towards where the woman sat, her long dark hair flowing down her shoulders and covering the half-hidden face, and the priest placed himself between her and the king as he continued, "Any news yet on Gallius' return?"

"No news, my lord," Serdos replied. Helping himself to a cup, he poured out a generous helping of wine and topped up the untouched cup of the woman who sat beside him.

"Well, let us hope we shall hear from him soon," Dedrick said, "for I know he will not let us down while he understands his daughter remains our guest." He looked along the table to where the high priest sat close alongside Daina, her eyes fixed firmly on the laden plate before her.

He knew she linked her imprisonment to her father's journey and her only chance of freedom on his successful return. He was also fully aware that the young woman had not been mistreated or had cause to say she had been, for his orders had been strict and were to be carried out only by his guards. He himself had ensured her cell in the depths of the dungeons had been given over to some comfort, but still, she remained a prisoner and would stay so until the return of Gallius.

A full plate was placed before Serdos, and the attending servants slowly withdrew from the hall after ensuring that the fire had been tended, the table candles lit and the drink flasks refilled. And the three were left to their supper, the gathering gloom of the hall falling around each of the seated figures.

"Do you think the weather could be causing his delay?" King Dedrick eventually asked, his voice breaking into the dull silence while his mind remained fixed firmly on the whereabouts of Gallius.

"Possibly," the high priest guardedly replied. Gently touching his chest, he felt the slight increase in the weight of the talisman. With this, it made clear that Roth, bearing his own token, was hopefully coming closer, and his confidence soared as he anticipated that the last Icon was approaching further into his reach. "But he is clearly on his way north, my lord."

The king looked down at his full plate, and taking a long drink from the mug sat close to hand, he nodded his head, and the two men began to eat. Eventually, as the woman saw little sense in going hungry when food was within reach, she slowly picked up her fork.

***

Much later, as she sat back in her prison, Daina reflected on the words spoken and took some comfort in knowing that Gallius would soon be back in the city. He had been gone well over sixty days, last seen by her in the throne room while seated alongside the king. And in all that time, she had been confined to this prison room and denied any access to the outside of the stronghold. There was no other to know or be concerned about her whereabouts, so she kept her strength and only hope alive in the homecoming of her father.

***

The blue water of the Highland Tarn was reached on the end of the third day after Gallius and the group had left the escarpment of the Great Eastern Waters and the weather remained cold with an increasing breeze. But at least it had stayed dry. Their following night, alongside the waters, however, saw a change in the elements, and the journey through the ranges proved to be less cordial, the cold wind blowing between the hills being accompanied by constant rain, and the nights had been miserable and dreary.

It took a further three comfortless days before the City of Muntani sat before them on the lesser steppes, the early afternoon light flooding across its darkened walls before disappearing beyond into the lands where the herds once roamed. The group was instantly glad to at last see a refuge ahead as they approached up the grassy slope to where the once thriving city of herdsmen and drovers sat on the beginning of the grassland plains.

***

The City of Muntani, with its domain of heath and grassland, had lain abandoned and deserted for many years over three decades, its previous citizens having fled into the forest of the north when civil disorder and the fires of lawlessness had spread and become too overwhelming. And while the people had integrated within their new found societies, their old city and way of life had been left to decay, and the expanse which once surrounded their homes and led off east remained unattended and overgrown.

The charred outer walls of the buildings still stood, but inside, the avenues had become crowded with saplings seeded from the vast northern forest on the higher steppes. The thin roots of these tenacious trees had slowly torn apart the walkways, and the once neat gardens and pathways were now unrecognisable in their neglect and ruin.

The gates to the city had fallen aside many years ago while the massive hinges remained rusting in the brickwork, and the wood of the doors had rotted to the ground and lay slowly turning to dust before its entrance. This gaping hole, left behind within the thick walls, guided the riders through into a wild and windblown area where another opening stood directly opposite.

Gallius immediately passed through this entrance, and turning to his right, brought his horse to a halt at an archway into what was once a courtyard. Here the market stalls had sat, and the voices of the people had once risen high. Now, however, the area stood silent and overwhelmed by the congestion and growth of numerous shrubs.

Dismounting, he handed his horse to Brann and moved towards an open doorway. Looking in, he saw that the walls of the room remained intact, and in the far corner, a part of the roof remained, its blackened beams protruding high over the undergrowth.

"We'll get an area cleared," he said, aware the afternoon was making its way to a close. Bending, he easily pulled out the seedlings at his feet, and throwing them aside, he began to free up an area around the entrance. "We shall make camp here tonight."

Brann was again tasked with the horses while Tragen and Darric joined Gallius in his job of tearing out and uprooting the overrun expanse. Within a short time, the doorway had been brushed clear, and a single walkway into the far corner was opened up between the shrubs. The simply decorated floor tiles, their surrounds chipped and soil encrusted, had now become revealed in their ruin.

"I have a good feeling about this place," Shuma said, looking around at the bareness of the scorched, burnt walls as she stood upon the broken slabs that had been torn up. "There is something timeless yet sad about this city."

"Yes," Anitta agreed, following the wise woman as

she moved further into the room behind Darric, "it feels as if it was once much loved and prosperous but is now alone in its wait."

They eventually cleared the mess into the corner, and the walls were cleaned off from the climbing shrubs, and they took time to collect their packs and returned beneath the shelter that the surviving part of the roof gave. With their backs to the walls of the marketplace, they could relax as the darkness encroached through the remaining trees.

While Brann left the horses to graze within sight of the ruined entrance, a fire was lit from the uprooted shrubs and the collected rotting timbers, and the bedrolls were positioned around its warmth and the damp and musty clothes left to dry off.

***

As the night closed in, none of the group seated around the fire could know or even judge the importance of where they sat, for this city in the long past had been the first to reveal its association with the Eight.

Here, within these very walls, the first of the divine beings collectively called the Ogdoad had been found, and the Icon of *Heh* had begun the rise of chaos throughout the land.

The Priest of the City, Johenn, had unwittingly stumbled upon the Icon in his attempt to extend the chapel, and in pulling down old existing walls, had opened up the surrounds which had stood for more than an age. Here, the statue had been purposefully hidden away countless years in the past and just forgotten about over the many centuries. Placed within a sealed casket and walled up inside the safety of the chapel, the everyday people of the city had been kept ignorant of their responsibility, and their rituals and devotion had turned to that of the lands around and the herds of cattle and sheep which grazed there.

Johenn, however, had taken the statue to the newly appointed high priest in the city on the high steppes in hope of finding out what it was. And Serdos, unwrapping the golden statue and seeing the emerald green eyes staring up out of the frog-like face, had been completely overcome once he realised what had been found!

Instantly summoning members of the brotherhood, he had claimed the statue as being one of the Eight and the search for the remaining Icons, never fully forgotten in their day-to-day prayers, had been rekindled afresh, falling upon the brothers in an even greater fervour.

Knowing the statue had been found within the confines of a chapel, Serdos restlessly contemplated where the others could have been hidden, and information had slowly been gathered. Over the years, small groups had been sent out on the hunt, some never returning while many came back empty-handed.

But eventually, the reports gradually became clearer, and the brotherhood further educated themselves and became wiser. And the captains and their scouts had been sent out with more purpose, their attentions becoming concentrated on certain places within the north and south.

In the course of time, the Icons were slowly acquired and brought secretly into the city, leaving behind them only the gathering clouds of chaos and disorder until finally, there remained only three to be collected, *Kauket*, *Amun* and *Amaunet*.

It had only been in recent years that the high priest had found certain evidence of a temple building in the distant City of the Fosse and dispatching a group of scouts, their hard-headed captain known for his harsh manners, they were given their orders. They had ridden fast in their search along the waterfalls of the Eastern Great Waters, the duty falling on them to return with either information or knowledge of the Eight.

Captain Steffan had done even better than that, for he had returned from the city bringing with him the Icon of *Kauket*, and it had joined its counterpart *Kek* and the others at the foot of the carved snake god along the alabaster ledge of the altar. *Amun* had next been collected, leaving *Amaunet* the last remaining Icon to be acquired, the Eighth Primordial Deity and the long wait for her could not come any sooner for the gathering Brotherhood of *Apep*.

***

Edgar again returned to his rooms, and summoning Tervic, one of his chief officers, he allowed the small, weasel-like man to remain standing while he pulled away the chair from behind the desk. Sitting down heavily, he spread his arms over the paperwork which covered the table top almost in its entirety and which, unfortunately, came with his job of warden. The room was chill, with a weak light sullenly flowing through a series of small high windows, but it remained in shadow even at the height of the day. As the flames burned low in the grate, he peered across the gloom to the man who was his main source of rumour within the city walls.

"Anything I should know about, Tervic?" the question asked in general as the prince poured himself a mug of wine and took a heavy sup.

"Comings and goings," came the reply. "Although mainly comings," he added, the recent arrival of outsiders to the city heading to the stronghold not going without notice.

"Have you heard anything about a statue?" Edgar

turned his enquiry, knowing that if the recently acquired knowledge were correct, then Tervic would be the one to add further facts. For the man held his position within the warden's household only on his ability to acquire and possess secrets and confidences, and one in which he excelled.

"A statue?" the man repeated, a puzzled look crossing his dark, lean face as he appeared surprised at the questioning. "No, sir, I haven't, but I will certainly give it my attention and do some snooping."

"Very good." The warden nodded. "And what about any captained groups?" His disappointment at the man's lack of insight was noticeable in his voice. "Are any absent or any been gone for some time?" Rising, he moved to the front of the desk, leaving behind the mess of papers and seating himself on its rounded edge, he slowly sipped his wine and watched intently as Tervic thought for a short while.

"There is one group which has been away a while," the little man finally said, and quickly he recalled its leader's name, "led by a Captain Gallius. I think they have been away from the hold for some months."

"Gallius," Edgar repeated the name which gave him no cause for concern, "isn't he just a Captain of the Escort? Why would he have been sent out of the city?"

"It's rumoured that his daughter is a visitor to the king's keep," Tervic suggestively added, his talent making known Daina's whereabouts, "been there since her father left, they say. Could be good enough reason!"

"Good enough reason, for sure!"

Leaving behind the officer with his grateful hand clasping a silvered coin for his efforts, the warden left behind his cheerless rooms and took the short flight of steps down towards the chambers and on into the crypts.

***

The fire burned brightly under the overhang of the blackened roof, and as evening turned into night, the group stretched leisurely around the cleared expanse. Gallius sat alongside Shuma, their backs to the corner of the hard stone wall as they talked. The shadows fell long into the surround, providing a feeling of dense enclosure about them as the forsaken City of Muntani lay spread around, the darkness having given back its dignity as the decay and collapse slowly receded into the dusk, and the crumbling walls disappeared.

"Two more days, and we'll be among the forest of the higher steppes, and the city will soon be in sight," Gallius briefed them, his face staring out over the flames, "and we need to have a plan ready before we see the main gates."

"Our return will be expected, Gallius," Brann clearly reminded him, "So there should be no problem getting back into the city."

"Yes, but I am a captain, and I should be returning with my compliment of scouts, not just the two of us and…" Stopping, he looked to either side of Brann where the others sat beside the fire. Seeing one older man, one younger, another man who was an unmistakable stranger and two women, he dropped his head, appearing for a moment to be lost for words.

Shuma gently touched his arm in some understanding, her hand remaining in place as he lifted his head before continuing, "…and once we do get into the city, I will need to have the Icon. I will need to show possession of it to gain entry into the stronghold." For him, *Amaunet* came first in his thinking only as means of access to Dedrick, and in ensuring that his daughter was alive and safe, and ultimately rescuing her from the king.

"What if you said it had been taken from you," Shuma suggested, her mind presenting another idea. "You and Brann could go to the king and tell him you had been ambushed yourselves and the Icon stolen from you in the struggle. You have the wound to prove evidence of your fight." Dropping her hand from his arm, she looked towards his right shoulder where, beneath the cover of his shirt, she knew the wound still parted the skin. "And all of your men, except for Brann, are dead. Killed in the encounter as far as the king needs to know."

Gallius' mind followed this thought through and could see the reasoning and possibilities in its thinking, and for many moments he stared into the reddened heart of the fire as he contemplated the outcomes this would obtain. The main one was surely that he would be able to see his daughter and check that she was free from harm, while the second gave them more time in which to assess their situation regarding the Icons.

"That sounds practical," he eventually said, turning and smiling at Shuma as his military mind worked over its feasibility, "but I shall need to give it some further thought and sort out a strategy."

"Would they not just send you back out again?" Darric clearly declared, his white hair forming a lightness about his face as he looked across the fire towards the leader. "You and Brann could be sent with even more scouts to follow these thieves and take back the Icon!"

"Possibly, but that would still give us more time, and that's what we need. Time to check out where the other Icons are and to make our plans."

"But what about us? Where does that leave us," Tragen asked, bringing in the remainder of the group, his voice dark and low as he sat between Darric and Anitta. "We need to be in the city with you!"

"Yes, but there must be some reason for your being

63

there," Gallius replied, knowing full well that strangers within the city walls would be questioned. "You are not from this city, and your presence there will be noted."

"Well, what about the talisman?" Malian suddenly asked, his mind pondering the meaning of these items and their association with the brotherhood. "Could they be of some help in our getting into the city and in your reaching the king?"

"I don't know," Gallius truthfully replied, his thought turning to that notion. But not being able to say too much in front of the others, he found it best to leave this questioning aside, and both he and Malian fell silent.

"But where does that leave us?" Tragen again finally demanded, his frustration becoming apparent as he thought about his nearness to *Naunet*, his city's Icon and the chance for her recovery.

"It leaves us with another two days' journey," Gallius strongly said, "and we should take our rest while we can." The leader lay down, turning his back to the fire and Tragen and the rest of the group, sensing that nothing further would be achieved from the moment, had to be satisfied.

***

Taking the stone steps from the wide opening in the hall, Prince Edgar followed the stairs down as they gradually narrowed, his long shadow falling before him as he descended into the lower depths beneath the stronghold. Here the air took on a more distinctly stale yet drier quality, as the fresher air from above rarely reached these areas.

Nearing the bottom, the heavy bars of the gates came into sight around the curve of the staircase. The guard who stood in the basement looked up uninterested as

Edgar came into view around the wrap of the stair but managing a swift salute, he unlocked the heavy bolt to allow the man to pass, and the warden entered the dungeons.

The king's brother had often been known to help himself to wine from the vaults, and there appeared no reason to think otherwise on this occasion. But this time, instead of turning right along the corridor after the gates and heading towards the vast cellars, he stepped to the left, where he knew the passageways entered a more clearly restricted area.

The dungeons and prison cells of the high city sat alongside the sprawl of storage rooms and vaults where the wine cellars sat, but the rooms where the prisoners were confined were found more in the far north of the underground area along a number of twisting and turning passages. The feeling of isolation was magnified and increased by the limited and cramped corridors leading off the main alley, and along these, Edgar followed the close passageway on its main route, the light of the flickering lamps lighting his way.

The tunnel eventually became more restricted, and the rooms on either side were mainly small and limited, each offering an increased feeling of isolation and imprisonment with their heavily locked doors having just a single barred window. But not all appeared to be occupied, and Edgar glanced through into each cell as he passed, noting any residents as they either slowly raised a head on his passing or else were unable even to call forth that response.

The warden finally came to a stop at the last barred door on the right, and looking through the open window, saw a young woman seated slumped on the edge of a bed, her feet tucked away beneath the thin mattress while a blanket lay drawn up around her shoulders and the long hair remained hidden and shrouded away under cover of a wrap. The interior of this slightly larger cell appeared overly light and lavish in respect of the surrounding dark, barren rooms, for a number of comforts had been provided on the king's orders. But the door was locked and secure, and Edgar did not have a key.

Moving on further past the other cells, the prison guards had made a room for their own comfort at the end of the passage, and Edgar pushed aside the half-open door. Stepping inside, he found the room empty, the white painted walls peeling in their dryness, while only a couple of empty beer mugs sat upon the bench, and the remains of a card game gave proof of recent occupation. Pulling the door closed, he walked back towards the locked door.

Standing outside the room, he brought his face closer to the aperture and peered into the prison room, noting the table containing its small provision of food alongside a water flask and the extra blanket which stood close to hand draped over the single chair.

"Are you the daughter of Captain Gallius?" he straightaway asked, his words unexpectedly echoing into both the stillness of the chamber and also back along either side of him through the passageway.

The girl was startled and jumped at the voice, the abrupt intrusion into her silence giving her cause for alarm. Rising, she quickly unwrapped herself from the blanket and came towards the door.

"Who are you?" she instantly demanded, staring blatantly at the face framed in the window, and then recognising the man, she took a step back. "Oh, I apologise, Warden." Her voice took on a slightly more courteous tone. "I didn't realise it was you."

Edgar would never have recognised her face, it being one of many that would be in the crowds of bystanders and general public seen in the course of his day-to-day. But she obviously knew his, and the slight trace of respect softened his approach, and the warden repeated his question in a less demanding tone.

"Are you the daughter of Captain Gallius?"

"Yes, I am Daina, Gallius' daughter," she answered, her voice rising in hope as she asked further, "Have you report of my father?" She moved back towards the grill of the door, and standing closer, Edgar could see the paleness of her face bordered by the rich texture of her wrap. A deep worry was etched across her brow, yet, her head was held high, and her eyes still held some fire, and in the asking, she did not belittle or demean herself.

But in answer to her question, he could only reply, "No, I have no news of your father. But I was hoping, Daina, that you could enlighten me on that issue."

"I would have thought you to be already in the know, sir," she said somewhat bluntly, her eyes remaining fixed upon the barred window, "being brother to the king."

"Well, not all information is passed my way, and some is knowingly withheld," he said, in hope that she might understand his position, "But in this case, I feel I need to be given a little insight." He then asked if she had heard any news of her father's arrival, finishing with, "That is all I need to know from you."

Daina, standing behind her boundary of the locked door, simply explained to the listening warden that she had little news herself, only recently hearing, by way of the high priest, that her father and his men were on their way back to the city. He should soon be returning within its walls, she explained, but of what their assignment had been, she knew nothing and was unable to provide any help in that direction. And the warden had to be content in what little gained knowledge he had gathered.

Returning along the depressing passageway, Edgar

reached the main corridor leading to the gate, and crossing over its width, strode into the wine vaults. There he picked out two of the better flasks of his brother's wine, and retracing his steps back, headed towards the stair.

The guard at the gate had changed, but the one who now stood to attention had been made aware that the warden was in the cellars and his sudden appearance up the corridor, the flasks tucked under his arm, came as little surprise as he passed through the barrier.

Retiring to his rooms where the wine was poured and savoured, Edgar sat at his desk and contemplated the imminent return of Gallius, and further questions were placed before him and spun heavy in his thoughts as the night lengthened into shadow. Until finally, the liquor made its mark, and his head dropped to the table.

CHAPTER FOUR

The Brotherhood of *Apep* had seen an increase in their numbers over the last few days, and a regular influx of visitors had arrived separately at the city gates summoned by the word of the high priest. Each had made their way steadily towards the stronghold where Serdos stood in wait atop the steps.

Greeting each new arrival, he welcomed them to the City of the High Places before guiding them through to where King Dedrick sat upon his throne, and here they had shown their respect either in deference or mere acceptance of his position, depending on the type of talisman worn. Most had shown deference, being *Hem-netjer*, a basic priest within the brotherhood, and the king felt some bond with these as they later stood at the back of the assembly.

At this first gathering within the palace crypt, Serdos led his *Hery-heb*, his lector priests, in their ceremonies. These priests, wearing the talisman of the snake within the snake, were the scribes and the brothers of the word. They also carried the books of ritual and prayer, and in their duties, supported the high priest and stood above the rest.

The gathered brotherhood so far had come together within the safety of the palace, and all were housed inside its confines and were content to remain within its walls. All except for Dedrick. For the king chose to return each night along the colonnade back to his stronghold and keep to his own customs when not at the gathering.

Here in his halls, he still retained some supremacy in his given authority, and his rule was never questioned by his attendants. But he had begun to feel somewhat put out by the actions of Serdos, and in the recent days, had felt even more secondary as more of the *Hery-heb* had arrived and increased in number. But the talisman had always implied the position of the wearer within the brotherhood and had forever been handed down from father to son, and in its long past, the kingship of the city had never risen above its first standing, and Dedrick struggled to be content with that.

***

In the early morning, Shuma arose from her sleep alongside Gallius, and crossing the courtyard, left behind the group and walked out into the front area beside the gates where the horses had been tethered for the night. Passing them by, they lifted their heads in curiosity and anticipation, but on seeing her continue eastwards into the avenue of the city, they slowly dropped their noses and relaxed back into their rest.

The City of Muntani lay before her in the light of the day, and her heart dropped as she witnessed its devastation. The walls of the houses and buildings were blackened by the flames, and here and there, roof timbers, charred as bones, poked up out of the rubble and grass-choked debris. And small saplings seeded from the northern trees had eaten into the paths and walkways of the streets, breaking apart the ornately patterned tiles and lifting their remains upwards. In the overrun gardens and backyards, the larger fruit trees, initially scorched and damaged by the fires, had in places, regenerated and flourished and stood surrounded by their own seedlings gathered around their base.

The main walls had somehow survived the blaze, their height being a backdrop to the ruin beneath, but they had become overgrown with trailing weeds and climbers.

Here the green of their leaves stood out against the scorched brickwork, and through this ruination and slow natural restoration, Shuma wandered her way into the city. Her mind instantly went to the terror and panic which must have driven the people out, and in the morning light, she found it easy to imagine the confusion which would have ensued.

Finally, she arrived at an area where the street widened, and the collapsed houses gathered around its wilderness. At its very centre stood a water well, the twisted metal of its pumping arm sticking upwards out of the decay, and about its brick walls, the invading bush and shrub had haphazardly become rooted in the dust and dirt which had gathered.

Looking at the city's downfall, Shuma was unaware of Gallius coming up behind until reaching her, he stood at her side and gently lifted her hand, and she turned to look up into his serious face.

"I've somewhere I would like to show you," he whispered, unable to raise his voice in the quietness which closed around.

Guiding her past the water pump and across the desolate streets, he walked the paths remembered from a previous time. Crossing the main arena at the centre of the city, where the square waterlily-clad ponds once stood, and the people had met in conversation, he led the wise woman into the alleyways beyond.

Eventually, he came to a stop before a row of separate buildings, their terraces leading around and down the sides, and his gaze looked fixedly ahead at the first in the row, the burned-out shell remaining of what was once a substantial house.

"This was the family home of my wife," he said, staring into the darkness which looked back at him from the lower windows, "and my daughter was born here."

"Are you also from here?" Shuma gently asked, realising she knew so little about this man. "From this city?" She too, now stared into the garden and along the weed-choked pathway to the open front door where the top rooms of the building, having fallen through to the bottom, could be seen amongst the blackened rubble.

"No, I'm from the high city," Gallius replied, lifting his head and looking up towards the higher steppes. "My family were originally merchants there, trading between these two cities. That's how I met my wife."

He went quiet as the remembrances of the past gathered around, and the stillness once again became a solid boundary between the ruin of the house with the lives once lived there and the two who looked upon it. As they stood side by side, the time between the long ago and the here and now seemed miles apart and would remain forever unreachable.

"What happened to her?" Shuma softly asked, breaking into his memories. For in realising she was seeing another side to Gallius, she felt confident in her asking.

"She died when Daina was born," his voice came strong yet with an undeniable warmth. "Not that same hour, but the following morning, so she knew she had given me a daughter."

He would never forget the smile that had crossed her face when she knew it was a girl, and she had slowly whispered the name "Daina" to him. Now in standing there and looking at the desolation of a past life, he knew that she would not want him to forever mourn, but would wish for his happiness and for him to move forward. Dropping his gaze, he turned his back on the ruin and looked at the woman at his side. Shuma returned his stare before grasping his hand again, and the two slowly returned amongst the ruined streets towards the city gates arriving back as the camp was awakening itself to the day.

After the morning meal, Brann and Tragen attended the horses, and the camp under the collapsing roof was abandoned as Gallius readied them to move on, and the group slowly gathered before the gateway.

"We shall have one more night in the open," the leader advised, their next stop being at the ridge between the plains of the lesser steppes and the woodlands that made up the higher ground. "After that, we shall be through the forest and at the city doors."

The group prepared to mount and be on their way but with one slight change to their previous arrangement, for Shuma was quick to jump up behind Gallius, and Malian found himself riding alone. The swap did not go unnoticed, and Tragen and Darric looked at each other, slightly amused, a sly smile crossing the face of the older man as he pulled himself up and settled into his saddle. Gallius, noting the look, quickly moved off and turning his horse, he led them back through the open gateway. Walking between its high walls and the distant towering tree-lined cliff, they followed the city around to the right.

Once past the city walls, the grass plains of the lesser steppes opened out before them, the lush, thick turf of the meadows spreading out into the east where the terrain remained as flat as the eye could see. The odd tall tree was dotted around, but the only real intrusion into this unbroken vista was the distant grey haze of the escarpment of the higher steppes which lay north in their direction of travel.

While the ranges of the mountains to the south marched away, their white-tipped summits meeting the far-off horizon, the horses were given the freedom of their rein, and with the feeling of fresh grass beneath their hooves they swiftly broke into a canter, the riders sitting tight as the moorlands passed alongside and the escarpment gradually grew closer as the day advanced.

***

The sharp knock disturbed the warden from his drowsing, and slowly rising from his couch, he crossed the room. On opening the door to the chamber, he found Tervic standing on its threshold, and stepping aside, he gestured for the man to enter. The room smelt of stale wine, and the two flasks chosen the previous day now lay empty in the cold hearth. As the prince retired somewhat casually behind his desk, the man furtively came to a stop again before the table.

"You were asking about a statue, sir," the informer immediately reminded the warden of their previous conversation. Going on, he quickly explained that on leaving the prince's rooms, he had personally taken it upon himself to do some investigating and although he had taken his questioning further afield than the stronghold, he had, unfortunately, come up empty and been unable to gather any real news. He had even resorted to the exchange of money, and the lady friends of a couple of the king's captains had claimed to have heard a few unguarded words and "statue" had possibly been mentioned. But the rumours had appeared too vague and unreliable even for his liking.

"But there's definitely something going on in the palace," he said, hoping to compensate for his lack of report. Having made himself witness to the comings of the recent strangers to the city, he felt able to warn Edgar of their growing numbers.

"Those visitors to the stronghold have all gone there," he further reported. "Not a one is lodging 'neath the king's roof."

The man had found this somewhat disturbing, and even Edgar appeared concerned about it.

"Where's the king now?" he quickly asked.

Edgar had last seen his brother in the main hall of the stronghold, and little had been said in their passing. The warden had wished to stop and talk while the king, seemingly impatient in his progress, quickly moved away. But Edgar noted a look that appeared out of place, a look of indignation alongside that of unease, and his many absences from within the stronghold were becoming of interest and had not gone unnoticed in many quarters.

"The king's in the palace," came the reply, "but he's still in his halls of an evening, and his bed chambers slept in every night I'm told." The man's eyes furtively took in the money pouches in the open top drawer, and he slowly looked away back up into the warden's watchful face. "But he's in the palace most days, there for many hours at a time, along with that high priest and those visitors."

Edgar purposefully nodded his head, his eyes focused upon the expectations of the little man, before slowly he reached towards the drawer, his hand coming to a stop just before his fingers touched the coin.

"And what of Captain Gallius? Any news yet on his arrival back?"

"No," Tervic quietly said, his gaze fixed on the motionless hand, "but the gate is being watched morning to evening for his return."

***

The last night in the open for Gallius and the group was spent on the ridge of the lesser steppes under the shadow of the high escarpment, where it slowly receded downwards to meet the plains. The only means of approach up onto the higher steppes had gradually gone from being open grass to becoming dense woodland. The night had again been cold and windy, but the moon gave some light across the steppe while the dark forest to the north had overshadowed their backs.

The talk around the fire became concentrated on their getting through the gates and into the city, and Shuma's earlier suggestion of the Icon having been stolen appeared to be at the forefront of their considerations. Gallius had given this idea attention as they rode out from the City of Muntani and thought it well worth the time spent, for he reasoned that it would surely grant an audience with the king. He could check that Daina was safe and get some idea of what had been happening since his departure. Hopefully, he could then make his report back to Malian on the Icons while any further decisions were being made.

This only left the question of how the rest of the party would get into the city and where it would be safe for them to stay while Gallius and Brann were in the stronghold.

"I think I may be able to help with that!" Anitta instantly announced. The heavily marked face, which remained strong in its looks, was wearing a more pleasing expression, for she suddenly felt that, finally, she could be of better aid other than just in her campfire making.

"I used to have family here," she further explained before going on to say that her mother's brother, a blade maker, used to have a workshop in the city and that she and her sister sometimes stayed there when they were children. She finished by declaring, "I think I will recognise where they lived. It was close to the gate, if I remember right. But, of course, he may have moved on."

"What was his name?" Gallius asked for he knew

many of the artisans, especially those with the capability for blade making.

"My uncle's name is Ladio. Do you know of him?"

"Yes, I know of him." A swift smile crossed Gallius' face. "He's a good swordsmith, I hear. And if my recollection is correct, you should find him in the first lanes on the right. But there will be little room for the horses," he added, "so they'll have to be left outside."

"What if he can't give us any shelter?" Darric asked. "It won't be safe for us to remain in the city!"

"No," Gallius was quick to agree, "then I think it best to gather provisions if you can and return to the horses." The forest held a lesser fear to him than would the overnight being spent on the streets, and he knew the remainder of the group would fare better outside the walls of the city. "Brann and I will check in the lanes first, and if you're not there, then we'll come to you in the forest."

The decisions for the next day were felt to be coming together, apart from the details of the loss of the Icon, and Gallius felt he needed to make the attack on himself and his men look more convincing. Checking his shoulder wound, he could see that the healing was many days in advance, and he knew it would not pass for a recently acquired injury. It would need re-opening, the pain having to be endured bringing with it more meaning and realism to establish their story.

"Shuma," he said quietly as he placed his hand across his shoulder where the touch of tenderness remained. "I'm going to have to open this wound up a bit. Will you help me?"

Going on, he further explained his thinking behind this harsh action, and the wise woman reluctantly accepted the dagger offered up. Knowing what was being asked of her, she was quick to find a finger-thick branch from beneath the edge of the forest. Cutting it down to size, she placed the bitter-tasting bar between Gallius' teeth, and pulling away the clothing from off his bowed shoulder, she exposed the drawn-in edges of the healing laceration.

"Bite down hard!" she advised before positioning the blade.

Without hesitation, she brought the hilt down, the knife's point re-entering the wound and slicing open the flesh which had begun to bind together, again allowing the blood to flow freely. Gallius had bitten down hard on the wood, but a suppressed growl of sheer agony came deep from his throat as the pain once again pierced through, and the torment rushed down his right arm. Shuma was quick to remove the knife, and Gallius, spitting out the wood, turned to look at the trauma.

"Will it pass, do you think?" she hesitantly asked, watching the warmth of the bright redness as it coursed once more down his chest.

"It'll do," he replied, loath to have the action repeated.

***

The remainder of the night under the stars led into the coldness of the early morning, and the following day passed by in their travel through the woods of the higher steppes. And in the early darkness of that late evening, the gates to the high city appeared in the distance.

Drawing them along the lined pathway, the thickness of the encroaching trees closed in around, and the track became bordered by boulders as it wound its way through the forest towards the settlement. The city itself stood high in a clearing, the structure of the walls built atop a natural mound which afforded it some protection, while a short slope led up towards the two solid wooden gates.

As the light faded throughout the forest, Gallius ordered that the four remaining horses should be left secure and safe within the woodland, and Malian and the others followed slowly behind both himself and Brann as they rode towards the city.

Joining and mingling with the few people returning from their wood collecting, Malian and the four walked surreptitiously alongside the heavily laden carts being pulled through into the courtyard area where the stables gathered close around its boundary. Here the workshops of the smiths lay off to either side.

Anitta quickly ducked away, and disappearing off to her right, steered them to where she remembered the bustling lanes of the smithies and the craftsmen were located. Leaving behind the busy yard, she passed unseen through the third door along and was soon thankfully being reunited with the long-lost family of her mother. Many tears were shed on either side as they were made welcome amongst the warmth of the braziers, and the cold of the night was soon left behind the closed door.

Gallius and Brann's return to the city, however, did not go without notice, for the two mounted men were the only riders through the gate that day. Dismounting somewhat carefully into the yard as the dusk of the night gathered further, they were quickly approached by Dedrick's men led by Captain Isaac.

"Captain Gallius!" Isaac challenged from the shadows, and striding across the cobbles, he ordered his men to take up place around the riders. "Welcome! We have been expecting you back for a number of days." The two greeted each other as old associates before Isaac continued, "The king asked us to look out for you and to escort you to the stronghold immediately. He's been getting overly anxious about your arrival."

Gallius and Brann were given little choice, and the

captain and his men were swift to leave behind the main gates. Escorting the two towards the stronghold, they first passed through the stables area and along the busy, bustling streets of the city, where the arena with its immense formidable structure eventually reared up ahead. As they passed the training ground, its walls surrounded by market stalls, the eager traders still at this later hour touted for business, and many of the citizens scurried around looking either for a bargain or something essential to their needs.

Finally, the steps of the stronghold lay before them, and climbing these, they were escorted into the halls of the main building and the two taken directly through to the throne room. Here Dedrick sat alone, apart from his two trusted and reliable attendants, who appeared almost invisible in their presence.

"Welcome back, Gallius!" the king declared loudly along the hall as the men were conducted into the room. But on nearing the throne, Dedrick looked down upon the two riders and their escort.

"Is this all that remains of your men, Captain?" he immediately demanded as the two were brought before him and Captain Isaac and his men quickly stood to one side.

"Yes, just Brann and I, sire," Gallius explained, coming to stand at the foot of the king's chair, his blood-stained shirt clearly visible under his jacket. "We were attacked many days ago, my lord. Attacked as we slept beneath the Mounts of Aquila, and the remainder of my men were killed."

"Attacked! Who by?" he was quickly asked, "And what of your task? Have you got the Icon?"

"No, sire, I'm sorry to have to report that it was taken, and we both here did well to survive and escape with our lives." Gallius' hand went to this shoulder, the nature of his injury being made evident in the unmistakable pain that crossed his face. His head, however, remained held high as he reported back, and he was unable to miss the instant change to the features of the king as he took in the news. He had expected Dedrick to show his intense anger, but he had also surprisingly seen a fear there, a darkness that flashed across his eyes, and after the temper of the king had somewhat subsided, he felt able to persevere with his account.

"There is more I fear that I need to tell you, my lord," he slowly added, "for I was also betrayed by one of my men." He paused for a moment before continuing, "But before I go on, I first need to seek some assurance, for you know I have concerns about my daughter. You promised you would keep her safe, and on my return to the city, you would give her back to me."

"She is safe, Captain. But you have returned empty-handed!" the king snapped back, his anger and rage deepening his voice and slowing his words. "But give your news, and if I feel it worthy of interest, then I shall keep to my promise, and she will be returned to you."

Gallius now felt able to tell of Roth's betrayal and also that of Marke and Rogan, who had attacked them in the Sleeping Caverns. He told of the loss of the Icon at their hands and their subsequent making off, leaving himself and Brann behind at the mercy of the swan women. And while the ensuing chase and final fight at the Median Bridge had witnessed the killing of Roth and the two brothers, it also, he explained, saw the return of the Icon back into his keeping. While he talked, the king sat motionless, his tall frame still struggling to control the emotions which played across his face as he stared intently at the speaker.

"Roth was my second-in-command and a lifelong friend," Gallius finally finished, "but he was a man I seemed hardly to have known." Retrieving Roth's talisman from his pocket, he stepped towards the throne, and handing up the metal disc to the king, said, "I have something here that I must show you."

Dedrick, who on recognising and realising what had been offered up, stared down in confusion at the gleaming token which lay in his hand and immediately he challenged, "Where did this come from?"

"This is what I found about his neck," Gallius continued as he stepped away, knowing an identical token was worn around the king's collar. "I think it's some sort of priestly regalia." He paused in his account as the token was let go, the disc falling into the king's lap, before he finished with, "And as he lay dying, he told me in his last breath that the high priest had ordered him to bring the Icon to him. To him alone and not to you!"

The king's head jerked up immediately as he heard the last words, and he glared in rage towards Gallius and was immediately out of his chair, Roth's token falling with a ring to the floor as the sentence came to its end. His anger was unable to be contained as the words struck, and he walked around his seat of power to stand at the rear of the throne, his long fingers gripping tightly the ornately carved back. But slowly, the storm died down to a simmer as many thoughts and speculations coursed through his mind, and returning to the fore, he bent down to retrieve the disc and stood before Gallius.

"But what of the Icon, Captain Gallius?" the king strongly demanded. "You said you were attacked, and it was taken. What has become of it?"

"I don't know, my lord," the captain lied. "It was seized by a band of outlaws and taken only for its value in gold, I would have thought." He let his head drop as the pain again darted its way into his arm and the aching throb of his injury increased.

Noting his discomfort, Dedrick turned away from his misery and slowly walked to the rear of the room. Looking up into the faces of his ancestors, the past kings of the high places, he felt the magnitude of his own kingship falling about his shoulders. Knowing that the coming days could bring with them many more questions, he placed the talisman in his pocket and hoped that at least this could provide some answers.

Returning to his throne, the cold stone eyes of the kings of past watching his progress, he sat in front of the silent assembly of his men, and directing his address to Gallius, he noted the tired and troubled face which looked back.

"Your injury needs attention," the king said in his dismissal. "Go and get it seen to, your daughter will be awaiting you there." The king's hand motioned for one of his attendants to come forward, and a message was given. The young man quickly left the room, his slight figure disappearing into the corridors behind the great granite statues of the former kings before it reappeared moments later, the message having been passed on.

Gallius, along with Brann, then turned and began to walk back towards the door through the avenue of Isaac's men before suddenly the king stood again from his seat and called out towards them.

"Brann, you will remain," he shouted his instruction. "And you too, Isaac. The rest of you are dismissed!"

The room quickly emptied, Gallius being the first to make his eager way through the doorway. While Brann and Captain Isaac returned up the hall to stand again before the throne as Dedrick resumed his seat.

"You know where this event took place?" he asked, instantly addressing Brann.

"Yes, my lord," Brann answered, his reply binding true the misleading words spoken by Gallius, "a good three days from here in the mountains. But they could be anywhere by now."

"Yes, they could be anywhere," the king replied, looking again at the token before his eyes lifted and he looked into the face of the man.

"Brann, I here declare you captain," he announced as the astonished tracker took in his immediate promotion. "And you are ordered to take a company of men at tomorrow's first light to reclaim the Icon. Do this for me, Captain Brann, and further honour and rewards will be yours for the taking."

Dedrick came forward, and placing his hand down heavy on the man's shoulder, he said, "Welcome, Captain Brann!" Before the hand was lifted and the king turned to the remaining man.

"Isaac," he addressed his other officer, "see that Captain Brann gets a bed for the night and see that his men are readied for the morning!"

***

Tervic once again had news for Prince Edgar, and approaching his rooms, he rapped sharply on the door and was allowed entry into the darkened chamber, the prince returning to the brightness of the fireside where he had placed his drink.

"Gallius is back," he straightaway reported, and closing the door, he left behind the brightness of the corridor and shuffled into the dark, coming to a stop at the front of the desk before continuing, "He's already been with the king; I saw him escorted in."

"Escorted?" the voice queried from the other side of the room.

"Yes, Isaac and his men were with him," he disclosed, his eyes slowly adjusting to the gloom, "but they've all just come out."

"Where's he now?" the warden asked, eager to be informed. "Has he gone to his quarters?"

"No, he's gone down to the lower halls," the little man reported. "He's carrying an injury, I would say."

The warden slowly finished off his wine, and paying the man his dues, he followed him into the lit passageway and headed down towards the main hall, where he took the stairs into the depths of the stronghold.

***

Many minutes before, on leaving Brann behind with the king, Gallius had also taken the steps down to the lower halls where the rooms of the healers and their attendants were situated. Here he hoped he could get some relief from his pain and some rest from his tiredness. Pushing open the first door where he could hear voices, he was welcomed in by the smell of the herbal infusions of the infirmary and the sight of his daughter.

Daina was already there, standing in wait next to the healer with her back to the darkness of the open low window. On seeing her father walk through the door, she was immediately at his side.

"Father!" she cried, rushing to greet him, and throwing her arms around his neck, she hugged him tight. And as the agony of pain in his shoulder was endured, his arms returned her embrace, and the fear and doubts of the days past were instantly lifted.

"Are you alright?" she sobbed, looking with worry and concern into the wearied face she thought she might never see again.

"I'm fine," he blatantly lied, wishing to delay any distress, "but let me look at you." Letting go, he held her away to see her in full as she stood before him. "Have you been well cared for?" he asked as his anxiety increased, and looking into her watering eyes, he saw the upset she held there.

"Cared for, yes," she gave reply, also not wishing to cause concern. "But the quarters have been a little stifling." She smiled deeply into his eyes, and once more, they embraced, their happiness holding them together and overwhelming them both by its force.

As they finished their greeting, Prince Edgar suddenly appeared in the doorway and on his entering the room, the welcome within immediately ceased. Jasan, the attending healer, quickly bowed his head, and Gallius and Daina were also expected to acknowledge his presence. Turning to face the king's brother, the father and daughter slowly nodded their respect.

"I heard you were back, Gallius," Edgar said directly, coming forward. The smell of wine was strong on the warden's breath as he stopped before the leader.

"Just arrived this day, my lord," the captain answered, his voice becoming more severe in its manner while his eyes stared blankly ahead. "I'm here to see my daughter and get a shoulder wound cleaned." Aware of who he was speaking to, he aimed to keep the explanation short and to the point, and in keeping with his meeting with the king in the halls above, he stuck to his story.

Edgar, however, needed answers, and guessing there could be more to come, he gestured for the healer to come forward. Instructing him to attend upon Gallius' wound, the room instantly awakened to activity as Jasan came forward and pulled out a stool for Gallius to sit.

"Let me take a look," he said, and in removing the clothing and examining the injury, it again caused bleeding, the aching throb once again making its presence felt down his right arm and weakening his hand as it lay in his lap. The man had seen many such traumas before in his long career, inflicted by both sword and dagger, and turning away from the damage, he called sharply for his assistant and gave his orders. Within moments the woman returned, bringing along a bowl of warming crushed herbs to pack the wound, and the discomfort of the healing treatment began.

While Gallius' wound was being attended, Edgar slowly walked the room, eventually returning to stand alongside Daina where she was holding her father's hand. And as the last piece of wading was packed into the gaping hole, the shoulder could finally be bandaged.

"That's it for the moment," the healer said, unable to do anything further. Wrapping away the surplus dressings, he advised, "Come, you can rest here for the night, and I will look at it again in the morning."

Gallius and Daina were taken opposite to where a small ward containing two beds, each standing to either side of the room with a table in between, would provide their overnight quarters, and Prince Edgar followed them through.

"Rest now," Jasan instructed, seeing Gallius onto the thin mattress and ensuring his comfort. "I shall see you tomorrow." Finally, he left, leaving the three together, and Edgar could, at last, ask his question as he paced between the two beds.

"What is going on here, Gallius?" he strongly demanded. "I've been hearing of captains being sent out and returning with statues, and there have been many recent visitors to the palace, and it's all being kept hidden and secretive." He paused as he looked down at the injured man. "I need to know what's happening here, and I order you to tell me your information or anything you may know!"

"Why do you ask me? Why should I know anything?" Gallius replied, laying back on the bed as the pain of the examination and treatment distracted him from the spoken words and the given command of the speaker.

"I ask because I know you know more," came the candid reply, "but I don't think you realise how in the dark I am. My brother, the king, is away at the palace most days and shows little concern for this city. My unease, however, lies with the people, and I sense that something is advancing upon us beyond our understanding."

This was the first time that anyone had mentioned the people and Gallius looked directly up into the troubled eyes of the prince as he turned in the doorway and came to a halt within its boundary, the bulk of his frame filling the opening to the passage beyond. But he still held some mistrust, and he was unable to disguise it.

"Father," Daina said from the far side of the room, seeing the uncertainty gathered around his features, "the prince showed concern for my well-being while I was held by the king, and I feel trust must be given."

"I want and need to know what is going on," Edgar finally demanded. Moving back into the room, he came to sit alongside Gallius and awaited a reply.

After many long moments, Gallius cautiously asked, "Have you ever heard of the Brotherhood of the Snake?" His soft voice echoed its words in the depths of the stronghold. But on seeing no recognition on the prince's face he realised he may have an ally within the city walls and gave Edgar a brief outline of their known information about the brotherhood and the meaning of the statues.

An hour later, Gallius could rest with his daughter close by and Prince Edgar, drawing the door to the ward closed, left the lower halls. Passing back through the body of the stronghold, he returned to his rooms and to another early dawn of sleeplessness and contemplation.

But this time, he felt he was at least less ignorant of the whole situation.

***

Serdos had given his final service for that evening, and on release from their ceremonies, the brotherhood had retired to the rooms of the palace where they had each taken up residence. Coming out into the dark of the night, the high priest walked alone between the splendour of the buildings and the small gardens, his back to the curve of the high outer façade as he returned to his apartment near the far northern wall.

Arriving there, he quickly noted the lamp already lit, and cautiously opening the door, he found his informant, one of the king's trusted attendants, standing discreetly within its bounds. His report was given swiftly and detailed in the information, and all of the recent activities witnessed in the king's hall were presented word for word in their full scope, and nothing was changed or omitted.

Serdos was given much to think about into the sleepless hours of the remaining night, but his main concern kept returning to how the king would have reacted to the betrayal of Roth and even more so to his accusing words that had been spoken in his dying breath. He knew Dedrick would be swift in his follow up, and he would need to be equally fast in his counteractions. Moving restlessly about his room, he sent word to his lector priests for them to gather at first light before quickly wrapping around his cloak. Pulling up his hood he headed out towards the stronghold.

***

The knock came quiet and discreet in the early hours of the morning as Captain Brann was preparing himself to join his men. On opening the door, he found Serdos, the high priest, standing on the threshold, his cloak wound around his thin body and the dark hood covering his face.

"I hear congratulations are in order, Captain Brann!" he straightaway declared, his voice hushed and low as he stepped unasked into the room. Walking towards the far wall, he stopped at the side of the table and placed a small flat parcel upon its surface before dropping the hood and disclosing his tired face.

"You have done well, Brann," he further declared, turning to meet the man's stare, "for I hear the king has guaranteed you many riches."

"He has that," Brann replied as he closed the door. Assuming that the high priest was here to wish him and his men well for the journey, he returned to his preparations.

"Well, I can offer you much more than he can," the amiable voice of the high priest suddenly stated as he looked around the spartan room where the king had housed his new captain. "In guaranteeing you all that he has already promised, I can also ensure your acceptance into the Brotherhood of *Apep*, and grant you command of all the armed men within these city walls." He stopped and looked directly at Brann's back as the man paused in his packing, and the words came reassuring and inviting in their tone as he finished, "All this I can pledge in my promise to you. But only if you return the Icon to me!"

The high priest picked up the parcel which he had so carefully laid on the table, and unwrapping the fabric, displayed the brotherhood's silver token for Brann to see, the meagre light of the room's lamp illuminating the intricacy of the snake-enclosed disc as it lay upon the cloth.

"It's yours if you so choose," his voice came cold yet confident before he seated himself at the table. And in the silence that gathered, he watched as Brann resumed his packing, using the remaining time to prepare for his first command.

Shortly afterwards, another knock was heard at the door, this time sharp and harsh in its delivery and the voice outside declared.

"Captain Brann, your men are ready for you!"

"I'll be there in a moment," Brann bluntly shouted back before swiftly glancing across to the high priest.

Serdos made to take his leave, and heading towards the door, he carefully opened it before stopping within the doorway and checking along the passage. Looking back to where the talisman remained gleaming in the light, he finished, "Think on and make your decision, Captain Brann." Turning, he left the door ajar and disappeared back towards the main hall, and on into the palace where he joined his gathering priests.

Brann had only a few minutes to make up his mind, and sitting alongside the table, the token spread out before him, he contemplated the propositions that had come his way. Eventually, he slowly stood and picking up the talisman he carefully placed the token in his pocket, lifted his pack and left his room.

CHAPTER FIVE

The dawning light between night and the new day saw Captain Brann and his dozen men gathering in the courtyard before riding out through the main gates of the high city. Here the forests of the higher steppes closed in around as the grey mist of the early morning floated beneath the boughs of the tall bordering trees. The group of riders and their packhorses had quickly disappeared along the coldness of the forest path, heading for the plains of the lower steppes, the pack animals appearing overly burdened for the supposed few days' ride back to where the Icon had been stolen. But Brann, having told his men that they would be pursuing bandits, had been quick to make clear he would not expect their quarry to be sitting waiting for them. His tracking skills, he explained, could see them journeying much further afield than anticipated in the chase, and it could be many weeks before they would again see the walls of the city.

Travelling swiftly through the forest, the hours passed by in all-out speed, and as the villagers at their backs began to awaken to the morning, the riders found themselves dropping down onto the vastness of the lower steppes and galloping on through into the grasslands.

***

Gallius slept well that night, his last vision being of Daina sitting alongside him. He had closed his eyes, knowing that his daughter was safe and he could finally relax and feel some ease from his troubles.

The following morning he was slow in his waking, the light in the room announcing that dawn had long passed. But as he shifted slightly in the bunk, he felt again the stab of pain in his shoulder, and slowly the creeping torment came back into his arm as he turned his head to look across the room. The mattress on the far side was empty, although evidence of its recent habitation could be seen in the disorder of the bedclothes. Looking further around, he noted the door into the room had been left ajar after Daina had left, and on further raising his head, Gallius could see out into the empty passageway beyond.

His daughter returned a little later as he was slowly seating himself on the edge of the bed, and as she pushed open the door, her arms holding a flat tray that contained fresh warm bread, cold meat and a hot flask, she noted the brief smile as the smell preceded her. Pulling up the small table between the two beds and tidying off her own, she sat down, and father and daughter breakfasted together for the first time in many months, the stillness of the room surrounding them in the unity of their meal.

Eventually, the day-to-day sounds of the lower halls began to filter through the door and into the comfort of their silence, and the assistant who had helped the night before hastened in to check on the well-being of the captain. Seeing that Gallius was up and had already eaten, she quickly withdrew, and moments later the healer appeared, a fresh basin of medicinal herbs in his hand, and he replaced her in the doorway.

Daina hurriedly moved out of his way. Taking with her the empty tray and laying it on the bottom of her bed, she sat down beside it.

"How are you feeling this morning?" Jasan enquired, his pleasant face radiating an encouraging smile. Moving aside the table, he placed the sweetly smelling bowl down and turned to face his patient. "Let's take another look at this shoulder."

Exposing the wound, Gallius felt the resurgence of pain as the thick wadding of herbs was gently removed, and the healer worked purposefully on the exposed injury, cutting away the dead skin from around the edges and staunching the fresh flow of blood as it wept out. Flinching a number of times and seeing his discomfort, Daina joined him to sit alongside and hold his hand while Gallius allowed his mind to focus on something other than the pain.

Swiftly his thoughts turned to the challenge that lay ahead, for he knew the coming upheaval would soon be placed upon the city where he sat, and he remained uncertain of its outcome and how it would affect those within these walls. The consequences went far beyond these borders and out into the cities they had passed and the people who endured within.

This thought proved too great to contemplate at that moment, and he moved on to other thinking. The face of the wise woman slowly came into focus, and as the healer skilfully used his blade, he turned his concentration hard on remembering the colour of Shuma's eyes.

***

Tervic had been lax in his gathering of the overnight news. But on finding out about Brann's departure, he had been quick enough to alert the warden, and Edgar had immediately felt the need to know more. Overnight his mind had been disturbed by Gallius' disclosure. Now, knowing of Brann's advancement to captain along with his hasty exit, it gave much cause for concern, and he felt a need to question Gallius further.

Returning to the lower halls, he arrived as Jasan was attending to the shoulder wound and was forced to wait while the damage was assessed and Gallius received his ministration. Finally, the healer renewed the packing afresh from the mixture in the bowl and sealed the wound. He then swiftly left to go about his daily rounds, and Edgar closed the door behind him and sat down heavily upon the bed opposite.

"I need you to tell me more about these statues, Gallius, and how they affect this city and its people," he straightaway demanded, the tiredness seen harsh about his face. "I need to know all of your story. From the very first moment that you were sent out by Dedrick."

Gallius saw that he might need to tell all from the beginning, but concern still remained about who to trust. Even Malian had agreed to keep full knowledge of their circumstance between themselves and Shuma, allowing the rest of their group to remain unaware of the full predicament. The prince, however, had shown his concern for the people and their city and appeared to be completely in the dark regarding the brotherhood. But still, Gallius held back until, finally, Daina's voice broke into his thoughts. Guessing the dilemma that her father was undergoing, she repeated her words of the previous night.

"Prince Edgar showed me his concern as I was kept confined, Father, and I again say we should give him our trust." She took his hand, and lifting it to her face, slowly laid it against her cheek as she turned to meet his gaze. Looking back, Gallius knew he could now afford to tell a fuller story. Yet, at present, he would still delay in mentioning the people awaiting him in the eastern lanes of the workshops and for now, only reveal the basic facts.

He went on to explain the order given for him to go on a quest to steal a statue, and the reluctance that he first held began with his outright refusal to go. Then, Serdos mentioned his daughter and Daina had been taken from him and used as his incentive.

Telling of the long journey with his men to the valley and the places they had passed through to get there, he spoke of the stealing of the Icon and their subsequent return along their trodden paths. He then spoke of the betrayal of Roth in the Sleeping Caverns, and the eventual fight at the Median Bridge where Roth was killed.

"He was my friend," he declared, "one who I had known for many years and who I trusted with my life. But in his trickery, I feel I no longer hold much store in either friendship or comradeship."

His story then became focused on the cities through which they passed on their return, and the tales gathered along the way told the devastating plight that had become the people at the loss of their statues. Finally, he spoke of the Eight and the brotherhood who were gathering them together.

"So, if you had returned with this statue it would have been the last one?" Edgar asked, his concern growing as he wondered on the situation this would have caused.

"It would appear so," Gallius confirmed, "for all the cities we passed, and others beyond my knowledge, have had their Icons taken, and each has been affected in some tragic form."

"But why are they being collected here?" the warden queried, unable to understand the importance of where he stood. "Why this city?"

Gallius then told the remainder of the story in full, bringing in the names of those who travelled with him and leaving out nothing that had been said or was known between himself, Malian and Shuma. And after coming to an end, the prince, along with Daina who sat quietly next to him, had been granted the complete story so far.

The room went quiet as the late morning light flowed through the window, and they each followed the path of their own thought. Gallius' thinking took him along to the group with which he travelled, and he knew he would have to take Edgar and Daina to see Malian.

"Will you trust me to take you to see someone?" he finally asked, coming out of his reverie. "For there is a person who I feel you should meet." Rising from his bed, he felt a sudden renewal in his strength, and even his arm felt less painful.

However, as the three prepared to leave the lower halls and return to the main hall, Edgar paused in the doorway and, spinning around said, "Before we leave, Gallius, I think you might be interested to learn of your colleague, Brann?"

"Brann, what of him?" Gallius quickly replied, his head turning as he suddenly looked to the warden in alarm.

"I've been told he left this morning with a company of men. Left on the king's orders to reclaim and return the Icon," Edgar enlightened, "and he's been made up to captain!"

Gallius' astonishment could not at first take in this seemingly second betrayal, but then the anger hit, and guiding Daina quickly through the doorway past the prince, he looked towards Edgar and said bitterly, "Then we have an even greater need to make our meeting, for I feel we can trust no one!"

***

Dedrick had sent out one of his spies to see off Captain Brann, and on his report back that the new captain had not been seen with anyone since leaving his rooms and the company had left seemingly unobserved, the king felt a little less troubled. The token, however, presented by Captain Gallius along with his words regarding Roth, still remained. Here was a cause of immense worry, and sitting at his hall table where his breakfast had lain untouched for many hours, he spread out the talisman and its chain before him and a strong urge to rise and face the high priest head-on had risen in his heart.

He had little inclination to attend that morning's services within the palace and so sat in fear and apprehension. But with an overriding anger slowly beginning to come to the fore as the realisation that Serdos wanted all the control and power for himself, his rage simmered and he knew he must act. His only option was to confront the high priest, and rising from his table, he picked up the talisman and headed off to the palace.

***

Malian and the remainder of the group spent the night at the home of Anitta's uncle, Ladio, and his wife, Brinda, and they had been made welcome and a room towards the back of the workshop given over for them to rest and sleep. They had been allowed access to the backyard where the grinding rocks for the sword polishing had been stacked against the back wall of the city alongside the fuel for the fires. And here the group sat the next day as they continued in their anxious wait for news of Gallius and Brann.

As King Dedrick had risen from his table to make his challenge on the high priest, Gallius had begun his walk back towards the main gates. Passing through the activity of the stables and the courtyard, he turned left and entered the eastern lanes with Daina at his side and Prince Edgar following close behind. Taking the walkway closest to the main wall, he headed down past the busy workshops of the swordsmiths. Reaching the third on the right, he knocked hard upon the wooden door.

It was opened by a woman who stood back in expectation of their arrival, but on seeing the figure of the prince, she immediately bowed her head as the three entered, with the two men stooping slightly to gain access as they stepped through into the workshop. Here the heat immediately hit them, the smell of smoke and flame appearing a constant as the blade smith and his apprentice worked the metal in the far corner. The intensity of the noise grew as they moved into the steam-filled room and were shown through towards the back where a slim figure could be seen standing in the open doorway.

"He's here!" Darric shouted back over his shoulder to the others as he saw Gallius appear out of the smoke.

The man's whereabouts had been their main topic of talk that morning, and they had worried about the lack of news from the stronghold, their thoughts turning to what would be their next step if nothing was heard that day.

The whole group now hastily returned into the fume of the workshop, pausing as they saw that the man was not alone. But he was quick to come forward to present Prince Edgar first to Malian as a person to trust and the altar tender quickly saw that they would have a powerful ally within the city and felt a sudden surge in the hope of succeeding in their quest.

Edgar was then introduced in turn to each of the other four, finishing with Shuma, who Gallius pulled to his side, his arm reaching around her waist. Finally, he turned and introduced his daughter to Malian and the group, and Daina was likewise made welcome. But on letting the two women go, he was quick to speak with Malian with an urgent need to pass on his news.

Drawing the man to one side and lowering his voice, he said, "Malian, I have put my trust in Prince Edgar, and have told him everything that has passed these last weeks. Everything, you understand," he emphasised, his dark eyes looking intensely at the older man, "and Daina has also been witness to my telling."

The altar tender nodded, and looking towards Gallius' daughter, who had walked over to them, he was thankful that at least part of their agreement in her rescue had been fulfilled and that, hopefully, it would predict an equally good outcome for the next.

Slowly reaching out, he smiled, and grasping the warm hands of the young woman who stood before him, he led her away through into the rear of the workshop. Moments later, the rest followed, and all moved out into the relative quietness and privacy of the yard and the freshening air of the late morning.

Gallius promptly told his news of his meeting with King Dedrick and his disclosure regarding Roth and the talisman, and finally, he came to the report he had just received from Edgar regarding Brann.

"He's been made up to captain and been sent out by the king this morning along with his own company of men," Gallius declared angrily, "and he's been ordered to return the Icon to the city!"

"Will he do this, do you think?" Shuma asked, sitting close by his side and feeling the hatred flowing through as a tenseness gripped his body.

"I don't know," he replied sharply. But in remembering Roth's treasonable actions, he felt he knew what the answer could be. "Although I expect he would for the right price."

"Then again, our concern returns to *Amaunet*," Malian suddenly declared, his fears returning as the agitation became apparent and he stiffly stood and paced the cobbled yard, "for Brann knows where she's been taken, and the safety of the swans in their Sleeping Caverns will be endangered."

He stopped at the far wall, staring at the moss-covered bricks, before turning and walking back towards Gallius. "Someone must go back and aid them, or at least give warning."

"I shall go myself," Gallius declared. But on standing, the weakness of his wound showed itself in his bearing and a look of doubt crossed his face.

"No, you carry your injury," Malian said, noticing the look as he placed his hand upon the arm of the rider, "and the pursuit must be fast and without delay. If the men left this morning, then their horses will be fresh and swift, and many miles can be gained in their first day's ride."

Turning to Tragen, he stopped in front of the large man who sat, arms tight across his chest, while his back was set firmly against the brick of the city wall, and here the slight white-haired figure of Darric sat at his side.

"Then it will have to be yourself, Tragen. You and Darric," the altar tender stated, his voice rising as he felt his authority returning. "You both have rested overnight and will be able to ride fast, and your fighting skills may again be called upon."

"But *Naunet* sits so close!" Tragen said, his anger and dismay evident as he realised the significance of the job being assigned. "I am within an arm's reach of her recovery, and now you say I must leave!"

"Your closeness will mean nothing if *Amaunet* is retaken," Malian instantly replied, "because as yet, you don't know the full story, for it has gone far beyond just the return of *Naunet* and the rescue of Gallius' daughter. Even if your own Icon were returned to its city, it would never again be safe while the rest of them remain here."

Malian explained to Tragen, Darric and Anitta the full details known to the rest. These being that all of the Icons must be split up and returned to their given cities in order for the chaos and disorder to cease throughout the regions and that the gods themselves had shown this to Malian in his dreams. This was the duty that they had placed upon him, and he, in turn, placed on each of them.

"You see the burden that has been settled upon us," Malian finished. "We have to rescue and return all of the Eight Icons."

"But do we know where all the Icons are!" Tragen demanded, his mind taking up a slightly different approach as he realised the devastation and disorder seen went far beyond the bounds of his own people and their city.

"I think I can help with that," Edgar replied. Going on to tell of his recent asking around regarding statues along with the news of the gathering at the palace of the priests, he finished, "They have been coming through the gates the past few weeks, and all have been met by Serdos, the high priest."

"Serdos," Malian repeated, his mind going back to the libraries in the valley and the books which stood there detailing the named clergy. "That name means nothing to me. But what of your brother, the king? Is he one of them?"

"I would say so," Edgar replied, "he's been spending days away from the stronghold of late, and he's always been in league with the high priest."

"Then this is where the Icons must be, and this is where we must concentrate and focus our plan." Malian walked towards the doorway back into the workshop, where the sound of the hammering had come to a stop. "But first, we must ensure the safety of *Amaunet* and the swans."

Turning back to Tragen, he instructed him, along with Darric, to prepare immediately for a return journey to the Sleeping Caverns. And while the two men swiftly disappeared into the workshop to make their preparations, the altar tender took Gallius' arm and drew him to one side.

"Is there another way out of the city?" he asked, aware

that the sight of two strangers leaving through the gate could warrant unwanted attention.

"Yes, I can show them the southeastern gate," Gallius answered. "It's not often used but lies close to here, just through the lanes and should lead directly back to the horses."

"Good, then that is one less concern."

They then turned to the situation within the city, and as they discussed their recently acquired information from Edgar, Daina came to stand close beside her father, and Anitta also walked over to stand before the men.

"I shall also be returning with Tragen and Darric," the swan declared, her voice giving no chance for any refusal, "for a fear now lies with my friends in the caverns, and they must be warned of their situation. And," she added, "I should be able to help the men in a swifter return."

She went on to explain that she knew a quicker way back into the caverns, one that was dangerous and not for the faint-hearted. But the climb up the rocks of the cliff face above the Sleeping Caverns and down into the lakes, although not being easy, was much more immediate than taking the route through the caves.

"If we have not caught up with Brann before the Median Bridge, then we shall need to make up time as they journey through the grasslands," she advised, looking to each of the men as they listened intently. "We can travel back along the Western Great Waters and up and over the caverns and down directly into the Lower Lake."

This way, over the roof of the caves, had been known for many years. Although rarely used due to the nature of the ascent, it had always been there and viewed as an escape route from their lake for the swans if needed. Now it could prove of use for their forewarning and their defence.

"That is well worth knowing," Gallius said, as the swan finished her disclosure and his tactical mind took on board the strategy behind the idea, "and one which I can see will be of use if Brann has given us the slip." He looked to Malian as he stood at his side before saying, "I think Anitta makes good sense in her demand, and she should go with Tragen and Darric. I feel her presence will be much needed."

"Good," the swan woman replied, knowing that, whatever their decision, she would not have been denied. "Then I shall gather my things and make ready, for we shall also need fresh supplies."

Moving away, she looked to where Edgar remained in talk with Shuma before Gallius' voice rang out across the yard.

"Anitta," he called out, "could you take Daina with you? She can help you with finding some provisions."

On hearing this request, Anitta stopped, and sensing there was more in the asking, she turned and smiled at Gallius before saying to Daina, "Shall we go and ask my aunt? I'm sure she can help us!" Holding out her hand, she waited for the younger woman to join her before they walked back into the workshop.

Malian now also had cause to feel that Gallius needed his own time, and saying that he would see how Tragen and Darric were doing in the packing, he left the man standing at the far end of the yard. Walking back towards where Shuma and Edgar stood on the opposite side, he briefly stopped, and speaking with the prince, the two followed the women through and returned into the building, their conversation continuing as the door closed behind them.

Shuma and Gallius were now left alone in the quietness of the yard, and the two were quick to cross the intervening space between. Reaching out, their arms encircled, and they kissed long and hard before finally parting. Gallius took Shuma's hand and led her to sit, their backs coming up against the coldness of the hard stone wall.

"I need you to do something for me," he said as they both settled. Looking into her eyes, he continued, "Will you look after Daina and take her back to the City of Muntani, to the place where she was born? The house that I showed you."

"I should like to remain here with you," Shuma replied, staring back hard into his face, her hand brushing the roughness of his cheek. "I can fight, you know I can."

"Yes, that I well know. But I need you both safe and out of the city," he reasoned, his fears now doubled as the wise woman made known her affection, "and then I can put my strength wholeheartedly into the task which I foresee ahead."

Shuma could see the sense that he talked, but her heart told her something else, and she was loath to leave him.

"Trust me, Shuma," he asked, the warmth of his fingers brushing against the softness of her lips. "It will be better for me if I know that you are safe. And remember, the distance between us will only be two days' ride!" He wrapped his arms around her once more and kissed her softly, the two remaining in each other's embrace as the slow minutes passed.

Inside the workshop, Tragen and Darric had collected their packs, and along with Anitta and Daina, they each helped in gathering supplies from the stores provided by Brinda. Assembling at the front of the building, they were joined by Malian and Edgar as they stood alongside in wait for Gallius.

Eventually, he and Shuma came through from the yard at the back, and passing once more across the swelter of the room, he opening the door and said sharply, "Are we ready? Then come, we must go."

Stepping out into the noise and activity of the workshop lanes, he walked to the right, his daughter at his side and Malian moved to stand at the door as each passed by.

It was time to say their goodbyes, and first Tragen and then Darric followed by Anitta, each received the blessings and best wishes for their safety as the altar tender embraced each in farewell. Until finally, Shuma stood before him. Now she also told of her own departure, and suddenly the hotness of his tears rose, and he felt a blurring of his vision as he looked upon the wise woman.

"Take care then, Shuma," he wished her well, his voice breaking slightly. "You know you will always have my good wishes." Enfolding the slight figure in his arms he said, "We have all come so far, and I hope we shall all remain safe."

"My good wishes will always be with you, Malian," she replied, and smiling back, she left him with one last instruction. "Please take care of Gallius for me." With that, she was gone, and Malian stood, hand raised in farewell as the group he had known from the valley separated, and they each went their own way.

***

The secret doors to the palace crypt were open to the king, the lector guard briefly acknowledging him as he passed. And slowly taking the steps down after instructing his two attendants to remain at the top, he moved towards the doors to the crypt and the entrance to the altar chamber. Passing the empty seats within the bowl of the cavern, King Dedrick approached the front where Serdos remained attending the Icons upon the alabaster pedestal, the figure of *Apep* spiralling in its stature above his head. Here another lector priest stood silently at his side, and his hand had briefly come up to alert the high priest to the sudden appearance of the king.

"Dedrick is here," he whispered before standing to one side, his robes stirring as he moved away.

The high priest stepped back from the altar with one last glance up towards the snake god and turning, he faced the deserted chamber and looked towards where the king approached.

Dedrick's absence from that morning's service had not gone without notice, and Serdos' own worries had again rekindled once he realised his lack of appearance. His thoughts had then turned to the actions which would need to be taken. But for the moment, he felt he could let the king play his hand and see where it took them.

"I require a moment of your time, Serdos," Dedrick strongly stated, stopping before the man. Glancing across to the lector priest who stood nearby, he quickly dismissed him, "And you can go!"

The *Hery-heb* immediately looked towards Serdos, and noting the slight response he moved away, choosing not to leave but to stand on the far side of the altar where the shadow of the snake blended him into the background.

"I hear Gallius has returned," Serdos began, his voice smooth and slick in its wording as he moved towards Dedrick, and wrapping his long cloak around, he stood before the king, the seven collected Icons gleaming along the raised ledge at his back.

"Yes, but empty-handed and with only one of his men," Dedrick replied, noting the tone of the high priest. "They had the misfortune to be attacked three days out from the city, and the Icon was taken by bandits."

He went on to tell of Gallius' account, unaware that the high priest had already been told of all said in the king's hall and that nothing he was saying was new to the man who stood listening. After informing him that he had sent Brann out again that very morning to trail the thieves, Dedrick was finally able to come to the crucial point.

"In regard to the rest of his men." He glanced across first to where the invisible lector priest stood before his gaze fell once more upon Serdos. "I've been informed by Captain Gallius that his second-in-command, a man called Roth, turned on him and attempted to take the Icon for himself." He looked intently at the high priest for any reaction, but Serdos returned his stare coldly and calmly, and he unhurriedly continued to explain Gallius' account of Roth's final words and their implication.

"Do you know of this man called Roth?" Dedrick straightaway asked, his voice demanding answers to the questions that Gallius had posed.

"No, I don't know him," came the outright reply. "Should I have done?"

"This was taken from about his neck." Dedrick brought out the talisman, and grasping the hand of the high priest, he dropped the token into his palm. "And it must have been given by someone."

Serdos turned the intricate token over and looked disinterestedly down at the piece of silver, his fingers picking out the detail around its trim.

"Perhaps he stole it!"

"Yes, perhaps," the king came back, "but that makes me concerned for the Icons. Perhaps someone will attempt to steal them!" Feeling that he would exercise more of his privilege, he said, "So I think I'll straightaway send you some of my guards to protect them and then we can be certain of their safety."

"No!" Serdos immediately shouted, his face filled with indignation. "None other than brothers are allowed within the crypt, and our orders do not permit such action." His anger made itself known, and his voice shook at the very suggestion. "And I shall uphold this ruling as high priest." Walking briskly away from the king, he turned his back to the darkness of the chamber before slowly saying, "We must keep to our practices, Dedrick! You know that!"

"Very well," Dedrick responded, but feeling he could press his requests further, he added, "then I command that the Icons are brought into the safety of the stronghold, for the vaults there are guarded well beyond these walls."

Serdos walked along the front of the altar as Dedrick made his demand, and stopping before the Icons of *Kek* and *Kauket*, the god and goddess of darkness, he swung around and looked to the king where the black shadows of the crypt had deepened in their intensity about his person.

"If that's your wish," he finally replied, realising that for this moment, he had to keep the king placated, and in so doing, agreed to his request, "we shall move the Icons tomorrow."

"Good, I shall send some men in the morning!"

Dedrick quickly left, retracing his steps towards the crypt door. Passing through and back into the realm of his own authority, he thought on the power he would hold the following day, before his thinking turned to Captain Brann and the hope he had placed on him for the recapture of the last Icon.

Making his way out into the light of the palace gardens, his attendants were both quick to join him, and following him through the northern door of the colonnade, the gate shut quietly behind him as he turned the corner.

***

Watching as the king made his way out, Serdos swung back to face the altar, his back to the overwhelming silence and smiling up into the sharp features of *Apep*, he was re-joined by his brother lector.

"He knows," the *Hery-heb* said, his voice echoing through the stillness.

"Yes, he knows," Serdos answered, the smile deepening across his features, "but the knowing will not be his for long."

***

Gallius led the four through the streets of the eastern lanes, and following the workshops to the end, he passed between the last two buildings, coming out into an area where the city walls closed in around the back of the dwellings. Here, the southeastern gate led directly into the forest, and unfastening the barred exit, Gallius pushed open the door and walked through into the calm of the woods. Heading around the side of the city wall, they turned south, and with the pathway to their right, moved through the trees back to where the four horses had been rested. Quickly finding them not far from where they had been left, the riders made ready to mount and be on their way, and Gallius pulled Shuma to one side.

"Look after her, for me," he said, the deep apprehension again crossing his features, "and look after yourself. I will join you both as soon as I can." They kissed, and letting her go, she sprung into her saddle, and Daina climbed up behind her, her hand reaching out to

110

her father as he stood by their side.

"Take care, Father!" she cried, looking down towards Gallius, and Shuma was quick to move the horse away as the hands of the father and daughter briefly touched.

Darric and Anitta followed, and as Tragen passed, his horse eager and ready for the off, Gallius held out his palm and the large hand folded around his before letting go. Wishing them all well, he watched as the horses disappeared into the trees before slowly returning back towards the city gate.

CHAPTER SIX

The gate of the colonnade closed softly behind Dedrick, and the stretch of the walkway that led off around the corner enveloped him in its unnerving silence while the bustle of the city over its high walls remained muted to the king's ear. Nevertheless, he had little cause to notice any fear in this well-walked route with its feeling of seclusion and its protected surrounds and, with this, it allowed his mind to wander.

His thoughts continued along the path of Brann's homecoming then returned to that of the Icons and his soon-to-be control and authority in their ownership before he all at once thought on the lies and deceit knowingly spoken and shown by Serdos, and he became incensed and flew into a rage.

Following behind, his two attendants, Esra and Jakob, walked at their discreet distance, keeping their pace in correspondence with the king as his stride quickened at the sharp rise in this sudden anger. On approaching the secured doorway into the stronghold and seeing that it remained closed as he neared, Dedrick raised his hand in instruction for the guard to open up.

"Open the door!" he shouted in demand, his indignation propelling him forward.

Seeing the king coming towards the door, the guard turned to face him, a questioning look briefly crossing his face as he stared past the man to where the two attendants advanced before it was replaced by outright hostility as the king came within his reach.

"Open the door!" Dedrick again ordered, his voice this time outraged by the lack of obedience shown. Stopping within the shadow of the doorway and the return back into the safety of his own realm, he felt a sudden fear come to the fore and instantly, he recognised the treachery.

The short blade bit deep into the king's chest, and thrusting upwards, found its mark close to his heart. In the shock of the sudden and unexpected attack, his hands reached forward towards the guard. Grabbing at his tunic, the material burst at the buttons and ripped open to reveal the silver token worn about his neck, and Dedrick stared at the known certainty of the high priest's betrayal. Slowly his knees gave way as the blade was withdrawn, and the warmth of the pain intensified while the cobbles of the colonnade stopped any further downward progress and his body came to lie at the feet of his assassin.

Immediately the two attendants rushed to the fore, and seeing what was occurring, both reacted in defence of their king, their daggers being drawn as they moved to protect him from further attack. The guard then raised his short blade, turning to the taller attendant, Jakob, in his first strike while ignoring the attack of the other.

The fight was brief, Jakob receiving a wound to his left forearm as he raised it in defence, and as the dagger had been brought upwards to slice down again and cause further injury, Esra had come up behind the guard. Bringing his blade around, he cut across the throat of the unwary man to silence any comeback, for in his giving of the nod moments earlier to carry out Serdos' order to kill the king, he had also been signalling the guard's own death. The body then dropped to the floor, the clatter of the blade preceding the thump as the figure hit the cobbles and the two attendants turning away gave it no more thought.

Rushing to the king's side and moving him onto his back, Esra could see that Dedrick was not yet dead, and his eyes looked up into the light of the afternoon sky, the scudding clouds above reflected in the widening stare.

"Get help!" he ordered Jakob as he placed his hand over the wound, appearing to press down hard as his colleague disappeared in a rush through into the main hall. However, on looking back towards the king, the trusted attendant removed his hand and let the blood flow freely, the redness of the royal liquid running down to pool in the cracks of the cobbles.

"Tell Prince Edgar...that Serdos is behind this," the king's voice came quietly as he stared up at his devoted aide. But noting the look of unconcern and apathy in the eyes of the man who stared back, he was quick to feel the coldness of the metal again as it entered his body. With a sharp plunge of his dagger Esra finished off the guard's work.

Looking across to where the guard had fallen, his silver token lying about his neck in its gathering pool of blood, Esra reached across and snatched at it, pulling it away before thrusting it into the pouch of his tunic. Then he awaited the return of Jakob, his concern for the dead king at his side causing him little anguish.

***

"The king's been attacked! The king's been attacked!" Jakob shouted on crossing the stone floor of the main hall. And his voice rose in panic as the emptiness of the chamber echoed his words, passing them along the passageways where they reached the ears of the stronghold's staff.

Finding Captain Isaac and two of his men coming through from the outside, he rushed towards them, yelling, "The king's been attacked!"

Running back towards the western doorway, the men quickly followed, loosening their blades as they overtook him. Charging through, they came upon the scene of the king's violation.

"The guard attacked him," Esra swiftly cried, his head bowed as he sat alongside, and looking down to where his hands lay covered in crimson with his apparent attempt to staunch the blood, he feigned his distress and dismay.

Dedrick lay motionless, his head turned to stare across at his attacker, and Isaac knelt quickly to check for any signs of breath, his hand briefly resting on the bloodied chest before he rose and turned upon his men.

"You two stay here and look to the king," he instructed his men. Then staring at each of the king's former attendants said, "And you too will remain and await my return."

Isaac turned back into the stronghold and setting off in search for Prince Edgar, he first checked his chambers before rushing towards the dining hall and beyond into the king's residence. Finding the prince nowhere around, he raced back to the main hall where the news of the king's attack was growing and making its way out onto the streets.

***

The gate in the southeastern wall had blown shut, and as Gallius opened it and passed through, he retraced his steps back around the buildings, which appeared close in proximity after the expanse felt beneath the overhanging trees of the woodland. The sound, too, had risen, and a general clamour was heard over the usual sounds of the workshops. The hammering of metal and the blasts of the furnaces had suddenly gone still as he walked along the lane and a feeling of unease grew with each deadened sound and step. Hurrying forward, he arrived outside the door that he had left earlier.

Seeing the wife of the blacksmith who worked opposite, standing in her open doorway, he asked, "Has something happened?"

Further along towards the courtyard, he could now see activity around the main gate, and his first thought went to Tragen and the group he had seen off many minutes earlier. And the thought briefly crossed his mind that they had already been stopped and forced to return to the city!

"What has happened?" he again asked, the demand made clearer this time.

"It's the king, someone's attacked the king!" the woman declared, and turning to where her husband worked within the dimness of the interior, she shouted back to him, "They say Dedrick's been stabbed!"

The blacksmith came to the doorway, the sweat of his day's labour dripping down his flushed face, and turning away from the captain, he spat thickly on the cobbles before his doorstep. Briefly nodding to Gallius, he disappeared back inside.

Turning, Gallius darted back into the workshop of Anitta's uncle and strode into the main area and on through into the back and out again into the yard where Malian and Prince Edgar sat in talk. The conversation in his absence had once more turned to the details of the brotherhood and the tokens and the situation in which they found themselves. But the two had quickly looked up as he rushed through the doorway, his stunned expression bringing an instant stay to their conversation.

"They say the king has been attacked!" he immediately disclosed, and stepping towards Prince Edgar, he thought about his protection. "We need to get you back to the stronghold, this city is no longer safe."

Gallius led Edgar back through the city streets, while Malian was advised to remain in the safety provided by Ladio and Brinda. The walkways and thoroughfares that were usually busy and bustling now appeared full of confusion and tumult as the news of the assault upon the king within his own stronghold was passed around. And many people had come out onto the pavements to stand and watch.

Arriving at the steps to the fortified building, Edgar was met by Captain Isaac, who was taking his search for the prince onto the streets.

"We have been looking for you, sir," Isaac straightaway said before swiftly asking, "Have you heard?" He stepped to one side as the prince took the steps two at a time and stopped to face him in the doorway, the dimness of the hall behind them seemingly pitch-dark as the light of the afternoon poured across the entrance.

"Is it true, Isaac? Has the king been attacked?" Edgar urgently challenged.

"Yes, sir, but I'm afraid it's much worse than that!"

"Dead?" he quietly asked, looking down at the blood-stained hand of the captain as it rested upon his blade.

"Yes, sir," came the guarded reply. "We've left his body where he fell."

"Show me!"

***

Isaac led the two through the growing turmoil filling the darkness of the main hall and across to the open door leading around to the palace, and as they passed through, Gallius picked up a couple more of the guards to attend upon the prince. The view through the doorway into the colonnade appeared to have become suspended in time, for the king's body lay where it had fallen, and his two attendants, along with Isaac's men, remained in position.

Edgar passed back into the light of the day, and could

see instantly that his brother was dead, for the face was already drained of colour, and the eyes glazed over. But instinctively, he dropped to his knee and checked for any signs of life. Finding none, he placed Dedrick's hands across the wounded chest before turning the head away from his attacker and gently closing his eyes, the stare of the dead man disappearing beneath the lids as they slowly stiffened. Dropping his head, Edgar gave a moment in thought to his older brother and the stillness which surrounded them was respected by those who stood in witness.

Suddenly a harsh voice broke into the silence.

"What is going on here?" High Priest Serdos demanded.

The recent noise from within the colonnade had made its way into the palace gardens, and the high priest, who remained in his crypt, had been notified that there had been an attack on the king and that his presence would be required. Arriving with his attendants to see what had occurred, he followed in the king's footsteps along the open corridor, and seeing the crowd gathered at the far end of the colonnade, he approached the door to the stronghold.

"What is happening?" he now shouted, noting Prince Edgar at his brother's side along with the two captains standing behind.

Scowling at the two who stood in the doorway, he glared hard at Gallius as he neared the fallen body, and the angry stare was returned as the captain advanced to stand close to the prince.

"The king is dead," Isaac said in answer to the question. And as he too stepped forward, coming to stand at Edgar's side, he finished, "He's been killed by his own guard."

Serdos quickly glanced towards where the guard lay,

and noting the clean cut of the fatal slash, he was thankful to see a job well done, and his thoughts and attention turned solely to the king and his preparation for the afterlife.

Watching as Edgar stepped back from the body, he was seemingly quick to assert his authority as high priest and all that would be expected of him at this time. And with his lector priests at his side, he moved forward to stand before the body of the king.

"He must be immediately moved," he made his declaration, "and taken away for preparation for the hereafter." Looking towards the two attendants, he nodded at the shorter of the two and said, "Come, Esra, you can help us prepare your master for his last journey."

"No!" Edgar quickly stated as he saw a sudden expectation cross the face of the attendant. "He will remain here." Looking from where his brother's servants stood, he stared angrily back towards the high priest before finishing, "These two are the only witnesses to what happened here, and they will both need to be questioned."

"Very good," Serdos conceded, his voice somewhat discourteous in its tone, "but you will grant my lector priests to take charge of the body?"

"Yes," Edgar eventually conceded, and looking down upon his brother, he gave his consent, "you may take him."

The body of Dedrick was lifted by the attendant priests, and Serdos led the slow march into the stronghold, the gathered crowd parting as they walked through. Here they moved off in ceremony beyond into one of the smaller antechambers leading from the hall. This was now given over to their ministrations, the king being placed within and the doors closed to preserve the secrecy and mystery of their profession.

Outside in the walkway, the body of the door guard remained, although at some point, it had been dragged to one side and away from where the king had fallen. Edgar had briefly checked for any signs of life there, but his throat had been expertly cut from ear to ear, and his lifeless form would be unforthcoming of any explanation.

"Take him away," he angrily instructed, wasting no further time upon the man. "And see that he is stripped and strung up for all to see."

The captains then concentrated on clearing up the colonnade area, and Isaac nodded his head to the two men he had left to attend the king. Assisting him in carrying the body of the guard unceremoniously out through the door and down the steps into the city streets, he personally saw that it was dealt with.

Gallius' thoughts, however, turned to the security of the stronghold and more so to the safety of the prince. Hurriedly he suggested they relocate to an area that could be better defended if needed, recommending the king's halls in the northern end of the stronghold. Gallius knew that these quarters would be an ideal place and could be well defended, for his recent visit before the king in his throne room had given him some insight into the layout within the building, and Edgar, knowing the rooms of old, was quick in his agreement.

"You two," Gallius demanded, staring at both attendants, "you will come with us." And as the prince returned through the door into the main hall, Gallius followed, and the attendants fell in line behind. The remaining guards, being last to leave the red-stained cobbles of the colonnade as they brought up the rear, then closed the door on the scene before they escorted the prince through the hall towards the doors leading to the king's residences. Halfway across, Gallius stopped, allowing Edgar to carry on, and turning back to the attendants, he spoke to the taller figure who had stood beside the king.

"Have you been injured?" he asked Jakob, noting the bleeding wound to his left arm. Glancing down, he saw the gash which cut across the forearm.

"Yes, sir," the soft reply came, "in defence of my king, sir."

Looking back to one of the guards, he instructed him to take the attendant to the lower halls for urgent attention and to bring him straight back to the king's halls after he had been attended to.

"Speak to no one," he advised them both. "No one, understand!" he repeated as they walked away. Turning he quickly followed Edgar, catching up with him as he entered the double doors into Dedrick's domain. Stopping the remaining guard before he also passed through, Gallius instructed him to gather straightaway further armed men who he knew he could trust and return immediately to defend the prince.

The king's halls consisted of the throne room, the king's chambers and the meeting room along with its dining hall. Edgar instantly walked past the first and took the door opposite into the meeting room where a large table took up the centre of the vast chamber, the tall-backed chair of the king taking its place at the top. Around the room, a number of seating areas had been placed close to the outermost edge, and two padded chairs sat on either side of the fireplace, each with a footstool. But the remainder of the room was stark and empty, even the hearth seemingly barren of timber, and the grate lay neglected.

"I've organised more guards, sir," Gallius urgently advised as he followed Edgar over to the fireside, "for your life may also be in danger."

Within moments, the ordered guard had swiftly

returned along with a number of his associates and the room was checked and secured, and the door leading through into the dining hall had been closed shut after the room had been inspected.

Esra, the king's attendant, had automatically gone to stand in his place at the side of the king's chair and was told to remain there and await the return of Jakob. Seeing that nothing further could be done for Edgar's defence, Gallius' thoughts returned to Malian and the urgency that was gathering for his safety, and he asked the prince to give him leave.

"I need to go and fetch Malian," he said, his haste and fear growing for the man who was a stranger within this city. "I have made pledge to ensure his security, and I must keep to my word."

Edgar had spoken in detail with Malian and knew in full the story which surrounded him, and on hearing the urgency in Gallius's voice, he was reminded of his significance and the need to keep him free from any harm.

"Yes, go," he immediately said, looking around at the men who stood in his safeguard. "But bring him back here where we can ensure his protection."

Passing the armed guards who stood at the double doors, Gallius walked back out into the main hall, there meeting Isaac, who was returning from his duty. The two men who had accompanied him had now been joined by two others, and each was well armed, the short blades in their belts complimented by the longer ones which hung at their sides.

"We've strung him up in the marketplace," the captain directly declared on seeing Gallius, his voice showing a note of satisfaction. "He's on show in the cattle yard."

"Good, we need to demonstrate the prince's control," came the reply, and nodding his head back towards where he had come from, Gallius indicated Edgar's location. "He's in the king's halls. Guard him well and let no one leave the room."

***

The people on the streets had increased in number, the word having gone around that the king was, in fact, dead. And Gallius made his way through the crowds from the stronghold and down past the eastern side of the arena. Eventually, he reached the stalls of the marketplace where the booths and covered trestles of the marketeers massed around the stockyards and butcheries. Arriving first into the cattle yards, he came upon the body of the guard.

Isaac had done an excellent job, for the remains were hanging upside down from a meat hook which would usually have held the carcass of a forest hog, his head dangling awkwardly from the severed throat as the congealed blood darkened against the whiteness of his features. His body appeared thin and scrawny as it gently rotated on the hook while across the chest, a sign hung from the hilt of an embedded blade which read "Slayer of the King" written in his own blood.

The crowd which had gathered in the yard was unused to such a spectacle, and after the initial shouts and jeering which accompanied the stringing up of the body had died down, the audience had gone quiet. Now the women began to take their children away back past the stalls while the gathered men folk had remained and talked of the wickedness that had fallen upon their city.

Pushing his way through the cattle yard, Gallius continued his walk into the back of the lanes and down past the numerous workshops before arriving at the doorway of Ladio. Here the blade smith himself was

123

standing outside, his neighbour's wife from opposite holding conversation on the king's demise. But on seeing Gallius, he was quick to stand aside and open the door, and the captain passed through into the back.

Malian was seated within the yard, but on seeing Gallius, he was on his feet and hurried towards the doorway.

"Has the king been killed?" he straightaway asked, the unbelievable news having been given to him by Brinda as soon as the report had been passed along the lanes.

"Yes, he's dead," Gallius replied, "and for the moment, in the guardianship of the high priest!"

"And what of Prince Edgar?"

"Safe within the stronghold," came the quick report. "But now we must ensure your safety, and for that, you must also be taken there. Get your things and let's go!"

Malian noted the urgency and hurriedly collected his pack. Thanking Brinda for her care and hospitality, and nodding his head to Ladio as he remained on the doorstep, he followed the man into the lanes. Taking the same route back towards the cattle yard, Gallius retraced his steps and Malian was taken through the city towards the stronghold and the safety of the guarded building.

Passing between the back of the stables and the side of the cattle yard and reaching its topmost corner, Malian caught a glimpse of the body of the dead guard over the outer fencing, but they were swift to pass it by in their haste to reach safety.

Reaching the stronghold, the doors to the king's hall were well defended, Isaac's four men having replaced the two who stood there earlier. But on seeing Gallius escorting Malian across the floor, they stood to one side to allow them both to pass. At the same time, Jakob was being led back from his treatment in the lower halls, a heavy dressing covering the deep injury. And on noticing

Gallius nearing the doorway, the guard stopped to hand him across, and the captain escorted both Malian and the attendant through the entrance and into the meeting room.

The guards within the room had reduced to four, one being Isaac, who was standing beside Edgar. The prince himself had given order for the fire to be set and lit, and was now seated before its warmth. But on seeing Gallius guiding Malian through from the hallway, Edgar had stood and made his way over to meet them, and the altar tender had expressed his sympathy at the loss of the prince's brother.

The group then moved towards the fireside, Edgar again returning to his seat while the other was given over to Malian. While behind him, Gallius took up his position, with Captain Isaac remaining in place, standing close to the side of the prince.

Edgar then ordered for the attendants to be brought forward, and Jakob was directed to stand before them, his back to the fire. At the same time, Esra reluctantly left the side of the king's chair and came slowly forward to stand alongside his colleague.

"Tell me exactly what happened," Edgar immediately demanded, looking to the two who stood apprehensively before him. For both knew they would be taken to task for allowing the attack and not preventing the death of their king.

Esra, the smaller and older of the two attendants, now recounted what occurred that day, saying that the king had not been to service that morning but had been to see the high priest later in the day. They were on their way back through from the palace into the stronghold when the guard made his attack. He told them that both Jakob and he were completely taken by surprise but rushed to the king's aid instantly and were upon the man before he could inflict any further injuries.

"He came for me!" Jakob added, his voice rising as his unease grew in the recount. "And as I fended him off, Esra came up behind and slit his throat."

"We both fought well, sir," Esra hopefully furthered the account, looking to support their fearlessness in the situation, "and once the threat had been overcome and the guard taken care of, I swiftly sent Jakob for help."

He looked towards Edgar before dropping his gaze. "But the king passed away in my arms before any aid could come." His head dropped, and he stared intently at the floor as the prince stirred restlessly in his chair, his cold hands gripping tightly the leather of the armrests.

The room slowly went quiet, and in those minutes Edgar began to relax. Reaching past the attendants to add another piece of wood to the fire, his hands remained close to the flames as the chill was dispelled from his fingers, and Captain Isaac moved across to where Gallius stood behind Malian.

"Do you think the guard was acting on his own?" he whispered, looking across towards where the prince's back was turned away from them.

"I would say not," Gallius came back, "but I think I know who is behind this."

Aware that not all were yet in the know of the brotherhood and its association with the snake god, he lowered his voice and directed his attention back to the prince.

"My lord, I think there are many here in this city who are oblivious to the increasing dominance of High Priest Serdos. But we must be seen to make our plans, and I propose we take some immediate action against this rising threat that he may pose to you."

"The high priest is very powerful," Edgar replied, sitting back in his chair before looking up at his captains and saying, "And I'm sure he has his supporters. We too, shall have to gather our forces which may take a little time. But now that we are aware of his possible agenda, what do you suggest we do?"

Malian instantly stood, giving the others little chance to reply, and standing near the two attendants, he was ready to give his opinion as one wise to the temple traditions and the rituals and routines of the ministries.

"I think, firstly, we must allow Serdos to continue in his service and attendance upon the king," he said, aware that the priests would serve Dedrick in their agreed undertaking. "For his body must be prepared for his journey into the afterlife, and nothing should prevent him from achieving this." He went quiet, seeing the slow understanding and acceptance of this advice on Edgar's face before he continued, "I also think this may calm any disquiet in Serdos' thinking, for he will certainly expect some retaliation if he suspects we know anything."

Malian's mind now went to the actions he must take to achieve his goal, that of getting into the meeting room of the brotherhood with its end result of gaining further information on Serdos' intentions. And he went on to tell the listening men of his purpose to join the brotherhood to achieve that aim.

"But you will never be granted entry," Edgar said, looking with genuine misgiving towards the man who stood before him, before adding, "and if you did get in, how will you explain yourself to the brothers?"

"Well, in answer to my gaining entry, then this should grant me access." Bringing out Mentu's talisman, he held out the token and looked down at the silver as it glinted in the light of the fire. "My face being new to the city should give me some anonymity within the gathering, and once I am accepted, then I can hope to be received as yet another brother."

"I feel that this is an unwise thing to do, Malian,"

Gallius agreed with the prince. Looking with growing concern at the older man who stood before them, he said, "I fear it is too unrealistic and too dangerous in its undertaking if you get found out."

"But you know we must have more understanding about the brotherhood and what their plans are!" he exclaimed.

Suddenly Jakob stepped forward, his reserve giving way to a sudden boldness he could no longer hold back, and standing beside Malian he addressed the prince.

"I have seen one of these before, sir," he said, looking at the token as it sat in Malian's hand. "There was one around the guard's neck, the guard who attacked and killed the king!"

"No, you must be wrong," Isaac quickly replied. "There was nothing about his neck. I myself supervised his body when he was carried out from the colonnade, and would surely have noted it when he was stripped." Knowing in full the measures given to the guard's body, he could be in some certainty of its absence.

"It was there," Jakob said resolutely, "I saw it when he attacked me!"

"Did you see anything like this?" Gallius swiftly turned to Esra, noticing a look of unrest and agitation beginning to build up in the anxious face of the attendant.

"No, Captain, I didn't," came the reply. "After killing the guard, my attention went only to my king's welfare. And one to which I should like to return if it please the prince. For it is our custom to stand vigil for both myself and Jakob." He bowed his head towards Edgar and continued, "Our many years of service as attendants will not end until we have seen and stood in witness of our king's body and all made ready for his funeral tomorrow."

Edgar saw no reason to keep the two attendants, for he

felt there was nothing further to be gained from them. Dismissing them with a wave of his hand, the two walked away from the fire to attend upon their king. But as Esra passed by Isaac, the captain noticed the light blood stain on the attendant's tunic pocket was appearing to get darker, and he shouted for the door guards to stop the man before he could leave.

"Are you injured?" he asked, following him towards the opening.

"No, Captain," Esra readily replied, "why do you ask?"

"Because there is blood coming from you." Pointing out the increasing blood stain, Esra stared down in disbelief towards the pocket where he knew the guard's token lay hidden.

"Search him!" Isaac immediately demanded, seeing the look of alarm which crossed the man's face, and roughly the door guards held him tight before rifling harshly through the front of the tunic. Finally, they pulled out the blood-soaked token, and the attendant was swiftly dragged back towards Edgar before he could attempt to escape.

"What do you know about this?" the prince demanded, his face enraged as he stared at the red-streaked silver talisman which was handed over. "And what part have you played in the death of my brother and the killing of this city's king?"

"I know nothing, my lord," the man pleaded, and crying out as the tip of Isaac's blade was felt at the back of his neck, he repeated, "I swear I know nothing!"

"Captain Isaac," Edgar strongly instructed, not wishing to waste any further time, "take him away and see what he has to say!"

The man was hauled across the room, his shouts of protestation slowly becoming silenced as Isaac removed him from the king's halls, and he was taken down into the vaults which housed the prison rooms. There he was shown the meaning of torment and given little option of renouncing any questioning.

An hour later, Isaac returned, and Esra was brought back into the meeting room between the arms of two of the prison guards, the groans and cries of pain at the many broken bones being ignored as they carried him briskly through the doorway. The small man was now beaten and bloodied about the face and head, and his blood-stained tunic was ripped and torn about the bruised body, his arms dangling uselessly at his side as the guards placed him before the prince. And Isaac, coming to stand behind him, instructed him to repeat his account.

"Tell Prince Edgar what you have told me!" he softly said, bending to whisper into the man's ear. Placing his hand across the man's shoulder, he squeezed down hard and a groan came from the attendant.

"I was commanded, sir, by the high priest," Esra immediately began, his voice shaking as the pressure applied increased his pain. And being unable to lift his hands, the blood ran into his eyes and blurred his vision as the prince's face clouded over before him. "I was ordered by the high priest to give the guard a sign as we came back along the colonnade. A sign for him to kill the king, and once he had done that, then I was to kill him!"

"And what about your friend here?" Edgar asked, looking to where the other attendant had been placed under guard, his face staring expressionless as the interrogation progressed.

"No, it was just me. Jakob was not party to any of my actions."

The attendant broke down, the blood-tinged saliva dripping from his mouth, and hanging his head, he was unable to stop the red liquid from splashing to the floor as he pleaded with the prince. He finally finishing by begging, "I was only obeying orders, my lord!"

Edgar furiously rose from his seat, and standing before the traitor, he fought to control his rage. Turning away from the beaten man, his temper at breaking point, he shouted over his shoulder, "Remove this man from my sight!" Quickly turning back, he glared into the face of the attendant, "And take him to join his accomplice!"

"I was only obeying orders!" the little man screamed as he realised his fate.

As the two prison guards quickly removed him from the room, silencing him with a blow to the chin, Captain Isaac followed, his given instructions clear and precise in his mind.

***

Returning some time later, Isaac found the room quieter, and Edgar, Gallius and Malian were all seated near the fire, the attendant Jakob standing close to hand for the prince.

"We've strung him up, sir," he knowingly declared, and glancing across to Jakob he stared long at the attendant to ascertain any reaction. Receiving none, he came to where the prince was seated. "We've placed a sign, so there should be no doubting as to why he's there."

"Good," Edgar replied, his rage having given way to an apathy, "but come and have a seat alongside Gallius, and he can explain more of what is happening here. For I'm sure, you are in the dark on some aspects."

Captain Isaac knew a little about the Icons, for it was himself and his scouts who had been sent out by Dedrick some untold time ago to find and steal the water god *Nun*. And they had been many months away from the city on their quest into the south. Eventually, they found their prize in the City of Caerule on the shores of the open sea, and their journey had been long and eventful in his remembering.

While the quietness within the room took on a more subdued tone, Gallius further explained to Isaac the meaning behind the Icons and their gathering together by the Brotherhood of the Snake.

Along with his own given quest to steal *Amaunet* from the valley and the disloyalty of his men, he told of his eventual meeting with Malian and his growing friendship with Tragen, Darric, Shuma and Anitta, who had travelled back with them here. Finally, he made clear the reasoning of how they had come to be seated in the stronghold.

"We originally came back to save my daughter and retake the Icon of *Naunet*, the Icon of the City of Lights, which is Tragen's city in the south," he explained. "But the whole situation has grown, and we find ourselves facing much darker days and harsher times."

"But who is this Tragen that you mention, and where are these others?" Isaac felt a need to ask Gallius.

"Tragen is one of the companions of Malian, and he has suffered more than most in his quest to reclaim his Icon," he explained, only touching briefly upon the suffering that he knew the man carried. "We have sent him back south, along with Darric and Anitta, to alert the women in the Sleeping Caverns of the impending arrival of Brann and his men. For there, *Amaunet*, the Eighth Deity, has been taken. And under their protection, we are relying on its safety." He made clear the task assigned upon the group heading south, saying, "Tragen is going to try and overtake Brann and his party of men who have been sent out by Dedrick to retrieve this last Icon. But now the king is dead, I feel right to assume that Serdos will obviously take control on his return should he succeed. Unless, of course, we can stop him!"

"Meanwhile, we must look to ourselves here within the stronghold because we may also be in danger," Gallius reasoned, his thoughts returning to their plan, "and I think it best if we delay any action until after King Dedrick has been laid to rest tomorrow in our custom." Looking towards Edgar, he quickly added, "And of course, you must also be crowned king, my lord. For then, all of the city's troops and militia will be in your power. Until then, I feel we must address our own safety."

"Well, we have the night to think on the matter," Edgar said in agreement, "and for the moment, I feel we should remain within the king's chambers." Rising from his seat, he continued, "There is a room down the hallway for both you and Malian to sleep, and you will be close by if anything occurs."

"The time is getting late, and nothing can be achieved now. So, yes, we should retire and wait for the morning."

Gallius then suggested that Isaac should stay at the prince's side to ensure his safety, and speaking directly to the captain, he said, "Until Serdos has cause to show his hand, we shall remain unsure of his plans or if he would want to strike or take out the prince. So, Isaac, I think you should stay by his side until tomorrow's ceremonies have finished."

Escorting Malian down the hallway, Gallius firstly ensured the placement of guards outside the main doors for protection of the prince. While Edgar, leading Captain Isaac and Jakob into his brother's chambers, closed the doors into the hall and thankfully watched as Gallius gave his orders with some certainty that they could take no further steps at that point.

King Dedrick lay within his casket, the table in the darkened room bearing the full weight of both body and box. Around the edge, several small rings of scented flowers had been placed along with perfumed tapers that smoked sullenly in the airless expanse. At the four corners, tall white waxy candles were lit, throwing the shadows of the four lector priests down along the ground as they stood, heads down in devotion at each edge of the table.

At the foot of the casket, Serdos himself stood, the high priest having already conducted his rites and rituals, with the jars containing the organs of the dead king already being shut tightly away in their ornate cartons.

As he waited, his thoughts turned to the king's attendants, for it was only right and correct that they should be present at this ceremony of their master. But they had not yet shown, and it gave him concern for this lack of protocol. He knew little about the tall attendant Jakob, but Esra had been his spy for countless years, and he had great faith in him and no doubt whatsoever that he would reveal or say anything even if pressed. For he had been faithful to the cause of the snake god and been well rewarded in the past and would soon be in the service of a new king and again performing his undercover duties.

CHAPTER SEVEN

Malian and Gallius found their room at the lower end of the hall where, in the long past, an area had been set aside for guests visiting the stronghold. It was not overly lavish, but the rooms within gave an enclosed space to sleep while the main area was adequately supplied with seating alongside a table. Both men felt some relief as they closed the door at their backs and placed their packs to one side.

"This should only be for one night, Malian," the captain stated, looking around at the simplicity of the apartments, "for once Edgar is crowned, then all the stronghold and the city itself will pass to him as king. He can then take control of the troops and the stronghold."

"But that didn't do Dedrick much good, did it?" Malian replied. Pulling aside one of the drawn curtains he peered into the sleeping corner beyond, the sheets and blankets folded at the end of the simple bed with its number of cushions placed to hand.

"No, I don't suppose it did," Gallius recognised, and allowing his discipline and instruction to take control, he finished, "But we are now all on our guard. So let us first get some rest, for tomorrow we need to remain on full alert, and it proposes to be a busy day."

The captain drew aside the heavy curtain of the alcove opposite Malian and, collecting his pack from beside the table, he returned to the cubicle and quietly pulled the curtain closed.

Malian too, retreated behind the curtained screen to make his bed and relax, and as he rested his head onto the cushions, his thoughts turned to the two groups who had left the city earlier that day. He kept alive some hope that Tragen and Darric would be swift in catching up with

Brann, and the women of the Sleeping Caverns would not be called upon to fight and risk their lives in their protection of *Amaunet.* But somehow, deep down, he knew it was a false hope.

***

Malian slept heavily, the tiredness instantly overcoming him and taking him deep into his dreams. There he found himself standing once more back at the Seventh Gate of *The Duat*, his feet floating over the golden waters in the Realm of the Dead as he approached the portal of the gateway. Here the god *Horus* stood once more before him, a staff held in his hands as his thickly feathered cape surrounded the broad shoulders, and the heavy head of the falcon gazed upriver of the flow and watched as he neared.

Coming to a stop, Malian noticed the change to the stone surround of the gateway, for the onyx was bare from its decoration, and the images of the crowns depicted in their sparkling stones had disappeared from its façade.

"Where are the crowns?" he asked the god, looking up in puzzlement into the beady eye of the falcon.

"IN THE SAFEGUARD OF THE GODS," came the deep voice. **"FOR AT THIS MOMENT, THE KINGSHIP REMAINS UNBALANCED AGAINST THE GREAT SCALES OF LIFE, AND WHILE THE CROWN HAS NOT YET BEEN BESTOWED, THE LAND REMAINS LOST AND WITHOUT ITS AUTHORITY."**

"But the prince is to be crowned tomorrow, and I shall be there to watch," Malian stated, his voice seemingly coming from afar as the god bent down to stare towards the floating body, the hooked beak moving this way and that as the hawk focused upon the weightless figure.

"**A NEW KING WILL BE APPOINTED, AND THE CROWN WILL BE GIVEN,**" came the assured reply, the eyes of *Horus* meeting those of the altar tender as he readily returned his gaze. "**AND THE GIVER SHALL DECLARE HIM KING!**"

The god raised his staff and brought it down with an almighty blow, and the echo flowed back along *The Duat* as he continued his declaration.

"**BUT FIRST, THE HYPOCRITE MUST BE OPPOSED, AND HERE YOU WILL BE CALLED UPON TO STEP FORWARD AND SHOW YOUR FORTITUDE. THE GIFT OF THE *SHEN* STAFF GRANTED TO YOU BEYOND THIS GATE WAS GIVEN NOT ONLY TO ENSURE YOUR PROTECTION BUT ALSO FOR YOU TO FAVOUR THE GODS!**"

Malian's dream then immediately went to the thought of Serdos. And knowing that, as high priest, he would be presiding over the ceremonies both of the internment of the old king and also the anointing of the new, he felt an overwhelming dread fill his body. Slowly the image of the man appeared in the gateway before him, but now it appeared somewhat out of proportion.

The overlarge head appeared hooded while the body slowly shrank in on itself, the clothes dropping off to reveal the snake beneath the vestments. While at the same time, a fleshless voice came out in a hiss.

"*There will be no stopping the rise of chaos, nor stopping the return of* Apep *and his followers, and all shall become witness to the disorder.*"

The form slowly began to fade, and finally, the voice disappeared into a whisper. The darkness beyond the gate then gathered and filled in, enclosing the space taken up by its presence, and Malian looked in towards the depths of the beyond.

"YOU MUST CONFRONT SERDOS, MALIAN," the great god spoke his order in finality, **"FOR THE GODS ARE WITH YOU."**

Turning his head towards the gateway, Malian slowly began to drift towards its opening, his feet feeling the coldness of the shining surface as his toes began to submerge. And as he passed beneath the portal into the darkness of the Seventh Gate, his knees disappeared beneath the waters, and sinking further, the great golden river eventually poured over his head.

Malian woke with a start, the sweat pouring off him as he sat up in the bed. The only sound he could hear in the dawning light was the harsh snoring of Gallius, and slowly he lay back down, his body shaking as the dream lingered alarmingly clear in his thoughts. Until slowly passing, the image of the falcon god faded, and he again closed his eyes.

***

Serdos had ordered an early service for his brotherhood that morning, for he knew the day would be long. Leaving behind his vigil at the king's side in the early hours, he followed the colonnade back through from the stronghold to the palace, pausing momentarily at the spot where Dedrick had fallen to look down in contempt at where the blood-stained cobbles remained in testimony of his death.

The king had always been seen as an obstacle in his rise to power, but recently had become even more so, the demands he made being the breaking point to which Serdos had found himself rapidly approaching. Now he was dead, there would be nothing nor no one to stand in his way. He gave little thought to the prince, only that once he was crowned, he would automatically be allowed entry to the brotherhood. But somehow, he never saw Edgar as being interested in doing so, and he brushed that possibility aside.

His hopes were now lying solely with Brann. On his return, either in his cause or in Dedrick's, for either would make no difference now, it would bring the last Icon into its rightful place and the Ogdoad, the Eight Primordial Deities, would again be reunited.

The preparations for the king's funeral had begun as soon as his death had been announced, and Serdos, passing through the top gate of the colonnade, was met by torch-lit activity in the palace forecourt. The palace buildings themselves had been built in a semi-circle around the raised platform of the enormous frontage, which made up the greater portion of the gated enclosure. And here, the body of the king would be placed in readiness for the service of his funeral before he was interred in the vaults alongside his father and predecessors. Here also, in the openness of the court and before the gathered crowds, the crowning of the new king would take place immediately after the funeral of the old. Thus marking and guaranteeing the continuation of the kingship within the city.

The high priest, however, did not linger in watching the preparations, for the dawn was on its way. Taking his route to the back of the buildings, he stepped purposefully through the attended door into the crypts and walked through under the activity of the forecourt above. There, on immediately entering the corridor down to the chamber, he was met by one of his senior lector priests who had been on his way out to see him.

"I have pressing news, Serdos," the brother straightaway said, his position within the association allowed him to use the high priest's name and be fully aware of the dealings within the palace. Stopping before the man in the walkway, he continued, "My lookout has been eager to tell me the news that the morning has brought." He moved closer to Serdos and lowered his voice. "He says that Esra, the king's attendant and one that I know has been useful in our cause, is dead and has been strung up alongside the guard who made the killing. Strung up and been well beaten, he said, by the look of the body."

"When did you hear this?" the high priest immediately said, his voice maintaining its composure while an unnerving feeling made itself known on hearing the report.

"Just now, I was coming straight to tell you!"

"Was he...tortured?" Serdos guardedly asked, the face of the attendant suddenly coming into his mind as he remembered his last meeting. In wondering if pressure had been applied, he was now unsure how it would have gone for him.

"It would seem so," the reply came. "His body had been well beaten and the arms broken. But the killing blow had been the same as the guard, throat slit, and the body hung upside down with a sign saying 'Traitor' hanging from his chest."

The two began to walk on further, following the slight slope of the tunnel downwards as the questions remained.

"Would he have talked, do you think?" the lector priest was quick to ask, aware that Serdos had been his main contact within the brotherhood and would know the man better than others.

"No," came the blunt reply, and in the saying, it gave Serdos some measure of comfort, and arrogantly he continued, "I feel we have little to concern ourselves with in this regard, for if he had, then they would have already acted!"

Reaching the door into the chamber, the high priest passed through first, followed behind by the lector and halting between the start of the seating, Serdos looked to the brother and said, "Let us now be about our business!"

The altar of *Apep* was waiting, its candles forever lit as the keepers maintained their watch throughout the day and night. Serdos headed that way, and passing between the seating, noted that some of the brothers had already gathered as the shadows of their bowed figures flickered in the light of the torches. Changing into his ceremonial gown, he presented himself before his god, the altar keepers standing to either side as he approached the foot of the statue.

In his hands, he held the means to prove the brothers' final pledge and ensure their commitment. Along the ledge of the shrine, he took out and carefully placed the metal brand, its depiction of the snake coiled around in its intricate serpentine figure of eight. And collecting together the red candles to form one mass of flame, he quietly knelt before the statue of *Apep*. Above, the great god looked down upon his congregation, his dark eyes staring out across the shadowed ceiling and falling upon the arriving devotees below. At the same time the bowed head of the high priest whispered his words of deification.

Finally, his words were over, and he stood to look up towards the carved serpentine form which embodied *Apep* before his gaze again took in the Icons where they sat upon the alabaster shelf.

"Just one more," he whispered, "and then the chaos and disorder of old will be once more unleashed."

The rest of the brotherhood had now assembled for their early service, and Serdos turned to stand before them, the light of the arrayed Icons swimming before the tired eyes of the men gathered in the conclave.

"My brothers," he began, his voice echoing loudly into the very back of the chamber as he walked calmly away from the altar's frontage. "This morning, we are gathered early in our meeting to send off one of our own. One who was also king within this city." He paused as he noted the passage of disquiet around the chamber before continuing, "And we shall also proclaim a new king. One who we do not recognise nor to whom we show our allegiance, and this has today brought us to our own juncture. A time in which we must renew our intentions within the brotherhood."

He looked to the gathered men before proclaiming, "The day that we have all been awaiting is growing ever closer, for *Amaunet* the Eighth Deity will soon be in our possession, and we are now each individually duty-bound to pledge our faith and fidelity to the great god *Apep*. And to show our loyalty to him alone."

The high priest turned back to the altar, and picking up the branding iron, he warmed it through the core of the flames, allowing it to rest there as the heat reddened the metal in its intensity. "Now is the time for us all to declare our oath and swear our allegiance. A time to demonstrate our true loyalty only to *Apep*!"

Moving away from the front of the altar, the red-hot iron held aloft in his hand, Serdos turned towards the gathered men, and ripping open the front of his gown, he bared his upper body. Wielding the brand, which had been held long within the flame, he placed the burning image of the Ouroboros, the never-ending serpent of destruction and rebirth, against his skin. And while the heat seared into the flesh above his heart, he spoke the words of covenant.

"With the bearing of this symbol, I give my pledge to you, *Apep*, the Serpent of Chaos, and present my allegiance as a brother in the cause of discord. And if

I should ever betray you, may this symbol of my oath be torn aside from my chest and my heart ripped out from within my body."

The brand was removed from his skin, the image of the snake forever scorched upon the surface, while the redness of the heat spread across his chest. And as the pain slowly condensed and concentrated its torment, Serdos quickly addressed his brothers.

"If any one of you here wish to withdraw or leave," he said, looking into the dark and silence of the hushed chamber as he replaced his gown, "you are here and now free to do so. But keep in mind that once you leave, the gates to these chambers shall never again be open to you, and the welcome of the brotherhood never again be yours to call upon. So think on and decide well!"

The silence remained, and the minutes passed without any stirring as every member of the brotherhood waited where they either sat or stood. With this they each became duty-bound to follow the precedent of Serdos. The lector priests were first to come forward and quick to make their declarations to *Apep* before finally, slowly standing in their seats, the remaining brothers, some appearing more eager than others, each came towards the altar. There receiving the mark of the brand, they pledged their loyalty and obedience to the snake god.

Finally, turning back towards the altar, the smell of burnt flesh filling the air, the high priest led the brotherhood in their usual morning service in the glorification of *Apep* and their anticipation of the coming chaos.

***

Malian had been the first to wake in the guest room, while the silence behind Gallius' curtain indicated that he still slept. And while the altar tender dressed, and quietly sorted through his pack, he went over and over the meaning of his dream. But always he came to the same troubling conclusion.

When Gallius did rise, he found Malian seated at the table, the *Shen* Staff given on his journey through *The Duat* placed before him. Although the look on the man's face was one of great apprehension, Gallius kept his silence. Seating himself opposite, he waited for him to speak and break the calm. Finally, the older man pushed his seat back, and looked down at the staff, its golden *Shen* ring encircling and giving eternal protection to its owner.

"The gods have come again to me, Gallius," Malian stated, his face looking across the table as the captain watched him. "And I have been enlightened that this gift was given with more than my own safety in mind." Placing his hand over the top of the circle, he continued gravely, "I have also been given my command and instruction for this day."

He went on to tell Gallius more of the detail of his dream, and that he had been challenged to confront Serdos before Prince Edgar's crowning. Seeing the sudden alarm rise in the captain's face he was quick to further his explanation.

"This will not suspend the ceremony," he immediately declared, in hope of putting aside any concerns regarding this, "for today Prince Edgar will be crowned king. However, I feel it may bring within our reach some development as regards the brotherhood." He paused as he thought further on his dream, but coming out of his reflection, he found that nothing more was to be gained and said, "What that will be though, remains with the gods for this moment and we must trust in them and wait and see what the day brings."

"I was thinking mainly of Prince Edgar's security, over his crowning," Gallius quickly replied, his military mind instantly going to the protection of the prince over and above the ceremony. Looking towards where Malian still sat, he also held a great worry and concern for him, for his dream could only take him into an unknown danger. And he finished by saying, "But we all must keep to our guard today, Malian!"

"He will be kept safe, Gallius. And he will be declared king," came the reply with some finality and reassurance on both of Gallius' concerns. "And for us, we can only wait to see what the day brings," Malian repeated. With that said, he rose, and placing the *Shen* Staff about his neck, he picked up his pack and made for the door.

***

Some of the other many residents within the king's hall had also been up since first light, and Edgar, accompanied by Captain Isaac, had already been down to see his brother lying in his confines. The lector priests, having returned to their positions after attending their morning service, briefly looked up as he slowly opened the door, and walking towards the central table, he had stared down upon the dead king recumbent within the confines of his funerary box.

The body of his brother had been dressed in the richness of his station, and the reds and golds of the clothing which covered his cold, stiffened body gave some warmth to the stark whiteness which had crept its way into his features and hardened his jaw. The lower part of the coffin was completely covered by a cloth of deep red wrapped tight around the king's feet and legs, and with the arms crossed gently over his chest and the dark balding head resting on a white pillow, it looked as if he lay asleep.

Edgar did not remain long within the room, for the sweet smell of candles and flowers was overpowering in its extreme as it fought off the stench of death. Feeling he had done his duty to his brother, he promptly found his way back into the main hall, the guard captain softly shutting the door as they both returned to the guaranteed safety and the fresher air within the meeting room in the king's hall.

Here Gallius and Malian had also made their way, finding that breakfast had been laid with Jakob standing at the end of the table, ready to be of service. But first, Gallius had walked around each of the guards standing at the doorways, and Malian went to sit near the fire as Edgar and Isaac entered the room.

"My brother would seem to have been well prepared," Edgar announced, as he noted the vigilance of the captain as he checked upon the guard, "and the city will soon be gathering together to witness his send-off."

Seating himself opposite Malian, who had stood on seeing his approach, the prince called the two captains forward. First addressing Gallius, he made known their duties of the day.

"I want you near to me today, Gallius," he declared, sensing somehow the tale that the captain had told of the devastation of the cities at the loss of their Icons and of the rise of the brotherhood was reaching further into his dominion. Looking to both captains, he ordered, "Both you and Captain Isaac are not to leave my side. You will be my escort in both services, understood?" His voice was steady and assertive in his demands, and each captain nodded their acceptance and were in no doubt of their directives.

The day continued in service and ritual, and after taking breakfast together, the group had parted. Captain

Isaac returned to his duty of guarding Edgar while Jakob escorted the prince along to his chambers to prepare for his coronation.

Gallius and Malian, however, remained in the meeting room, and here the captain spoke with the altar tender on his protection and the importance of his staying for the meantime unknown to Serdos.

"You shall remain here while Dedrick is honoured and interred," he instructed, "for we don't want Serdos to see you before the coronation. After this has been seen to be done, then word shall be sent for you to join us along with the other captains."

Malian was in full agreement with this, and in knowing that he would be unable to face the high priest before the service of crowning had begun, he was prepared to wait for word and bide his time.

Finally, as the grey sky darkened, Prince Edgar walked along the king's hall with Captain Isaac at his back, and passing the door to the meeting room, he instructed Jakob to wait with Malian. Gallius then joined Isaac in protecting Edgar, and falling in behind the prince, he placed himself alongside his colleague.

***

The enormous double gates to the palace courtyard had been folded open and then folded back again to reveal the complete frontage of the palace. These buildings, where the high priest lived and where the gathered brotherhood had slept, curved around the back of the forecourt, while on either side, the gardens led off. Beyond the buildings themselves, the tall outer wall of the palace formed a backdrop to the vaults and mausoleums of the past kings and queens and here would be the eventual resting place of Dedrick alongside the bones of his father.

Dedrick's open coffin had been brought around and through the colonnade in the early morning, the four lector priests lofting high the heavy casket once it had been carried through the walkway and brought around into the courtyard. Here they slowly and reverentially bore it through the gardens before it was set down at the front of the raised area.

The city's throne from which Dedrick had ruled sat behind his casket towards the back of the platform and stood empty apart from a cushion on which the crown of office sat, it having been brought out and placed to take its part in the crowning of the new king. While the sword of ceremony lay at its side.

To either end of the platform, two seats had been placed, one on the right for Prince Edgar to sit while he awaited both his brother's funeral and his own inauguration, and the other on the left for Serdos to rest while his lector priests prepared the courtyard for each differing ceremony.

Outside in the city, the crowds had already begun to take their place in front of the entrance, the folded gates appearing to determine the limit of their admittance, and the city folk seemed somehow unable to step foot over this imaginary line that barred them further access. Here, the dark greyness of the day surrounded them, but somehow, this seemed a fitting backdrop for Dedrick's funeral.

As Serdos, wearing his black robes of ministry, approached the end of the king's casket, the light faded even further, and a cool wind fed its way through the closeness of the gathered crowd, and each of the watchers pulled their cloaks about them.

The ceremony for the king's burial was brief and began with Serdos blessing his body with water and oils, as was their custom before he spoke a few words over the dead man. The lid was then brought across over the top, and the wooden pegs were hammered to hold the cover down. There was no singing, and little more to be said about the old king, and the occasion was over in minutes, the four pallbearers returning to take up their positions at each corner as Dedrick was lifted and taken off the stage.

His internment was to be conducted out of sight of the main crowd, and Serdos, leading his four priests off the platform, was followed only by Prince Edgar and captains Gallius and Isaac as they walked behind the casket around to the back of the buildings. Here they paused before the opened vault which awaited, the yawning darkness of the tomb standing in wait for its new occupant. The casket was slowly lowered, and placing the foot end into the opening, the lector priests gradually slid forward the whole of the box to run alongside the coffin of the last king. Dedrick's body disappeared into the dark to lay alongside that of his father, the doors closing behind him with a clang.

The group returned in their parade back to the frontage of the palace and the waiting citizens, where in their absence, the throne of the city, along with the crown and ceremonial sword, had been brought forward to take up the centre of the platform. The seat of the throne itself had been further raised on a podium to ensure and guarantee its observation by the assembly.

Edgar, however, walked past the chair upon which the crown sat and returned to his seat on the far side, for he knew he would need to be called forward and anointed by the high priest before he could take up his position on the king's seat of authority. And with Gallius and Isaac standing behind him, his other captains, along with Malian, had joined them, and they all gazed across the frontage towards where the high priest had sat down, his gowns of black being replaced by those of silver. While his lector priests gathered in a cluster at his back.

The watching crowd was soon becoming restless, and while the wait dragged on beyond their endurance, a voice could be heard shouting from the back while another was quick to join in. But seeing Serdos slowly rise from his seat on the left, the silvered robes catching the light which had begun to brighten, the gathering once more gave its respect to the occasion, and the increasing commotion quietened down.

The high priest stepped towards the throne, a heaviness in his tread seeming to slow his momentum. Stopping before this representation of nobility and power, he lofted the sword, and walking to the very edge of the raised shelf, he first addressed the watchers before calling on the prince to make his claim.

"The old king is laid to rest," he began, looking into the faces of those gathered within the gateway, "and Dedrick has been honoured by your presence here to witness his funeral." He paused as a few heads bowed in response before continuing, "Yet here we remain, for now is the time to anoint your new king!"

Turning to face the opposite end of the platform, Serdos looked across to where Edgar sat with his captains gathered close around, and lowering the sword to touch the stone of the raised courtyard, he once more lofted it and made his appeal.

"Come forward, Edgar, and assert your right and authority to sit this throne!"

His voice echoed fully across the courtyard as the wind carried it back towards the city. "Present yourself and be crowned before and in the presence of your people."

He turned to stand in front of the crowd, and looking at the gathered city folk, he extended the sword out towards them before bringing it slowly down and bowing his head.

Edgar, rising from his chair, suddenly felt a hand placed gently on his shoulder, and looking up, saw it belonged to Malian who had come forward to stand at his side as Serdos made public his demand.

"Please wait, Prince Edgar," he said, his voice soft as he lifted his hand. Moving away from the gathered group, he stepped out into the openness of the platform.

Instantly turning to Gallius, with a look of surprise crossing his face, the prince's eyes held a look of question and a search for an urgent explanation, and the captain was immediate in his response.

"All will be revealed, my lord!" he said, bowing his head slightly to encourage the prince to accept the delay. "Please keep to your seat." Turning away, he watched as Malian moved further towards the high priest.

The watching crowd had gone completely quiet, for the prince that they all had known as their warden and who was often seen on their streets had remained seated. While a stranger to their city was walking towards the throne, his plain drab clothes giving little to the pageantry that they had expected. The day, however, suddenly became brighter, and the silvered gown of Serdos rustled against his body as he slowly turned away from the expectant people to look to where their eyes had all become focused on the advance of the outsider. And on seeing Malian instead of the prince, he stepped back from the edge of the platform and turned to face the man who was unknown to him.

"What is this interruption?" he straightaway demanded, his expectation of seeing Edgar causing him first to be surprised before his anger took over. "How dare you interfere with this ceremony!"

He glared across at the approaching man as he moved

back towards the throne. "Who are you? Explain yourself immediately," he ordered, and looking around to his lectors, he gestured for them to attend him. Stepping forward, they were fast to come to his aid, their short blades remaining covered but close to hand.

"Malian is my name," the altar tender sternly replied, his serious eyes looking piercingly at the high priest. Walking towards the group, who had taken up their position, he arrived to stand a distance away from Serdos.

"I am the keeper of *Amaunet*, the Eighth Deity," he stated in declaration, "and I am here, this day, at the command of the great god *Horus*." Staring with intent at the high priest, his strong words seemed not only to be directed at him but also to encompass those who stood at his side. "I am here, at his bidding, to confront you before the people here, in the violations and wrongdoings you and your brotherhood have wreaked upon the cities of this land!"

He paused in his speech while the crowd took in his words, and a restlessness in the ignorance of the long-forgotten and unknown gathered throughout the company.

"I have seen with my own eyes the devastation brought about by the theft of the Icons," he continued, his voice rising in its passion, "and the increase of the disorder which has become widespread across the lands in their absence." He glared at the high priest before looking around at the assembled crowd. "And here, within these walls, the actions of your brotherhood have brought about the events leading to this day. To the death and burial of your king!"

"What is this talk of treachery?" Serdos demanded, his great anger forcing him to step forward in his rage. "How dare you talk to me like that! What proof have you got to bring this before me and to blacken the names of my brothers who have served this city well for so many years?"

Malian slowly took a talisman out of his pocket, and throwing it down at the feet of the high priest, he spoke harshly, his bitterness unable to remain hidden as he spat out his accusations.

"This was found about the neck of a friend who I trusted with my life, one with whom I had travelled and one who I had looked to and depended on." The token of Mentu gently spiralled around before spinning to a stop, the talisman facing upwards, showing the snake within the snake symbol of the lector priest. "And this one was taken from another who would have killed in your name and to your order." Malian threw down Roth's token, which landed with a clatter on top of the other.

The high priest glared down at the two as they lay accusingly before him, and finally Malian produced the last token collected and hurled it down to join the others,

"And this is the token taken from about the guard's neck, the guard who killed King Dedrick and which was found upon the person of his attendant whom I am sure you know well." He looked down at the silvered symbols before declaring, "All of these people are now dead, but they each wore these tokens and have been branded as traitors. And all were members of your brotherhood, the Brotherhood of the Snake."

"That may well be," Serdos smoothly replied, knowing he had been placed in a position where he must explain himself. But in mentioning the word snake, he thought it possible that Malian knew little of its association with the god *Apep*, "But these are no proof of your accusations of treachery or your allegation that we have caused any wrongdoings in other cities." Quickly stooping to pick up the tokens, he passed them back to one of his priests and continued in his speech,

"These are mere markers of rank and position within our brotherhood, nothing more."

"I am sure that is how they appear," the altar tender stated, "but I know that your brotherhood is intent on collecting the Eight Deities and destroying our world of order and once more bringing forth chaos. And that is not something you would be declaring before the people of this city!"

"The people of this city know well who I am," the high priest growled his reply, and turning to face the gathering, he lifted his head to smile upon the growing restlessness of the crowd, "for my face is known in the streets and markets. But who are you? You are nobody!"

Turning back towards the throne, the high priest stared towards where Edgar sat, his guards collected at his back, and their faces appeared fixed in their interest as the proceedings between the two men played out before them.

"I am here with the blessing of the gods," Malian eventually replied, as Serdos once more looked his way, "for I have been granted their protection, and in so doing, they have ensured the security of the Eighth Deity. Under my instruction *Amaunet* has been taken beyond your reach, and the chaos you so readily dealt out has been brought to a halt."

On hearing this, Serdos was unable to hold back a sly smile, and a sneer of contempt and disregard for the man's words crossed his face. For he knew they meant little and Brann was on his way from the city and would be seen to achieve his goal.

"Well, Malian, they may be well-spoken words, but what more can you do to prove these accusations!" Serdos' raging brought about a sudden response, and bringing forward the ceremonial sword in his defence, he looked at the solitary figure of the unarmed man who stood only feet away.

"I shall speak for the gods!" Malian answered in certainty, and likening the movement of the high priest, he brought out the *Shen* from his robe and held out the short staff before him, and in the doing, allowed the gods to take over.

The body of the altar tender began to glow, the soft light beginning in the ring of the *Shen* before slowly cascading over the staff and up and over his arm to eventually envelop the whole of the man himself. The light grew rapidly in its height and range, and in its place, the immortal body of *Horus*, the great sky god, made its presence known before the throne of the city, his great beaked head towering up into the sky.

Immediately on witnessing the start of the transformation, Serdos had stepped back in some urgency, and as the image before him grew in its stature, he stared up in fascinated and horrified disbelief. Dropping the ceremonial sword at his feet with a clang, he retreated still further, heading towards where the chair upon which he had so recently sat was positioned to the left of the throne.

Stumbling backward, he aimed to retain his balance as his ceremonial robes wound about his legs. But as he reached the left-hand side of the platform where his lector priests had begun to drop to their knees, he stumbled again. Coming up against the front of the chair, he continued his gaze, witnessing the final configuration as the representation of the enormous falcon head sitting atop the body of a man came into being, the great robe of feathers swirling into place. And coming to a halt, he remained standing, frozen in the presence of the noted god.

Over in the gateway, the crowd gathered at the palace had dropped to their knees, and the commotion of voices that first began as the image started to appear, went into a deep silence. This slowly spread over the whole of the city and encompassed the palace where the scene on the platform had somehow become stopped in time. Prince Edgar and the guards, positioned to the right, had all fallen forward and now knelt, and on the left, the lector priests and the whole of the gathered brotherhood were also bowed down, all apart from the high priest.

"STEP BEFORE ME, SERDOS," the deep resonating voice of the god sounded out its order as he looked down. And the forceful tone of the command was heard throughout the city and into the forests beyond. **"FOR I AM HERE TO CALL YOU TO JUDGEMENT FOR YOUR ACTIONS AGAINST THE PEOPLE AND THE CITIES OF THIS LAND."**

With eyes blazing, he glared down upon the silver-robed figure of Serdos as he remained fixed in position. But slowly and with much reluctance, the man was forced forward and began to walk, his unwilling feet bringing him to stand within the presence of the god.

Staring up into his face, he looked upon the power and greatness held within this most symbolic of Deities, for *Horus* was known throughout the nation, and in his bearing, he epitomised the meaning of kingship and guardianship. The beaked head now slowly looked away from the high priest, and turning to face the kneeling crowd, he looked over their bowed heads towards the city, his intense gaze taking in the surrounds within its encompassing walls.

"YOU HAVE COME HERE TO SEE A KING CROWNED," he spoke, the words arriving in the minds of those who stood within the boundary of the gate. **"BUT ALSO YOU ARE HERE TO BEAR WITNESS TO THE ACTIONS OF THIS MAN WHO STANDS BEFORE ME, AND OF THE MEN OF THE BROTHERHOOD WHO**

CALL HIM HIGH PRIEST."

Horus then continued to address them, his voice ringing out in accusation as he explained to those gathered about the fall of the cities. Each one he named in turn, along with the name of their Icon, and the details of the atrocities borne at their loss were given in graphic detail. Nothing was left out as the desolation caused was told in its harsh and precise recount.

Finally, the statement of charge came to an end and *Horus* turned back towards where the Brotherhood of *Apep* knelt in congregation at his left. The lector priests also stooped before him, and here none could deny their association, for their white robes singled them out, and each knew they wore the brand of the snake.

"THESE ARE THE MEN," *Horus* declared, looking down upon the heads of the gathered priests, **"THE MEN OF THE BROTHERHOOD WHO ARE ALL GUILTY OF COMMITTING THESE CRIMES, AND I HEREBY CALL THEM TO RISE AND FACE THEIR RETRIBUTION."**

The whole of the brotherhood were compelled to take to their feet, the white robes of their vestments rustling in protest as they rose to stand in the company of Serdos, their high priest.

Placing himself before the people of the city, *Horus* lifted his head and proclaimed the punishment of the gods so that all could hear and behold their justice.

"TODAY, SERDOS, YOU AND YOUR BROTHERHOOD, IN ABANDONING AND CAUSING SUCH GREAT SUFFERING TO THE PEOPLE OF THE CITIES, HAVE BEEN SEEN TO FORFEIT YOUR LIFE ON THIS EARTH, WITH YOUR PLACE IN THE AFTERLIFE NO LONGER FORETOLD OR GRANTED, AND EVEN YOUR WRETCHED SOUL WILL BE FORBIDDEN TO WANDER.

"IN YOUR ACTIONS, YOU HAVE SEALED YOUR

OWN FATE AND THAT OF THOSE STANDING ALONGSIDE. KNOW NOW THAT YOU WILL ALL BE PURGED AND WIPED CLEAN FROM OUR HISTORY BY THE SUFFERING AND TORMENT OF FIRE, AND YOUR NAMES WILL NEVER AGAIN BE SPOKEN!"

The god had now ensured that there would be no destiny or resurrection in the afterlife for the members of the brotherhood, and looking into the terrified faces and knowing there was no escape for them, he made his final request. Lofting his staff of office into the sky, the tip reaching upwards towards the motionless clouds, his words came out in challenge to the snake god, *Apep*.

"I, AS GUARDIAN GOD AND PROTECTOR OF THE PEOPLE, NOW CALL UPON *APEP*, THE GREAT SERPENT, TO HEREBY ACKNOWLEDGE HIS OWN, AND IDENTIFY EACH OF THOSE PLEDGED IN HIS NAME.

"IN MY STRENGTH AS SON OF *OSIRIS*, KING OF ALL THAT EXISTS HERE AND IN THE BEYOND, I MAKE THIS DEMAND AND ORDER THAT IT IS FULFILLED."

The great god brought the staff down upon the platform, and the whole of the ground shook under his feet as the shocks coursed their way into the depths before they radiated out under the city.

Reaching the very lands of the high steppes and into the beyond, the command was heard and obeyed. The Brotherhood of *Apep* were now caused to be singled out by their own god, and the brands so recently received and endured in his name slowly began to weep upon their chests. The blood of each man coloured the white of their garments as it oozed its insinuation of guilt.

"EACH OF YOU HAS BEEN RECOGNISED BY *APEP*," *Horus* declared in notice of the brothers' blemished robes, and peering down onto the blood-soaked cloak of Serdos, he finished, "AND NONE

SHALL GO UNPUNISHED!" The staff was once more raised and brought down in delivery of the sentence, and looking away from the condemned men, the hawked head of *Horus* looked over towards where Prince Edgar remained on his knees, head bowed. His guard captains stood to either side, and at his back, their armed men fanned out behind them across and out into the courtyard.

"ARISE, EDGAR," the challenge came, **"AND INSTRUCT YOUR MEN TO TAKE CONTROL AND REMOVE THESE OFFENDERS AND RID THE WORLD OF THEIR EVIL."**

Prince Edgar rose, his eyes briefly glancing nervously and with awe towards the god, while his captains got to their feet around him and the troops at their back sprang up like a wave across the water.

"Gallius, Isaac," the prince quickly ordered, turning to the two stood on either side, "you shall remain with me." His tone then grew harsher as he raised his voice and made known his urgent command. "The rest of you see that these men are taken away and imprisoned in the stronghold, and tomorrow we shall see to their punishment." Stepping back, he once more seated himself, and the captains hurriedly went about performing their duties.

The brothers were now beyond themselves in terror, for all realised their wrongdoings in the name of *Apep*, and whether knowingly or unknowingly performed, they had been placed before them. Some tore in frenzy and panic at their clothing, trying to remove the evidence of their wickedness, but their hands snatched uselessly, and the clothing remained seared to their skin. The pain of the burning brand as it burned itself into the bleeding flesh gave some small insight into the impending suffering and being but a taster of what was to come, the men became terror-stricken.

Now for them, there was no escape, for the group of brothers were soon surrounded by the captains and their guards, the sharp blades of the officer's swords corralling the men together before leading them off across the frontage of the platform. Here the image of the god remained in place, and the crowds continued to kneel at the gates as they passed before them.

Serdos had taken the lead of his men, his cloak of blood wrapped around his shoulders, and with head held high and seemingly distant from the distress of the others, he walked slowly past where the prince sat. Stopping to look down, he glared at Edgar and appeared about to speak, before the point of a blade was felt at his back, and Captain Cormack was quick to move him along.

The brothers disappeared out of the palace along the colonnade, the gate leading towards the stronghold banging shut while the doors into the great hall were hurriedly opened to receive them. Then the steps leading down into the dungeons yawned darkly ahead, and the priests soon found themselves behind the locked bars of the prison cells.

***

The condemned men of the brotherhood had all been taken away, and the people of the city had been seen to witness the charges of their crimes and the penalty for their actions. On return of the captains, along with their men who had seen to the imprisonment, they could all now turn away from one bizarre spectacle and return to the matter of the other. That being the crowning of the new king along with all its expected accompanying ceremony.

Jakob, the last king's attendant and one who had been seen to attend upon Prince Edgar, appeared from behind where he had stood alongside Malian and where the captains returned to stand. Walking before the gathered crowd and the image of the great god, he crossed the platform in silence to settle alongside the right-hand side of the throne.

Removing the red velvet cushion topped with the crown from its position upon the seat of power, he held the symbol of royalty outstretched between his hands, ready for Edgar to be crowned king. Looking out into the crowd, he glimpsed the faces of city people he had known of old, and he held his head high in pride at his given assignment before the voice of the god once more took charge in the absence of the high priest and caused him to bow his head and look to his duty.

"COME FORWARD, EDGAR, AND MAKE YOUR OATH BEFORE YOUR PEOPLE. FOR ONLY AFTER MAKING YOUR PLEDGE CAN YOU RECEIVE THE CROWN OF THE CITY," *Horus* declared as the crowd raised their heads to witness the start of the coronation. And as the prince slowly stood from his seat, his plain robes indicating his position at that moment, he looked around at his gathered men. Receiving their many nods of support, he walked towards the seat of sovereignty, and his Ceremony of Succession began.

The ritual of investiture was seen by all assembled and began with Edgar, right hand raised to make his word of honour, standing before the city's throne. While at his side Jakob, holding the crown-topped cushion, had moved forward to stand in support. The pledge was made to serve the city for the good of all of its people, and to be seen to uphold and strengthen the laws within which their society prospered.

But as he spoke, he found his mind frequently going to the same words spoken many years ago by his brother, and he hoped to be better in keeping his promise. Finally, the oaths had been proclaimed, and Edgar seated himself on the throne while Jakob moved to stand alongside, his arms starting to grow weary as he held out the cushion before him, the precious, ornate contents heavier than imagined.

"THE PLEDGES HAVE BEEN GIVEN," the voice finally declared, "AND I NOW CALL UPON YOU, JAKOB, TO CROWN YOUR KING AND, IN DOING DECLARE HIM THE NEW RULER OF THIS CITY." The god looked down upon the little man who stared back, unbelieving in what he had heard. And a sudden dread filled the heart of the attendant as he stood transfixed in hesitation of the enormity and the honour which had been placed upon him.

"CROWN HIM KING, JAKOB," the order was repeated, "FOR ONLY THEN WILL HE HAVE BEEN SEEN TO BE CHOSEN BY AND FOR THE PEOPLE OF THIS CITY."

Realising he had little choice in the matter, the lowly attendant stooped, and placing the velvet cushion on the floor, he very carefully and hesitantly removed the ceremonial crown from its position on the pad. Returning to stand, he reached upwards and cautiously placed it with great care and respect upon Edgar's head before lowering his arms and bowing his head before his new king.

"THE CROWN IS GIVEN AND RECEIVED," *Horus* announced, his words continuing to fill the minds of all those who stood witness, "AND A NEW KING NAMED BEFORE YOU! BUT NOTE WELL, I ALSO CHARGE AND GIVE EXTRA DUTY ON THIS DAY.

"I NOW PLACE A TASK UPON YOU, EDGAR, TO RETURN ALL OF THE STOLEN ICONS BACK TO THEIR GOD-GIVEN HOMES. I ALSO ORDER THAT YOU AID AND ASSIST THESE BLIGHTED CITIES IN THEIR RESTORATION TO THEIR PAST

AND FORMER GLORIES."

Edgar, listening to the god's decree, lowered his head in acceptance of the orders, and looking to Jakob at his side, he smiled upon the bowed head before looking back to the god as he made his final declaration.

"**ARISE, KING EDGAR,**" *Horus* proclaimed. "**LEAD YOUR NATION WELL AND BE TRUE TO YOUR OATHS!**" As the voice spread into the heart of the city, the staff was brought down upon the shoulders of Edgar, and he was anointed before his people.

The new king slowly rose before the kneeling crowd, the crown of office sitting neatly upon his head while the city's throne formed an elegant backdrop, and gazing upward once more into the huge beaked head, he gave his word of honour.

Vowing that he would carry out his wishes to return the Icons and look to the welfare of the people affected by Serdos and his brotherhood, he announced that no time would be lost in achieving this and restoring the cities to their once-known splendour.

The great god, having seen that honesty and truth had been done in both the destinies of Edgar and of those within the brotherhood, now gently began to fade. And a wind that had been absent throughout the services slowly began to gather, drifting the edges of the feathered cloak and blurring the vastness of the image. Finally, it allowed the impression to collapse in on itself and once again reveal the figure of the altar tender, who slowly toppled over and met the stretch of the platform.

Malian lay flat out, his face hidden by the hood of his cloak and his arms spread out before him as the vision of the god disappeared in the wisps of the wind, and Gallius was quick to rush forward to attend his friend and ensure his safety. Finding him insensible, and locked in a deep trance, he was unable to do more than arrange for his removal from the platform and out of the courtyard.

As the city folk began to rise, their tired knees feeling relief from the hard ground, Malian was picked up and carried into the comforts the stronghold. The people then moved back and away from the spectacle and from where the throne again stood empty on its raised platform. Returning to their homes, they spoke of what they had seen, aware that this day, which had been one of fascinating and unbelievable sights, would never again be witnessed in their lifetime.

CHAPTER EIGHT

Brann had ridden on through the dark, for he sensed the import of his undertaking to retrieve *Amaunet,* and he wished to be quick and successful on his return back to the city. Both Dedrick and Serdos had each expressed an urgency in his quest and whichever way he chose, he felt it could only be to his benefit. As yet, though, he had not made his choice, and his reasoning went this way and that as he rode. Unaware for the moment that he was being pursued, he remained concentrated on the journey ahead and let the decision lie.

***

Many miles behind, Tragen also led his group well, swiftly following the steps he knew Brann would have taken. Making fast progress, they too rode on through the night, eventually witnessing the morning light coming up and reflecting off the distant City of Muntani. Here the brisk breeze blew through the grass of the plains, and the lesser steppes spread out around them and away off into the stretch of the hinterland.

On reaching the fallen gates of the city once again, the horses were brought to a stop, and Shuma and Daina were quick to dismount. Not wishing to hold up the others in their pursuit, they briskly lifted away their bags from their horse and were short in saying their goodbyes.

"Take care, Tragen," Shuma said in direct farewell. Coming around to the warrior's side, she stretched out both of her gloved hands and grasped the bulky arm of the large man as he remained astride his horse. "Be swift in your chase, for many are depending upon it," she reminded him.

Tragen was sharp in nodding his head in reply, but the hand placed over hers was gentle in its grip. Shuma smiled up into the tired face, which had become so familiar, the heaviness of the dark around his eyes giving a look of resolve in his pursuit, and quickly letting go of his arm, she again bid him farewell.

Now turning to Darric, who had dismounted to rearrange the packs on the horses, she felt an overwhelming sense of departure come over her as she tightly hugged him. On his release, she looked hard into his face, and although the look returned was encouraging, the white hair of the young man framing his slender features, she also saw an awareness that concealed his apprehension.

"Farewell to you also, Darric. Take care," she ordered, her voice appearing somewhat harsh to disguise its concern, "and keep a watch out for Tragen. For your eyes are much younger than his," she gently teased hoping to lighten the separation. Quickly loosening her hold, she turned to the last rider.

"Look after them, Anitta, and lead them well. For you know the lands of the Sleeping Caverns, and our hope lies in your swift guidance. And please," she appealed to the swan, "see that my mother knows that I am safe and that I send her my love."

The four horses moved off, the three somewhat lighter as the fourth had now become the pack carrier and taken the burden from the others. Turning their backs to the two women who stood, hands raised in farewell in the ruins of the city, Tragen, Darric and Anitta rode away towards the lower ranges.

Shuma and Daina slowly turned away from their parting and eventually walked through the open gateway and made for the arch that led to the covered area the wise woman had left only days before. Guiding Daina through the rubble and overgrown shrubbery of the neglected buildings and through into the birth city of the younger woman, they both remained unaware that far behind them on the higher steppes in the City of the High Places, the day had already started with the funeral of Dedrick. A new king would soon be crowned, and change was forthcoming.

***

The stronghold, like the rest of the city, remained on edge. The ceremony the people had just observed had been beyond anything they could imagine, and their amazement and wonder were without explanation. Even so, doubts and uncertainties about what they had actually seen would soon inevitably be playing into their minds. And the city folk would, over time, look to each other in question, and their reasoning to the testimony of the day would be brought to challenge. But for now, within the dining hall of the royal domain, a modest meal was held in celebration of the new king's coronation.

The staff of the kitchens had been given short notice, and been rushed to prepare for the occasion, but the most was made of what was to hand. Attending the new king at this simple table would be the men and women of the household, along with the captains of the guard, and all had assembled in the main hall to await the summons of the stewards.

But first, after being in witness of the god's presence and his words regarding the brotherhood, King Edgar felt a need to face the high priest. Standing before the great doors to the stronghold with Jakob at his side and his captains at his back, he waited while Gallius attended to his friend before he looked to venture down into the dungeons.

On Edgar's orders, Malian had been placed within his own chambers in the king's hall, and Gallius had seen to it personally that he had been made comfortable and had all the care and consideration he would require. There appeared little more that he could do for the sleeping man, for the altar tender lay in a complete trance, his body flat upon the comfort of the bed with the covers folded around the stillness of his frame. His breathing, however, was healthy and stable, if a little shallow, which was of minor cause of concern to the healer, who was quick to attend. He was tasked to remain at his side throughout the night, and Gallius had to be content to leave him under his supervision. Knowing that the day was not yet over in its ceremony, the captain was keen to return to the main hall.

"How is Malian?" the king immediately asked, seeing Gallius appear through the crowd. "Is he being looked after?" His last sight of the older man was of him being carried away through the doors before he disappeared along the hallway, and he had been sharp in his order for him to be attended.

"He's resting, sire," Gallius replied, stopping before Edgar. Bowing his head, he gave respect to the man who was now his king before he continued, "Jasan is tending upon him."

"Good," Edgar answered, glad that his order had been carried out. But as he returned the look of his captain, he became aware of the boundaries that his kingship had suddenly placed around him. Taking Gallius by the arm, he led him off to one side and away from the looks of the guards.

"I have a great need to see Serdos," he whispered, an anger rising that he fought to hold down. "Before yet another minute passes, I must confront him and ask on the accusations placed upon him!" He glared at Gallius, and knowing that out of his captains, he was the only one aware of the full story, he ordered, "Come with me, and we shall see what he has to say!"

The two left behind the rising noise of the hall, and disappearing down the curving stairway into the vaults, they were instantly allowed access through the gates. Following the corridor around to the left, their footsteps took them along the twisting tunnels into the domain of the prison.

***

The high priest had been given his own cell, damp, dark and run down, into which he had reluctantly walked before turning to stare at his jailers. Folding the bloody cloak about himself, he sat down upon the cold stone of the floor, and lifting his head, he watched as the door closed, the heavy bolts grating as they were drawn across into place.

Around him, the lectors and those of lower rank had been packed into two smaller chambers with little thought given to their crowding. Each could only stand as they were pushed through the doors, which swung heavy and ominously at their backs. A silence had then fallen around, and while they waited within the darkness of their fear, the ceremony to crown the new king had taken place in the sunlight above them. Finally, the image of *Horus* had slowly disappeared on the breeze, and the crowds had gone back to their homes.

***

Peering through into the gloom, Edgar could barely make out the figure of Serdos. But as the high priest raised his head, he caught a glimpse of the pale flesh of his face as he looked towards the door and found that he dared not enter. His anger had grown with each step taken, and he was unsure of his reaction if the door had not been between them. Gripping the bars to the small square window, he brought his face close to the opening and snarled his accusations towards the seated figure.

"You had Dedrick killed, didn't you?" he shouted his allegation, his hands twisting around the cold metal of the bars. "You had my brother killed!" he repeated, his voice echoing into the room. "And a king's life was forfeit in your judgement. And for that, you have been sentenced to a cruel and agonising punishment. Sentenced by the gods themselves, and in that, I shall see their work done." He paused as he controlled his rage before eventually demanding, "Do you have anything to say for yourself?"

The high priest slowly rose to his feet, the stained incriminating robe left to drop around his frame. Approaching the door, he smiled towards where the window encircled the face of the king, and his stale breath reached Edgar on the cold draught seeping between the bars. Slowly he moved away to lean against the back of the thick wood of the door.

"Dedrick was weak and greedy," the high priest softly replied, his voice showing little concern for the life of the past king. "Of that, Edgar, I am sure you were well aware, for you too held little love for him." Bringing his face back to the opening, he looked into the enraged eyes that blazed before him and spat out his words. "It is only through me that you now stand there as king, and through me, you would have stood in his place before the lord of chaos and disorder, and all that he was giving to the brotherhood could have been yours."

"You talk of chaos," Edgar answered back blatantly, his words ringing out into the dark of the cell, "and of disorder, and speak as though it should be pursued. But many men and women have died under those pennants, and I would see that changed!"

"But chaos and disorder IS the way of man," Serdos shouted his testimony, his anger rising as he found the man spineless and lacking in his wisdom. "For even in times of peace, he always seeks to better himself at the cost of others. Note well that some, like ourselves and your brother, would do anything to surpass or improve their very essence." He faltered as he realised the futility of continuing his argument, and looking into the king's eyes, he made his admission.

"I have rid the world of your brother, for he would have so easily seen the same done to me," Serdos concluded, his mind fully aware of his words and their implication for himself along with the brothers who had each been fated. "So I struck first!"

Edgar punched the door in his rage, the blow causing the thickness of the wood to tremble slightly while the suddenness of the violent action sent Serdos reeling back into the dark, which enclosed him in its denseness.

"Well, tomorrow I shall strike," Edgar declared, feeling little pain for the moment from the impact of the door, "and you shall remain in witness to the suffering and destruction of your brotherhood before you are also released forever from this life."

He turned to look along the length of the tunnel to where he knew the rest of the brotherhood remained, and raising his voice, continued, "All involved and held here in these cells are thus condemned and will be wiped clean from this earth, and their names shall never again be spoken. *Horus* himself has declared your manner of punishment, and I will see that it is fulfilled!"

He moved away from the door, knowing that his words would have been heard by all and striding past the cells, he ignored the pleas and petitions from the priests who stood close behind their barriers and who had also been witness to the words of their high priest.

Walking back through the dungeons, the two men briskly passed the many doors to the cells, the silence following them as Edgar thought on the words of Serdos. But eventually, Gallius broke the quiet by speaking of the Icons and the importance of the task placed upon the king, which through him was also placed upon the captains who had over countless years been responsible for their collection from the many blighted cities.

"They shall all have to be returned," Gallius stated, the words of *Horus* ringing out in his mind, "and with some speed, I feel. For I think we will need to begin their severance to dispel this growing turmoil."

"Yes, that I agree, but first, we must find where they are," Edgar replied, the scuffed knuckles of his hand beginning to throb with pain as the anger slowly died down. On reaching the steps, he and Gallius returned to the main hall, emerging out where the gathering of people once more surrounded them and where Jakob stood in wait.

"Surely Jakob must know of their location?" Gallius reasoned on seeing the king's attendant. "He would have been wise to the comings and goings of Dedrick. At least he may know where the brotherhood met, and that may give us our starting point."

"A starting point. Yes," the king replied, but on seeing the faces turn his way in expectation, he finished, "However, let us leave it for the moment. We have a celebration to attend, so let us enjoy the occasion!"

***

The festival dinner was soon over for the king, and at his wishes the guests to his investiture meal were urged to remain and enjoy the beer and conversation. And as he, along with Gallius and Jakob, took their leave and made their way towards the colonnade, the dining hall persisted in its merrymaking. While deep within the city, the ordinary people celebrated in their own ways, and within the prison cells, the brotherhood thought on in ever-growing panic of the coming morning.

Jakob, carrying aloft a lamp to light the way, led King Edgar and Gallius past where Dedrick had fallen and round into the palace courtyard. Following the curve of the building around at its back, he brought them to the door that opened into the crypts. The door was neither locked nor barred, and pushing it open, Gallius stepped inside, lofting high the lit torch.

Followed by Edgar, he retraced the footsteps of the brotherhood downward along the dark corridor while Jakob brought up the rear, and quickly they came upon the entrance to the main chamber. This door, too, was shut but turning the heavy latch that held the barrier closed, Gallius slowly pushed open the door to reveal the lamp-lit enclosure which was the domain of Serdos and the Brotherhood of *Apep*.

To each side, the lamps remained lit, and as the three moved down the aisle, their shadows were thrown wildly across the bench seats. Ahead the altar reared up in its dominance, with the statue of the snake taking up the centre of the cold white shelf, while along the ledge, the Icons sat in wait. The silence was overwhelming, the warmth and smoke of the lamps giving the air a hazy bitterness that was savoured on the tongue and crept its way into the back of the throat before being expelled on an outward breath and returned to the encircling vapours.

The Icons lay before them, spread out in their couples

173

on either side of the effigy, their diminutive size seeming vastly out of proportion to the value placed upon them. The three stood staring at the collection as it glowed golden between the red candles, the light of the flames below shining upwards onto the features and reflecting the colour of the precious stones of the eyes.

Gallius was the first to speak and break the silence, and his voice held a certain tone of admiration coupled with an urgency that was readily recognised.

"We must begin to return these immediately," he stated, his eyes moving back and forth along the sill as he sought to take in the gravity and importance of that which lay before him.

"But how do we know which one is which?" Edgar asked, his face shining in the heat blazing up from the lower shelf. But as he looked for the first time at each of the figures, he noted the difference between those bearing the head of the frog and those of the snake. "They seem to be in pairs, like male and female," he said, "apart from that one." He pointed to the one on the very left where the solitary statue of *Amun* awaited that of *Amaunet*, the ruby eyes of the frog looking out in expectation towards the seating area.

"The captains must surely know which is which," Gallius replied, as he too looked to the empty place where the Icon he himself had stolen would have eventually sat. "We will need to get them down here to pick out and identify the ones they took. But for now," he suggested, sensing no alternative, "I feel we should leave well alone and keep them here."

The three stood for untold moments, each in their own thoughts as to the ceremonies and services that had gone on before this altar. Until finally, Edgar looked up to the towering figure of the snake god, the large hooded head reaching out and over the seats below. At the same time, the cold harshness of the eyes stared down and the wide open mouth showed its array of razor-sharp teeth as an aura of pure evil fell down in the rain of candle smoke. Slowly averting his eyes, he placed his hand on the attendant's shoulder and gave his order.

"Extinguish all the candles, Jakob," he said, his eyes beginning to burn and itch in the gathering mist curling down from the roof.

The three men turned away, the lights of the torches being snuffed out one by one as they walked back to the door. And as the altar of *Apep* gradually descended into darkness, the serpentine figure of the god disappeared into the shadows before vanishing completely into the gloom.

***

Coming up out of the crypt and back into the welcoming freshness of the afternoon light of the courtyard, the talk remained with the Icons and a need for their safety. Before eventually, as the walk took them through the gardens, it turned to the god-given task of the following morning, that being the sacrifice of the brotherhood and the death of High Priest Serdos. Reaching the gateway into the colonnade, Jakob stood to one side as the king passed through, followed by Gallius, and slowly closing and fastening tight the gate to the palace, the Icons were left behind in the gathering dark.

"I'll let you see to the guard for the Icons," Edgar said, taking the turn towards the stronghold. Looking down the length of the walkway, he followed in the last footsteps of his brother and made for the doorway into the hall.

"Very well, sire," Gallius replied as he followed. "But what of the other? What of the god's ruling on the brotherhood?"

"It must be done swift and quick," Edgar declared, stopping before he reached the door, "and more importantly, away from the city. And for that, I have already instructed Captain Steffan to prepare a place in the north. Hopefully there, the stench will disperse through the trees, and any noise should be confined and out of earshot." He looked hard at Gallius before continuing, "The decree of the god will be carried out and witnessed, and announcement will be given. But I hardly think the spectacle is for the eyes of women and children!"

Gallius was quick to agree, and with his thoughts suddenly turning to Malian, he asked to be given leave to check on him before returning to his duties.

"Yes, go," Edgar said, turning back towards the door, "and leave your duties until the morning." Pausing again before entering the open doorway, he finished, "But let me know if he wakes."

The king returned to his guests, leaving Gallius to make his way back into the residences, and here he was again met by raised glasses as he re-joined in the celebration of his kingship.

***

The first morning of the new king's reign began with Edgar rising before dawn. And quickly waking Jakob, who had slept in the anteroom, they walked the short distance along to the sleeping chambers in the king's hall. Entering the room where Malian lay and where Gallius had spent the night alongside his friend, they found the two asleep. The captain lay sprawled on the second bed, his exhaustion of the past days causing a complete collapse, but the king appeared indifferent to this and was swift in waking him.

"Time to rise, Gallius," he declared, pulling away the blanket that covered the man, "for the time to do the will of *Horus* has arrived, and we must be both speedy and vigilant to do his command." The king turned and left, his instructions given to the waking man for him to be swift in joining him in the main hall.

Gallius was quick to rise, the heaviness of sleep being washed away by the coldness of the water which he splashed into his face. Checking hastily on Malian, who had neither woken nor moved during the night, he further prepared himself for the task ahead before finally stepping out. Finding the king at the main doors where he stood with the assembled captains, the group descended the steps from the stronghold, and making their way out into the northern woods, they aimed to carry out the orders of the gods!

***

Confined within the cells, and with the gathering panic of a long sleepless night, the brotherhood had each agreed to remove their talisman with the hope of distancing themselves from Serdos and the god *Apep*. And a collection of tokens had been pushed through the bars of the doors and now lay scattered along the deeply trodden floor of the tunnel. Through these, the high priest was the first to make his way, his feet kicking aside the metal rings which drew his eyes downwards in regard to the rejection that his men had handed out. Looking through the bars at the frightened, terrified faces as he was manhandled past the doors, he sneered at their cowardliness and sedition and roared his anger into the confines of the passage.

"How quick you are to throw aside your loyalty but you each wear the brand of *Apep* upon your chest, so willingly placed there by pledge and by fire. And by fire it will be removed from your body. Remember your oath," he shouted over his shoulder as he was pushed along further down the darkening tunnel, "for today your hearts will be blackened and roasted, and *Apep* will feast well off your flesh!"

His voice disappeared along the confines of the passage leaving behind the stunned silence of the cells before a slow sobbing started and the torment and agony of the waiting began.

The guards summoned to collect the high priest began their quick march out from the stronghold and into the empty streets where the dark of the early morning greeted them. And passing the vacant taverns and closed-up beer halls, they moved out through the northern gate where the forest of the higher steppes went off into the far distance.

Now the denseness of the trees gathered around was lit only by the torches carried by the leading men, and after many long moments of walking, they finally stopped at the edge of a clearing. Here Captain Steffan and his men had been charged to prepare the pyres, first having hunted further north and west than anticipated before they found a likely open area to build the bonfires.

The scouts had been swift in their clearance and construction, and now a number of huge hastily prepared mounds of wood took up the main area and stood in wait, their central stands pointing up into the heavens. While in between each of these, a further supply of gathered branches and wood was stacked to supply and kindle the blaze and maintain the heat and flames of the obliteration.

The eyewitnesses had arrived at this setting many moments before that of the guards and stood silent and cold amidst the trees. King Edgar stood positioned at the fore while his captains had initially spread out further around. But on seeing the approaching lights, they all gathered to one end, and through this, Serdos was seen and brought forward. Passing the glare of the flaming rush lights surrounding the bonfires, he was escorted towards an area where a simple single post had been driven into the forest floor. Here he was stripped of his main clothing before being tied for the forthcoming spectacle, and the stage was made ready for his own witnessing.

The brothers had now also been taken out from their cells, some walking with an acceptance of their fate while many of the others were dragged out screaming and fighting, and the guards had to be more than forceful in their control of the prisoners as they dragged them out and through the city.

Beyond into the woods, the forest lay with a quietness around, but slowly the bird song of the daybreak was heard on the edge of hearing. And as the frightened and beaten brothers were brought towards the glade, this sound was replaced by another. The array of torches that stood around the expanse hissed their intent and gathered in strength as the priests were brought through and out into the open. Here it became a thunder and roar to the ears of the terrified men.

The pyres were directly ahead of them, their harsh starkness adding to the overwhelming alarm that gripped the entire group, and some dropped to their knees in horror. These were then dragged forward along the rough ground to the base of the bonfires and thrown down while others collapsed around them in extreme dread.

The priests were stripped of their robes, some already torn to tatters, and the blood-stained raiment of each was tossed aside. Baring the accusing brand of *Apep* on their chests, they were each hauled up off the ground of the damp woodland and lofted high were tied tightly to the posts, their feet buried deep within the sharpness of the surrounding branches. As the panic of their realisation became apparent, and the cries for pardon rang out, their understanding that any chance of reprieve was long gone and, finally, their words slowly dwindled until silence fell upon them.

The priests of *Apep* stood all together in their circles, the whiteness of their semi-naked bodies surrounding the standing posts, and as the light of the morning spread further between the trees and the dark of the night disappeared into the beyond, the guards began to set the flames.

Thrusting the rushlights between the boughs and lighting the damp kindling placed at the heart of the bonfires, they first saw a steady grey smoke begin its initial climb past the bare legs of the condemned priests. The cries of the men rose again as the fumes thickened, and the crackling of the scrubby twigs pushed up the small yellow flames to light the thicker branches placed around their bare feet. Quickly the cries turned to screams, the high-pitched shrieks magnified over and over again as their flesh began to burn and sear in the blazing heat and the skin of their legs turned black and blistered even as the men remained alive to their agony. Then the flames crawled upwards, reaching towards their chests until, finally, the whole of each of the bonfires was ablaze, the dwindling cries turning into the howl of the inferno as the flames leapt high into the reddening sky and many minutes passed as the bodies were allowed to burn in their ferocity.

High Priest Serdos was now the only one of the Brotherhood of *Apep* who remained alive, and the witnessing of the bonfires appeared to give him little cause for concern for the torment and suffering of his brothers. But the realisation of seeing them executed in such a manner had made him aware of his coming misfortune and imminent misery. Standing tied to his post and surrounded by his own little bonfire he made one last plea to King Edgar, who he could see standing across the clearing.

"I am your high priest, Edgar," he shouted above the roar of the flaming bonfires, "your high priest and your minister to the gods." The stench of smoke pouring off the burnt bodies made him choke, and he struggled to finish his sentence. "And through them, I have served this city well and wanted only the best for our people." He began to cough as the light wind drifted the fumes across the clearing. "And this is the way that you have treated my men and me. Do you have no conscience?"

"This is not my will, Serdos, it is the will of the gods," Edgar shouted back, his hand briefly removed from across his face, "but I would not have you go alone into the fire." Turning away from the blazing pyres, he looked to the guards at his rear. Raising his hand, the beaten dead body of Esra was brought forward and carried across the clearing to be thrown around the base of the piled wood at the man's feet, the glazed eyes of the old king's attendant staring upwards. Nodding his head quickly, Edgar indicated to the guard standing alongside, and the flaming torch was brought down into the heap.

Serdos looked down into the dead eyes of Esra and knew he would receive no pardon here in this gathering. Seeing the slow advance of the flame through the rotting leaves and around the dead body below him, he was quick to first feel the heat of the gathering blaze before the lick of fire scorched across the underside of his feet and flicked around his toes. An agony of excruciating pain shot through his whole body, and crying out to his god, he writhed in the torture of the increasing heat and torment. As the red of the flame increased, he continued his supplication to *Apep*, and the wind gusted up to fan the snaking flames encasing him in their embrace until eventually, with a final roar in his ears, the wretchedness stopped, and darkness took him.

The smoke and flames pouring from around Serdos snaked their way up into the air, the overhanging branches of the trees disappearing amid the vapours gathered high above. And the blaze lingered long in its rage as the scouts added more wood to the fire. Even as the scorched body of the high priest slumped forward, the ties holding him to the stake burnt through, his body was thrust back onto the pyre, and more wood was thrown over the top to further encase his burning bones.

"We stand in witness of the punishment declared by the god *Horus*," Edgar stated, his voice small yet decisive as he sensed the disquiet surrounding him before he finished, "and in that, we should hold no account for today's acts or add any blame to ourselves." Marching away from the sight and reek of the burning bodies, he gestured for Captain Steffan to attend him before ordering that the fires should burn through the day and any skeletal remains of the Brotherhood of *Apep* should be smashed to dust and scattered far and wide through the forest.

The will of the gods had now been seen to be accomplished and witnessed, and the observers turned away from the smoking clearing and returned through the forest to the safety of the city where the folk of the town were rising in their ignorance to a red dawn, and the day was beginning its new chapter.

CHAPTER NINE

King Edgar had returned through the woods with his captains, and once inside the city walls, they made their way back into the stronghold. There each had briefly gone their separate ways to change out of their smoke-permeated clothing and throw off the dirt and stench of the dawn, which they felt had settled heavily upon them. And the need to scour and wash away the recollection of the bonfires was accomplished before they began to reassemble at the king's command in the main hall.

Gallius, however, had followed Edgar and Jakob through the double doors into the king's chambers, and while the king and his assistant returned to the royal apartment to freshen up, he walked back along to where Malian still slept. Finding Jasan already there, a sudden relief swept over him as he stood smoke-saturated in the doorway.

The healer had returned at the break of day, and after gently repositioning Malian, he dampened his lips with water. Unable to do little more than that for the sleeping man, he sat to one side and remained there. Gallius moved around the room, and after removing the ingrained clothing, he sluiced his head and face, over and over, with the fresh water in the bowl before returning to the bedside, his face dripping as he wiped away the moisture.

"I shall be with the king this morning," he informed Jasan. "But you must send word and let me know immediately if he wakes." Seeing the nod of agreement, he bent once more towards the sleeping figure. Noting the slow, deep breathing, he felt reassured in his leaving, and turning away from the bed, he left the room to the quiet of the morning.

The captains had all returned into the presence of King

Edgar and were there joined by Captain Steffan, the smell of burnt flesh hanging over him as he strode in direct from the forest. Taking a cup of cool beer from the steward who stood near the main doors to the hall, the captain was glad to exchange the taste of ale over that of charred wood and seared meat which had invaded his mouth. His tongue felt coated with bitterness, and he quickly drained the cup in one go before joining the group as they stood near the door to the colonnade.

Edgar took charge of his captains, and gathering them about him as they stood within the vaulted hall, he spoke to them as witnesses to the events of the last few days and those of the long ago past.

"I know that each of you here has been responsible for doing the king's wishes in times past with regard to the Icons," he began, and looking around at each of the men, he saw the realisation and remembrance of their actions again being recalled, "and each of you, I'm sure, was well paid to keep his tongue." A slight murmur quickly fed its way through the little group before silence again descended. "Gallius and I have already seen those you stole which helped Serdos and his brotherhood gain their overall control. But now we need you to single out the ones you brought to the city. For the orders of the god remain, and we must be quick in carrying out his wishes."

Edgar turned to open the door, and finding that Jakob had already begun to perform the act, he led his men out into the light of the morning. The captains were eager to follow, and passing through the doorway, were soon being led along the walkway and around into the palace garden. Here Gallius had already put in place two of Isaac's men to guard the crypt door, and the two stood to attention as the king approached. Saluting as he passed through, they each looked suspiciously down into the dark passage as the captains descended into the blackness and disappeared into the depths before they let the door close quietly behind them.

Jakob had brought a torch, and lighting the one placed in the bracket near the doorway, he handed it to Gallius as he led them back into the crypt. The captains seemed ill at ease and unaware that even such a place existed, and as the candles under the altar of *Apep* were lit, the slow advancing brightness quickly shone upwards and across the Icons as they stood along the alabaster ledge. The men gathered before them, the group standing in silence as the enormity of the tragedy and overall impact of the stealing of each of these Icons fell around. Looking upon the golden figures, many differing thoughts filled their mind until, eventually, the quietness became overwhelming, and Edgar broke the spell.

"Can you remember which ones you stole?" he quietly asked, his voice coming out in a whisper. Seeing the looks of unease turn into doubt in the faces of the men as the Icons sat close beside each other, he continued, "I know for some, it may be many years since the order was given and your actions carried out, but I'm sure you must remember."

Captain Gregory was first to come forward, for the Icon he had been commanded to steal was the last that had recently found its place upon the altar and which now stood by itself on the very far left. Placing his hand on the cold edge of the shelf, he indicated the frog-headed statue as being the one that he had taken from the Mountain City of the Fortis. The Icon of *Amun* could then be discounted by the others, its ruby eyes shining out from the oddly shaped head, and their attention became focused further along the ledge as the heat of the candles added to the stuffiness and the air once again became tainted by the smoke.

Captain Cormack was next in recognising and

identifying the Deity he had taken so many years before from the shore-lined City of Delmar. This city was positioned in the west, on the very edge of the sea's limits and had risen high before the vast oceans. But on the loss of their Icon *Hauhet*, the waters seemingly abandoned the shoreline, and the sands of the bay grew large and led away into the far-off distance. For the citizens, a feeling of complete apathy in all its aspects had descended upon the city and soon the people had, like their seas, even abandoned each other!

Standing along the very right-hand edge of the altar, Cormack peered down at the two Icons that took their place together, the snake head of the goddess standing to the right of the god as the green eyes of both reflected the light of the candles collected in their gaze.

"This is the one I took," he admitted, looking at the small figure, unaware of its given name. "This one here with the green eyes and the head of a snake." He pointed to *Hauhet* as the other captains moved closer, and each looked at the collection of statues. Now being able to discount the two already chosen, they easily began picking out their Icons by the shape of their bodies, either frog or snake, male or female and the colour of their eyes. And the statues and the cities from which they had been taken were slowly spoken of and identified.

Eventually, this left one remaining unclaimed statue, the Icon of *Heh*, which stood next to the statue of *Hauhet*. And in this one, the whole of the story of the Deities was bound. For this one was unknowingly the one that breathed new life into the search for the Eight and started off the whole catastrophe which had now culminated in the bonfires in the northern woods.

Heh had been found in the City of Muntani on the lesser steppes and given in tribute by the Priest Johenn, and here it stood accusingly at the end of the shelf, the blood red candles of the altar casting their shadows across its emerald eyes.

"Tomorrow, we must begin to split up these Icons," Edgar said, the words of *Horus* resonating through his mind as each statue had been recognised and claimed, "and we can begin by returning each of them to their cities. With that, I ask you to ready yourselves and your men to accomplish this." He paused, looking at the dark faces of the men as they stood before the altar. And in remembering the exacting words of instruction given by the god, he continued, "But prepare yourselves for a long stay. For you all witnessed the words of *Horus*, and the task fallen upon me, I now pass down to you. I command you to help in the rebuilding of these cities left devastated by the loss of their Icons."

His focus and words of responsibility were then passed to each of his captains, and as he looked into the shadows surrounding his men, he felt the heaviness of the burden that he was placing in their hands. "But be aware, some will be in more dire need than others, and the impact of their loss may have been disastrous. Therefore your time away could be far, far longer than imagined."

The immensity of the situation and challenges placed upon them now came to the understanding of the captains. And as each once more looked to the golden Icons sat upon the alabaster shelf, they could hardly refuse the bidding of a god and accepted it as given.

"But we must leave the Icons here, for the moment," Edgar quickly stated, aware that his order to his captains would require further thought and preparation before they went rushing off. "You cannot just up and go, for you need to prepare your men before they leave the city. We shall have to sort out a plan on how to go about their partition and return."

He walked away, Jakob following him up the aisle

between the seating, before he suddenly came to a stop. Looking back, he glared upward towards the head of *Apep*, his eyes narrowing as they dropped to where the candles beneath gave out their glow. "But first, you can begin by tearing down that atrocity!"

The altar of *Apep* was dismantled, its heavily carved sculpture of the snake being first removed from the plinth. And as Captains Nathan and Ullric stood atop the altar, the Icons and candles already having been taken down from the ledge, they lowered the heavy serpentine figure into the arms of the waiting men below. Slowly, it was carried aloft and up through the passageway and out into the courtyard.

The figure, on seeing the light of day for the first time in hundreds of countless years, then began its decay. The once finely carved representation collapsed into many crudely chiselled pieces before falling through the hands of the captains, as in meeting the freshness of the morning air, it dropped to dust across the palace ground.

The Icons themselves were replaced atop the ledge, although not in their pairs but haphazardly along the plinth, and the red candles were discarded across the floor, the men's feet kicking them beneath the seating as they moved around.

The captains, having been seen to be given their orders, were then quick to leave the closeness of the vault behind and immediately went about starting preparations for the next coming days. Their aim was to swiftly organise their troops and prepare maps to make their return journeys with the statues. This, in some cases, had been such a long time ago that the campaign had been forgotten over the years, and the memory would need to be refreshed.

Gallius returned up the passageway out the chamber, and being last to leave, he extinguished the candles on the lower shelf. Taking up his torch, he softly closed the door, once again leaving the statues to the dark of the crypt.

Coming up into the courtyard, he found the king awaiting him, with Captain Isaac standing at his side, and along with Jakob, the four walked slowly back into the stronghold. Passing through the main hall, Gallius was quick to ask to take his leave of the city for an urgent need to check on Shuma and his daughter had suddenly risen in him, and after the upsets of the day, he wished to delay his departure no longer.

"You have my permission, Gallius, for I feel we have done enough for the moment," Edgar consented, his mind desperately trying to push aside the morning's work as they came to a halt at the double doors of his chambers.

"First though, I should like to know from both of you your thoughts about returning these Icons. How best would it be to begin, do you think? For I feel we need to get ourselves organised quickly in this regard."

"I agree, sire," Gallius replied, having already given the situation some thought, "and in my thinking, I feel it best not to send all of the men out together. That, to me, could in itself cause its own problems within the city."

The soldier in him saw the strategy of moving all of the troops at the same time as not being the easiest or the most efficient. He had always worked with fewer men, which he found easier to deploy and control. He felt justified to further advise, "I feel that with a couple of smaller groups, then the closest cities could be the more obvious to remedy in the first. These would be the cities of the Fortis and of Delmar. They should surely fit as being the ones nearest to here. What do you think, Isaac?"

Both of these cities, the two men knew, stood many long weeks' ride away, both in a westerly direction. But in being closest, they could at least begin the breakup of the Deities, and Captain Isaac was quick to agree with Gallius on his suggestion.

"So it's Gregory and Cormack," Edgar stated, remembering the sight of the two captains as they had, in turn, pointed out the red-eyed god *Amun* and the green-eyed goddess *Hauhet*. Suddenly, without warning, he again witnessed the flames of the woodland bonfires burning before his eyes, the flickering flames dancing around the men's feet, and he heard again the cries and screams of the brotherhood as a half-imagined smell of scorching flesh filled his nostrils.

Wearily, he wiped his hands across his face, and feeling that he had seen enough of the day for that moment, slowly said, "Can I get you to see to it then, Isaac?" Seeing the swift nod, he walked through the doorway before turning back and finishing, "And, Captain Gallius, you are free to go. You have my approval to take one of the horses."

The two men were left in the main hall, and Isaac quickly acted upon his given instruction. Taking his leave of Gallius, he met Captain Cormack as he strode down the steps of the stronghold, and swiftly escorting him towards the arena, they found Gregory already massing his troops.

Passing on the king's instructions for both men to make their preparations for the morning, he was able to return to the king to make his report before being given leave with permission to prepare his own men.

***

Returning to his room Gallius checked on Malian, and finding no change in the altar tender's slumber, he was quick to take his leave. Packing his bag in haste for his travel through the woods, he arrived at the stables near the main gates and found the king had already given his orders. One of Edgar's best horses had been saddled and stood in wait while a packhorse was alongside, ready for the off, and Gallius, briskly tying on his bag, was soon bidding farewell to the city.

***

As the late morning light fed its way past the smoking, smouldering bonfires and through the still woodland to the north, the captain found himself riding south through the closeness of the forest that gathered around.

Following in the footsteps of Tragen, his thoughts led him along the route the warrior, Darric and Anitta would have taken in their pursuit of Brann before his wonderings moved on to the outcome of the inevitable encounter. Knowing that the two groups, each travelling south in their chase, would be unaware of events in the north and would continue on their given course, Gallius hoped for a swift conclusion.

***

Shuma had seen that Daina was made comfortable on her bed roll beneath the overhang of the fallen roof, but that first night was cold and miserable in the wind that whistled across the plains and through the city, and the two women had huddled together to keep warm.

The following day the wise woman vowed to find them better accommodation, and rising early into the dark of the dawn, she wandered her way through the forlorn loneliness cloaking the city until she eventually reached the outer wall. Looking out across the lesser steppes, the morning had begun to dawn red across the grassy plains, and Shuma felt a deep unease sicken her before eventually a feeling of elation took its place.

Watching the white clouds scud their way across the lightening sky, she stared across the moving tops of the grasslands into the far distance for many moments. Slowly dropping her gaze, she turned back towards the fallen city, her need to find a fitter place to sleep suddenly returning to the fore in her mind.

Walking back through the desolate streets, she finally found one of the older buildings that would suit them better. Stepping inside for a closer inspection, she found the roof completely enclosed, and the thicker walls offered hope of greater protection and a safeguard from the wind over and above that of their last night's shelter.

Hurrying back to the front gate, she found the younger woman already awake, and they were quick to move their camp. Shuma led the way bearing the packs, while Daina followed, carrying the bed rolls as they walked towards the town centre. Once inside their new home, they found a dry-level spot to place their baggage and began to make themselves as comfortable as possible before stopping briefly to sit and eat their morning meal together on the doorstep in the rapidly warming breeze.

***

Later that evening, as the rays of the setting sun splayed out along the western border, Gallius could be seen making his way towards the wise woman and his daughter. Once through the woods, he had stepped up his pace amongst the grasslands, his mind having become utterly focused on seeing both women. And he rode hard through the heaviness of the pasture, the packhorse managing to keep pace with the horse given by the king.

As the last dying rays disappeared behind the western

mountains, the darkening clouds suddenly opened up and fell away, their lower layers scudding across the sky and appearing to be within touching distance above his head as he moved onward. Above in the ebbing daylight, the moon slowly began to rise, and shining its light down between the tattered remnants, the sky finally became clear, and Gallius could arrive in its guidance once more at the gates of Muntani.

The city was completely quiet, and riding through the opening into the stillness, he began first by checking the place where the group slept on their way north, knowing that Shuma would have initially thought of there to rest for their first night. But finding no one, he left the horses and began his walk through the moonlit streets, calling out the names of the two women into the silence as he moved inwards along the torn-up pavements. Eventually, as he began to chill and a great tiredness came upon him, he was rewarded by the sound of his daughter's voice.

"Father is that you?" Daina called out into the dark, a weak light suddenly shining out into the avenue as she held out the glowing candle before her. Recognising his voice as he made his reply, she said, "We are in here, Father." Opening the door further to guide him towards them, he entered the shelter of the living quarters and was quickly made welcome by both of the women.

Returning later to check on the horses and collect the supplies, he and Shuma were able to have a moment together, and they held each other tight, exchanging kisses as they stood close in the darkness of the city walls.

But Gallius was swift to pull away, his hands untangling themselves from her soft hair, as the need to enlighten Shuma of the last days rushed to the forefront of his mind. While they walked back along the windblown streets, he told of the events that had taken place in the city which slumbered in the north.

The wise woman had to stop on hearing the news of Malian, and she sat down in distress upon a half-tumbled wall as the shock came over her. Slowly taking in the words, she stared off down the road and into the darkness of the distance, while the cold breeze swirled around and pulled at her rumpled hair.

"How is he?" she eventually asked, turning her worried face to the captain. Remembering the incidents in the past when the altar tender had been visited in his dreams by the gods and the places those dreams had taken him, she knew it could have a great effect on the body and mind of the man.

"He has the full attention of the healer," Gallius confidently replied, and in the hope of reassuring her further, said, "and the king will ensure he is well looked after."

A sudden relief from her worries came over her as she took in his words, but this was quick to turn back to a new alarm. For in knowing that the Icons held within the city were safe beyond the possession of the brotherhood, her thoughts returned to that of her mother and the Icon of *Amaunet* held within the Sleeping Caverns.

Now a great unease came upon her as she thought of Tragen and the others she had said farewell to only the day before. They would be heedless of the recent development and remain in pursuit of Brann on his task appointed by King Dedrick. This now appeared to be a chase that could so easily be stopped before the two groups even came within range of the swans, and she quickly asked, "Has the new king sent out a rider to recall Brann or to notify Tragen of the events?"

"No," Gallius replied, "they would not be able to catch them in time, for they would be too far ahead." Seeing the look of dismay cross her face, he continued, "We must trust Tragen to ensure the safety of the Icon and of the women assigned to guard her, and in that, I've much confidence in his ability and that of his companions."

Hearing this news, however, her heart sank further before the memory of the warrior as he sat astride his horse made itself known, and she smiled up at Gallius. The smile, though, held a certain sadness, for she thought of the sights which he must have so recently witnessed. They must indeed have had some effect on him, and although he seemed not to be changed or troubled as he spoke of what he had seen, she could see deeper into his spirit.

"Yes, I too feel we must trust Tragen," she positively said, before asking, "But what about you, how are you?" Looking up towards the tall figure, her worry became a genuine and deep concern for his well-being, and she reached out to him.

"I am fine, now that I have seen you," his words came in reply, and lifting her from the hardness of the wall where she sat, he once more took her in his arms, and they again embraced, holding each other in the rubble of the crumbling city as the light of the moon shone down.

***

As the morning sun rose high the following day, Captain Gregory led his team towards the main gates of the city and there found Cormack and his unit already positioned in readiness, the taller man standing to one side impatiently awaiting the arrival of his colleague. The two captains then returned to the stronghold, where they met with Isaac on the steps of the building.

Edgar awaited them inside with Jakob standing ready at his back, and the small figure, who had seemingly become a constant, now appeared more at ease with his new master. As the king once more took them through into the palace confines, the group found themselves again before the doorway to the crypt. The two captains followed behind Edgar as he led them down the passageway, the darkness within being pushed aside as the light of day flooded down from above.

On reaching the bottom, they lit the torch brought with them and returned into the blackness of the vault to look upon the Icons. These remained along the alabaster ledge, but whether in their same position or not, the men could not say. For some movement appeared to have taken place and they now stood gathered towards the middle of the wide shelf where the statue of *Apep* had risen up. A coupling, too, had seemingly begun to take place as the gods and goddesses were compelled to pair up in their dyads while the heads of each of the statues were positioned looking out into the darkness.

The two Icons, the god *Amun* and the goddess *Hauhet*, were swiftly removed from their location, and wrapping each in layers of cloth with a final wrapping of calfskin, the two were given to the men who had initially stolen them.

Then the responsibility was placed upon them to do the will of the gods, and they quickly tucked the parcels in their packs and made ready to leave. Turning away from the Icons as they stood staring out into the crypt, the men began their march past the seating towards the doorway. But it felt like they were walking through a heaviness, for the air around had thickened and condensed as the eyes of the Icons stared icily at their backs, the glow penetrating the minds of the men as they struggled to reach the doorway.

Finally, Edgar led them through into the passage, and the door was closed with a decisive clang, and the coldness of the force that followed was immediately lifted. Once outside, the fear was banished even further, as climbing back into the freshness of the morning, the crypt door also closed behind them, and the openness of the palace courtyard drifted the breeze around as they made their way back towards the stronghold.

The two captains were then brief in bidding their king farewell, and with good wishes from the other captains ringing in their ears, they walked past the arena. Returning to their waiting men they then began to move out of the city, and taking their mounts forward, their troops followed close behind.

In the rear, the small carts filled with supplies driven by the artisans and skilled craftsmen came slowly, the rough wheels following the tracks of the horses. These few men, along with their apprentices, had been seconded to help in the rebuild of the cities, and all had been advised to say their farewells to family and friends in the hope of their swift return. However, none knew how long they would be away, and as the woods of the higher steppes drew them south through the landscape, the sounds and shouts of the send-off gradually faded and then stopped.

The passage was slow for the two groups leaving the City of the High Places, and as that first night began to drop its chill and dank mist upon the heads of each of the men, the southern edge of the forest still lay many miles before them. Their camp was made beneath the overhanging boughs of the trees and the next morning seemed long in its coming.

Starting again early the following day, it saw them eventually reach the boundary of the forest. Dropping down into the lesser steppes, the progress of the carts became easier. As the rutted tree root paths of the forest became grassland the wheels of their wagons rolled along swifter over the flatter land.

In the City of Muntani, towards where the two teams of men slowly rode, Gallius had awoken on his second night in the desolation of the ruins to the brightness of a sunlit morning. His extreme exhaustion and tiredness of the last few days had finally been replaced with a feeling of renewal. The deep sleep that had fallen upon him this past night had seen him almost comatose in his slumber, and in this state, his many fears had been discarded in the comfort given by its oblivion.

The woman's head lay softly against the bareness of his right shoulder, and although the wound still gave him pain as healing continued to take place, he endured it to have her closeness. Her face was covered slightly by the dark hair falling over her eyes, and gathering around the softness of her chin, it gently fell across her neck before disappearing beneath the stitched edge of the blanket as it rose evenly at each breath. The captain carefully moved to one side, and letting Shuma resettle amongst the warmth of the blankets, he slowly rose and left the woman to sleep.

Walking into the room to the back of the building where his daughter had been sleeping, he found Daina's bedroll empty. Quietly making for the door out into the brightness of the day, he came upon her seated along the front wall of the house opposite. Hearing the door opening, she raised her head to look to where her father stood.

"I didn't want to disturb you," she immediately shouted across, seeing her father raise his hand as the glare of the morning light fell across his face. Looking upwards, he saw that the sun had risen high in the sky, and he had slept long into the day's beginning.

Stepping over the threshold of the doorway, he slowly

walked towards his daughter across the avenue. Seeing his approach over the cobbles, the younger woman continued in her explanation, "You still seemed wearied from the efforts placed upon you in the north, and I thought it best to let you sleep. But I knew you would be all the better for it this morning."

"Thank you for that, Daina," he answered, as he joined her in front of the fallen-down building that led off in a low collapse to both left and right, before eventually merging into the subsided debris of its neighbours. "I do feel fitter and less exhausted today."

The father and daughter sat alongside each other amidst the rubble, and a quietness concentrated around them, uniting the two as they sat in the warming sun. Around, the breeze blew in off the grasslands fanning the weeds that grew tall in the gardens surrounding the streets, and the hush of its passing broke the silence.

"I like Shuma," Daina eventually said, her voice soft and faint as she turned to look across to where she knew the wise woman remained asleep.

"Good," came the reply, as a light smile crossed his face, "I am pleased about that. I like her too, and I'm hoping she will be around with us for some time." He touched his daughter briefly on the cheek as she smiled back at him. Remembering she had never known her mother, a sadness overcame him, and he wrapped his arms around her, holding her close for many moments as the sun continued its rise into the cloudless sky.

The door across the avenue took its time to open, but when it did, Shuma stood there with her hair tied back off her face. Gazing over to the figures as they sat atop the wall, their shadows slanting backward into the scree of the debris, she shouted across that breakfast was prepared if they were ready to eat.

The three reunited, each taking their plate of food out

into the open. Feeling the warmth of the sun on their shoulders they sat with their backs to the wall of the building, the clear sky of the steppe land high above their heads as their talk turned to the day that lay before them.

"I think it is time we should return to the city," Gallius soon said, the empty plate sitting before him as he watched the wind whip the dust up into the air. Having seen the complete ruin of the buildings in the light of day, he realised they could not stay there for long. Plus, he knew the two women should now be safe to return back within the walls of the northern city.

Over and above that, his mind was forever wandering back to Malian, and time had been spent wondering if he had yet awakened. He also knew that Shuma's thoughts were troubled in that respect and was not surprised that both she and Daina could find little reason to disagree with this suggestion when it was made, and after finishing their meal, they were quick to rise and vacate the ruined house that had given them its shelter.

The early afternoon sun, slowly arching overhead, saw the three returning through the grasslands, the City of Muntani again being bid farewell as the captain led the two women, both seated atop the pack horse, through the fallen gates and back along east towards the stretch of the plains.

However, it was not long after their leaving the city before, in the far distance, the troops of Cormack and Gregory came into view as they made progress west along with the wagons. As Gallius raised his arm in greeting and the groups came together, the two men made him aware that the Icons had finally begun to be separated and distanced once more from each other.

The smaller group, however, did not delay the passage of the two regiments as they met within the sweep of the pastures, for they knew the next stop for the slow-paced wagons would be the city they had hurriedly left that morning.

After a brief pause to exchange words, the two companies parted, and each headed either west towards the mountains and a precarious journey into the lower ranges or back towards the forests of the north.

The three heading north to the City of the High Places were quicker in reaching it than those who had recently left, riding on through the dark of the night and arriving at its entrance as the herdsmen led their flocks down from the main gates. Here the young men shepherded their animals out, and a hurry overtook the beasts as they rushed forward to lower their heads and graze upon the stunted grass. Finally, the greyness of the forest beneath the overhang of the trees slowly led the sheep inwards, and they disappeared, followed by their drovers.

Leaving the horses back at the stables, where the grooms and stable lads of the city were beginning to wake, Gallius led the two women to the stronghold where they found the main hall astir with the cleaners which kept the king's residence swept and clean. Quickly passing these by, Gallius led the women through the double doors into the king's chambers. Leaving Daina in the safety of the meeting room, he and Shuma walked on to where Malian lay, there finding the healer still in residence.

Jasan had remained with Malian all this time, sleeping and taking his meals within the room and only leaving his side to wash and freshen up. But on the early arrival of Gallius and Shuma, he saw an opportunity to take his leave for a while longer, but first, he gave report.

"He still sleeps," he said, holding the rigid hand of the patient, "and there has been no movement within his frame, for his limbs appear fixed in a stiffness I have not seen before in my time!" He looked with concern at the still body of the altar tender as it lay, solid and immovable, within the bed. "It's like he's in a trance, suspended within his own essence." Looking down upon the pale face, Jasan gently shook his head before turning away. Walking purposefully out through the door, he left the two to consider the man who lay before them and to stand watch over their friend.

"I've not seen him like this before," Shuma said as she worriedly sat down at his side. Closing her long fingers around his hand, she felt the severity of the rigour as the fingers remained unyielding in her grip. "His dreams have always taken him far, that I know, but on waking, he was always unchanged in his manner." She brushed aside a stray hair that had fallen across the whiteness of his features, and she wondered where he was.

"You must remember he was completely taken over by the god," Gallius reminded her, for the sight of *Horus* as he emerged skyward from the very being of the altar tender remained fresh to his mind, "and it must have had cause to affect him this way."

"Then let us hope it will just be a matter of time," the wise woman stated, looking down into the placid face, "and a matter for Malian to deal with by himself. We can do no more here than what has already been done." Placing the hand gently upon the bedspread, she stood, and walking back to Gallius, kissed him. Running her hand alongside the stubble of his bearded chin she looked up with concern into the captain's face.

"I will stay here a little longer if you need to be elsewhere," she said as they moved apart, the warmth of the man's caress lingering across her lips, "and if Daina wishes to join me, she is most welcome."

The two were then parted by their duties, Gallius first ensuring that food and drink were taken in to Shuma as she kept vigil in the sick room, while for him, the day stretched ahead in varying parts of the now waking stronghold.

The wise woman settled herself in Malian's company and made ready for his awakening, and as she watched intently the rise and fall of the altar tender's chest she was joined by Daina, who opened the door to admit the servants from the kitchens carrying their trays. Walking over to the window seat, Gallius's daughter sat herself in its bounds as a silence returned to the room, and the door was again quietly closed.

***

Unknown to those who sat around him, the soft voice of Shuma as she showed her concern had slowly begun to filter its way into the depths of Malian's deep sleep. Hearing the tenderness of her voice as she spoke to him, the darkness around began to fade, and a lighter grey steadily came to the fore, and Malian gradually began to open his eyes. Shuma was standing at the base of his bed, the wise woman staring back intently as she saw the first flickering movement of his eyelids.

Eventually, his eyes were fully open, and although he lay staring up at her, he appeared unable to move or speak. The words were there in his mind, yet the thought did not give way to any actual expression, and the struggle to make himself known quickly gave way to overwhelming frustration. Silently he screamed the words in his head as the woman looked on in expectation, blind to his inner battle until finally he was overcome with weariness, and slowly he reclosed his eyes and let the darkness once again take him.

CHAPTER TEN

Edgar had heard of the homecoming of Gallius as he sat at breakfast and immediately sent Jakob out to find him, giving him orders that the returning man should be straightaway brought before the king to make report.

Finding the captain walking the short distance along the hallway from the guest quarters, Jakob had first waited as Gallius put forward his request for food and drink for Shuma and Daina and then, making known the king's instruction, he guided him directly across the intersecting aisle. Leading him into the back of the dining room through the frequently used servant's entrance, he was swift to be seen to do Edgar's bidding, and having done his duty, softly closed the door behind him.

"Welcome, Gallius." Edgar was quick in his greeting upon seeing the captain brought before him. "Did you see Gregory and Cormack on your way back?"

The captain came forward, lowering his head in respect to the man. On seeing the king extend his hand in signal for him to join him alongside on the bench, Gallius unknowingly placed himself where Serdos had once sat, and the two met in friendship at the long table.

"We passed on the lower steppes, sire," he was able to inform as an aide came forward carrying a plate, "but we did not hold them for long. They appeared somewhat overly burdened by the wagons, and they had need to reach the city walls that we had left that morning before the nightfall caught them up."

"Good." Edgar smiled as he saw the keen man begin eagerly on the serving that had been placed before him. "And yes, it will be slow going for them," he conceded, the smile leaving his face as he remembered the troops would be somewhat taxed in their swiftness by the presence of the civilians. "But it's good to know that we've made a start to part these symbols of the brotherhood, and this city has begun to feel lighter for their absence."

He looked down at his breakfast, the dish nearly empty of its contents before his eyes suddenly moved to the spread of the map that lay between himself and the captain.

Pushing forward the chart of the northern lands, he placed his finger carefully down upon the outline of the Eastern Great Waters, which snaked across the scroll, announcing as he slid his finger into place over the parchment, "Here is where we shall be returning the next statue."

He looked to the captain as he stared downwards to the indicated spot, further stating, "It is to be sent out today and restored to its rightful people, and the city from where it was stolen will be rebuilt and given back its dignity."

The next nearest city was that of the Fosse, which Gallius had passed both on his way south and back northwards and which lay across the plateau on the cliffs of the Eastern Great Waters.

Captain Steffan, the leader initially tasked untold time ago to steal the Icon of *Kauket*, had informed the king the night before that his men were ready and the wagons loaded ready to be off. His desire to leave and make redress had grown within him since witnessing the bonfires and the morale within his detachment had risen in expectation of the coming action after many months of seeming inactivity within the city walls.

"It's the City of the Fosse," Edgar advised as the two contemplated the lands spread before them, "do you know of it?"

"I know of it," the man replied darkly as he slowly

placed his fork down upon the plate, "and I have passed it in my travels. But I've never had cause to enter its walls."

His mind went to the overheard talk between Shuma and Darric and their telling of the people within those confines who had been wreaked and devastated by a blindness since the loss of their Icon. Then bringing his focus back onto the plate laying before him, his thoughts looked to other avenues before turning to the king's safety and the overall security within the city where he sat, and he felt it the right time to speak.

"Do you not feel it unwise to send out any more of your captains, sire?" he slowly said. Turning to face Edgar, he began to put forward a worry that had been growing in his mind. "They will be away for many months, and I fear it may weaken the civil defence within this city. And you, as a new king, must be seen to have charge within your own walls."

He thought for a short while before making his suggestion. "What about the second-in-commands? They must be as much in the know as their captains. Couldn't we send them out instead?"

Edgar gave this some thought, and noting the look of unease in the face of the man opposite, he slowly nodded his head as his thinking turned this way and that. Eventually, seeing the reasoning in which the advice had been given, he sat back from the table and looked towards the far corner where the adjoining door led into the meeting room.

"Steffan is in the next room, ready for the off," he informed Gallius, knowing the captain would have been unaware of who was leading the next group out, "and we shall put the suggestion to him. Only," he hesitated, "I judge the timing may be too short to make changes to leadership now. But let us place the idea before him and see what he has to say."

The breakfast came to an end with both men pushing aside their plates, their eyes once more becoming drawn to the mountains, lakes and immense plains as they stared down upon the map. Here the vastness of the terrain depicting their northern lands spread out before them, ending at the wrinkled and rough edges of the scroll. While the contours bled off as the outlines of the boundaries to both the Eastern and Western Great Waters snaked along the bottom margin, and the top disappeared into the endless woodlands up to the northern and eastern bays.

"I wonder how it goes with Tragen and those who journey with him?" Edgar suddenly asked, as seeing the lines on the scroll brought to mind the group as they trailed south in the steps of Brann. "Do you think they will have been quick in their accomplishment?"

"I don't know," Gallius honestly replied, his eyes taking in the simplicity of the innocent lines, which in reality, he knew disguised the harshness of the extreme terrain, "but they have often been in my thoughts. For they travel with little knowledge of what has happened since they left." He remembered the last time he had seen both men as they rode away into the woods alongside Anitta. And the sight of the warrior sitting astride his horse had filled him with a hope for all of their safety. "Still, I have much faith in Tragen to swiftly bring the chase to an end." He paused as he remembered his encounter with the women on the Lower Lake. "I know that in the women of the Sleeping Caverns, we can guarantee a harsh reception if Brann makes it that far!"

A silence enclosed the two as they each allowed their thoughts to wander, but in both minds, the image of a woman kept returning to make itself known over and above the others. In Gallius' case, it revolved around the face of Shuma, while in Edgar's, the face of Daina was slowly becoming engraved.

"What of your daughter?" the king now clearly asked, his gaze fixed firmly on the outlines of the plateau which lay before him. "Did you find her safe and well?"

His voice showed more than just a regard for Gallius' daughter as he slowly pushed aside the scroll. Rising from his chair, he remembered the paleness of the young woman he had first seen standing at the barred door in the cells of the stronghold. Turning towards the other man, he smiled in expectation of the reply, and the captain, aware of the concern given in the younger man's voice, found himself returning his smile.

"I found Daina well and in good care, sire," he answered, and noting the look of consideration along with the interest that played across the king's features, he quickly nodded his head, and turning away gestured for Edgar to take the lead.

The door out of the dining area was opened, and the two walked into the meeting room where Steffan, readily dressed for his journey, quickly stood from his fireside seat. Crossing back into the main stretch of the vaulted room, he joined the two at a small table, where after greeting the returning captain, they met to talk. The discussion was immediately brought to focus on Gallius' proposal regarding the deputies, one which he urged and insisted that Edgar and the captain should consider.

Steffan was at first loath to relinquish the command of his men. However, as the exchange in conversation took place, he slowly became aware of the worry that Gallius was holding. Coming to realise that it made greater sense to take this approach, he was quick to concede and accepted the ruling.

The king then instructed the two to inform the remaining captains of the change in plans, and he gave them the power and privilege of advancing their deputies.

After doing that, Edgar declared, they were to report immediately to the stronghold for further conference, while the deserving second-in-commands were to be given outright authority over their men directly on promotion. Given that most of these men had been in their position for some long time, all would hopefully be happy with the advancement and the extra dividends their betterment would bring.

***

Many hours later, after the meeting of the captains in the king's hall had been concluded, Gallius returned to the room where Malian slept. On nearing where Shuma still sat at his side, she quickly turned to him, her tiredness disappearing as a look of hopefulness crossed her face.

"He's opened his eyes!" she stated as Gallius arrived beside her, and standing, she quickly kissed him and took his hand. As the two stood side by side at the bedside looking down upon their sleeping friend, Jasan also returned, his weariness seemingly alleviated by the pause in his long vigil. Now, with his arms full of fresh bedding and bags of dried herbs to sweeten the air, he approached the bed, and Shuma anxiously repeated the words to him.

Quickly checking on Malian, the severity of the tension in his limbs appeared slightly lessened in its extreme, and a certain softening in the features around the mouth gave reason for an expectation of revival. The healer nodded his head in much relief as he stepped back from the bed.

"Good, good," he said slowly, hoping that the worst was behind not only for the altar tender but also for himself. Looking around into the concerned faces, he finished, "We should begin to see a gradual improvement, but it may still take some time!"

***

The improvement was indeed unhurried, and in the intervening days in which Malian awoke fully and regained his strength, three of the five remaining Icons had been sent out from the palace, the newly advanced second-in-commands eager to show their skills in the newfound leadership of their men.

Within the city, the lessening influence of the Icons over the people had also begun to slowly initiate a change. The obvious feeling of subjugation placed upon them over many years and unaware to most, as they led their everyday lives, began to lift as the kingship of Dedrick, and the grip of Serdos and his brotherhood, were removed. A disquiet and unknown nervousness took its place and began to emerge within the people of the city and those whose lives had begun outside of its confines.

Amongst the many overcrowded citizens who lived alongside the high city walls and who worked in the back streets, many could remember the life they left behind long ago in the City of Muntani. And a resurgence to return home to the lands of their descent, and hopefully a better existence, began to gather at a pace as a discord between the city's people became noted.

This first began around the market stalls and bars, eventually giving way to more general disagreements that saw trouble arising between neighbours in their once friendly courtyards and which spilled along the pavements within the inner areas.

A desire to leave the City of the High Places behind inevitably saw the unsettled people collecting around one person. His name was Earold, a man who had struggled and worked hard for his family for many years, as had so many like him. But he was quick to turn a phrase and rapidly found an increasing audience eager to hear his words in the disquiet of the backstreets, and with that, he crucially needed to know more from Gallius on his return to the city.

The two men met in the marketplace, the captain having received a note asking for a chance to talk from a man whose name was fast becoming noted around the stronghold. However, Gallius was not quick in leading the man in his hope of returning home and was more than forceful in passing on the devastation he had seen within the once proud City of Muntani.

Time after time, he did not hold back on the destruction he had witnessed, endeavouring to stress the work and commitment required to bring the city's crumbling ruins back to within a standard of living. But as they walked past the stalls within the market, Earold appeared not easily deterred and showed an even greater readiness to rally the people. Gallius, sensing that unrest was inevitable, was glad he had insisted that the other captains remain, for he could foresee disorder and turmoil ahead.

***

The afternoon that Malian found the strength to rise from his bed, unknowing of events in the north, Tragen, Darric and Anitta arrived at the Median Bridge between the Western Great Waters where the stretch of the seas met those leading off east. The group they were chasing had navigated the water a day before over the cobbles of the bridge before disappearing into the stretch of pasture as they rode into the grasslands and on towards the Sleeping Caverns.

But for the three, they could travel no further that day. The journey taken in pursuit of Brann had taken its toll, and a weariness fell over them as they reached the clearing of the crossing. The night was spent on the hard ground, but the following morning found them rising refreshed, and the three were prompt in breaking up their camp. Thankfully finding the canoes which had remained hidden in the shadow of the bridge alongside the water's edge on their race northwards, they rushed to ready themselves. Then relieving the horses of their bridles, they turned them away into the surrounding woodland before rapidly taking to the craft and setting off back along the water's edge. Here they were swift in battling the waters of the Great Western Sea as the high tide of the morning aided them in their rush, and they pushed the canoe southwards with great urgency.

Eventually, the following day, they neared the outpouring of the underground stream they had left countless weeks before. Anitta pointed to where the high domes of the Sleeping Caverns reached down towards the water's edge, and the nose of the canoe was brought around and up onto the gravelled shoreline of the cove where they had so briefly rested.

"Follow me," Anitta ordered. Quickly jumping from the craft and hefting her pack out from the front, she turned to the two men, "but have a care for the way up is steep, and you will need all of your energy to maintain your safety."

Walking to the back of the cove, she pushed her way in past the accumulation of boulders and found herself on the other side where the beginning of the path led upwards. She had climbed this way before as part of her training many years ago, up through this stack known as the Caminus. But then she had been much younger, and a fear of tight spaces was one that had never bothered her.

Looking back towards where Tragen stood, she knew well the extreme confines would be troublesome for him.

His bulk would give little room for negotiating the tightness of the terrain, but his strength, she hoped, would outweigh that, and he would surely be able to pull himself through and skywards to where the light of day shone down through the fissure.

The two men joined her, and looking up, could see the stricture into which they would be climbing. The start of the path was a sheer crawl upwards between the walls of a chimney-like structure that disappeared over their heads, and Anitta showed the two the best way to climb. Taking the lead, the swan woman pushed her pack high above her head, wedging it into place before she brought her arms up to find the first hand hold. Placing her back against the rock wall, she braced herself within the flue. Bringing her legs up taut, her feet set against the opposite wall, she slowly inched them upwards. Sliding her back into its next position, she began to climb higher, her pack being pushed further up as she advanced.

Darric stared up, and watching how she placed herself, began to mimic her actions; and following close behind, he started the slow climb upwards. Tragen remained in the rear, and although his size and bulk may have been a drawback within the confines of the tight stack, his overall height gave him a much greater reach over the others. Pulling himself into the opening, he allowed the two to get slightly ahead in their ascent before he began to crawl up, his massive arms hauling him skywards. While around, the closeness of the walls caused a shower of grains and larger rock fragments to fall and cascade over and below him as he moved ever higher.

The climb was tough for them all, but on finally reaching the top, their bodies and clothing covered in the dust from the walls of the vent, they found themselves once more in the light of the day with the wind whistling up from across the seas that lay far below. Here the gentle curves of the cavern's hard roofline arched away, the smoothness of the weather-carved humps giving them an unlikely and deceptive appearance of soft creamy drifts of sand.

The top of the Sleeping Caverns led the three eastwards across towards where the valley walls would eventually drop sheer away into the Lower Lake, and while they hurried over the roof, the winds followed along, carrying with them a salty tang. The grasslands to the north could be glimpsed as they crossed over one intersecting mound into the next, while the sand dunes in the south bordering Lake Cannis and beyond into the High Rush Plains lay hidden downwards and at a distance of the undulating ridges.

The sun had risen high in a cloudless sky before they neared the sheer drop down into the bowl of the lake, and coming cautiously over this final ridge, a tall figure could be seen against the clear skyline of the valley's perimeter.

"Get down!" Anitta suddenly whispered, and grabbing hold of Darric's arm, she pulled him to the ground, while Tragen dropped to the floor behind them, the dust flying up as he felt the harsh grittiness of the surface hit his face. Flattening themselves into the landscape, a silence encircled them, and the wind disappeared into the east.

Moments passed before Anitta slowly raised her head over the gentle contour of the bank, where she could see the figure in more detail. It was calmly turning its head to scan the northern horizon; its gaze became fixed as a soft cloudiness was seen gathering amidst the grasslands. But the covering which hid the face, along with the curved sword held in the hand, immediately gave away a connection with the swans, and Anitta felt a relief wash over her.

Rising, she indicated for Tragen and Darric to remain in position and shouting out to the woman she made herself known. The swan woman instantly brought her sword up and around to face the threat she imagined was before her, but on seeing a familiar female figure, the hands of the lone woman bare from weaponry, she brought her hand up to her face. Pulling away the covering that concealed her features, Anitta immediately recognised her as Mia, one of the swan guards and the awareness was returned.

"Anitta!" the figure exclaimed, the blade dropping to her side as the woman moved forward. "I did not expect to see you here!"

"We came up from the sea," Anitta stated, and moving forward to meet the advancing figure, the two women were quick in exchanging their greetings. Turning her head to indicate their direction of approach, the returning woman shouted for Tragen and Darric to join her.

But as they rose over the ridge line and came into view, Mia was swift in replacing her veil, the cover giving her anonymity and hiding away her character in the presence of the men. In further explaining that they had come up through the Caminus from the Western Great Waters, Anitta stressed the urgency they had to speak with the Black Swan and the two women hurriedly turned to the advancing haze which blurred into the north.

"See, Brann is nearing the northern entrances," Anitta said, the certainty of the dust cloud becoming more noticeable as the riders disturbed the dryness of the thick soil, and the very earth itself was thrown into the air. "We must swiftly let the others know."

Leaving Mia to continue her task of observation, Anitta led the men down through the roughcast stairway, which started close by the precipitous drop into the lake. And taking the deeply cut steps carved into the rock of the caverns, they found themselves eventually coming out at its base into the light of the Lower Lake near the western edge of the valley. Following the path around the waterline, they arrived before the doors of the Enclosure, where in making themselves known, the Black Swan came out to greet them in eagerness for their news from the north.

Wrapping her arms around Anitta in welcoming her home and greeting the men with a smile, Olor Ebon led the three away from the doors into the sanctuary. Walking with them further along the lakeside, they came upon a place to sit and stare out over the lagoon, the caverns on the far side of the Lower Lake staring back out of their darkness.

Anitta quickly explained the events that had led them back there, and while the sun shone its light across the white tops of the burnished water, the Black Swan listened intently, her head still as she heard of the betrayal of Brann and his nearby arrival with his men back at the Sleeping Caverns.

"I had put out guards because I had a fear something might happen!" Olor exclaimed as Anitta finished her telling, and turning to the large man who sat alongside her, said, "And the swan wardens are always ready to protect our borders. But, Tragen, you are a warrior and used to the practices and methods of these fighting men. How do you think we should meet this?"

The question came as a surprise to the three who sat there, for the women of the caverns had always seen to their own security and defence. However, as Tragen looked back into the intent dark eyes that stared unwaveringly into his, he saw the need to reconcile their differences. He recognised her wish to lower the barriers set by custom and to include them all in the protection of *Amaunet*.

Looking back across the water, the soldier within came to the fore, and his thinking turned to battle plans used in the past. And while the traps and subterfuges given over to man's domination over man played through his mind, he finally came to a decision.

"I feel an ambush would be our best way to deal with this," he put forward, "for surprise is always best used on the unsuspecting, and that will hopefully give us the edge." His gaze came back to the shoreline where Darric and Anitta sat in a growing state of readiness. Yet unknowing of the terrain within the eastern edge of the Sleeping Caverns, he looked again to Olor and asked, "Would there be a place to set one up within the caverns?"

"They will be coming up through the lower passages," she answered in explanation, knowing the direction the men would have to follow, "and we could make use of our archers to create an ambush there."

She went on to say that on her return with *Amaunet* to the Sleeping Caverns countless days before, she had seen fit to place warden guards within the lower passages and had put the Sleeping Caverns on alert and in readiness for attack, for the outcome for those travelling northwards from the Median Bridge had remained unknown to her. Finally, she concluded that the remaining swan women at the lakeside could be swift in getting themselves ready and would not stop short of their duty.

"That sounds good," Tragen voiced his agreement, "You can prepare your women, and we will all make good use of the lower caverns!"

The conversation was concluded as the Black Swan rose, and even as the sun began to set in the west, she was seen to give her order for the women to arm themselves, and the Lower Lake of the Sleeping Caverns became a hive of activity, the protection of their home given priority over and above their everyday labour.

Anitta had been charged with remaining alongside

Tragen and Darric, for even given approval from the Black Swan, they continued to be men within a woman's domain and would still require surveillance and supervision as they moved around. Knowing, however, the need for action which all three consciously hungered for, she was swift in guiding them away from the activity of the darkening lake.

Leading them through into the tunnels and along the paths that the swan wardens had already taken in their quest to protect themselves, they followed the glow-worm-lit passages and the three took up their position in the entryway to the coldness of the damp caverns which led towards the mouth of the openings in the grasslands.

Around them, the swan wardens had also prepared well and lay in wait unseen in the shadows as the semi-darkness of the caves worked in their favour. The presence of many hidden and interconnecting channels between the main tunnels gave them an advantage over the unwary men, and there in the darkness of their realm, the night passed, and they sat tight within its silence.

***

Outside, Brann had come to a halt, for the last days had seen him urging his men forward through the thickness of the grasslands in the heat of the day and the cold of the night. And as the nearness of the openings to the caverns had been seen to rise up before them in the early evening light, he guided them forward. Arriving in utter exhaustion at the entrance, the need to rest overcame them all.

The men had thrown themselves to the ground just as soon as the horses had been relieved of their saddles and left to their own care amongst the grasses. And each slept the sleep of the bone-weary on the hardness of the turfed lawn, which encircled itself around and in front of the mouth of the gaping darkness.

Early the next morning, they rose somewhat refreshed but with a wariness for the next stage of their course. Leaving the horses to the care of one of the younger men, they reluctantly walked to the back of the raised lawn and entered the confines of the Sleeping Caverns, Brann taking the lead.

"I don't like this, Captain," his second-in-command whispered as they felt the warming sun disappearing from their shoulders and the coldness of the passageway took its place. "This feels like an easy spot for a trap!"

"That is what I am hoping for," Brann abruptly muttered. "I want the women to know of our presence! The quicker they find us, then the quicker we can be returning north with our prize."

"You mean us to get captured?" the man answered in surprise, his voice hushed on his cold breath as he glanced towards his leader.

"Yes," Brann simply said, and quickly looking back, he let the man in on his subterfuge. Smiling slyly, as he saw the idea become recognised and take its place in the mind of his deputy, he turned away and walking forward, harshly shouted out into the dark, the aim being to give away their whereabouts to the swans.

The cold gloom quickly encased the men in its unsociable atmosphere, and the light at their backs, their only escape route back into the grassland, was soon dwindling to a pinpoint before it disappeared altogether. The men felt the weight and growing unease of their confines as the enclosing proximity descended upon them, and their eyes took time to adjust to the dimness.

Eventually, the obscurity cloaked itself around and became clammy, the moisture of the tunnel walls becoming more evident as the low roof gave off its ghostly glow. Around them, the eerie silence occasionally gave way to the sound of the rush of fluttering breeze that coursed up from the grasslands and passed through the chambers higher up into the caverns. Thankfully, the passageway appeared fairly straight with no noticeable shafts or crosscuts leading off, and so progressing slowly, they moved forward, unaware of the eyes that watched their advance.

***

Tragen and Darric had seen fit to reposition themselves close to Anitta, and waiting silently alongside the women in their hidden passages, they had seen out the night.

Tragen could smell the men as they passed, their stale sweat hanging heavily off them, and signalling to Darric with an incline of his head, he slowly moved back up the intersecting tunnel. Guided by the glowing strip of orbs that lit up the middle of the canopy, he made off towards the corner of the large damp chamber where the passageway would lead the men directly into its opening space.

Darric quickly followed, and taking up position on the opposite side of the doorway in the darkness of the shadows, they both waited as Brann and his men unknowingly approached the opening into the higher caves. Behind them, several of the swan wardens had emerged from their unseen tunnels, and now following noiselessly in their wake, they brought up the rear and cut off chance for any escape.

The group eventually reached a junction in the passageway, a shorter channel to their right sloping upwards and leading into what looked like a cavern, while the one leading to the left remained tight, the headroom encroaching even further towards the floor.

Stopping briefly, unknowingly watched by the swan wardens who stood silent in their darkness, they took time to drink from the flasks and whisper their growing disquiet into the gathered gloom.

Finally, Brann made the decision to lead his men to the right, for the breezes appeared more in favour of taking this route, and stepping through into the small passageway, he moved forward into the expanse of the chamber. Here the sweep of the walls disappeared into the shadows, and the soft light above lit only the core of darkness.

Again he let his voice ring out as his men anxiously followed, a fear rising as the reek of mildew and humidity forced its way into their senses. And as the vastness of the unknown depths of the chamber remained concealed, the darkness continued to hide the growing restlessness that gathered around.

Suddenly a complete silence descended, and even their footfall quietened as the soft glow from above dimmed slightly, and the surrounding darkness inched its way inwards. Shouting out again to alert the swans of their presence, Brann led his men into the descending hush, and as the growing shadows cloaked them, they came to a stop within the coldness of the passing air, and here they waited.

Ahead, a glow began to gather over the rising ground, and the shape of the Black Swan appeared gradually out of the gloom, her face covered by her dark veil and the black cloak thrown about her shoulders. Surrounding her, the swan archers, with their arrows already positioned within their bows, fixed the tips of their darts unwavering upon the men before them. While behind in the darkness of the upper passageway leading off to the side, the disappearing breezes eagerly sought their way out into the upper chambers.

"Why have you returned to my caverns?" Olor Ebon declared, her voice ringing out and giving no option for refusal as she stepped out from within the safekeeping of her escort. Approaching the waiting men, the increasing glow above her head lit up and followed her advancing figure.

"I am here at the request of Malian and your daughter Shuma," Brann began his bluff, "for they sent my men and me south many days ago on an urgent errand."

"And what would that errand be?" the voice came back directly, the black lace of the veil moving slowly as the words were spoken into its confines.

"To return yourself and the Icon, which you hold, back into the safety of the north!"

The Black Swan stopped, the light outlining her in its ghostly glimmer as she stood tall before the collection of men, and dropping her head slightly to one side as if pondering on the response, she said, "But why didn't Malian send Tragen on this charge?" Bringing her head forward, her unseen eyes looked upon the treachery she could see growing in the face of the man before her.

"The warrior has been wounded in the overthrow of the king," Brann quickly said, expecting such questioning while continuing to play his deceit. "But all is safe now within the city, and the task has fallen upon me to take you into its security."

"Liar!" a voice suddenly roared out, the echoing word angrily rebounding its way through the dark.

Recognising directly the sound of Tragen's voice, Brann's manner instantly changed as he realised his plan had somehow gone awry. Swiftly knowing that the whole subterfuge and pretence was up, he turned away from the Black Swan and moved to face his men, ordering them to arm themselves as the imposing mass of the warrior appeared out of the shadows.

The fight, however, was over for some of the men before they had a chance to move. Although they initially appeared equal in number to the women, the Black Swan had instantly turned away, and returning to where her archers stood, they were joined by the wardens from out of the hidden passages and the men were outnumbered. And as the Black Swan shouted out her order to defend the caverns, a volley of arrows was immediately loosed. The arrows of the swans were quick in finding their targets, and soon the bodies of the wounded littered the coldness of the damp floor, and those injured beyond aid were soon put out of their misery by the quick stroke of a dagger.

Towards the rear, Tragen struck, and roaring his rage into the confines of the cavern, he tore out of the blackness, slashing and scything his blade at the remaining men who had turned to face his fury.

Darric, however, had swiftly moved through the dark of the shadows to attack from the side and followed by the swans who rushed through from the lower passages, their short blades drawn in support of the two, they cut off any escape route for the men.

Brann remained standing and advancing through his fallen men in a fury, his blade worked to fend off the assault of the swans in his attempt to reach Tragen. On seeing his aim, Darric was quick to sidestep from the clash, and yelling his rage towards the older man, he sped forward through the conflict. Suddenly he found himself with the prospect of coming face to face with Brann, but first he had to deal with an unknown man who stood in his way. As the man brought up his short sword to meet the downstroke, Darric plunged his blade deep under the ribs before removing its bloodied length with one easy stroke. Bypassing the falling figure, he strode to meet the violence of the advancing man.

The two met on the edge of the light, their blades flashing in and out of the shadows as they turned and fought with such ferocity while, around them, the fight took on its own life within the confines. But from across the chamber, Tragen turned to see the blow coming, the sharp blade being brought around low and crosswise as Brann suddenly moved backward to make space for the hit. Shouting his warning, he tore across towards the shadows, the darkness slowing him in his advance.

The slash caught Darric full across the stomach, the edge cutting easily through the cloth before reaching the tightness of the vulnerable skin beneath, where the blade bit down hard. The young man cried out as he dropped to his knees, and his sword fell alongside, clattering to the floor as the glow of the lights cut across its crimson surface.

Tragen was immediately upon Brann as he lofted his blade, ready to cast the final blow, and the warrior took him off guard as he caught him full on from the side. Knocking him hard into the shadows, the two were quick to rise and meet in combat. Facing each other, they brought their weapons forward, and the blades met in an almighty clash as they fought hard, the rage equal in both as the darkness hid their encounter. The violence could only be imagined as the figures moved between the dark and the light, the flash of sword and ring of metal giving evidence of their confrontation.

Finally, the warrior made his move, and catching Brann in a savage cut across his upper arm, his opponent immediately dropped the hand holding the sword, and Tragen played his attack. Catching Brann across the chest and slicing open the shirt, he scored the skin crosswise as the man fell, the feel of the damp cold of the cavern wall at his back, stopping his drop. Knowing he could not escape, he stilled himself in exhaustion, and his head hung down as he fought for breath. But on feeling the cold metal tip of Tragen's blade slide beneath his chin, he lifted his eyes to look up into the dark enraged face.

"I was not expecting you to be here!" he gasped, his breath coming forcefully as he struggled to stand in the overhanging shadow of the huge man.

"I should not *be* here," Tragen snarled back, his voice echoing within the quiet that was growing at their backs. "But for you, I should be heading south. Returning *Naunet* to my people and restoring their lands to a once-known glory."

The whole of Tragen's anger and frustration now became focused on the very tip of his blade, and he slowly advanced it into the man's throat, the point piercing the vulnerable skin as the pressure increased.

"But for you and your greed, I would be many miles from here, and our paths would never have again crossed." He stopped, his eyes catching a glimpse of metal against the white of the man's chest and looking down to where his blade had already made its mark, he saw the token.

The cloth of Brann's shirt lay open, and around the neck, lying across the slashed chest, the talisman given by Serdos could be clearly seen as the blood seeped its way around the silvered edge before slowly trickling through the snake-enclosed disc and down the man's chest. Reaching out in his bitterness to grab it, Tragen pulled hard on the chain and forcefully broke its connection from the man.

"I see you chose your side!" he roared.

Casting the disc to the ground, he let his hand slowly push forward, the tip of the metal finding its mark as the rush of blood poured down Brann's front. The blade was then slowly withdrawn from his throat, and seeing the stream of fluid cascade to the floor, the man's body gradually followed it down and collapsed to the ground at the warrior's feet.

The fight was over, the bodies of the men lying across the dampness of the wet and now blood-soaked cavern floor, and as Tragen rushed quickly back to Darric's side to help his friend, the swans gathered themselves around Olor Ebon and made ready to leave.

The injury of the young man was beyond help, and Tragen, glancing down to where the blood poured forth, could only press his large hands across the gaping wound in an attempt to stem the flow. But feeling the warmth and extent of the thick fluid running between his fingers, he gradually released the pressure and let the life continue its slow weep out.

"Come, my friend," he softly said, "let us leave behind the darkness and look to the light!" Nimbly picking up the body, he followed the Black Swan back up through the upper passageways, and alongside the surviving swans, they carried their injured out of the dark.

The light of the early afternoon was slipping across the waters of the lake when the swan wardens emerged back into its brightness, and around the lake's edge, the armed women dropped their defences as they saw the wardens return. The Sleeping Caverns were now safe, but the cost for the women as they brought out their wounded was counted as the injured were taken to the sick bays, and the severity of each was assessed, and their wounds stitched and dressed as required.

Darric was still alive, though the blood-soaked tunic to his front gave little hope for his survival, and Tragen laid him down on the hard soil of the reed-edged waterside. Placing his folded cloak beneath the white hair, which now appeared tinged with red, he sat down at his side and took up the cooling hand as the breeze blew through the rustling greenery.

"We'll rest here for a while," he said, more to himself than to the mortally injured man at his side, "for the job is done, but we must soon make haste in returning north."

"I fear I shall not be going further with you, Tragen," Darric softly replied, his voice coming out as a whisper as he looked up into the stern face that stared off across the water, "but I am thankful to have learnt from you and feel favoured that we fought alongside." With that, he gently closed his eyes, and moments later, the life of the young man was gone in one last shallow breath and the body that lay at the warrior's side became just a husk stripped of life's essence.

The losing again felt like the grievous loss of his sons, and Tragen's anger and sadness raged through him even as he remained in stillness beside the beauty of the water. Finally, Anitta found him seated beside the lifeless body of the young man, the limp hand still within his grasp. Kneeling at his side, she gently removed the connection which remained between the two, and taking a firm hold of his hand, she pulled him to stand and turned him to face her.

"Come, Tragen," she said, her soft, warm hand taking the place of the dead man's as she walked him away, "you have said your goodbyes, and we must now join the swans in giving thanks for our success."

The body of Darric was left at the water's edge, the arms crossed over the chest with the clothing positioned to cover the severity of his injury.

As Tragen and Anitta joined the women gathered around the waterside in the last of the evening rays, the lake slowly becalmed as a stillness settled itself across its mirrored surface, and the caverns around its rim appeared overly large as they stood duplicated in their inverse reflection. The Black Swan positioned herself at the head of her women, and turning to face out over the water, she raised her arms skywards, showing her face to the heavens and allowed the hush of the evening to cloak her in its serenity.

The goddess *Tefnut* emerged from the middle of the lake, the waters dripping from her crimson-clad body as she rose into the darkening sky. Slowly bringing her hands together before the assembled crowd, she blew gently upon her fingers to release a cloud of luminous droplets which drifted skywards, their little lights glowing brightly against the blackness of the night before they dropped to the water's surface.

Expanding over the water, the lights began to gather at a pace, moving this way and that as they raced onwards before they finally reached the lake's edge and stopped. The brightness clustered towards the area where Darric lay, and here they became stilled before slowly increasing and intensifying, covering over and around his body as the brilliance surged in its force before slowly they rose again as a whole into the darkened sky.

When the glow had gone, receding back across the water, the body of Darric had disappeared, the only image left of his presence being a shallow dip within the folded cloak of the warrior where the dying man had lain his head.

Finally, the goddess too, faded out of sight, the lights collecting around her as the body sank beneath the solid surface of the calm water. As the night-time breezes gently returned to ruffle the edges around the reeds and the swan women of the Sleeping Caverns turned away from their lakeside, Tragen's anger was allowed to slowly subside with the thought that Darric was now at rest alongside the gods.

CHAPTER ELEVEN

In the north, Malian felt a great sadness descend upon him as he awoke in the early hours to the sounds of the stronghold stirring from its slumber. Laying silently within the confines of his bed, a great longing to return home gathered and overwhelmed him in its intensity before it slowly subsided, and he turned over and tried to settle. But unable to sleep, he finally rose, and slowly walking the cold stone floor of his room, he let the dawning light gather around him in his unease, and the darkness slowly banished itself to the corners of the room as he thought on the past few days.

Since that first morning of his awakening, Edgar, the king, had regularly appeared at his bedside, for on hearing that Malian had opened his eyes, Edgar eagerly checked on his well-being and gave his grateful thanks. Passing on his recognition for the part the altar tender played in the overthrow of Serdos and the Brotherhood of *Apep,* he stated that without his presence that day at his inauguration as king, and his transformation by the god *Horus* witnessed by the whole of the city, the release from the grip of the brotherhood would never have been lifted. He placed the whole of the staff of the king's hall at his service and then left the tired man to regain his health.

Malian, therefore, concentrated on his well-being, and in the time he had been recuperating, he received further visits from Edgar. But his main caller was Gallius, who kept him updated and informed of news within the city, and his strength grew noticeably during their visits. However, given the attention that Shuma and Daina also afforded him, he expected little less of himself, and in his goal to fully recover, looked to his own improvement.

Looking around at the pleasing surroundings he came to a halt at the end of the bed and slowly seated himself upon its edge. He knew he must soon be away from this place and returning south. He had been told on his wakening, all that happened since the god *Horus* had appeared at the ceremony, for the spectacle that unfolded before the crowds had gone completely unknown to him as he stood in the trance cast by the god.

The news of the overthrow of Serdos and his brotherhood came as a surprise before becoming blurred somewhat by the telling of Brann's double-crossing. The traitor's race southwards, followed hastily by Tragen, Darric and Anitta, had upset him greatly, and he often lay awake in prayer hoping that *Amaunet* would be safe and still awaiting him in the guardianship of the swans. For beyond, in the valley, he knew his people would still be living in belief of the recovery of their Icon and the return to a life more commonplace and in keeping with its traditions.

Sitting in the growing light, the overpowering feeling of restlessness continued even as the feeling of sadness faded, and he felt ready to make the journey back into the south. The urge to be away from this place alongside that of his increasing vitality gave him great need to meet urgently with Gallius, and on hearing the door open as the attendants arrived to pull back his curtains to the morning light, he was quick to declare his request to speak with the captain. While unknown to him at that moment, Gallius too, had a strong need to speak with him.

***

For many days now, within the confines of the city walls, the feeling of restlessness had continued to grow and had come to the fore in the mind of Gallius. And with his increasing awareness of the rising troubles, the need to remove the final two Icons appeared the only way in which to lessen the grip and ease the tension that remained. As Malian slowly regained his health and strength over the long days and nights, the captain eventually went to see the king, and their talk had taken them late into the night.

Finally, the two walked the colonnade back towards the palace, and again entering the darkness of the crypt, they stood before the forsaken altar of *Apep*, where two statues were all that survived along the ledge of the fallen shrine. Here the silence surrounded them in their solitude as they stood defiantly glaring out into the pitch darkness of the once flame-lit cavern. These two were *Heh* and *Naunet*, and their Icons stood in wait, each seemingly with their own purpose, and as the king looked upon them, his thoughts turned to these remaining statues. Knowing that *Naunet* would eventually be returned to the keep of Tragen, his attention turned to that of *Heh*.

"We must return this one back to Muntani," he said, pointing to the frog-headed statue as its bulbous eyes stared back, the deep green, lit by the light of the torch that stood blazing before it. "But it cannot just be taken there and left!" He looked to Gallius, who stood tall at his side, and the man appeared deep in thought while a heaviness hung off him under the weight of his cloak, and his reply seemed long in coming.

"Yes, it must be returned," Gallius eventually acknowledged, his agreement given as his idea once more presented itself, "and you are right, it cannot just be left." He paused as if waiting for the right time to continue. Turning towards the king, he felt able to put forward his suggestion. "But perhaps the resurgence of the people wishing to reclaim and rebuild their old city could be an opportune moment for us. What do you think?"

The idea came as a complete surprise, and Edgar's immediate thought had gone to Earold, who he knew remained a constant source of upset in Gallius' attention. The man was tenacious in his dream to restore the dilapidated city, but unknown to the king the vision that could be Muntani had itself grown within Gallius. Thinking of the possibilities as the days passed, he could now see a way to reconcile the settling of both issues and bring about a stillness from the public disorder within the high city and return a sense of pride to its people.

"You mean that we should give Earold free rein with his aspirations?" Edgar stated, anxiety and uncertainty noted in his tone as he said the man's name. Muntani was the closest city in the north, and the thought of its sudden regeneration gave a cause for concern which the king felt was justified.

"Yes…and no," Gallius said calmly, sensing the unease and recognising its cause, "but you know the situation with these statues will only be resolved when they leave this place and the quicker they are gone, the better, in my thinking."

He looked to where both Icons glared defiantly out into the surrounding dark before continuing and making his final proposal. "However, by witness of my own eyes, I know the City of Muntani is in such ruin that aid will be required there for many years. So in my opinion, it will be beneficial to station a garrison there. One to help with the rebuild, as well as in keeping the peace."

"That is more to my liking," Edgar slowly replied. Knowing he would not just be handing over the city to Earold, but could continue in office as king and be able to keep a close eye on his nearest neighbour, he let the concern go and looked to *Naunet*. "But what then of this other statue? Do we wait for the return of Tragen?"

"No, I shall be taking that south myself," the captain declared, for his mind had become clear on this action, and the wait for the warrior's return could not, he had judged, be guaranteed. Already he had spoken long with Shuma on the subject, and she had been swift in agreeing with his decision, adding that, in her thinking, their undertaking should not be delayed for overly long.

Edgar gave both of Gallius' plans some thought, but eventually, seeing the reasoning and sense behind each of them, he stretched forward to pick up the cold Icons of *Heh* and *Naunet*, which weighed surprisingly heavy in his hands. Turning away from the now empty, desolate altar, he relinquished both to the captain and handed over the obligation. "Very well, Captain Gallius," he finally said, "I shall leave all of that to you."

The altar of *Apep* and its crypt within the palace were left to silence, the last two statues seeing the light of day after untold time in the dark. As they were brought out, the doors were locked fast behind, the keys taken away to be concealed from the eyes of man, and the story of the brotherhood appeared to come to an end.

However, in the following days, Gallius had to reconcile his plans, and having spoken again with Shuma about travelling south and Earold in regard to the City of Muntani, he now only needed to speak with Malian. On hearing that the altar tender was asking for him, he strode through the king's hall in the early morning and made known the recent events and the undertaking they would soon be making.

***

In the south, the night had been long for Tragen as he slept restlessly beneath the cooling arch of the cloudless night sky, his mind enacting, over and over again, the fight as it played out before his closed eyes.

Rising early the following day, he spent many moments looking out across the lake, which had seemingly returned to its activity, the boats of the swans moving across its surface as they awoke to the day, before finally he lowered his head in farewell to Darric. Walking along the lakeside he went to meet with the Black Swan.

Olor Ebon and Anitta were found sitting outside the dark opening to the Enclosure, the fresh morning sunlight warming them as it radiated its light from the east. The heads of the two women appeared bowed and close in talk and their voices seemed hushed on the stillness of the air.

"I will be returning north immediately," Tragen shouted to them, as he strode along the water's edge, "and I must make ready in great haste."

On hearing his approach, the women were quick to stand and joined him on the gravelled pathway, the taller of the two coming to stand before him as he stopped.

"We knew you would not linger," the Black Swan said wisely, her face remaining uncovered before the man's gaze as he stood over them, "but you will not be travelling alone. Anitta, too, has shown a willingness to return north with you, and I hope you will accept her wish to accompany you."

The warrior looked down into the upturned face of the woman he had travelled alongside, and recognising a growing feeling that he once thought dead to him, smiled and nodded his head in acceptance.

"I shall be glad of her company," he replied, the older woman looking on, glad of the response, "for her skills and guidance along the way have seen a hard journey made just that bit easier, so she is very much welcomed."

"Then I shall leave you to make your plans," Olor

Ebon said, turning away, "and I shall be looking to mine."

The Black Swan left the water's edge where the two remained in the growing light of the morning. As the activity increased around them and across the waters of the Lower Lake, their talk became focused upon their travel back towards the northern city.

"How will we be making the journey?" Anitta straightaway asked, her immediate thought going back to the canoes and their travel up the Western Great Waters that they first made together. "For we need to be quick on our return into the north, and knowing the lands through which we will be passing, we need to ensure our supplies."

"Well, let us first see what Brann has left behind for us," Tragen replied, knowing the rider would have been foolish not to have made his preparations, "for he too would have wanted to be swift in his ride north and he would not have left that to chance."

With that, he and Anitta returned through the lower caverns, the floors of which had been washed down from the blood spilt in the fight. While during the night, the bodies of the dead scouts and their captain had been removed and taken away to the lake's eastern end, where they joined the bones of the long-dead men who had fallen over countless years to the women of the swans.

⁎⁎

The scout tasked to remain behind with the horses in the grasslands before the Sleeping Caverns had slept a cold night in the entranceway. After hearing the initial shouts of his captain fade into the darkness, the man had settled himself into his job, awaiting the return of his comrades. On hearing the sound of approaching movement along the passage, he rose in expectation of seeing Brann, his expression of relief quickly turning to alarm as Tragen appeared out of the shadows. Swiftly arming himself, he stood in readiness for a fight.

"They are all dead, my friend," Tragen straightaway shouted to him, seeing the blade held ready. Fearing nothing from the little man who stood before him, he continued, "And their flesh lies as fodder for the birds. But for you, I shall give a choice."

The warrior came before the man, his own blade still sheathed at his side and his arms crossed before him.

"You can fight me here on this grassy lawn in the light of the morning sun, and your body will surely join those of the others. Or you can accompany us back northwards and aid us as best you can in our travel." He watched as the beady eyes took in the stature of the man standing before him, and the mind of the young fighter thought on his chances. Slowly he lowered his blade, the tip coming to rest on the lawn of the raised platform before he threw it to the ground and raised his hands.

"Good choice," Tragen said. Coming forward, he picked up the weapon and held it out before him, the sharp point coming to rest over the man's heart. "What is your name?"

"Blake," the reply came, the man looking into the dark eyes of Tragen as his own blade was held to his chest.

"Well, Blake," the warrior said, "I shall give you my trust, but know that if I find it wanting, then we shall have this talk again. Now put down your hands."

Lowering the sword, he moved the point away and handed the blade over before turning to look out across the long grassland where the horses' heads had lifted in notice of the voices.

Now his means back north was seen to be guaranteed, and he finished by looking back and saying, "Right,

Blake, in your first effort to assist us, I want you to organise the horses. We shall be back soon and will be straightaway heading off."

***

Trekking back to the upper caverns, Tragen was becoming impatient to take his leave and be on their way. Arriving back at the waterside, they found a number of swans standing next to Olor, and the Black Swan appeared ready in her warm cloak, a pack positioned at her side. Here also, two of her trusted attendants stood ready to accompany her.

"We shall also be coming with you," she declared, indicating the two. "I wish to see my daughter again and know that she is safe. But my friends here would not have me make the trip alone."

"Well, thankfully, we have found horses and supplies left by Brann," Tragen informed her, "and there is enough for all."

But on looking at the women, he noted their long cloaks, and the light clothing, which seemingly wrapped itself around them, and he quickly pointed out, "However, we shall be travelling swift, and there is little room for over-decoration in our dress."

"You will not be held back, Tragen," the Black Swan smiled as she noted the scrutiny. "We are all good riders and know, full well, the harshness that awaits." Nodding her head, the two women pulled to one side their covers, indicating that they were adequately and sensibly clothed beneath their cloaks, and although they wore veils over their faces, they appeared sturdy in their bearing.

"Very good," the warrior said, looking away, "then let us make haste."

The group turned to follow Anitta as the swan woman

led her associates along the water's edge. Tragen, however, had an urgency that he needed to address before they left the Sleeping Caverns, and lagging behind the women, he fell in step beside the Black Swan as she brought up the rear.

"What of the Icon? Where is *Amaunet*?" he quietly asked as he looked to those who strode before him. The life of Darric had been given to ensure its safety, and he needed to know it had not been given in vain.

"She is hidden away," the reply came in a whisper, "safe even from the eyes of the women who guard her. For in my experience, I have come across the obsession of devotion, and the rage and fervour in which it can be manifest, and it seems best not to first place the temptation."

"But what if anything should happen to you?" Tragen anxiously asked. "How would Malian, or anyone else for that matter, know where to find her?"

"This morning, I feel that question needs no answer," she replied as they reached the opening to the passageway, and stopping before entering the darkness, she turned and extended her hand over the water. "For look, even the waters of the Lower Lake appear somewhat brighter, and in my heart, I feel the lifting of a terrible weight. It gives me great belief in a favourable outcome."

The warrior stopped at her side, his gaze taking in the vista across the reed-edged water where Darric now rested. But the feeling the Black Swan described somehow went unnoticed in his own heart, and following Anitta back into the tunnel, they left behind the clear waters of the lake to their stillness.

As the blackness surrounded him and the proximity of the walls closed in once more, Tragen found he could only whisper to himself, "Let us hope that you are right, Olor!"

The party quickly deserted the Sleeping Caverns, the sound of farewells and good wishes of the swans following them along the passages as they left, and once back in the grasslands, Tragen found that Blake had been true to his word. The horses stood packed, saddled and ready for the off, and the group was soon riding back towards the Median Bridge, where beyond its boundary, they would move northwards.

In the north, while Tragen felt the harshness of the lush grasslands beneath his feet and the sun reached its point in the sky, Gallius had been seen to leave Malian and Shuma behind to begin their travel preparations as they sat in the king's hall. Marching through the double doors out of the stronghold, he had straightaway gone to seek Earold.

Finding him again in the market, he made known the decision for the following day and the man was completely overcome, his joy being unbound at the thought of the return to Muntani. But Gallius was quick to bring a seriousness to the situation and aimed to offer his guidance as they hurriedly walked away from the bustle of the marketplace back to the man's house.

"You will need to be taking many food supplies," he advised as they passed the stalls laden with a variety of produce. "Also wood for building and tools for breaking soil," he now considered, not knowing what preparations the man had already made. "For although the stone lies around plentiful along the ground, the dereliction there is probably beyond your imagining, and the hard work needed to begin the regeneration will be backbreaking."

Gallius had said these words on numerous occasions to the eager man but knew Earold would have little idea of the scope of work and commitment needed to rebuild. However, he was pleased to hear the man's reply as they reached the small row of ramshackle buildings on the southeastern wall that he called home. Here on either side, the homes stood unkempt and grubby behind their tiny gardens, their small windows dirty with grime as they looked out into the cobbled lane. But Earold's was tidy enough, and some intention of neatness had been made. Placing his hand on the roughly painted gate, he stopped to face Gallius.

"My thoughts and measures have already taken note of your oft-given advice, Gallius, and for that, I give you thanks," the man said. "But in my reckoning, it will be best if we are only small in number to begin with, for then our needs will be simpler." His face turned quickly away from the captain to his doorway in his longing to give the news to his wife. "I have already chosen those who have the skill, expertise and passion to begin the restoration, and they only await my word." Opening the gate, he moved off the lane and onto his own little pathway.

"Wait for one moment, Earold," Gallius demanded, and taking hold of the man's arm, he pulled him swiftly back through the gate. Bringing his face close to his own, he held the man in position before him as he spoke, "There is more to tell in the rebuild of this city and plenty that is in the dark to you." The tone of the man's voice gave cause to take note of his words. "Your return comes with more than just the restoration of the city buildings of Muntani alone, and now is the time that you must listen well."

He went on to tell of the Icon of *Heh* and its return to the city from whence it came, as stated and demanded by the god *Horus*. And with that, he placed upon Earold the obligation to firstly ensure its safety over and above that of anything else done within those city walls. He stated that the building of a place for the Icon to sit in shelter and security must be swift in its construction as decreed.

Finally, he let the man go and dropped his fists to his side, but Earold stood his ground and stared for many moments straight into his eye before slowly lowering his head in consent. Raising it once again to look upon the captain and seeing that action as giving his agreement, Gallius felt able to play his final card.

"However," he cautiously stated, "the king would not see you take on this burden alone and would like to aid you and your people in their safe return to the city." The stare of Earold became fixed as silence descended upon them, and continuing in its calm, Gallius declared, "With that, he has seen fit to allocate a number of his men for you to use as you will in your undertaking." He explained that he had assigned Captain Nathan and his company to travel with the group and aid them in their relocation, and already a collection of carts were in readiness to transport the people and their goods.

As he spoke, the man standing before him looked deep into his eyes for any sign of deceit or trickery in all that was being said. Finding none and realising that with any dream, the reality could be somewhat different and compromises would need to be made, Earold assuredly gave his agreement. For in the main, his people would be finally reclaiming their lands and could once more take pride in their community, and his dream of returning home would be seen to be achieved. In his thinking, more than likely, the king's men would probably not overstay their welcome and would soon yearn for the fires of their own homes.

"We shall be ready for the morning, Captain Gallius," Earold finally declared, and as he stepped back from the man, he turned instantly away from the rickety gate and rushed inside to instruct his waiting wife.

Later, after the excitement had eased its emotion

somewhat, Earold had gotten down to the fundamentals of their leaving, and having gathered his chosen men to disclose the unbelievable news, he advised them in their immediate preparation for the next day. Then he walked briskly off to the stronghold in a great hurry to meet with Captain Nathan and check on the organising of the carts. Satisfied with the preparations, he finally came home, and sitting with his feet up at the fire, looked around in the quietness of the building that surrounded him.

After leaving Earold, Gallius swiftly left behind the backstreets and walked back to the stronghold in great relief that there had been little questioning around the placement of the troops. On his return to the main hall, he found an eager messenger awaiting him with an order to attend immediately upon the king in the meeting room. Rushing into the apartments at the rear of the stronghold, he found Edgar in the large chamber, Captain Isaac standing at his side. Joining them as they stood at the top of the meeting table, Edgar appeared keen to lead them towards the fireplace to a more sociable setting where the three men positioned themselves before the cold hearth in the ease of the arranged chairs.

"How's it going?" the king keenly asked Gallius as they enjoyed the comfort of the seating. "Will you be ready for the off?"

"All the preparations are underway, sire. I've already spoken with Malian and Shuma, and they are presently organising themselves," he established. "And Captain Nathan and his men have been instructed to stand prepared in the arena. While just this last moment, I've returned from notifying the man Earold. So now," he went on, glancing across towards where the king sat in his chair, his head placed against the soft cushioning of the backrest, "I only need to look to myself. But we will be set for leaving tomorrow," he confirmed.

"Good," Edgar said, coming forward in his chair and staring into the empty fire grate where a number of charred logs had left their pitiful remains, "and the city here should soon be feeling the lighter with the removal of these last two Icons." He stood, and turning to face the men, his mind went to their other dilemma as he looked at the officers before him. "But how goes it with the people? Will we be seeing an exodus from the city streets?"

"No, not at this moment," Gallius was quick to advise him. "Earold has informed me he is only taking those deemed of use in this early time, and I feel that your men may well outnumber them in the first."

"Well, that may be for the best in these initial days," Edgar conceded, his mind returning to the Icons and his awareness of the urgent need to remove the last two statues, "for perhaps the man may regret his decision once he sees for himself the task ahead and possibly be tempted back to the shelter of these walls once the reality is made known."

"I think that to be hardly likely, given his zeal," Gallius declared, looking intently at the king as he stood before him. "And in all honesty, we know we need him to succeed, and in placing of the troops, they should clearly help in that fulfilment. The Icon of *Heh* must be taken back to its entrusted city just as surely as the others must be restored to their own."

The king dropped his head in thought, and looking to the floor where the rug beneath his feet lay pockmarked from the many red-hot embers past spat out from the fire, his mind went straightaway back to the blazing bonfires in the northern woods. The smell of burning flesh again surrounded him in its severity, and he knew he would never be free from the recall.

Bringing his focus back to the here and now, he stared

at the edges of the frayed mat, the coldness of the grey flagstone floor disappearing off under the seating towards the far corners, and he purposely tore his thoughts away from the past traumatic days and returned to the moment.

"Well, we shall have to leave it at that for now," he finally said, knowing that Gallius could do little more.

Raising his head, he appeared to come around to the reason for his calling of the meeting between himself and the two men. First, turning to where Isaac remained upright and honest in his seat, he fixed his gaze upon the man before him.

"Well, now, Captain," he began, his voice returning to its authority, "you have certainly become a great asset to this city, and in my recent advance to king, I feel a new position would be best awarded and in keeping for your actions." He remained looking down to where Isaac had come slightly forward and where a sudden look of expectation crossed the darkness of the man's face. "And I think the office of Chief Captain would sit well with you. For with the recent increase in the number of your rank, I need a steady hand to keep control."

Turning, he reached up to the mantel over the fireplace, and bringing down a short sword that had been resting along the shadowed ledge, he instructed the captain to stand as he brought the piece forward. Isaac was quick to rise to his feet, stepping away from the chair as he rose tall before the king, and as Edgar extended the blade towards him, the weapon was quickly turned, and the hilt presented forward.

"In keeping with your new office, Chief Captain Isaac," Edgar said, as he handed across the blade sheathed within its heavy leather scabbard, its highly ornate silver-topped handle decorated with various intertwining branches protruding out of the confines. Removing the metal dagger from its cover, Isaac extended the blade upwards to look upon its simplicity where the clean lines of the metal shaft met the hilt, and a glint of light from the high windows caught the sharpness of its neatened edge.

"I feel favoured to be given the privilege of being first to this calling," Isaac replied, his eyes leaving the glare of the burnished metal and meeting those of his king. Replacing the blade within its casing, he made known his promise of duty to Edgar. "And I shall do my best to justify the honour and trust given to me on this day, sire." He stepped back before bowing his head and returning to sit alongside Gallius where the captain remained, he placed the scabbard at his side and waited in anticipation in the silence that had descended.

Finally, Edgar spoke again, his voice echoing into the vastness of the room. "Well, that is the first dealt with, but I also have a need to look to the duty of warden, for on my becoming king, the position has made itself available. I can think of none better than yourself, Gallius, to take over from me." He walked away from the cold hearth towards where the captain remained in silence, staring up towards his king, for the words caught him completely off guard, and he appeared stunned by the prospect of his promotion.

"So, Gallius, how would that suit you? For I should like to offer you the position of Warden of the City and all the concerns and duties that office entails." Looking at where the man sat, taking in his words, and knowing that a refusal could not be forthcoming on his request, he ended, "I know that first, you will need to go south, for you have unfinished work there. But on your return, it would please me if you would take up the position full-time in its commission and leave behind the service of the guard."

Gallius was given little time to think, and on the

king's request for him to rise from his seat, he saw Edgar removing the ring that had sat his finger for many years. Passing it over to the captain, he bestowed the authority of the city upon Gallius, and with that, his long captaincy within the guard became a feature of the past.

King Edgar's delegation of duties came to an end, and removing the three goblets that Jakob had seen fit to place in readiness to one side of the hearth, he presented the two standing men each with a brimming cup of wine, and they drank together in celebration of their new appointments.

Seating themselves once more before the fireplace, they talked of the past few days within the city walls. However, the talk quickly turned to the topic of Gallius' forthcoming travel to Muntani and his journey beyond into the south, unknowing of what lay ahead. And he spoke of his concerns in regard to the two who would accompany him along the way.

"Be assured," he recognised, "I have no doubt or misgiving with Shuma if it comes to a fight," he explained, knowing well the skills with blade and bow that the wise woman possessed, "but Malian is no warrior and his strength remains a concern to me after so long a time in his trance." His gaze dropped to the half-empty cup, and he slowly swirled the remaining liquid around as he thought on his last sighting of the altar tender.

"I have four good men I could recommend to accompany you," Isaac was quick to promise, "all known to me from past merit and excellent scouts with fine fighting skills if you feel a need to take some troops along with you." He finished his drink to the bottom, and turning to place his empty cup along the mantel, made ready to leave before continuing, "Just let me know, and I can have them fit for the morning!"

"I had already been thinking along the same lines,

Isaac," Gallius quickly replied as the chief captain turned back, "and four scouts would seem adequate in number both in maintaining our quickness in speed southwards and also for their expertise in combat. For after the City of the Fosse, we shall be going into unsure territory as we move forward, and the smaller our outfit, the better."

Gallius further explained that his main fear in journeying beyond the city on the Eastern Great Waters was meeting Brann and his men returning north. There they would be in the vastness of the lower northern lands, and any action was more likely to be ambush in nature rather than full on. The battle skills and techniques of the scouts offered by Isaac would, therefore, be of a necessity and indeed called upon to play their part under those circumstances.

The newly appointed warden wandered away from the fireplace in thought before slowly coming back to where the men remained. Finally lifting his half-empty cup to the chief captain, he said, "I shall leave it to you to ensure their readiness for the morning then, Isaac!" Draining the cup of its bitter contents, Gallius turned from his king and went to take his leave alongside Isaac.

But as the two men made ready to depart, Edgar asked Gallius to remain, and walking back over to the hearth, he seated himself and turned to watch as the heavy double doors into the hallway closed softly behind the chief captain. The room turned to quietness as the warden returned to stand before his king.

"There is something further we need to discuss before you leave tomorrow, Gallius," Edgar finally spoke out, his voice taking on a slightly hesitant quality as he looked directly at the older man. Rising, he quickly continued, "For I think you know how I feel about your daughter, and I should like to formally ask if I could take Daina in marriage and make her queen at my side?"

The request did not come unexpectedly to Gallius, although Edgar noted a look that fleetingly crossed the warden's face, and he was anxious to add, "Know that I have not made you city warden because of your daughter, Gallius. No, that position has been granted because of your loyalty to my people and me. And should you have refused my offer today, then I would still be asking the same question of you at this moment."

Edgar went on to explain his growing love for Daina and his wish to make her his wife, and Gallius heard in his voice the passion and desire that he once held deep within his own heart. Given the love known and shared in the past, he knew his daughter would be happy in the union with the man who stood before him.

"I would never dictate the course of my daughter's future," he was happy to disclose, looking to where Edgar remained awaiting his reply, "and if Daina's heart is agreeable to the match, then it is not for me to stand in her way."

"Daina and I have already spoken long on the subject," Edgar informed, a smile crossing his lips as his mind went over the many times they had talked, "but she feels that in my asking, and your giving blessing, it would be more in keeping to custom."

"Well, in that then, my blessing is given," the warden said, "and I wish you both a long and prosperous life together." Gallius came forward, his arm extended in approval of the union, and the two joined hands at the fireside.

The king then guided the warden towards the dining room, where Daina had sat long in wait and anticipation alongside the length of the table. However, on seeing the two come together through the adjoining door, all her worries and doubts suddenly fell away. Rushing forward, she first embraced her father before her arms found

Edgar, and turning, she led them towards where a modest feast awaited them in celebration.

The three sat along the bench, the two men seated on either side of the woman, while Jakob purposefully and eagerly waited on his king and future queen, and the warden enjoyed the company of his daughter and her prospective husband, knowing that in the morning, he would be saying farewell.

Time passed quickly in the company of the two younger people, but finally, Gallius could delay no longer and rose purposefully as the afternoon moved on and the urgency for him to prepare himself for the following day took over. Standing at the table's side, he bent to kiss his daughter on the cheek before turning to Edgar.

"I know she will be safe in your care, sire," he acknowledged as he raised his glass to the couple who sat before him. Finishing his wine to the last, he placed the cup carefully back beside his empty plate before turning away and leaving behind the remains of the occasion.

Returning hurriedly to his rooms, Gallius began his preparation for the coming morning, his main concern being the two statues that had been handed over by the king and which had since been wrapped away out of sight in the saddle bags that stood ready by the doorway. He knew that *Heh* would soon be handed over and left in charge of Earold in the city on the lesser steppes, and with that, he felt an end to the worry and concern for that Icon. But with *Naunet*, the future remained less sure, and the coming days could see their expectations change, with plans having to be rethought as each one passed.

In Gallius' mind, it now all came down to Tragen, Darric and Anitta and how they had fared in the south. If they had been able to stop Brann and his men and *Amaunet* remained safe within the charge of the swans in their Sleeping Caverns, then they themselves would be swift in returning north. And they should meet with them as their journey southwards progressed, and the reunion would be favourable in its making.

However, if things had not gone well and Brann himself was heading north with the Icon, then there would be further bloodshed. For unknowingly to those in the south, time had moved on, and the outcome in the north had already played out to its end, and for the returning traitor, his journey back would be in vain.

Sitting himself down on the bed, he suddenly felt a great need to speak with Shuma as he stared down at the warden's ring that sat upon his finger. But he knew that she would be absent from his side that night, her attentions given over to her own and Malian's readiness for the morning.

Later with the thought of her in his mind and the vision of his daughter seated happily beside her future husband, the darkness of night and the languor of the late evening was not long in making itself known, and the warden slept.

***

The following day was quick in arriving, and Gallius rose early to ensure the readiness of the groups he would be leading south. On entering the main hall in the stronghold, his packs carried light by his side, he found Malian and Shuma had already beaten him to the start and stood ready at the open doors. The two were packed, and an eagerness to be away could be seen in their faces as they turned to meet his look of surprise.

"Welcome, Warden," Malian was quick in his greeting as he saw the tall figure appear out of the gloom, "Shuma has told me your good news, and I give my congratulations on your promotion."

"News travels fast," Gallius immediately replied, and smiling as he came forward, he kissed Shuma briefly on the cheek before his attention went to where the altar tender sat watching their greeting, "and you are certainly looking up for the travel, Malian."

"I am ready for the off, Gallius," came the confident reply. However, a certain frailty could still be heard in the tone of voice, and Gallius instantly looked to Shuma as she came to stand at the older man's side. Returning his smile, she gave a reassuring nod, and placing her hand upon the seated man's shoulder in support, the two looked up positively at the warden to confirm their determination, and Gallius had to concede.

"Well, if you are both ready, let us be making the most of the day!"

The three were quick to make their way down the stronghold steps and walked through to the arena where their horses waited. Here they were quick to offload their bags and bundles and take a view of their travel companions. Alongside, in the openness of the square, the troops of Nathan's men stood assembled in their ranks.

A steady trickle of Earold's followers had also begun to gather, and packs and basic fixtures had already found a place alongside boxes of tools on the horse-drawn carts that sat in the cool early light of the morning.

Eventually, as the sun continued its slow rise amongst the surrounding trees, the bustle of activity died down, for the carts were fully laden, and no more could be piled aboard the creaking wagons. Excess packs were lofted on the shoulders of the men while their womenfolk held bundles before them and the children carried what they could. Finally, the morning's silence slowly fell across the arena, and all waited in anticipation.

The whole of the assembly was now under Gallius' discipline, and he became brisk in his manner and authority to move along the collection of wagons with its following crowd to the city gates. Here in anticipation of their departure, besides the opening into the cool shadows that filled out the woodlands beyond, they found King Edgar and Daina in wait. Opposite them, alongside the gateway to the eastern lanes, four scouts from Isaac's troop had also gathered. Standing ready beside their mounts to join Gallius and ride alongside the Warden of the City, they were quick to mount upon seeing the arrival of their leader and fell in place before the troops of Captain Nathan.

Gallius, Malian and Shuma then took their leave, coming to stand before Edgar to say their farewells. And Malian, looking at the crowd gathered before the stable buildings in the courtyard, extended his hand to the king in his departure. Knowing he would never again set foot within the walls of this high city, he felt overcome with the occasion.

"My thanks for your care and hospitality, King Edgar," he said solemnly, his voice somewhat strained as he took the firm hand held out towards him. Bowing his head in respect, he felt he could say little more at that moment, and words appeared to be beyond him.

"My thanks clearly go to you, Malian," came the immediate reply as Edgar stepped closer towards the older man, and taking hold of both hands, he held them tight and stared honestly into the altar tender's eyes. "I give my thanks, Malian, mine and also those of my people who have seen your actions. You have released this city from the grasp and evilness of the brotherhood, and their intent to cause chaos has been stopped forever. Without you, we should all possibly cease to exist, so our thanks are surely poor in respect of the deeds you have done."

"For that, I feel we must surely thank the gods," Malian maintained, his eyes staring back into the honesty of the young man's face as he remained holding his hands. "They were the ones who showed me the way and through me did their work, and for the moment, we still have that to finish and must be fleet in returning all of the Icons back to their homes."

"In that charge, then, I shall not keep you from your duty, Malian. But know that with you, I send my wishes for your speedy homecoming and an end to your uncertainty." The two released their hold, and turning away from the altar tender, Edgar looked to Shuma, where he smiled and hugged her. Wishing her well for a safe journey, his gaze took in the man who stood at her side.

"Be swift in your actions, Gallius," the king advised, looking to the warden as they shook hands, "for this city will watch for your safe homecoming, and I especially will be eager for your return." Stepping back, he took hold of Daina's hand, and bringing it up to where his warm breath hit the cold of the morning breeze, he kissed the long fingers, which had become chilled, before allowing the hand to drop.

Daina instantly rushed forward, and wrapping her arms around her father, she wished him well as she grasped him tight, the feel of her arms and the sound of her voice close to his ear held long in his memory. Holding her away from him, he stared for many moments into her face before his hands gently let go, and turning, he marched back to his horse.

Gallius mounted, and leading off down the slope from the city gates, he bid a farewell to the city for that moment, and the darkness beneath the northern woodlands gathered around as they moved slowly forward. Later that day, the ridge between the lesser and higher steppes was reached, and the dip of the evening sun in the west found the wagons camped within the edge of the grass plains.

Behind them in the forest of the higher steppes, in the king's City of the High Places, the power of the Icons slowly began to fade as the last statues were finally carried away beneath the gates, and the streets and houses within the boundary walls become quietened in their restlessness as the departure home began for the people of Muntani.

***

In the north and the south, the two groups had now set off on their journeys, unknowing of the events that had occurred beyond their sights, and as the group in the south travelled within the grasslands back towards the Median Bridge heading north, Gallius had already arrived at the city gates of Muntani. Here at the broken down walls of the ruined city, he quickly left the troop of king's men in the charge of Captain Nathan.

Earold and his first arrival of eager followers had finally returned to the place they called home, and the Icon of *Heh* was escorted back through the ruined streets of its previous known domain. A lightness had then flooded across the decay and destruction while the shining rays of its brilliance lit up the grassy plains of the lesser steppes beyond, before gradually it disappeared into the distance where the flattened land led off into the east.

Gallius, Shuma and Malian were then free to head further southwards carrying *Naunet*, and as the four scouts followed close behind, they descended towards the lower ranges. Here the plains ended, and the mountains collected around as the light in the city at their back faded into the horizon, and a stillness cloaked them as dusk descended.

CHAPTER TWELVE

The City of the Fosse appeared as dusk began to fall across the lower northern lands. And as the bend of the canyon guided the tired group from the south around its smooth contours, the swiftly flowing river turned towards the city, and the vast levelness of the ground came into view as the gates stood off in the distance. Here the rocks and stumps of dried palm trees littered the ground and began to slow their progress as the darkness gathered, and the group suddenly found themselves hungry and eager for rest.

Although Tragen, Anitta and Blake had all travelled within this region before and knew its scope, the area was unfamiliar to Olor Ebon and her companions, and the uncounted hard days of the journey from the Median Bridge were beginning to make known their cost to the swans, and the women soon tired. Moving forward, the horses began to stumble their way through the gloom, and as Blake brought up the rear leading the pack animals, Tragen knew he would soon be stopping for the night.

On seeing the light of the burning lamps blazing out on either side of the tall palms gracing the gates of the far-off city, Tragen came to an abrupt halt, disturbed at their sight, and dismounted to stand beside his horse alongside the noise of the water. Previously the city on the water's edge had stood dark within its landscape, and that alone had given its concern, but now the lights at the gates appeared even more worrying. For they implied occupation, but by who remained an uncertainty, and Tragen stared towards them in some hope of understanding as they lit up the darkness.

"I'll go and take a look," Anitta volunteered, knowing Tragen was undecided of his next move, "for I feel we need to know what has happened here, and I already know the lie of the city," she reasoned. "But let's first get closer, and we can make better judgement."

The group dismounted amongst the rubble of the barren land, and navigating the horses towards the city lights and keeping the flowing water at their left, they made gradual progress across the plain as night fell upon them. Finally reaching a nearer point, Tragen brought them to a halt, and Anitta sped off into the shadows.

Seeing that the open gateway was unguarded, the swan woman still felt a need to keep herself unseen, and hugging the city walls, she slipped through the gaping entrance. Staying within the shade, she moved forward until she could stand beside the palm-lined waterway which cut the city in two.

Around her, much seemed as previous, for the streets and walkways were seemingly empty of people, but the lights that hung from the underside of the roofs of the galleried colonnades now lit up the pavements beneath. The doors beyond, which Anitta remembered as being boarded over, had now been released from their obstructions and appeared freshly painted. The whole of the city felt lighter, and a sweeter smell filled the air, for the decay and discarded debris seen when she was last here had been swept aside.

While the sound of the flowing river coursed strongly in its waterway between the two banks, the woman stood briefly in uncertainty of what to do next until a name came to mind.

Leaving behind the walkways, she quickly made her way to the north bank across the plaza, and finding again the streets of the workers, she headed down towards the sixth door in the block of little cottages. Here some of the doorways still remained boarded, but stopping before the entrance on the right, she knocked hesitantly and stepped away as she heard noise within.

"Who is it?" came a voice.

"Doctor Ansan, is that you?" she whispered, coming forward. "It's Anitta, I was here with my friends some time ago, and you were kind enough to offer your hospitality to us. Can you let me in?"

The door was suddenly jerked open, and the doctor, who she remembered as being stooped and squinting, stood tall before her, the certainty in his returning sight giving him back his dignity. Raising his lamp, he took note of the woman before him, the scarred face now being seen that had once been veiled by his own blindness. Quickly stepping aside, he motioned her in before softly closing the door.

"Welcome, Anitta!" the greeting came as the man looked shocked and surprised at her arrival. "You have turned up at a most fortunate time, for the gods have smiled on us since we last met. My sight and that of my wife and children slowly return. And it is all thanks to the restoration of *Kauket.*"

He placed the lamp upon the table where its light lit the small room, and Anitta noted the change to the drabness that had, in her remembering, cloaked the space. Now, the smell of freshly picked flowers infused the air, and the glow of a fire warmed the interior.

Ansan went on to explain the days that had passed in the city since the arrival of the new king's troops from the north. For with them, they had brought back the Icon, and it had been once more placed back within its shrine, and the city began its slow resurrection on her homecoming.

The troops were also charged with cleaning up the city, and the bodies of the long dead were removed from behind their boarded doors, their remains buried with some dignity. The homes and the areas around the plazas had finally been wiped clean of the dirt, and the stench of death that had descended was washed away and replaced by a feeling of hope.

"It's taking time with people's sight," he ended, "but each day sees improvement, and it will just be a matter of time for that to come right for those of us who remain."

Anitta told of her travelling companions, and leaving aside events in the south, recounted their journey back towards the City of the High Places and the need for news from the north.

"Come then," Ansan finally said. Grabbing his coat, he opened the door to the cool night. "You must speak with Captain Brook."

Leading Anitta out into the darkening street, he took her back towards the waterway, and walking in the company of the doctor up to the city gates, she crossed back over the plaza. Ansan eventually led her down to where the captain and his men had made their station in the buildings alongside the southern boundary wall, and finding the captain at rest for the night, the doctor was quick to wake him. Presenting Anitta as a friend from the south who wished to talk, he left, bidding the two goodnight with the hope of speaking again with the woman in the morning.

Brook, wrapping his cloak around his shoulders, seated himself beside the fireplace where his long sword stood upright, sheathed in the shadow of the wooden surround. Watching the swan as she sat carefully before the dying embers, he looked intently at her damaged face. But, with no concern for his stare, the woman swiftly introduced herself as a friend of Gallius, knowing that if the captain came from the city in the north, he should certainly know that name. And the giving of it should provide some assurance of her own identity and hopefully some promise towards her safety.

"Yes, I know Captain Gallius," Brook slowly acknowledged, "and he told me I may expect a visit by a group travelling up from the south!" Bringing the cloak up around his throat, he made himself warm as the chill night gathered.

Remembering the time before he had left the City of the High Places in the north bearing *Kauket*, he recalled that Gallius had taken him to one side. There he had been told by the captain that two groups of riders had fled south, one led by Brann, the other by a man named Tragen in his pursuit, and there was the expectation of the return northwards of one or other of them.

Now leaning forward, he stared intently into Anitta's eyes before finishing, "But he also gave warning that they could be either of two parties, one to be trusted, the other not. So," he questioned, glaring harshly at the tired woman, "which one are you?"

Anitta gave her account of those who trekked north with her and mentioned Tragen by name, but for the present, she remained silent on their mission at the Sleeping Caverns.

However, on hearing her tale, the captain was reassured by her story and was as equally brief in his telling of the events prior to leaving the city in the north. He did, however, give news of the old king's death and the rise of Prince Edgar to king, and he spoke briefly on the overthrow of Serdos and the beginning of the return of the Icons.

Seeing the sudden eagerness in the woman's face at their mention and her impatience to rise, he quickly brought the conversation to an end.

"Go now, and bring your friends into the warmth," he instructed, and placing more wood upon the hot ash within the fireplace, he watched as the flames gradually caught and the brightness lit up the room, before slowly rising, he went to gather his men.

Anitta was swift in exiting the city gates and returned to the group as they sat unknowingly and cold within the darkness of the scrubby landscape. Giving account of her findings within the city walls she went on to tell the astonishing news from the north.

As her report came to its end and the silence once more gathered, Tragen became quietened on his hearing mention of the Icons. In knowing of the return of *Kauket* back to the City of the Fosse, his thoughts had gone directly to *Naunet*, and as the darkness hid his face from those who sat close by, the stillness of his breathing gave little indication of the confusion gathering in his mind. Suddenly he rose, and taking up his reins, the warrior set off towards the gates, and the others hastened to fall in behind.

Approaching the city, they could see Captain Brook and a number of his men awaiting them under the glare of the lights from their torches. The men appeared armed, their short swords sheathed at their sides. But as Tragen and the weary figures of the tired riders slowly appeared out of the darkness, the flickering brands were held aloft and the travellers greeted with hospitality as they stumbled forward.

"Welcome," Captain Brook immediately said, stepping ahead of his men as he saw the bulky figure of the warrior making its way across the uneven ground, "welcome to the Fosse, Tragen."

The two met under the gateway of the old city, the twin tall palm trees reaching high above their heads, casting their waving shadows out into the dark. And as Tragen came to a stop before Brook, he was quick to extend his hand and make known his demand and urgency for news.

"What has been happening in the north, Captain?" he

straightaway requested, and grasping hard the man's hand, his tiredness seemingly left him, and an intense need took its place. "Anitta says you have spoken about Serdos and his downfall," he quickly continued, "and also that of his followers, and I urgently need to know your account of the past days!"

"Well, let us first get into the warmth, friend," Brook said, hearing the need in the man's voice. Turning to his troops, he gave order for them to aid the visitors with their horses while he led the group through into the city. As they moved down the southern wall to the buildings claimed as a garrison, the night was left behind as they entered under the overhang of the colonnade.

Seating himself back in his office, Brook watched as the travellers put down their packs at the door before moving towards the warmth of the blaze, where the veiled women were quick to stretch out their cold hands to its glow. Looking up to where Tragen remained anxious in his wait before him, he began to talk.

"Serdos and his brotherhood are all gone!" he declared, seeing the duty he had to tell his tale. "And I was there to bear witness, Tragen. I was there when the bonfires were lit under the feet of the traitors." His mind quickly went back to the clearing in the forest, and the smell of the burning wood and the shriek of the men as their flesh seared in the increasing flames came vividly back to mind. "When the cries of the brotherhood turned to screams, I stood and looked upon their agony, and being given command to add more fuel to the fires, I did my duty as did others, and we heaped the timber high!"

Tragen had gone quiet while Brook spoke, but there was no missing his relief and satisfaction in hearing of the timely end to Serdos and his men. Without them, and their desire to gather together the Icons, Tragen's family and the whole of his city would still be alive and prosperous and not just a memory. With that, the warrior had little sympathy for the way they had met their end, his only regret being that he had not been there in witness.

"Now, what of the Icons?" he pressed as the man stopped in his tale, and the room once more became quietened around the tiredness of the travellers.

"To my knowledge, all have been returned," came the quick reply, "or are being returned." Noting suddenly the fatigue that fell across Tragen's face, Brook finished by saying, "But let us speak again in the morning. You all look in need of rest, and my own bed cools in the lateness of the hour."

"No!" Tragen demanded, his face darkening in annoyance as a growing need for further clarity made itself known. "I have a great wish for you to tell me all that you know of recent events in the north." Looking around to those who stood close by, he added, "And I have need to know how my other friends fare. Only then will I be able to rest myself."

The captain could see a long night ahead, but noting the exhaustion that hung off the wearied bodies standing either side of the large man, he indicated to them and said, "Well, I think we should at least let your companions find some rest while we continue our exchange." Calling forward his second-in-command, he instructed that the group be found beds within the station's upper rooms, and the office of the guard gradually quietened as the last were led out and the door closed behind.

The two were left before the fire, and Captain Brook insisted that Tragen should sit before he would talk any further, and the large man took off his cloak before placing himself down in the comfort of the chair opposite. Stretching his long legs towards the hearth he felt the warmth slowly replace the cold.

Brook told further of the news from the north, starting with the death of King Dedrick, before moving on to the day of Edgar's inauguration. There in his own witnessing, he had seen the splendour of the appearance of the god *Horus* who in his whole embodiment had culminated around the small figure of the man Malian as he stood before the city's throne. From here, he went on, the great god had appointed his task upon the new king to return all of the Icons to their cities, but first, he had dealt harshly with the Brotherhood of the Snake.

Before the gathered crowd of the city's people, he had placed his judgement upon High Priest Serdos and his followers after their condemnation by their own god *Apep*, and this, Brook continued, had finished with their taking away and eventual fiery end in the clearing of the northern woods.

In closing his report, he came to the message that Gallius had given him and which was to be passed on only if he should meet up with the warrior. This was that he, Gallius, was waiting for the altar tender to gain his strength before they left the north carrying with them the Icon from Tragen's city. They would head for the Sleeping Caverns, and this message had been left in the hope of their encounter happening either out on the road as they journeyed southwards or else here at the city on the water.

Finally, sitting back from the heat of the fire, Captain Brook, having given all he knew, finished in his telling and looked to where the large man sat in his silence. However, listening intently as the captain spoke, Tragen still felt little relief, and he remained long in thought as the realisation that *Naunet* was safe made itself known. Yet until he held her in his own hands and knew she was secure, he felt unable to make any plans for a journey home.

"But what if it should be Brann sitting here in my place?" he suddenly pressed after that thought had come to mind. For he needed to know if Gallius had thought the same and made plans for such an event. "Did Gallius give instruction for that?"

"Yes," Brook slowly nodded. "I was told that if that was how it had played out in the south, then I was to detain him and his men if we should meet or he should enter the city. But if they passed us by in the dark of the night or they got away, then I should not give chase but continue my duty here and leave the fight to others."

The light was appearing in the sky when Brook had eventually finished, for Tragen asked again for every detail to be told of the days prior to the captain and his men leaving the city. And in some points, he needed to hear the telling twice over, especially in regard to the Icons, and more specifically in that of *Naunet* before he felt satisfied in his mind of her safety, and he could at last feel some ease.

Looking into the flaming fire, he suddenly felt the long days and nights slowly drop their weariness over him, and complete exhaustion took hold. Brook saw that he had fallen asleep in his fatigue, his dark head reclining back against the edge of the seat, and placing another log within the depths of the blaze, he rose to find his bed and left the man to rest.

***

The next day, Anitta was early to leave her room with the promise of seeing Ansan again, but first, she felt a need to witness more of the city. Walking across its breadth in the light of the fresh morning, she saw the reawakening from the darkness that had cast its ruin within these walls.

There were now people seemingly about their daily business, and along the plazas and paved walkways there was a neatness and freedom from the blemish of litter she had seen previously. Crossing the main bridge from south to north she wandered along the paths as they led beside the rushing water.

Following the flow downwards, she eventually left behind the city and stepped into where the stretch of river flooded out into rivulets of intertwining canals. Here the creeks and ditches crisscrossed the delta of the Fosse. Racing on, they poured over the cliffs, and the waters thundered down into the Eastern Great Waters, moving ever west to east. The morning was bright, yet the murkiness on the horizon clouded the far distance while closer along the cliff edge, the teeming waters threw up their spray and a rainbow of colour was caught within its haze as the rays were captured and scattered by the mist.

As the brightness increased in the east, she dropped her eyes from the spectacle, and turning away, left behind the views across the waters and returned to the city. Arriving back at the street where the doctor lived, she found some of Brook's troops had already torn down the last of the boarded doors and were swiftly bringing out the desiccated remains of Ansan's nearby neighbours.

The doctor stood watching from his doorway, his head bowed in respect as the men passed by carrying the covered bones of known friends, and once again, he appeared stooped in his posture as he leant against the wood, his eyes following the stretchers as they moved up towards the main street.

"Such a tragedy has happened on our doorstep," he called out to Anitta as he saw her approaching from the opposite direction to the troops, "and for want of sight it could not be brought to a halt!" Stepping onto the pavement, he walked to meet the woman as she moved closer, and on reaching her, said, "Come inside, Anitta, and again meet my family."

The swan woman spent the remainder of the morning with Ansan and his family. And his wife Mari, who had previously hidden herself away out of sight, now seemed happy to meet and make the visitor welcome as her children played around.

While the doctor sat and told Anitta of the good fortune that had come upon them, he explained that with the sudden appearance of the king's troops and the return of *Kauket*, there had begun a recovery within the city. He made clear that hope had been given to the people who remained, for her arrival had seen a turning back of the darkness that had crept into every home, and lightness was once again felt within the city walls.

"We return to some normality," he eventually said, as he watched his wife move around the room, her sandy hair brushed back from her face as she looked to where two of the young boys sat upon the bench, "but so many have gone and those that remain, recover slowly." The doctor's voice held great regret and dissatisfaction in his inability to aid and assist those around him, and he finished by saying, "I feel that progress may still be long in its making."

"But you will continue to see progress, Ansan," Anitta said, her hand reaching out to touch the edge of the man's jacket in encouragement, "and men of your kind and skill will once more be called upon in their capacity to heal, and the city will be thankful for your ability." Smiling, she hoped that her intent to support and reassure the man had been taken as it was meant in its giving.

As the morning filled with the noise of the children, Anitta too, finally found some rest and taking comfort in the company of the family, she let the worries of the past days fade.

***

Tragen slept long into the day, but on waking stiff and uncomfortable in the chair where he had been left for the past hours, he found that Anitta had returned to the troop's station and now sat opposite with an eagerness to talk. Passing on her discoveries found in the lightness of the day, she busied herself in making the warrior a drink as she told of her recent findings.

"The city is slowly recovering," she said, watching as the man cautiously sat himself up from his rest, "but for the everyday people, it's taking its time. I fear that for some, there may never be a complete regaining of their full sight."

Handing over the warm cup, she watched as the warrior hurriedly finished down his drink in his great thirst. "But I feel this surely indicates some promise for each of the cities in the return of their Icon, and that must give you a reassurance."

Hearing this, Tragen felt able to relax a little, and having listened to the account from the north and knowing that in return of the Icons to their given homes there would be seen some recovery, it gave further hope for his own people. Now though, he could only rest, and the group would take the remainder of the day to recover from their travels.

The Black Swan and her companions chose to remain in their rooms after a brief walk about the city while Blake was reunited with men of the guard that he already knew.

Later, Anitta escorted Tragen around the city, where he witnessed the greatness of its build and the recovery of its people. However, unknowingly to them, as they walked safely within the city walls, Gallius and his group approached step by step closer from the north, and as the night fell over the lower northern lands, they arrived close by along the edge of the eastern cliff.

***

Malian, Gallius and Shuma, along with their four scouts, had made good progress southwards over the days and nights as they pushed themselves on. And finally making their way along the cliffs towards the City of the Fosse, they arrived at the end of the day close to the water's edge, where the start of the gorge led around and inland into the canyon. Here they made their camp for the night as darkness fell over the water.

The following morning they rose early, and with an eagerness to see the last of the cold and openness of the plateau, they broke camp as soon as they had eaten breakfast and made ready the horses. Yet great anxiety and doubt still hung over them, for although they rode with the expectation that Captain Brook and his men would be awaiting them, an uncertainty remained in their minds as to who else would be there within the bounds of the city walls.

The events in the south were still not yet known, which meant it could be either Tragen the warrior or else Brann the traitor who would stand within the city gates to greet them on their arrival, and for all that travelled south, it meant an unknowing fear still endured. This was more lasting especially for Malian, for until he had sound proof that *Amaunet* was safe, he could find little or no rest.

Leaving the cliffs of the Eastern Great Waters behind, they moved into the hushed silence of the gorge that led through into the canyon where the towering ranges of the lower northern lands reached down to the waters. Following the mountain's base around its contour, they suddenly came out onto the far side across from where the City of the Fosse sat away in the vast spread of the flat land.

Turning the horses' heads into the oncoming wind blowing in from the east, they quickly headed towards the distant bank, moving across from the far side of the canyon as they splashed through the water. And as the deep distance drew closer and the river rushed along at their left, the walls of the great city gradually neared, and Shuma suddenly became aware of the activity around the gate. Turning to Gallius, who rode at her side, she gave warning as they made their way onto the dusty plain before the city walls.

"I think we are expected," she announced, raising her hand into the blustery wind to point to where a liveliness appeared within the opening leading into the city. But as she spoke, a further burst and roar of wind blew the coarse sand up into her face, and the vision before her became blurred as it stretched ahead.

Gallius immediately alerted the scouts riding at their back to prepare themselves, for the activity seen could not yet be recognised, and the four loosened their blades in readiness as they moved up alongside the warden while Malian remained in the rear.

Nearing the gates, however, Shuma suddenly lifted herself forward in her saddle and shaded her eyes against the rising sun. Squinting into the gusty wind, she peered towards where a tall, dark-robed figure stood awaiting them in the shade and shelter of the city wall, a hand raised in greeting as it watched the riders draw near across the windblown expanse.

"I think Tragen must have been successful in his task to alert the swans at the Sleeping Caverns," she exclaimed, turning to smile at Gallius, "for I think I see my mother!" With a great rush of happiness forcing its way through her, she urgently pushed her mount forward.

Slowing the last few yards before the gates, she brought the horse to a halt, and quickly dismounting, rushed to embrace the Black Swan as they met again in greeting. Behind them, Gallius and Malian carried on slowly forward alongside the scouts and eventually, passing by the embracing figures, they rode on through the open gates and into the entrance.

The warden now entered the City of the Fosse, where previously he had passed by, not wanting to know of its troubles. Finding Captain Brook and his men waiting on the southern side of the gate, they brought their horses around within the palm-fringed courtyard. Seeing the immediate salute of the officer who stood before him, he brought his hand up in response, and the horses came to a stop.

Further down to one side of the gates, Tragen and Anitta could be seen sitting in the shade of the overhang of the building in readiness to leave the city that morning, their aim being to continue heading north. But on seeing Gallius and Malian appear at the top of the pavement, they both rose and strode up together to meet them and stopped before the gateway.

"We had organised ourselves to make a start in hope of meeting you on the way," Tragen explained after they had exchanged greetings, "but you appear to have beaten us to it!" Coming forward, he smiled and grasped the hand of Gallius before suddenly glancing anxiously to the side where the altar tender sat his horse. Quickly turning aside, his manner changed, and he dropped his voice and looked apprehensively up to the warden before saying, "First though, I must talk with Malian, for there is no wasting time in pleasantries until I have spoken with him."

Walking around to the opposite side of Gallius, he stopped before the older man and aided him in his dismount. He knew that his news would be both bitter and sweet to impart, and the quicker in saying, the better in his own mind. But Malian appeared equally as quick in his own thinking.

With his feet having barely touched the dusty ground of the Fosse, he turned his face and begged a question of the large man who towered over him. "What of *Amaunet,* Tragen? Is she safe*?*" he anxiously asked.

"*Amaunet* remains safe, Malian," the warrior replied, seeing the look of long-held hope in the altar tender's face become exchanged for one of relief as the news was received. Then in making further his greeting, the warrior hastily embraced the friend he had missed since his sudden departure from the north, and Anitta joined them in their coming together as the three were once more reunited.

"But where is Darric?" Malian suddenly asked as he pulled away from their greeting. Missing the youth of the younger man, he looked around eagerly for a glimpse of the white-haired figure amongst the gathering crowd before his eyes returned to the face of the warrior, and he looked hard into the sadness held there. "Where is he, Tragen? Has something happened to him?"

Malian was told that Darric was dead. And as Shuma and the Black Swan walked their way through the arch of the gates, the feeling of joy for the wise woman in her reunion with her mother turned to one of great sorrow as she saw Malian standing in great distress before Tragen. On hearing of Darric's end, her own shock went deep, for she had known the young man since first setting off from the valley and had seen such change in the youth over the many weeks of their journey, and their friendship had grown over the time.

"Is there somewhere we can sit?" she urgently asked, coming forward to support the distraught man, and wrapping her arms around the weeping figure, she quickly glanced across to the captain for answer.

Leaving behind the city gates, they were escorted by Brook away from where the sound of the running water rushed in its channel and taken down further into the city, and the others were quick in following on behind. The group were led into a set of rooms that stood below the troop's station along the southern wall, and the large building, which had once housed a wealthy merchant and his family long since gone, was given over in its entirety to the arriving visitors.

As the captain took his leave, the Black Swan entered the room, and striding forward towards Shuma, she placed herself on the opposite side of the distressed man, and the two women offered what comfort they could as they stood in wait. Gallius then commandeered the situation.

"You must tell us exactly what has happened, Tragen?" the warden immediately demanded as he dragged together several seats so that all could sit.

First ensuring that Malian was seated and supported on either side by the wise woman and her mother, he turned to Anitta, noting she had already placed herself the other side of Olor. He was then able to seat himself down next to Shuma, placing his hand upon her in his support as he gently let his fingers rest along the warmth of her arm.

Tragen stood before them, the large cold fireplace at his back, and looking into the anxious upturned faces, he began to reveal their encounter with Brann and his men within the Sleeping Caverns. He started by telling how Brann had entered from the grasslands and had been seen to practice a deceit upon the Black Swan in order to claim *Amaunet*. But in their knowing of his impending arrival, the meeting had quickly turned to a fight within the darkened chamber.

As he spoke, he was often seen to glance over to Olor Ebon for her agreement and support, for in her having been there along with her swan fighters and having been witness to the violence, she knew the account which he told was true. And as she sat in silence and listened to the report, she was seen to nod her head many times to endorse his words.

Finally, he came to Darric's death and told of his bravery shown in his meeting with Brann and the fight that ended with the younger man losing his life.

"Darric fought well," Tragen finished, "and with that, I saw to it and made sure that Brann received his just punishment."

Malian had sat in silence as the story was told, his weeping having given way to such a vast feeling of emptiness. On hearing the exact detail of the death of Darric within the Sleeping Caverns, his thoughts went back in time, and again he was standing before the chair of High Priest Set'al in the Closed Court of the valley. In his remembering, he again saw the dark-haired lad who had stepped forward and now found difficulty in reconciling that with the man the boy had become in the swift passage of time.

His thoughts then moved on to his first seeing of the now white-haired man as he stood alongside the warrior on the beachside at Lake Cannis, the two racing up and down the dunes as Tragen instructed him in his training. Observing the quickness in which the boy had grown in such strength and maturity, he could find little to compare the two except in their behaviour. But in his recognising that Darric had been touched by the gods, he thought he must surely now rest amongst them.

As he remained in his recollection, the Black Swan had risen unawares as she sat at his side, and in giving further light on Tragen's account, added her report of the ceremony at the Lower Lake's edge in the closing dusk of the day. Finally, she came to the end of her witness and spoke of the goddess *Tefnut* and her receiving of the body of Darric into the waters of the lake, and Malian heard her ending words. Realising he had been right in his thinking and could take comfort in knowing that the man was at peace, he turned his thoughts back to the present day.

"I would like to be going home," he softly said, lifting his head as the room became quiet and each fell into their own thinking. Wiping his hand across his tired face, he pushed aside the great sadness, and his focus once more became on the here and now, and he finished, "but first, Shuma, will you collect my pack for me, for I have something which I need to do."

The wise woman was quick to leave his side, realising what he was thinking. Returning straightaway, carrying the small pack that both Malian and Gallius had each carried in turn close at their side as they journeyed from the city in the north, she handed over the heavy sack to the altar tender. Letting the package rest in his lap, he held his hands tight around its shape until, finally, he carefully unbuckled the straps.

"I restore this back to your keeping, Tragen," Malian said, lifting the wrapped statue from where it had lain hidden away within its dark confines, "and all here know that many may have lost their lives over it. But in putting our trust in the gods, we can wish that peace will be granted in its return."

Tragen carefully took the bundle from Malian's outstretched hands and, unwrapping the statue of *Naunet*, brought the small Icon with the sapphire blue eyes staring coldly from its intertwining head out into the glare of the morning's brightness.

At long last, he held within his grasp that which he had so long searched for and, suddenly, words were beyond him. The events and happenings around this one small figure all at once flooded over him with their dire images of the past burning their way across his mind. Overwhelmed by the intensity of his feelings, he hastily left the room.

Taking with him the object which was the embodiment of his own great despair, as well as being the bringer of hope for his people, he walked back into the light of the day holding her tight and swearing she would never again be lost.

Malian now felt overwhelming exhaustion fall across him as the door behind banged shut, and even his tears had no more energy to flow, for a complete fatigue likened to that which had gripped him before hastened itself within his limbs. Knowing he needed to let his mind and body rest, he looked up to the warden.

"Gallius, I must lie down!" he pleaded, and suddenly sitting back, the weariness pinning him deep within his chair, his head dropped forward.

"Yes, I feel we should all rest ourselves today, Malian," Gallius urgently agreed, his concern for the altar tender increasing as he looked upon the prostrate man, "and hopefully tomorrow, we shall feel keener to start the day afresh and with a new vigour." Turning to look to Shuma for her assistance, his glance was returned with a reassuring smile, and he felt able to leave the room to the charge of the women.

Knowing that his own call to feel some ease would have to go unanswered for the present, for there were doubts that plagued his mind and questions still to be asked, an overwhelming need to be out in the freshness of the air suddenly played over him and following after the warrior he swiftly made for the door.

Shuma took Malian upstairs, settling him into a light and airy bedroom at the top of the stairway in the upper storey. Here he lay for many moments staring at the cracks winding their interweaving way side to side along the flat ceiling as the wise woman pulled the curtains across to shut out the glaring light of day.

"Take your rest now, Malian," she said, turning back towards the bed, "and tomorrow you will feel the better for it." Reaching down to kiss his cheek, she softly drew the door closed, and returning down the stairs, left the man to continue his contemplation until, slowly, the sounds coming from the ground floor became muted to his ears and wearied sleep took over.

***

Below, where Gallius had come out into the bright sunshine of the advancing morning, a strong urgency to speak man to man with the warrior had come over him. He had a belief that there was further to report on the traitor Brann and that Tragen had news to disclose, which he appeared loath to mention before the gathered group.

Leaning up against the doorway, he waited his time, watching as the warrior stood within the shadows of the colonnade as carefully he rewrapped the Icon, tucking it away deep inside his jacket before finally turning to where the warden stood in wait.

"I shall carry it back close by my side," he said, aware that Gallius had been witness to this action. "And in knowing that she is near me, my mind shall be at peace, and its weight shall not be a burden."

"You have travelled far to reclaim that which was stolen, Tragen," the warden said, his concern being made known as he straightened up from his repose, and coming forward, he joined the man who stood in the dimness of the shade, "and you now have an eagerness, like Malian, to be heading home."

"That I do," the large man replied, his voice sounding uncertain as he drew his jacket around him, "although what awaits me, I have no real idea. But I must travel back with a belief and longing that some of my people remain and that my city will recover. And if I return only to find bare dust, then I shall call upon the gods to help me rebuild!"

"Then let us be happy in *Naunet*'s return. But first, let us take a walk," Gallius suggested. Nodding to the taller man as they both looked across at the walkways opposite, their sight was drawn onwards and beyond into the palm-lined courts and plazas that could be glimpsed in the far distance.

"Let's follow the river down," Tragen replied, putting aside his long-held doubts for that moment, "for Anitta says I must look upon the river's end before I leave this city and let my sights take in all its splendour!" His voice, having mentioned the swan woman, held a lighter tone, and Gallius could see a hint of a smile play across his features as they moved out into the sunshine and headed up towards the gates.

Guiding the warden up towards the pavement, Tragen and Gallius fell in step, and keeping the palm-lined river walkway on their left, followed it down through the city past the bridges and open spaces where a number of people could be seen crisscrossing the water of the Fosse. However, some still held their hands across their eyes to shield the sunlight glare of their returning sight. While many more walked assuredly through the streets and the sound of their chatter and the high-pitched voices of the children once more filled the air.

"Is there more I need to know about Brann?" Gallius was suddenly eager to ask as they passed by unnoticed in the main by the city folk, for all were now well used to seeing the dress of the northern men, although the size and manner of the warrior caused some to stop and stare as they made their progress.

"Only that I fear he did not expect to see me in the Sleeping Caverns," Tragen replied, "and in that, I am glad that my presence cut short his plans."

"What about his decision? Did he declare his affiliation and make known his intent to you before you killed him?" Gallius asked.

"I would say that the man had made his choice," Tragen replied, his hand going to his chest. "Once I had him on the ground, I found this about his collar."

He produced the talisman torn from Brann's neck, for having thrown it to the floor in the heat of rage, he had seen fit to retrieve it before carrying the body of Darric out of the dark. It had then lain within his breast pocket since that time. Not forgotten but just hidden away, and handing it across to Gallius, the warrior felt a certain relief that it had left his possession.

Their walk took them to within the boundaries of the city walls, and on stepping through the gates, they found themselves in the same spot where Anitta had stood only the previous day. This time, however, the horizon was clear to its end, and the sheer blueness of the sunlit sky met the calmness of the waters spread out in its distance before them. Closer, the concentration of the city's waters remained in its run to the edge of the cliff and here, the thin mist of its fall climbed high into the sky before dropping back upon the lushness of the land below.

"This sight is certainly one to fix in your mind," Gallius had to admit as the brightness and sparkle from the vast waters hit his eyes, and he brought up his hand to shield his face. "And one which I've never seen before in my wanderings. Come, let's get nearer to the edge."

The two slowly walked forward, the slabs of exposed rock between the interweaving canals becoming stepping stones for them as they first crossed sideways and then crossed back in their attempt to move ahead.

Until finally, they reached the very edge of the cliffs. Here the two men cautiously looked down deep into the plunging water, and the spray of its return settled around their shoulders as a dampness fell cold about them. The push of the breeze at their backs meeting the up-current draught off the face of the cliffs made them brace themselves from its compelling force, and here Gallius stood and raised his arm, holding out the last talisman over the watery abyss. Slowly his hand spread out, and for a brief moment, the token hung before him as the chain gradually worked its way through his fingers. Then with a flash of silver, the disc, with its intricate snake carving about its edge, dropped into the waters below.

In this disposing of the last reminder of the Brotherhood of *Apep*, Gallius felt a certain end to the whole catastrophe that had beset the lands in both the north and the south, and a surety of a job finished fell around his shoulders.

The two were then quick to turn their backs upon the wonder that lay before them and which had now been committed to memory, and walking back through the streets of the city, returned to the house that sat in the shadow of the southern wall and the calmness that had descended.

***

In the late warm dusk of the evening, Shuma and Olor Ebon walked the expanse of the plaza beneath the tall palms, their arms linked as the sound of fast-running water accompanied them on their stroll. Here Shuma told her mother of her love for the man from the northern city and that they would be returning there in the morning.

"I am so glad you have found that happiness, Shuma," Olor said, stopping to sit beside the flowing water, "and for me, my own joy has been rekindled in our meeting." Taking her daughter's hands and holding them tight within her own, she felt the warmth that flowed through the youth of the soft skin. Raising them to her lips, she kissed the fingertips before gently releasing them, whereupon Shuma let them slowly fall into the softness of her lap.

"I have realised my life has been so empty since I left both you and Tellia behind," Olor went on, "and my mind has been thinking long on the missed days which I shall never know. But there are still days to come, and I must not let them slip beyond me." A quietness fell as she stared into the depths of the passing waters, and in her mind, the time wasted in the unknowing years of her two daughters sped by at an equal pace, and the feeling of indifference and disdain in their passing became washed away by the soft murmur of the running water.

"I know you will be happy and safe with Gallius," she said, her eyes remaining captivated by the moving stream, "and I wish you both a long life together. But for me, I feel it is time to return to the valley." She lifted her head as if in sudden awareness of her words and declared, "Tomorrow, I shall be returning with Malian into the south, and we shall carry on our travels together past the Sleeping Caverns and journey further beyond their borders."

The two women spent the remainder of the evening sitting close together under the darkening sky, and at times the silence separating their talk was all they needed to feel a deepening of the bond between them. Eventually, tiredness along with a desire to rest overcame them both, and reluctantly they returned towards the city gates, where the blazing lights outside of the merchant's house guided them down to where the others had settled for the night and where their beds stood in wait.

***

The ending day in the City of the Fosse led into the night and the brightness of the following morning was quick to come and saw Shuma seated once more beside her mother, only this time beneath the colonnade outside of the merchant's house. Beyond them, up towards the gates where the water flowed its way through, the activity for the morning's departure was making its progress.

Anitta and the two swans sat further up in wait within the shadow of the troop's station, their bundles having already been placed in readiness outside the city gates. Alongside, in the shade of the palms, the scouts who had journeyed south under Gallius' order had also made ready and packed up their mounts. They also stood in wait, their number having clearly increased as the presence of Blake made their sum up to five. But all seemed in equal eagerness to be off with a swift return back to their families in the north while, opposite them, the horses of the group travelling south also stood with an impatience to be away.

"Will you take something back to Tellia for me?" Shuma requested, looking long at her mother before reaching down into the pack placed carefully at her side. Lifting out her hands from its depths, she brought out the wooden Shabti doll her sister had given with her love such a long time ago. Leaning across towards the other woman, she held it out in return. "Tell her that it served me well, Mother. For you, yourself, were first to note its value, and in that recognition alone, it made known the kinship between us and our relationship was reclaimed in its bringing us together."

The Black Swan gently took back the doll, and looking intently at the exquisite carving, that at one time had been seen clearly defined as a man, found that it had once more remodelled itself to show the female form, the long finely chiselled hair and upturned smile of the mouth showing an uncanny likeness to the wise woman who sat close by.

"I shall return it with the very love that it was given in its first place, along with that of your own," Olor answered, accepting her daughter's charge gladly, before suddenly asking, "But do you not feel she may think me poor compensation in replacement of her sister?"

"No, never!" the wise woman declared. "You are her mother, and I know that she will again feel the love you had to push aside long ago. Yes, I know she may be troubled by my absence," she further said, aware that the close bond between herself and her sister would be set at odds by her long distance away in the north, "but with you, I send my love and the understanding that she will always be with me." Her hand came up briefly to touch her chest as she looked again upon the Shabti doll, and in her eyes, the features had now remodelled themselves into that of Abu Salama, and she steeled herself to place her final appeal.

"And will you also give my love to Father?" she asked, an uncertainty showing in her voice as she looked up intently from the doll into the dark eyes of her mother. "He is a good man and has been a good father, and I hope, in your meeting, you will both find some peace from your long separation."

"I just hope in seeing me he will not shut the door on my return," the Black Swan came back, "for so many years have passed for both of us. His in seeing the time pass as his children grew and mine in the years unknowing of them. But for each of us, I hope that in the passing, we have both grown wiser and deeper in our thinking. And yes." She paused to smile into the face which would forever remain etched within her mind. "I shall give him his daughter's love."

***

The two groups gathered beneath the shade of the palms as the morning moved on, the gates of the City of the Fosse open wide at their backs as the soft canyon wind blew, its flurry following the watercourse down on its relentless journey to the open sea. Here Captain Brook stood in ceremony surrounded by his troops as they watched the goodbyes.

Gallius and Shuma had said all they needed to say to Tragen and Anitta the night before as the four sat beside the warm, roaring fireside in the companionship of the merchant's house. And while a simple good wish and farewell with a shake of the hand were all that was required between the two men as they parted, for Shuma, the leave-taking of both the tall warrior and the swan was more emotional in its showing. The three hugged for many moments, and while they each said their goodbyes, Gallius took his own departure of Malian, holding the man long, unknowing if they would ever meet again. Finally, the warden let his arms drop and the two parted, and Shuma, stepping away from the warrior, moved forward to take his place within the altar tender's arms.

"It's been a long journey, Malian," she said, her voice sounding taut and emotional as she held back her tears, and wrapping her arms around the weary body of the older man, she held him tight within her embrace, "and I'm loath at this moment of our goodbye to leave you

284

when you have still such a journey to make in your return home."

"But I do not go alone, Shuma," Malian replied gently, "for you know your mother will see me safely back to the valley, and I also have the warrior at my side to ensure no harm or misfortune shall come my way."

"You will be well looked after, I know, Malian," she acknowledged, and looking to where Gallius stood in wait, she quickly kissed the man on his cheek before saying, "and my love goes with you."

"Take care of each other," Malian said, looking deep for many long moments into the wise woman's eyes. "I wish you both much happiness."

"My love goes with you, Malian," Shuma repeated, the tears welling up as she spoke, "and you shall always be in my heart." Kissing the man on each cheek, she let her hands drop, and taking a step back, she watched as he turned away from her. Crossing the dusty forecourt before the gates, he joined the figure of Tragen as he stood beside the restless horses, and her mother now stepped forward.

Shuma remained long in her mother's enfolded arms, for both appeared unwilling to part until Gallius saw their dilemma. In hoping to ease the situation, he called over to Olor's veiled companions to join him, and in gathering the women together, the mother and daughter found the strength to let go, and he was able to give his address to the three swans.

"If any of the women of the Sleeping Caverns have a wish to return home to their families in the north," he declared to Olor and the two as they stood close by, "then as Warden of the City of the High Places, you must tell them that I gave my word that all will be made welcome and no harm or prejudice will befall any who choose that course."

"I shall pass on your words, Gallius," Olor immediately said in reply, her long cool fingers still clinging tightly to those of her daughter at her side, "but for many, the Sleeping Caverns have become their home, and the past is a place they do not wish to revisit." She paused briefly, remembering the distress and grief held by many of the women she had left behind. "Time heals, that I know, and for some few, that may mean a desire to return home. But with that, we must allow each to make their own judgement." Hearing her own words, she now felt able to let go her daughter's hand, and presenting it forward towards the man who stood before her, she joined the two together while smiling across at the warden. Then she bid them much happiness in their farewell, and finally letting go of Shuma, she quickly followed the actions of Malian and the group of women turned away, returning to where Tragen stood in wait beside the altar tender.

***

The first group to leave from the City of the Fosse turned south, and as the five horses fell in line behind the mounted warrior, Gallius and Shuma stood together alongside the flowing water. Seeing the figures dwindle towards the distance, Gallius was quick to jump astride his horse and turning to look back at his scouts, he gave his order for them to mount.

"Let us too be on our way!" he urged, and pulling the horse around from the entrance to the city, bid a hasty farewell to Captain Brook before turning his head north. As the six men moved slowly out of the shadow of the palms, he set his sights and thoughts on home while behind him the wise woman hesitated for many moments longer, her hand held aloft in goodbye as she watched the darkening shapes slowly disappear. Until finally, she could no longer discern Malian and the Black Swan, and the blurring figures became part of the endless scenery against the walls of the dusty canyon. Turning away and quickly mounting, she sped off after Gallius.

CHAPTER THIRTEEN

For those heading south, many days passed before the mounds and ridges of the approaching Sleeping Caverns slowly arose out of the mist of the grasslands. As the riders looked across the waving tops of the greenery, the terraced lawns before the darkened openings spread out their invite, and they swung the heads of their mounts towards the nearest in an urgency to seek the shelter and security that they knew lay beyond.

Their trek had been long, but in eventually leaving behind the horses within the freedom of the lush grass, the caverns once more welcomed them back. And the returning swans, alongside the company of the two men, walked their way back through the dim passageways.

Passing the place where Brann and his men had met their end, Tragen briefly stopped to lower his head in remembrance of his friend Darric. But he did not linger before swiftly following the lead of Olor where they were taken further through the tunnels. Steering them onward, she eventually moved downwards once again and finally they walked out into the brightness that met them on the lakeside.

Here they were received by some of the veiled women who had been alerted to their arrival by the lookouts who still stood watch atop the caverns. And the welcome was loud and cheerful as they assembled in the light of the morning to greet once more the return of their Black Swan and her two companions. Anitta, too, was well received for she was also well known and had been missed by many of the women.

However, Malian and Tragen had stood discreetly back, knowing their place among these women as they met again in their friendship. Finally, the Black Swan pulled away from the hugs and embraces, and taking the pathway along the busy lakeside, she led the two men past the women working at the water's edge and took them westwards towards the Enclosure. Arriving at its dark doorway Malian was quick to step forward and stop her before she disappeared into its depths.

"You said that *Amaunet* is safe, Olor," he eagerly asked, and unable to hold back his longing, he grasped her arm to hold her tight and stop her further advance. "You said she is safe, but I have a great urgency to see her, to calm the restlessness that fills my mind. I cannot wait any longer!" he demanded, his face filled with impatience until suddenly he realised his gesture was unsuited to the moment, and his grip softened, and he let go of her arm.

"She lies in safety, Malian," the Black Swan gently replied, aware that his action was not meant with any ill will, "protected beyond the eyes of man and any who may have looked to see harm fall upon her." Turning away from the anxiety she saw in the face that looked back questioningly into hers; her gaze took in the vista across the lake, which she knew she would soon be leaving behind. "But, know now, Malian," she said in finish and with hope of giving the altar tender some comfort, "she lies closer than you may imagine."

Walking towards the water, she slowly bent forward and reached her fingers into the coolness of the lake lapping against the reed-lined edge. Rising, she let the clear liquid drip from her fingertips, and as the last drop fell back into place, the waters of the Lower Lake quietened and became still within their shoreline. On the lakeside, the hush spread, and the swan women turned away from their work to stare out across the water as Olor Ebon raised her hands. Softly whispering her words, she called forth the goddess from the deep and in so doing brought back the Icon of *Amaunet* from the darkness of its refuge into the light.

The goddess *Tefnut* slowly appeared in all her splendour, the red sun disc that sat atop her head breaking the calm of the water as it pushed upwards into the sky. Malian and the swan women had been witness to her presentation before on these waters but still, the magnificence of the goddess as she rose out of the depths and the waters of the lake fell away caused them to drop to their knees as she looked down upon them in her divine right.

"WELCOME, MALIAN," she said, her dusky voice entering the heads of those bowed down before her manifestation, and the echoes of her words moved throughout the Lower Lake and resonated beyond into the passages of the Sleeping Caverns. "YOU HAVE BEEN LONG AWAY ON YOUR JOURNEY INTO THE NORTH, AND MUCH HAS HAPPENED IN THAT TIME THROUGHOUT THE LANDS. BUT ON YOUR RETURN, I RESTORE INTO YOUR KEEPING THAT WHICH WAS GIVEN TO ME TO WATCH OVER AND PROTECT."

Slowly uncrossing her arms, she brought together her hands and held them up as if in prayer before gently opening them to reveal the tiny golden statue held safe within her palm. "HERE IS THE EIGHTH DEITY," she declared, "THE ICON OF *AMAUNET*, THE LAST OF THE EIGHT STOLEN BY MAN. AND I GIVE CHARGE HERE, ALTAR TENDER, THAT IT REMAINS YOUR UNDERTAKING TO RETURN HER TO THE VALLEY AND RESTORE HER TO THE PLACE DECREED BY THE GODS."

The goddess's stark gaze switched from the Icon held before her, and taking in the bowed heads of those gathered below at the side of the water, she continued her address, "THIS YOU MUST ACHIEVE, MALIAN, FOR

ONLY ONCE SHE SITS BACK AMONGST HER PEOPLE WILL SHE BE DEEMED TO HAVE BEEN RETURNED. AND THE FORCES OF CHAOS AND DISORDER THAT LINGER IN YOUR LAND WILL BE FOREVER BANISHED, WHILE THE UNION BETWEEN ORDER AND BALANCE SHALL AGAIN GOVERN OVER ALL."

Gently reclosing her hands, the statue held within them disappeared into a shimmering radiance that flooded through her fingertips as the Icon dissolved into the brilliance of a gleaming shower of dust. Falling to the water's surface at *Tefnut's* feet, the Deity's light sped its way across the lake towards the stooped figure at the far-off edge.

The Icon of *Amaunet* emerged as the glowing brightness gathered, condensing itself before the downturned eyes of the altar tender as he remained kneeling, and the snake-headed female Deity finally reappeared within reach. Stretching down to pick her up from the grass bordering the lake's edge, Malian once more looked upon the figure that had been the cause of all his hardship and worry. Feeling a sudden rush fall over him as he once again touched the warmth of the statue and felt her weight in his hands, he stared into the dark ruby eyes. Dropping his head, overwhelmed by his relief at knowing her safe, he gave thanks to the goddess.

"My gratitude for keeping her sheltered in your care goes beyond any words that I speak here," he said, his voice growing stronger as he cautiously lifted his head to witness the imposing image of *Tefnut* stood before him. On seeing the goddess rising from the waters, he was swift, however, in showing his respect and dropped his eyes downwards again as she returned his stare. "And in your charge to return her to my people, I herewith declare my life in its accomplishment," he went on, giving his word as he held *Amaunet* tight within his hands. "But you must know that I came here with the help of the gods. And with their guidance through *The Duat*, the Gates of the Dead, the long miles from the valley to Lake Cannis were accomplished over the stretch of one night. With that, I stand here before you, unsure of the way back and unknowing of the miles that may lie between."

Suddenly the great tiredness that had come and gone over the days since being touched by the god *Horus* fell around him, filling his mind with such lethargy as he thought on the journey ahead. Feeling the ground rise before him, he collapsed towards the lakeside, still gripping the Icon close as the waters of the Lower Lake abruptly stopped his fall, and the goddess gave back her answer.

"KNOW NOW, MALIAN, THAT THE GODS WILL SURELY HELP YOU IN YOUR RETURN," she said, looking upon the man who lay prone before her within the clear water at the Lake's edge. **"FOR I HEREWITH GIVE GUIDANCE THAT YOU MUST HEAD EAST ALONG THE LOWER LAKE AND TAKE THE PASSAGES DOWN BEYOND THE SACRIFICIAL SANDS.**

"HERE THE *SHEN* STAFF GIVEN TO YOU BY *HORUS* WILL BE YOUR POINTER, WHILE THE LIGHT OF *RA* SHALL BE YOUR GUIDE HOME."

Her voice ceased, and in the sudden silence that flowed across the water, she once more crossed her arms, and the image of the goddess began to slowly fade, the red of her dress turning first to the warm pink of the rising sun before, finally, even that had dissipated.

The lake once more returned to its own life as the swan women rose one by one from their knees, and the sound of the water resumed its ceaseless lap against the reed beds as the song of the birds once more returned, filling the air of the bright day.

Tragen rushed immediately to Malian's side, his concern for the older man matching that of the Black Swan, who also came forward to aid him on seeing his struggle to rise. Noticing the altar tender, white with exhaustion as he first knelt looking back across the vastness of the lake to where *Tefnut* had stood, the two helped him stand further and seated him beside the water. Each remained close at his side while the strength and vigour returned to his limbs and the colour once more flushed his face, and many moments passed before Olor turned to him to speak.

"Well, Malian," she declared as she noted the Icon clutched to the man's chest, "you have been seen to be given your task, and the gods have given you direction. Now an early start for tomorrow seems ensured, so let us make the most of this day each in our own way and to the best of our means."

***

Malian and Tragen were taken across to the far northern side of the Lower Lake, each carrying close beside them the Icons of their people, and here they were reunited with the men left behind on their journey north.

The three elders who had made the far side of the water their home had unwittingly, in the months past, been taken captive by the traitor Roth and held hostage, and at the Sleeping Caverns, abandoned as sacrifice to the swan women. Here they had met Malian, but on his god-given quest to rescue *Amaunet*, they had remained behind on the lakeside, and their fate had been left in the hands of the swans.

Finding that Rusan, Petrus and Claud had remained in

293

seclusion over the water, and in that time, Claud had settled in his distress, and a healthier look taken place over his emaciation, the two travellers had been made welcome. They were told the women on the opposite side had seemingly kept their distance but had been good enough to ferry across basic food and essentials as needed, and Malian was thankful for their regard.

Here they were also reunited with Theroc, who had joined his friends in isolation, and who they had last seen heading south with Olor Ebon across the Median Bridge.

The welcomed men settled for the night in the caves, which the elders had made comfortable in their time spent within the caverns, and as they met over a simple meal, the elders told of the unchanging days that had passed as they rested within the domain of the swan women.

That said, the conversation turned to Malian, and in his telling of the events in the north and the outcome of the days spent at the high city, he left no story untold.

Tragen listened, nodding his head in agreement at Malian's words, and the altar tender finally came to an end in confirming that there was still one last journey to be made. And that was one they would all be making, for the morning would see them returning south, and the elders could finally hold some hope of going home.

***

The night on the southern side of the lake was spent in the Enclosure, for the Black Swan had summoned a gathering of the women, and they had all seated themselves within its bounds. Closing the doors to the growing dark of the outside world, she told of the news from her travels beyond their borders.

"A new king sits the throne of the north," she told the

swans after telling of her journey to the City of the Fosse, "and of him, I know little. But of the new warden, I can give more report. For he is a man known to me and also to some of you who sit here within the safety of our caverns."

Coming to the edge of the dais, her tall figure rising before the gathering, she continued, "His name is Gallius, and he is a man who has shown his worth in my eyes, and I would deem him to be fair amongst most men."

Watching as the women received the spoken words, a slight murmur of disapproval passed through the group bearing witness to their continuing dislike of man. She knew that for some, there would be no world beyond these walls and struggling to continue in her message, she went on, "He has sent word through me to the women here of the Sleeping Caverns who once may have called the high city home." Her voice echoed into the silence that had closed around. "His words are that if any of you should wish to return to your families, then no prejudice or judgement will be awaiting, and all will be made welcome." She paused while the words repeated themselves around the chamber before closing, "I pass his message to you and give claim that he is a man of his word. But I judge you should each make your own decision in this matter."

Finally, she came to her main reason for having gathered them together, and slowly pacing across the platform she had so often walked, she looked into the unveiled, upturned faces that looked back at her, and for some, she knew her next declaration would be of concern.

"Tomorrow, I shall be leaving these caverns," she calmly announced, "leaving in the company of the man Malian and his friends, and I will be returning back to my home in the valley where I aim to live out my days. With that, I make call upon you to appoint a new Black Swan to take my place and wear the mantle of leadership."

Turning away from the astonished assembly, she swiftly unclasped the brooch that held together the black robe worn for untold years and let it drop to the floor of the platform. Removing her symbol of authority, she placed the necklace of silvered rings atop the cloak, and stepping away with no feeling of regret, left them in wait of their new wearer.

The voting was quick. Over and done in a matter of minutes as swan Gina, known for her intense dislike of men, proved to be favoured by the many who would forever hold their prejudice. Given that there was little doubt in the outcome of the election, she was swiftly called forward out of the women who gathered around to assume and take on her new duty, and all appeared happy with her choice as their new Black Swan.

Leading her up and onto the dais, Olor bent to pick up the discarded necklace, wrapping it around the woman's throat before draping the dark cloth about the shoulders of the new keeper of the Sleeping Caverns, and attaching the brooch, she let the cloak fall around the woman's body. The burden of responsibility passed from one swan to another in this performance, and stepping back, Olor was immediate in turning away and leaving behind the platform.

As she moved down onto the main floor before the front of the seating, the swans rose in recognition of her years of guardianship. Striding towards the large doors, she walked out onto the dark of the lakeside and left the Enclosure behind.

***

The boat taking Olor Ebon eastwards across the lake arrived before the sun had fully risen, and the men of the caverns stood in readiness for the journey outside of the cave above the lake's edge, their packs standing at their sides in an eagerness to be away. Tragen was surprised to see that Olor was not alone, for Anitta sat alongside her paddling the boat, and both were dressed in their travelling clothes.

Striding down the slope, the warrior came quickly forward to the shoreline where the swan women were alighting and taking the arm of the younger woman, he led her to one side and walked away along the water's edge. Leaving behind them the activity at the boat, they eventually stopped, and Anitta turned to focus her gaze out over the lake, her scarred face mirrored in the clear water that lay at her feet, and Tragen asked her why she was there.

"I am here initially as companion to Olor," the swan woman replied, unsure of how her words would be met, "at least until we reach the valley. But beyond that, my days will be mine to choose, for I shall not be returning here to this lakeside."

"What do you mean by that?" Tragen directly enquired, very much surprised at her disclosure before suddenly remembering she had kin in the high city. "Will you be taking up the warden's offer and returning north to your family?"

"No, that would not be my first choice," she replied, her tone firm as she raised her head fleetingly to look up at the man standing tall at her side. Again looking out across the lake, her voice took on a more thoughtful tone as she continued, "We have travelled far together, Tragen," she cautiously said, "and with the time we have spent together, I have found you to be a trustworthy and good man. I would consider it a privilege if you would let me continue on your journey with you beyond the valley!"

Tragen instantly looked down in surprise at the request, for he had not expected this from the woman who had already accompanied him far and been witness to his basic nature as both warrior and a man skilled to life on the land. But knowing that, in her own right, she too was competent in the ways of fighting and a woman unafraid of hardship, he knew well her capabilities might be called upon.

However, he thought long and hard on how to reply to her asking while the two continued their silent stare out across the water.

Finally, he said, "It would be an honour to have your company, Anitta." And a brief smile crossed his lips as they turned to each other. "But you must know that we will face many difficulties in our travel south from the valley. In the time that I have been away from my land, I am unknowing of what other disasters may have befallen it, and in that, I remain unsure of what lies ahead for us!"

"I know the journey will be difficult," the woman replied, her light eyes taking in the gaze looking back out of the heavy face, "but I would hope that in the coming days, I may be of some comfort to you and be of assistance. In my being at your side, I know you will not continue your travel alone!"

Taking hold of her slim shoulders, Tragen looked intently at the woman who was standing before him. Smiling down upon the disfigured face, he saw beyond her injuries, and pulling her close within his arms, he suddenly realised he was thankful for her wanting to join him because he too longed for her to remain nearby.

***

Along the shoreline, while Tragen and Anitta spoke their words to each other and now remained long in embrace, Malian too had paused to talk, feeling a need to speak with Shuma's mother as she stopped beside the boat.

As they journeyed south from the City of the Fosse, she often told of her desire once more to look upon the valley, and they had many times talked of their lives lived there. Now taking her to one side, he needed to know that her resolve was still strong in her intent to return before they set off.

"What of your duty here to the women of the Sleeping Caverns, Olor?" he asked, knowing that in her deciding to travel south with them, it meant giving up forever the life she held long within this place as well as the security found within its borders. "Are you sure you are making the right choice? For you are surely needed here as Black Swan to all who call this place home."

"That is no longer my name, Malian," the tall woman replied, a hint of sadness heard in her voice as she helped him carry over the men's packs. Briskly she began to stow them away under the seating and continued, "Another Olor Ebon now oversees the Sleeping Caverns, and a new Black Swan will be protector and guardian over these women who found sanctuary here from the outside world. I am now able to leave this place knowing that it is in fitting hands." She stopped suddenly in lofting high the last pack, and placing it down carefully on the seat, stared out across the vastness of the water towards the caverns on the opposite side.

Now she wondered on the coming years for the women she would forever feel she was abandoning. "I just hope that my purpose will remain strong, and in my deciding to return to the valley, it will prove to be worthy of my letting go of the life here." Turning away from the home she had known for untold years, she smiled towards the altar tender with an aim to leave this past behind.

"But what now is your name?" Malian suddenly asked, giving thought to this question as he realised the woman beside him had instantly become nameless to his eyes. "What do I call you if you are no longer the Black Swan?"

"I shall still answer to the name Olor for the present," she replied, aware that his uncertainty was to be expected in her changing role. "But for the time being, my birth name will remain known only to myself and those who have spoken it in the past."

Placing the final pack beneath the bare boards, she turned to where the man waited, and extending her arm to help him clamber over the side, she joined him as the boat was seen to be packed with all of the traveller's belongings. Now they waited as the last of the assembled elders climbed aboard and took their places to man the paddles.

The shoreline along the northern side of the caverns instantly became barren of the men who had called it home for many long weeks, and a peacefulness fell over the backdrop of the caves that opened wide above their heads.

On seeing the waiting boat, Tragen and Anitta finally parted, and returning along the water's edge, the two walked close as they re-joined the group. Stepping aboard the craft and taking their places in the rear, it was pushed away from the shore, and moving out into the depths, they sped off eastwards.

The thick wooden blades now propelled them forward, dipping into the waters of the lake as the sun rose in their faces, and once again, the men witnessed the lushness of the Eastern Lower Lake. The vast reed beds slowly appeared out of the dawn and filled out its brim, while before them, the sands at the top of the cove gradually came into view.

This time, however, they were not passing this way to witness the Rite of Redress and were able to enjoy the sense of travel under their own exertion. And in the warmth of the sun that rose higher as they were carried forward, the men felt a sense of control returning over their fate.

Eventually, the cove of bleached sand lay ahead and met the boat as it came into the shallows of the eastern bay, and all those seated were quick to lay down the paddles. Gathering their packs, they climbed out, leaving the craft to lie empty and abandoned to the elements at the lake's margin.

Ahead, the burnt bodies of Brann and his men lay piled up on this eastern shore, their blackened bones meshed and fused together by the heat and collapse of their pyre as it died down. Already the windblown sand had begun its invasion, and the bones at its base protruded at odd angles from the ever-shifting shoreline of the lakeside.

Nearby, and to one side further up the beach, another body of bones lay in its own soft sand pile at the base of a short stake, and as the men passed by in witness to the past decrees of the swans, the remembrance of the death of the elder Tarnik fleetingly crossed their minds. But quickly striding past, he was once more forgotten, and his memory discarded forever into the past, and they lifted their heads to look upwards.

Above them, the interconnecting caves known long to the swan women as the *Eyes of Horus* yawned wide along the top margins that made up the backdrop to the staged scene below. And the group swiftly moved forward to make their way towards these over the ridges that drew them upward in a flurry of sand and fine dust.

Reaching the uppermost fold, where they stepped out

onto a solid slab of granite running along the length of the dark openings, they waited for the last to reach safety as, one by one, the men made the summit. Pausing briefly to view the beauty of the Lower Lake, they took the chance to gather their breath after their exertions before the women were quick to urge them to continue their progress. Then they each decisively and with little regret turned away from the waters below, and the realm of the swans was finally at their backs.

Accompanied by Anitta, Olor led off through the middle cave of the openings without even a backward glance, for their final goodbyes to the women of the Sleeping Caverns had already been said as the swans gathered along the southern bank of the Lower Lake. Both knew, as the bright light of the day faded at their backs, there would be no returning for either of them. Seeing their keenness to be away, the elders and the warrior were equally quick in their following.

Disappearing into the descending shadows, their eyes took time to adjust to the dark that met them, while behind on the bank above the lake, Malian remained longer in his pause and looked out across the vastness into the west. Finally, with words of farewell to the swans on his lips, he lifted his pack, and walking away from the sight of the sparkling sun as it moved its way across the reed-lined beauty of the lake, he too slowly vanished into the cave and let the darkness fold itself around.

Directly ahead, the image of the sky god *Horus*, depicted in his human form with the head of a hawk, appeared out of the gloom, the beaked face carved deep into the stone of the granite as its sharp eyes pointed off southwards to the left. Around the man-sized figure, the writing of the Ancients flowed skilfully across the smooth surface, and the cartouches of the long dead remained as a reminder of their name. The figure itself had been painted between the carved lines and appeared as fresh as the day when brush was first applied. Here the group collected as they looked upon this portrayal and awaited the altar tender as he stepped out of the light.

"Here is our starting point, Malian," Olor said with great satisfaction as she looked up at *Horus*. "This is your signpost home!" Her hands gently touched the white outline of the god as it suddenly shone brightly before them, the ochres and bronzes of the yellows deepening while the rich reds increased in their brilliance. The blues that ran along the god's head appeared heightened as Malian approached, and the presence of the *Shen* Staff was felt within the very image itself.

In the god's left hand, he held away from his body the Staff of Divine Power, an emblem of authority in his kingdom, while in the other, an *Ankh* was gripped tightly at his side to symbolise life and infinity. But there appeared no depiction of the *Shen* Staff within the painted image, and Malian stared for many moments in search of the distinct shape of the short staff topped by a circle before he bent to remove the golden *Shen* from his pack.

Standing before the sky god, he clasped the pointer and held it out towards the rock face while the rest of the group stood close by, their emotions rising in the sure hope that an event was about to take place before them.

Nothing happened for many moments until, gradually, the bronze shading across the god's chest deepened in one area beneath the painted ornate collar, and the outline of a *Shen* became evident in the granite as the surrounding colours faded into the background. Stepping forward and running his empty hand across the surface, Malian could feel the deep depression developing within the smoothness of the cave wall. Raising his other hand holding the symbol of the *Shen*, he placed one inside the other, the solid form fitting perfectly the indented shape carved out across the chest of the god.

As the two symbols came together, the doorway into the beyond sprung open amidst the writing that lay along the left-hand side of *Horus*. Widening slowly, the smell of long stale air within the confines beyond rushed out to meet the freshness within the cave.

Immediately, Malian removed the *Shen* from its hollow. Hurrying forward, he rushed to enter the chamber that stood beyond the opening door, and Tragen, trailed by the women and the elders, quickly followed. The group found themselves at the top of a stairway, a number of deep steps cut roughly from the rock leading directly down into where a glowing light showed the beginnings of a passage. Overhead, in the generous carvings that decorated the domed ceiling rising high above, the circles depicting the sun god *Ra* glowed in their illumination of the chamber. At the same time, along the walls, the all-seeing Eye of *Horus* pointed the way down.

Time now stopped for the seven who followed behind the lead of the altar tender, and the count of footsteps was soon lost as the unadorned walls of the passageway led them on in a continuing march in the Light of *Ra*, its confines constantly changing as they journeyed onward. For in some places, they had to stoop as the roof dipped its way along before it rose again, and they could move on the quicker.

Eventually, in the guidance of the glowing lights of the god, they became aware of a pinpoint of brightness in the far distance that gradually grew as they stepped closer. And in the untold time it had taken to span the unimagined distance from the passage's dark beginning, they finally stepped out into the brilliance of its end, and Malian once more found himself back before the First

Gate of *The Duat* where the ferryman and his boat stood in wait.

Here he again gazed upon the river that ran silver through this first stretch before it moved on in its changing colours along the Realm of the Dead, and overhead, the blackness of the painted star-studded sky formed its arch high above. Along the walls on either side of the water, the gods and goddesses remained in their rich and vibrant parade before their laden tables as they strode forward into the beyond.

Malian and Tragen had witnessed this spectacle on their journey north, but still, the feeling of awe and amazement gripped them as they again looked upon the start of the Seven Gates. However, for the rest of the group who found themselves first time on this path, the sight they beheld was beyond anything they had ever seen or imagined, and fear, as well as wonder, gripped them tight.

"What is this place?" Anitta whispered in astonishment to Tragen as she came out of the glow-lit passage into the splendour of the waterway, the light surrounding the boat dazzling her as its beams radiated out and across the mirror of the silvered expanse.

"We are in *The Duat*, the Realm of the Dead," the warrior replied softly, looking around with fresh eyes at the overwhelming grandeur that filled the entire space. In remembering that he had first seen this place from the confines of the boat, he could now give study to the vessel and its oarsman who had transported them along this path and through the gates.

The boat *Meseket* lay upon the waters before the First Gate of *The Duat*, and Lord Aken stood tall and shadowy in its stern, surrounded by the Light of *Ra*. Before him, the vague images of the souls of the recently dead were packed tight within the confines of the boat and were set silent and stopped within time as they awaited the beginning of their testing journey through the gates.

"Step forward, altar tender," the Boatman challenged looking across at those assembled in stunned silence before him on the path. Raising his hand, he beckoned for the man to come closer, and Malian moved to the river's edge. The hand, however, remained raised in invite and knowing he was being asked to enter the very waters of this underground world, he looked down upon the silver stream where his reflected image of uncertainty stared back. Hesitating briefly, he slowly sat himself down upon the bank, and lowering his legs, stretched to feel for the bottom.

The waters of *The Duat* enclosed themselves around, reaching up towards his waist as he moved downward into their warmth. But they went no deeper, and Malian's fear slowly subsided as the thick liquid of the river enclosed him in its embrace. Wading forward through the density of the flow, he made towards the strengthening light of the heavily laden boat.

Reaching the barge, the Light of *Ra* blinding him in its intensity, he held his hand over his eyes to shield them from the brilliance while gazing up through his fingers towards the towering figure of Lord Aken standing tall and imposing above him in the boat.

"You have something you wish to give me!" the Boatman declared, his voice deep and penetrating as the confines of *The Duat* intensified the words spoken. Bringing his head around, he dropped his gaze to the figure that stood at his feet, and out of the Light of *Ra*, Malian finally saw the face of the ferryman, and a smile crossed his weary face.

"I return this back into your keeping," he said, taking off the *Shen* Staff that had protected him and given its service in his search for *Amaunet*. Holding it aloft, he gave back that which had been granted upon him by the hawk god on his reaching of the Seventh Gate.

"I restore it back into the keep of **Horus,"** the Boatman said, reaching down to take the small staff from the raised hand before tucking it away into his broad belt, *"and in its return, I give to you the words of the gods!"*

The ferryman knelt upon one knee, his head bowed forward to address the altar tender, and the two remained in close talk for many long moments. Slowly he rose to stand once more, and Malian raising his hand in farewell turned away from the radiance of the boat.

Walking forward to where the others remained frozen in their continued amazement, he headed slowly back the way he had come, his gaze intent on reaching the safety of the far bank. But looking along and further to the right, where the river narrowed, and the path led towards the First Gate, a large pile of white rags, stained and discoloured by a red tarnish, could be seen entwining over and around a vast mound of blackened residue of bone which lay before the Gate. Malian halted in recognition of its sight, and the Boatman was quick to proclaim.

"Behold those who knew not the word to pass through the Gate," he said, his voice coming directly to Malian as he looked upon the despised and scorned souls of the men. *"Those who had neither the goodness of heart nor sympathy of spirit for their fellow man, and for that, they have been deemed wicked and worthless by the gods. They shall forever lie here before this First Gate in ignorance of 'Aaru', The Field of Rushes, and their names shall never again be heard."*

Here unmistakably to Malian were the waiting spirits of the Brotherhood of *Apep*, for upon the white cloth that bound them together were clearly the red stains of blood that the wearers had shed at *Horus'* command in acknowledgement of their own god. And at the head of this assembled stack of detritus, two vague distorted images lay upon the shingled ground. One being the black and tainted soul of High Priest Serdos and the other lying close by, the hate-filled spirit of King Dedrick, both denied admission into the afterlife by their corruption and left to rot forever in clear sight of the wonders they knew they would never attain.

Knowing full well the destruction and heartless deeds these men had inflicted upon the people of these lands and the hunger for greed that had soured their very souls, Malian found that he could easily give them no further thought. Looking away from their decay, he continued his walk back through the waters while the barge of the dead slowly pushed away along the stretch of silver and the Boatman began his eternal journey of escorting the sun through the hours of the night.

Arriving back at the bank to join the waiting group, Malian looked up to see that Tragen had quickly come forward to assist him, and taking hold of the hefty arm extended out, the altar tender emerged from the waters of *The Duat*. Here the silvered droplets that clung to the edge of his cloak fell away onto the bankside, there joining and chasing each other back downwards towards the vastness of the river.

"What did he say to you?" the warrior quietly asked, looking in question to where the boat was being steered towards the distant portal of the First Gate.

"Only that the gods have seen fit to give their thanks and gratitude in our undertaking," came the reply, a slight smile crossing his face as he looked first to where the boat shone its brilliance out across the water before his glance returned to the warrior who remained before him, "and they have wished all of us well on our continued journeys!"

Tragen glanced away from the splendour of the receding vessel, its mirrored counterpart moving slowly in the reflection of the silvered waters, and turning towards Malian, stared into a face at odds with the words spoken. The feeling that more could be said briefly crossed his mind, but not wishing to press the matter, he let the moment go, and leaving the man to his thoughts, joined the others in their wait.

The *Meseket* moved away into the distance, and Malian watched its radiance fade as the light slowly dimmed and vanished towards the First Gate, and solid darkness fell in behind. Finally, he turned away from the receding boat and led the group further along the illuminated path beside the richly painted walls. Following it along to its end, they met an imposing wall of white granite streaked with countless dark veins that rose before them, blocking their way. Looking to find their way out, Tragen swiftly came upon a flight of steps to one side, the unevenness of the treads creating a hazardous spiral stairway that cut up behind the massive wall.

Malian then led the group around this solid block, taking them slowly up the echoing staircase until finally, the light of *The Duat* escorting them in its glow as the winding climb became easier, they walked out of the Realm of the Dead. And with much gratitude for the protection along this route, they thankfully, and beyond any doubt, left behind the Seven Gates.

CHAPTER FOURTEEN

Nightfall met them as they came out into the valley, and Malian stopped to take in the air, that at many times over the past troubled months, he felt he would never have again encountered. A sudden rush of confusion overcame him, as in his astonishment, he took in the warmth of an early spring night, the mild air bringing to mind the subtle smell of orange blossom in the courtyard of the temple tenders. Overhead in the vastness of the heavens, the stars shone clear and bright in a cloudless evening sky, and a small moon shone down, reflecting on the water ahead.

Before him, the valley spread away from the middle lake, stretching down the lowlands to the meeting place where he knew it joined its two neighbours, and the combination of the three would lead off as one south towards the canyon and beyond to where the wetlands lay and the city rose up on its eastern ridge.

"I've brought her back," he softly whispered in sincere notice to the sleeping expanse before him. "And in carrying out my undertaking, I have achieved her return and give promise that the people will once more rejoice in her protection."

Looking around at the group who remained in his guidance, he instinctively moved out of the shadow of the overhanging cliff and stepped back into the place where he felt both he and *Amaunet* belonged, while the others, seeing his conviction, were equally clear in their following.

Behind them, the backdrop of the valley head soared high above, and the gateway to the stairs they had climbed out of the underworld disappeared under the cloak of its protection as they moved away from its exit, the entranceway simply vanishing into the background, leaving no trace of its existence.

To their front lay the stone-covered bay where Malian and the group of travellers had made camp close beside the water's edge as they reached the end of the snow-clad valley so many uncounted months ago.

Now though, he and Tragen were the only ones out of the eight who had been witness to this place, for the rest of the group had journeyed along differing paths and had never passed this way. But the sight which lay ahead filled all with great hope after the unnerving paths recently trod, and each eagerly moved down towards the shore where the draw of a lighted fire could be seen.

This was on the very same spot where Malian and his companions had attempted to sleep in the cold wintery darkness, and beside the glow that flared into the surrounding gloom, a familiar figure could be seen looking upwards of the shoreline.

"Psamose, my old friend," Malian cried out into the dark, as on nearing the light coming off the water, he recognised the hooded figure who sat beside the blaze, "you have surely not been waiting here throughout this whole time?"

"No, that I haven't, Malian," the pilgrim replied, his voice hushed as he slowly rose to his feet. Taking up his walking pole, he came away from the fire and strode up the beach. "But as I sat in the great House of Salama, I knew you were coming back, and I knew it would be soon."

The two older men met each other in an embrace of friendship, their arms holding fast around as they let their greeting linger for many moments. Time had played its change on both of them, and in their hold, they each made note of its passing. For Psamose had gained an increase to his girth while he rested at the great house, whereas for Malian, the opposite could only be said. The ordeals endured could be felt in his spare frame and were noted by the pilgrim as the two parted, and he looked hard into the tired face before turning to regard the people who stood around.

"But where are Mentu, Shuma and Darric?" he asked, his eyes eagerly searching the nearby figures who stood out from the shadows. "For I only see yourself and the warrior who left behind these shores. Have the others not returned with you, Malian?"

"No, they have not, pilgrim," came the wearied reply. Malian's voice filled with sadness as he led the man, who had journeyed with them from the City of the Vallenti, forward towards his companions. "There is much to tell of the passing weeks and much that will cause upset in its telling," he continued. "But let us put that to one side for the moment. First, you must greet Tragen again and meet those who have travelled this last passage with me. Then we can retire to the comforts of your fire, and we shall talk."

The warrior stepped forward from the group as Malian and Psamose swung their way, and greeting the tall man in his powerful voice, he held him in a firm grasp before letting go. This allowed Psamose to turn to the four elders who stood alongside the women. Theroc he knew from his visits to the city, and he swiftly took his hand and welcomed him back to the valley, and in turn, he extended his hand to each of the three who he vaguely recollected. But of the women, he was unfamiliar, and Malian was quick to make their introduction.

"Here is Olor," he said, presenting the taller woman, "one who has travelled from the Sleeping Caverns in the north. She is returning here to her home in the valley after many long years away."

Olor hastily stepped forward, wishing to curtail her

introduction, for having heard Psamose mention the House of Salama, she felt a sudden reluctance to make known her destination. Only she and Malian knew of her past, and unknowing of how her arrival would be received, she wished to keep it that way for a little longer.

"I am here, Psamose, to stay with relatives," she quickly said, glancing across to Malian for his agreement, "and to see the valley where I grew up. I have been many long years away, and my recollection of here has faded somewhat over time." Her eyes looked away across the water before returning to the questioning face of the pilgrim.

"Well, welcome back, Olor," he greeted her, his cold bony hand grasping the warmth of her long fingers, "and I hope you will find your memories again. You have arrived in time to see the blossom return upon the trees, and the days grow longer in their span." Seeing the glance that had passed between the woman and the altar tender, and wisely feeling that there was more to this return, he let go of the woman's hand, feeling the slight shake that accompanied her grasp. Turning back towards Malian, he let the past be and the introductions moved on.

"And this is Anitta," Malian deftly said, instantly turning the attention to where the scarred woman had come forward to stand alongside the warrior, "a woman who has been of great value to our group along its journey and one who will travel further with Tragen as he returns home into the south."

"Welcome to the valley, Anitta," Psamose said, smiling directly into the face etched by the scars of her earlier years. Noting the stance that Tragen took as the woman stood at his side, he shook her hand in friendliness, and turning away from the group, he looked to Malian, saying, "Come now, friend, let us all sit beside the fire, and you can tell of your travels beyond the valley, and I can tell you mine."

The whole assembly fell in behind the older man as he led them back towards the water line where the fire blazed out into the dark, and the man's voice continued in his explanation of his own journey as they moved forward and settled around its warmth.

He told of his days after the disappearance of Malian and the others as they vanished into the dark cloud that had fallen across the water. Recounting his travels back through the wintery valley, he had returned along the Neferu Passage before finally finding security at the House of Salama, where he had been welcomed back. There he had remained for many long cold weeks.

"I have only been back here a few days in wait," he explained, "for in seeing a change fall across the valley I knew you would be returning soon."

He had travelled for three lonely days out from his stay at the House of Salama, the six horses he brought along with him being his only company en route. But as one well practised in his journeying alone, he had little fear of the solitude and travelled in expectation of meeting again those last seen disappearing before his eyes.

"So you knew we were coming back?" Tragen asked as the pilgrim seated himself before the fire.

"Yes, that I did, Tragen. The valley itself told me!" He looked out across the darkness of the water as the light of the fireside gave out its glow. "You see, the bitterness of the cold was seen to change, and the heavy weight of the clouds disappeared overnight in a last flurry of winter before the sky emerged in clearness above the valley rim. Finally, the sun appeared weakly in the eastern sky." He looked to the south towards the lowlands that stood enclosed within the valley, and the warmth that radiated back from its steep sides gave evidence of his words.

"The land has been seen to be slowly renewing its vitality," he continued, "for the sun slowly grew in strength, and a thaw was seen to set in along the valley bottom many days ago. With that, I held out hope of both *Amaunet's* return and your own." He looked to the group who sat settled beside the blaze, and his focus turned again to where Malian sat. "But what of your story, my friend? You said there is much to tell!"

The fire became their focus as the altar tender told of all that had become them since they disappeared into the mists leaving the pilgrim alone beside the dark waters. And in his address, he left out none of the hardship, betrayal and dismay that had befallen their journey north. Even in his telling of the overthrow of Serdos and the brotherhood, with the rise of Edgar to his kingship and the return of the stolen Icons, his voice never wavered, only holding a certain sadness that somehow wrapped itself around and held him tight within its bounds.

Little joy, however, was heard in his words until he spoke of the finding and rescuing of the Eight. Here he gave news that in the toppling of the brotherhood, the Eight Deities had been guaranteed reinstatement back to where the gods themselves had decreed their placement, and the stability across the lands and the restoration of the cities would once more be assured in their return.

In the end, he came to his return journey and that of those who sat around, back to the valley through the underworld with the Icon, *Amaunet*, and he praised the help the gods had given them along the way.

Listening intently, the pilgrim saw the mark that all this had placed directly upon the man who sat before him, for even as he spoke, his skin appeared pale and translucent, and a weariness of the world hung heavily off his thin shoulders.

The remainder of the night was spent at the top of the

narrow lake, and Malian could at last find sleep again under familiar stars that slowly moved their way overhead. As the moon descended into the west, the growing lightness of a new dawn fell across the sleeping group, and a whisper of wind blew its way across the still water, murmuring its soft voice into the far corners of the valley.

That morning, Malian opened his eyes to the warmth of a weak sun climbing its way into the clear morning sky above the eastern lip of the lowlands. Eventually rising to witness the start of the day, his feet again took him back along the water's edge. Here he looked out over the middle lake. This had seemed so dead on his passing by in the winter that cloaked its stark border. But now, a transformation had taken place, and the lifeless black veneer had been replaced by a clear green expanse. The beginnings of regeneration could be seen as the light green tips of the reeds pushed up along the bank, rising in clumps further out where the lake ran shallow down its middle. Above the water's surface, a cloud of insects competed for space within the air as they dipped and dived in the morning breeze that swirled gently above, and behind them, the swooping birds followed in their dance.

***

Their journey through the vale took them along the waterside, where the middle basin led towards the joining of the three, and the river gorge could be seen opening into the south. Here at the merging of the waters, the group headed upward. Leaving behind the warmth of the valley bottom, they took the trail towards the western ridge that moved away from the vastness of the northern lakes.

Reaching the cave that began the start of the Neferu Passage, the light that guided their steps began to disappear westwards, and a sudden chill fell across the shoulders of Malian and Tragen as they arrived at where the winter still lingered in its grip upon the higher slopes. Remembering their pass through the tunnel as they came north, they both held a certain trepidation of their return along its route, and a wariness took hold on approaching the yawning darkness of the entranceway.

The cavern on this side, which led into the passage, was recalled as being harshly cold and barren as they sat huddled together after their traumatic experience along the tunnel. But this now appeared more favourable, and the night was spent in some comfort beside a warming fire in preparation for making the journey back through the passage the following morning.

This was quick to come around after a great tiredness had overcome the travellers, and all slept well until the light of the new day awoke them to its brilliance, and Malian risked a look beyond the confines of the cave.

His remembering of the Neferu Passage had been of an overwhelming feeling of panic and frenzy, combined with a dank darkness and an absolute foul stench. But the finding on this return was somewhat different.

On entering the tunnel that following morning, he found the air dry and dusty, the light from his flaming torch picking out the crude carvings adorning the walls. Yet a smell lingered, and Malian promptly stopped before his senses recognised that it was not now repulsive, and more resembled staleness and great age. Walking a little way forward into its softly winding channel, he had time to see that which he had missed on the panic-stricken flight northwards.

Here at the entrance, the carvings were all of *Ptah*, the god of sculpture and craftsmanship, and looking forward along the chiselled walls, the subject remained the same. Seemingly the blind young woman Neferu had attempted to make amends for her offence to the god and had aimed to pay homage to his great gifts by repeating only his name to the exclusion of others. The carvings were crude, but even in their simplicity, they had art, and Malian ran his hands across the marks that appeared as fresh as the day the unseeing girl had picked up her chisel but which he knew were there frozen in a time that had long since passed.

Later, the camp was broken within the cavern at this northern end, and the horses led slowly through the tunnel entrance, their footfall echoing along the shaft. And the day was counted in each step taken forward while time outside measured itself in the passing of the sun across the sky. In the world beyond their confines, the snow sustained its slow melt from off the upper slopes, and the valley's rebirth progressed.

Eventually, the journey ended, and another cold night was spent at the opposite end of the passage. The next day, however, soon arrived and began early, and the long stretch ahead continued further south, the first few hours leading down towards where the canyon filled the central valley. Beside the edge of the gorge bordered by the thick sloping forests that Malian remembered as being heavily snow-clad, they found the pathway free along the margins of the ravine.

Time passed quickly before they reached the orchards of the valley-side estate, where they turned off and headed upwards of the river track. Finally leaving behind the sound of the rushing waters, they moved on through the regenerating trees to where the great house appeared out of the afternoon brightness. Their eyes dazzled as the streaming sun cloaked the western side of the canyon, and pouring across the cultivated land, it fell over the façade of the House of Salama.

Immediately Olor felt a fear and worry grip tight as the walls of her home came into view and remembrances of her last sighting of its grandeur played across her mind. Wrapping her veil tight about her head, she covered her face again from the eyes of man, and sitting upright on her horse, followed restlessly behind Malian and Psamose as they moved towards the vineyards.

The gates to the house stood open for their arrival, and a small crowd appeared collected in a huddle, the early evening sun casting their shadows backward against the cream-coloured walls. Ahead the squat figure of Abu Salama, his hand lifted in greeting, stood before them with his rich cloak thrown off over his shoulders, showing the broad sash wound tight about his thick waist.

"Welcome back, pilgrim," came his raised voice as he stepped away from the gathering to meet the travellers. "And to you too, Malian, for Psamose said he would not be returning alone. With that, I have a need to look upon my daughter." He glanced across to the others as they came to a stop, and not seeing Anitta as she rode behind Tragen, he noted only the male riders of the two-up horses that had come to a halt.

"But where is she?" he asked.

Looking to those mounted atop the horses, he anxiously asked again, "Where is Shuma, Malian? Did she not return with you?" His eyes were suddenly drawn to the hidden female whose mount sat behind the one bearing the older man.

Olor slowly peeled away the cloth that shrouded her face, and feeling troubled and unknowing of how this meeting would go, she carefully answered his question.

"Our daughter has remained in the north, Abu," she gently said, her voice sounding nervous in the overwhelming hush that had fallen around them, "and in her place, I hope my return here will not cause you disappointment!"

"Fae!" Abu Salama gasped in shock and complete surprise as he looked into a face long thought lost to him. His hands quickly came up to cover his open mouth before they fell suddenly leaden to his side. "Fae, is it really you?"

Rushing past where Malian and Psamose sat their horse, the little man hurried forward to the side of the woman who had long been absent from his life. Reaching up with heavy arms towards her, he brought his hands together as the tears fell across his face. Begging her forgiveness over and over, Olor reached down to gather in his trembling hands. Climbing off her mount, she embraced her weeping husband and let the tears fall from her own eyes.

The two appeared out of keeping with each other, for the woman's height only seemed to exaggerate the smallness of the man. Still, the great joy and happiness of their meeting was unmistakable, although for Olor the homecoming was bittersweet.

The young woman who had left this place so long ago had returned changed by the experiences and happenings that had filled her life, and to hear her given name after so long a time seemed at odds with the woman she had become. But from now on, she declared to herself as she stood holding tight to her husband, she would put aside the past and answer once again to the name "Fae" and would accept the role of wife and mother.

Surrounding them, the group of riders, on seeing them embrace, moved forward towards the gateway wishing to give them their privacy. Entering the courtyard, they left behind the couple holding each other in sight of the walls of their great house, and the reunion of husband and wife was allowed to flourish in the homecoming.

Finally, Olor pulled back from the welcome and seeing that they were alone, she looked to where the dark windows of the house watched down silently, and her thoughts went swiftly to her two daughters.

"I have a gift from Shuma which I must give back," she quickly said, unable to hold off from seeing the one she had left behind.

As the couple once more kissed, she turned away and reaching back inside her pack, she brought out the Shabti doll. Holding it close to her chest, she said, "And before anything else, I must see its return."

"Come then, Fae," the man said, his hand extended in support, "you shall give back your gift and see the woman our beautiful daughter has become!"

The man and woman entered the courtyard of the great house together, and while the others dismounted and took down their packs, they left them behind in the charge of Abu's staff, and the two disappeared into the cool darkness of the hall. There they both climbed the stairway up to where Tellia sat in unknowing wait beside her window, and in the meeting of mother and daughter, the years lost were quickly forgiven, and blame was left in the past.

***

That night was spent in the warmth and comfort Malian remembered from his outward travel. And while Abu and Fae were absent for the most part, they did join them for the evening meal and their daughter Tellia was carried down to complete the gathering.

Malian could finally look upon Shuma's sister and found that the two were somewhat alike in cast. The hair for both was black, while the features of the younger, being close to the likeness of Fae, appeared more delicate than that of her older sister, but it was in their structure that the separation was most notable. The body and upper limbs of Tellia were covered by her clothing while her lower half remained hidden under a blanket of delicate white lace, and in reaching upward to grasp the hand of Malian, her hand appeared weak and slightly out of shape.

"You have returned *Amaunet* to us in our saving, Malian," she graciously said, looking up towards the altar tender, "and in that, our house gives you many thanks. But..." She hesitated, her face becoming troubled as an agitation set about her. "My mind is in a turmoil. I have lost my only sister, who has been a constant in my life, and I have gained a mother who I long thought dead!"

She dropped her hand to her lap, and taking up the Shabti doll that sat there, she stared at the carven image, which in its return, had brought such confusion. Seeing her distress, Malian seated himself at her side, taking the young woman's hand into his as she held tightly onto the doll.

"You must know that your sister would one day make her way in life, Tellia," he wisely said, softly squeezing her delicate hand in hope of giving some comfort. "But the bond between the two of you will always be there as long as you speak her name. However, in regard to your mother," he continued, "I cannot tell you how to feel or where to begin in your settlement, and can only say that you must both take your time to get to know each other. In the meeting of strangers, it is always best to find a common ground, and with that, I should look to your mother for her guidance."

He let go of the woman's hand, finding she had placed within his one of the figures from within the Shabti, and looking closer, he saw the carefully sculpted figure of *Horus*, the beaked head carved deep and intricate within the face of the wooden body.

"To keep you safe, Malian," she said, smiling upwards as the fleeting image of Shuma fell across her face, "and to give you comfort on your journey."

***

The evening moved into the night, and the next morning followed, and the farewell for the onward travellers saw them once more before the gates of the great house. Malian now said his goodbyes to the master and mistress, who stood close together to see their leaving.

"I shall always think of you as the Black Swan," he said as he stood before the tall woman, his eyes looking deep into hers as she stared back long and hard into his tired face. "For the name, 'Fae' sits at odds within our friendship."

"For me too, Malian, the name of Olor Ebon remains strong," came her reply, a brief image of the Sleeping Caverns playing itself before her eyes. But in hoping she had finally found peace within her life, she was quick to push it aside. Looking to the future, she took her husband's hand and held it tenderly within her own. "But I shall aspire to let it weaken and allow my given name to mend times past," she finally said as an overwhelming feeling of lasting departure fell upon her. Reaching forward, she kissed Malian on the cheek and wished him well, her hand raised in send-off as the horses eventually turned away.

The group moved off from the great house, the vineyards channelling them back down towards the canyon, and Malian had given Psamose the comfort of riding the lead animal one-up, choosing himself to ride the horse that Olor had vacated.

Given the increasing warmth of the day, the beginning

ride through the blossoming vines was filled with the sound of the droning bees as they moved fitfully from one flower to the next, and the ride was leisurely at first. Later the gorge opened up before them, and again they turned the horses' heads south to follow its track and allowed their pace to quicken.

Their next stop found them at the giant cedar tree that had long ago given its protection against the cold as Psamose guided Malian and his companions northwards along the valley. Again, this was a region known only to the pilgrim, the altar tender and the warrior, for the others who followed into the stillness of the surrounding clearing had never been witness to this or ever seen such a sight.

The diverging pathway led to either side of the enormous base of the tree while the trunk of the cedar disappeared upwards. Here the pilgrim led them away beyond the drop into the river and around the backward path to where a great opening into its interior appeared darkly between the spread of the massive roots.

Inside, the tree was as Malian remembered it on his first visit, although now the hollowed interior gave them a cool place to rest in the heat of the ending day, whereas on their first passing, warmth was what was required, and there the tree had been equally obliging. The log benches also remained, their position appearing unchanged again in his recall and looking upwards into the rising height of the tree's core, he thought of the long night spent there. The vision of the young man Darric tending his horses came directly to mind as he sat himself down under the protection of the tree.

Malian's thoughts had often turned to Darric as they journeyed south from the City of the Fosse, where he had heard of his death at the hands of Brann. And in passing back into the valley, he found his reflections growing stronger of the fighter the young man had become. In his remembering, he felt great sadness at such a loss and remained troubled by the boy's end.

However, as he sat within the safety of the great tree and peered up into the lofty heights, he recalled their talk as they sat on the lakeside after their journey through *The Duat*, and it brought to mind how Darric acknowledged his change from boy to man as he lay in the Light of *Ra*. He felt that now, in his own knowing of the gods, he could, at last, accept that the youth had been changed beyond the physical and that his time in this world would be short, and in that, he had to let it be and find some resolution to his sorrow.

***

The following days saw the group turning west and heading up close to the coldness of the valley's rim, where the drifts of snow still lingered, before they moved east to follow the track down. Here the wetlands and marshes led across towards the City of the Vallenti, and an urgency to finally return within its walls had increased for those who called it home. The requests for rest, which along the way had been many and frequent, diminished as they wished to move forward quicker and reach its sanctuary.

The great city appeared out of the surrounding woodlands, its walls reaching high as the ground rose slowly from the forest's edge. And as Malian followed behind Psamose guiding his mount across and up the softly grassed banks that began its footings, he looked away from where the great doors stood open high above, back to where the others followed out of the dense forest. Seeing Tragen and Anitta bringing up the rear, the packhorse following close behind, a sudden and pressing realisation swept across him and made him come to a sudden halt on the lush slope that ran ahead.

In his overwhelming undertaking of the return of the Icon back to his city, he had seemingly forgotten that the warrior had his own venture to complete and *Naunet* would remain exiled even after *Amaunet's* safe return. Having stopped his horse before reaching the entrance, he let the others pass in their excitement to enter the gates and waited as Tragen came up over the grassy bank.

"I fear I have been lax in my overlooking that you, yourself, carry a burden, Tragen," he said as the two riders and the trailing pack horse reached his side. "You have remained silent these many days on your own duty and the responsibility you carry, and these still lie ahead for you. And will remain so even as we rejoice in *Amaunet's* return."

"We each have had our troubles to think on," Tragen replied, knowing that the task for Malian had taken its toll over the past weeks. Therefore, in not wishing to further add to the man's distress, he had remained quiet on his own worries. "But, in my witnessing that the return of each of the Icons has brought restoration and rebirth in the cities, it gives me great hope in what I might find in my own. My mind has seen a growing ease of late, and this duty has become a little less taxing in my thoughts."

"Then come and see *Amaunet* returned to her rightful place," Malian said, his eagerness to see her back within her temple taking hold and causing him to set off up the grassed bank. "Then you can take some time to resupply and gather your strength for the journey ahead!"

"No, I shall not be entering your city," the warrior sternly replied, his wish to move on overcoming his desire to rest. "We remain well stocked with dry provisions, and the light lingers, so we must make the most of the day." He brought his mount alongside the altar tender, bringing the two in step, and taking hold of the man's arm, he quietly said, "So, let us ride together to the forest's edge, and there we can say our farewell."

Malian came again to a stop, but this time at the city gates, and leaving behind the rest of the group as each turned to say their goodbyes to Tragen and Anitta, he turned his horse away from the sanctuary that the city held. Following behind the warrior, they walked beneath the towering western walls. Here the huge carvings of the gods led to the very edge of the city, and the forest began its steep climb away up the valley side before it extended out into the barren lands and off into the south.

On reaching this point, the altar tender stepped down from his mount, and turning to where the swan and the warrior had gotten down from theirs, he first wrapped his tired arms around the young woman. Giving her a tight hug and whispering long in her ear, he kissed her scarred cheek in farewell, and taking down his pack from his trusted horse, he handed across the reins. Turning to Tragen, the two stood long in their embrace before they could part, each not wanting to take their leave. Finding that words did not come easy in the parting of friends, it was many moments before Malian finally broke the silence.

"I know you have got many more days of hardship in front of you," he said, his hand holding tight that of the warrior, "but I wish you well in the return to peace for your people and your city." Looking deep into Tragen's eyes, he stared long into the depths he knew would hold such sorrow and anger for many years before he finished. "And my hope goes with you that you find some answers for your daughter. Remember, look to the gods for guidance, for they will be there for you if you need them."

"I shall take your words with me, Malian," Tragen

replied, a smile crossing his face as he looked down at the tired figure stooped before him, "but I shall not say them back. For I know the gods have been with you on your journey, and they surely remain with you this day."

Having said their goodbyes, the two held each other for many more moments. Slowly they parted, and the onward travellers mounted their restless horses and moved off. Watching as they headed south, Malian stared deep into the darkness of the overhanging trees as the woodlands bordering the valley's sides enclosed them, and he stood long after they had disappeared from his sight.

Turning, he eventually walked back under the stares of the colossal gods. The great despair that had fallen over him once more descended as he thought on the betrayals and losses witnessed over the last months. His remembering first brought to mind the falseness and deceit of Mentu, one who he understood to be a friend and companion before his reflections led on to the loss of Darric, which had affected him so badly.

Now in saying his farewell to Tragen, he felt a finality as the separation of the group that had set out northwards alongside him from under these walls was seen to come to an end. The pilgrim Psamose was now the only one left of the four who departed this city with him such a long time ago, and without him, the start of his journey would have been impossible.

Coming to a gradual stop, he looked upwards at the massive carvings etched deep into the sloping walls surrounding the city until the ache in his neck became too much, and he dropped his eyes away from their gaze. Then with his head bowed, he slowly continued the walk back towards the gateway.

Reaching the wide opening into the city, and carrying *Amaunet* over its threshold, the overwhelming sadness he felt lifted slightly as a lightness took its place. Feeling the great burden lifting off his shoulders, he knew his task ordered by the gods would soon be seen to be completed in their eyes.

His return through the gates of the city was greeted by the whole of the remaining townsfolk, who had come to a sudden stop as his name had been shouted. In acknowledgement of his return, many had gathered before the gates to welcome him back, their happy faces showing much more than gratitude at his homecoming. As he now walked along familiar and thankfully snow-free walkways and lanes, his feet crisscrossed paths strode in the past, and eventually, he reached the place where he long ago entered the Open Courtyard of the elders. There he found Set'al, the high priest, in wait and robed in all his finery.

Alongside, Psamose the pilgrim stood with the remaining elders positioned beyond on the steps in wait to receive him and all held warmth within their smiles, which lit up their features.

Coming forward, the high priest welcomed Malian back, and raising his hands and thanking the gods that he had been successful, he spoke first to the altar tender and then to the assembled crowd.

"You have been victorious in your god-given task, Malian, and our words of thanks may seem poor to your ears," he exclaimed. His voice rose, and he addressed the gathering of the city's people, "But all here shall remember your name and give gratitude to you on the homecoming of *Amaunet* and for both the redemption of our valley and the saving of our people!"

Malian stepped forward as the rush of cheers and shouts surrounded him, and holding out the wrapped Icon, he handed the tightly bound bundle to the high priest, placing the package into the outstretched hands.

Here it was slowly unwrapped from its confines, and the golden snake-headed goddess once more saw the light of day.

As Set'al held her aloft to the waiting crowds, his eyes filled with tears as he reflected on the suffering and death that had engulfed the city in her absence. The devastation and misery for his people had been immense, and all hope had been in the hands of this simple altar tender that stood before him. Looking down upon the small man, his head bowed in such tiredness of his hardship, he knew that only in Malian's returning of the statue to its rightful place would he see his task complete, and the man could then find peace.

"It will be your honour, Malian, to replace *Amaunet* where she belongs," he solemnly said, his hand stretching forward to hand back the golden statue. "Come, let us return her immediately to her ordained place and fully restore the balance of her powers within the valley."

Stepping down, High Priest Set'al led the group in escorting Malian and *Amaunet* along the avenues towards the temple, the elders falling in behind, while around, the cheering crowds followed in their exuberance. And here, within the grandeur of the valley's temple, the homecoming for the stolen Icon, the Eighth Deity, was cloaked within its ceremony as the doors to the inner sanctum opened and Set'al walked through. Malian was escorted across the marbled floor and through the temple's gathered clergy into where the shrine stood beyond its screen.

The curtains to the sanctum of *Amaunet* had been drawn back, the intricate golden figures of the gods depicted upon its veil gathered and draped together at either side of the candle-lit entrance. While beyond, the granite ledge sat directly ahead above the altar of the Deity.

Here the high priest and the guiding group of elders came to a halt at the threshold of the screen, and Malian paused briefly in recognition of the occasion before stepping over the portal into the quietness of the sanctuary. The shrine of *Amaunet* sat before him, enshrouded in its many offerings that had been placed in the hope of her return, and slowly parting these to make space along the ledge, he reached forward. Thereupon he returned the small statue to its plinth, the ringing sound of metal against stone echoing in Malian's ears as the feet of the solid gold statue once more fell into their time-worn position.

"I return you, *Amaunet*, back to where the gods past placed you in their division of the Primordial Eight," he whispered, his hands shaking as he finally released his hold, "and in your restoration, let the forces of good and tranquillity once more govern in this world."

Stepping back, he looked up, staring long into the ruby eyes while around him in the land of the great city and throughout the valley, a completion in the recovery from the devastating tragedy of chaos and disorder was seen to be banished. There, as the last of the snows of winter that hung tightly to the upper valley melted away in the growing warmth of *Ra*, the people could rejoice.

***

The ceremony over, the entrance to the outer temple was left open, and all came to give thanks as the remaining day was seen to lead into the night. For the jubilation at *Amaunet's* return would overtake the whole of the city in its celebration, and many brought offerings to show gratitude.

But Malian, feeling overwhelmed by the event and torn between elation in reaching this point against the great loss of his friends, wished only for some peace. Finding his tiredness and need for quiet reflection had taken the lead in his thinking, he let the elders escort him back through the gathered people and out into the warmth of the evening, and here, Psamose came to his side.

"Malian, shall I ask the head of the elders to find you a guest bed in the Closed Court to rest for the night?" the pilgrim suggested as he stood close, aware of the exhaustion cloaking the altar tender. "Then tomorrow, we can find you fresh rooms, and you can settle yourself."

"No, I think I shall sleep again in my old bed," Malian thanked his friend, "for I have always found that my old bones fit its shape well. And given the places I have slept over these recent long months, I feel that in my tiredness, a certain comfort will be given even in its simplicity."

"Very well, but at least let me walk with you, and I can see you through the city and safely to your door."

"No, I can find my way," came the reply, an overwhelming weariness edging Malian's voice as he held out his hand to Psamose. "It is a path I have long trodden, and I need no guide."

The two parted, Psamose wishing the unlikely saviour of their valley a good and restful night as he moved away towards the noise of the celebration, leaving Malian to wander alone through the crowded lanes. Witnessing the joy at *Amaunet's* homecoming and slowly making his way to the stone corridors surrounding the courtyard of the Solar Scarab, he finally found himself back at his old rooms. Slowly opening the door, he stepped thankfully inside and let the quietness surround him.

Seating himself upon the bed and hearing the familiar creak of the boards, he felt a sudden comfort and relief in their hold. For although in looking around him, the room remained simple in furnishings, it was a modesty of his own choosing and one that gave him ease.

The last uncounted months since he awoke in this place to the dawn bell now played themselves over in his thinking, and the days that had passed ran clearly through his mind as he wondered why it had fallen upon him to take on this task. He was still none the wiser as to why the gods had chosen him, but he now let it be, relief and satisfaction edging the weariness that slowly overtook him.

Looking down, he stared again into the face of *Horus* as it sat upon the carved Shabti held within his hands. And remembering his last sighting of the great god as he appeared to him in the guise of the Boatman, he remembered the final words spoken as he stood beside the barge in the ever-flowing waters of *The Duat*.

"You have travelled far, Malian, and in doing, have fulfilled the greatest of tasks that the gods had placed upon you, and the peoples of these lands will be forever grateful for your struggle and sacrifice.

"Know now that we shall meet again very soon, and in the witnessing alone of my presence, your worries and toil will all be over."

Carefully shifting to the middle of the bed, he stretched out and placed his heavy head upon the pad that lay hard and cold beneath. Covering himself over with the sparse blanket, he first brought its heavily stitched edge up towards his face, the roughness of its simplicity feeling coarse against his chin before he turned it down across his chest. Placing his hands carefully along its border, he held the Shabti doll tight within his fingers.

He was exhausted, and an irresistible urge to sleep held him in its grip as he slowly closed his eyes. As the quietness of the night settled around, he allowed his body to become still and let the dream take him.

The silvered waters of The Duat *lay ahead of Malian, the Boatman seemingly waiting alone. And stepping once more aboard the* Meseket, *the Shabti of* Horus *held tight within his hand, the altar tender looked upward to where the great sky god himself stood within its stern in place of the Lord Aken.*

"You said you would come yourself, Horus,*" Malian softly declared, the familiar face of the falcon staring down with its sharp eyes, towards where he stood small before the feet of the god.*

"Yes," came the leaden reply, the voice sounding like far-off thunder, "for I made promise to you that, come your time, I alone would be your guide and guardian through the gates into the lands beyond."

Picking up the massive paddle that lay at his side, the god thrust it deep into the silvered waters, and the boat was set in motion along the river.

The Seven Gates of The Duat *all lay open before Malian, and no challenge was forthcoming as the boat slowly moved forward beneath the doorways and along its changing colour. Finally, the last stretch was reached, and the golden waters leading to the Seventh Gate turned into the blue of the heavens as the final door was passed, and the boat came to its resting stop.*

"Behold the 'Field of Offerings'," Horus declared, as the stillness surrounded them and the abundant fields known as Aaru lay in sight, "and here your everlasting life will be one lived in truth and light, and your soul will exist in all eternity."

The Field of Reeds spread its infinity before him, a light, warming breeze playing through the grass while the ever-brightness of the sun poured its rays across the unending expanse.

In the far-off distance, Malian could hear voices, the sound of laughter and lightness drawing his feet forward as he first turned and placed the Shabti doll at the feet of the god before stepping out from the safety of the Meseket. *And as the meadows of the beyond slowly closed themselves around, he thankfully left behind him all the tiredness and sorrow shrouding his soul, and turning to say farewell to the god* Horus *as he stood watching, he raised his empty hand and let the rushes embrace him.*

***

The morning sun rose over the valley, and the young man instructed to wait upon Malian knocked quietly before gently opening the door to where a stillness appeared to fill the room. The unmistakable absence of sound immediately gave cause for concern, and quickly moving forward into the cool greyness that cloaked the early morning, he suddenly stopped before approaching the bed where the altar tender lay.

Malian was cold, his face set waxen in a soft light smile, and the weariness that had settled upon him now appeared gone as he lay upon his back with the sparse bed cloth spread evenly about him. The pale hands that once held the Shabti remained crossed over his still chest, but the lifeless fingers lay empty and interlaced in prayer. His lids remained slightly open as he stared upward towards the ceiling where the dust motes floated in the day's dawning sunlight, while the glassy gaze of his empty eyes appeared focused skyward, seemingly past the present as he now looked into the beyond.

***

Far in the north, Shuma awoke from a disturbed dream where Malian had walked beside her, his hand resting gently upon her arm as he guided her through the growing vines around her father's great house. And in the distance, the figure of her mother could be seen, her head bowed low as she tended the plants that trailed around their supports.

"The valley is safe on *Amaunet's* return," the altar tender said, his voice filled with a happiness never before heard, "and with the balance of order achieved throughout the valley, the task placed upon me by the gods has been accomplished, and I can go to my rest."

Stopping, he reached across to pluck away a green leaf from a vine, and placing it in her hand, he raised her fingers to his lips. Gently kissing them, he bid her farewell as an immense feeling of loss wrapped itself around. Moving away, he turned, and walking slowly back towards the house, step by step, disappeared into the distance.

***

Rising quietly at her awakening, Shuma left Gallius asleep on the far side of the bed, and looking across the room to where the light from the large window cast its spread over the wooden floor, her gaze fell upon the small table that sat close by. Stepping over to where she knew only a bowl of dried flower petals stood, she looked down upon the shaped image that now sat there.

The carved Shabti doll stood beside the scented bowl, and taking up this small wooden figure, she placed it aside, finding beneath it a large green vine leaf, its fresh and pungent smell rising as she recalled her oft-taken strolls amongst the vineyards of home. Grasping this symbol of life's growth and regeneration, she walked slowly to the window and looked out into the brightness of the new day.

About the Author

Glennis Goodwin was born in Staffordshire and from an early age was often told she had a wanderlust about her – her nose was always in one book or another, whisking her away to some far-off land! Anything to do with the people or wildlife of Africa always held an attraction, and in the early 1980s, she was fortunate to find herself living and working in Zambia, which lasted for five years before she returned to the UK.

In her working life, she has gone from Nursing to Retail and from Academic Publishing to PA, but she never lost the feeling Africa gave her, and in those years, she had several holidays in Egypt and Kenya. Egypt was fascinating with all its Ancient history, and walking around the Temples of Luxor and Karnak, she imagined herself back in those days!

In 2004, after a change in personal circumstance, she aimed to return to her Nursing career and, combining that with her love of travel, went to New Zealand on a refresher course. Settling into life over there, she continued to further her career, met her new husband and made her life there.

Sadly, a brain haemorrhage and slight stroke ended her study, but after her recovery, she found herself wanting to write, something she had longed to do but never seemed to have the time for. Returning to the UK in 2017, she settled down at her computer, revisiting an idea put aside years previously, and over the following months, the tales of The Eight Deities of the Ancient Egyptians came to life in the story of Malian, the altar tender.

Currently, she is working on her third book, *In the Footsteps of Ra*, which continues the story of the gods of chaos and tells the tale of Tragen, the warrior.

www.blossomspringpublishing.com

www.ingramcontent.com/pod-product-compliance
Lightning Source LLC
Chambersburg PA
CBHW020903200626
46814CB00001BA/156